SPARKS OF AMBER

BOOK 3

THE CORRINGTON BROTHERS SERIES

LEESA WRIGHT

Copyright © 2022 by Leesa Wright

All rights reserved.

No part of this book may be reproduced in any form or by any electronic or mechanical means, including information storage and retrieval systems, without written permission from the author, except for the use of brief quotations in a book review.

Publication Assistance by:

Michelle Morrow, M.S.

*To the women who came before me. Your strength, determination, and sacrifice were not in vain.
To the women coming into their own.
You can do this…*

CONTENTS

Chapter 1	1
Chapter 2	8
Chapter 3	12
Chapter 4	23
Chapter 5	29
Chapter 6	36
Chapter 7	48
Chapter 8	58
Chapter 9	64
Chapter 10	72
Chapter 11	80
Chapter 12	87
Chapter 13	97
Chapter 14	104
Chapter 15	120
Chapter 16	133
Chapter 17	147
Chapter 18	157
Chapter 19	167
Chapter 20	180
Chapter 21	190
Chapter 22	203
Chapter 22	213
Chapter 23	225
Chapter 24	237
Chapter 25	248
Chapter 26	258
Chapter 27	266
Chapter 28	275
Chapter 29	290

Chapter 30	300
Chapter 31	308
Chapter 32	315
Chapter 33	322
Chapter 34	330
Chapter 35	348
Chapter 36	357
Chapter 37	362
Chapter 38	378
Chapter 39	386
Chapter 40	395
Chapter 41	405
Chapter 42	415
Chapter 43	425
Chapter 44	430
Chapter 45	444
Chapter 46	451
Chapter 47	457
Epilogue	460
Midnight Mist Is Coming Soon	464
About the Author	469

SPARKS OF AMBER

Copyright © 2022 by Leesa Wright

All rights reserved.

No part of this book may be reproduced in any form or by any electronic or mechanical means, including information storage and retrieval systems, without written permission from the author, except for the use of brief quotations in a book review.

Publication Assistance by:

Michelle Morrow, M.S.

CHAPTER 1

SOUTH VIETNAM. JUNE 1969

Camera in hand, her heart thudded in her chest as she crawled through the dense brush. All around George Irelynn Cross, a tense firefight played out across the lush jungle. Bullets whizzed by, striking the tree above her head, sending a stream of shredded bark and chunks of splintered wood to ping against her helmet. Ducking, she squeezed her eyes shut. Holding her helmet, she prayed for dear life and the shooting to stop. Eventually, the screams of the battle with the Viet Cong fell to an eerie silence. Lifting her head, she viewed the carnage of the shredded jungle around her. Rolling to her back, Irelynn adjusted the F stop on her camera before taking a deep breath and rolling back over to get the shot she wanted. Peering through the heavy foliage, she snapped photos of the soldiers spread out on the ground in front of her. Their young faces with old eyes told the story of grit and the will to survive.

The team leader, Sergeant Mallory, whipped around at the staccato beat of the camera shutter. He gave her a scathing glare. "Quiet," he hissed.

"Great," Irelynn mumbled. "He's pissed again."

Embedded with the U.S. Army south of Da Nang, South Vietnam, she had more than one run in with the cantankerous soldier. He didn't like her or the job she did, and she didn't care for his misogynistic attitude either.

Someone had thrown a can of blue smoke marking their location. The familiar whoop- whoop of a Huey chopper filled the sky above. Finally. Irelynn breathed a sigh of relief, anxious to return to the Army base at Da Nang and then on to Saigon, where she had a small apartment above a family run grocery store.

She peered down at her dirty fingernails, her body odor wafting up to taunt her; she shuddered in disgust.

"God. I stink," she whispered.

A young black soldier crawled up next to her. "Hey, Jonsie."

Jonsie chuckled. "Man. You are in deep shit."

Irelynn grimaced. "Nothing new there."

"He doesn't like reporters in the field. Especially chicks."

"If he calls me "Doll" one more time," Irelynn grumbled. "Oh, he's called you way worse than that," Jonsie said.

"Never to my face," she replied. Glancing over. "Geez, Jonsie. You look like you're bringing half the dirt from Vietnam back to Da Nang."

"Shit. Like you're not covered in the same swill. Come on. Keep your head low and run like hell. Sarge will have his foot up my ass sideways if I don't get you on that chopper in one piece."

Irelynn looked up as the chopper hovered above them. "What's that rope ladder they're dropping?"

"Fuck, there must not be anywhere to land. We've got to climb up to him."

"Climb? Oh shit. This... is not good."

"Nope. Not good at all. Run like the devils chasing you and climb that rope," Jonsie replied. "Whatever you do, don't look down."

Gripping her helmet to her head, Irelynn ran with Jonsie on her tail. A few men were already climbing the rope as it swung back and forth. Reaching the ladder, she started the climb up. Avoiding bullets from the enemy whizzing by, the chopper lifted from where it had hovered. Two men and Irelynn were left clinging to the rope dangling in the draft below the moving aircraft.

Irelynn's arms burned as she reached for the next rung. Above her, the men called out encouragement to keep climbing. Sheer determination filled her, and she pulled herself up to the next rung.

Keep going, girl. It's just like climbing the rope swing on the redwood trees at home. A large gust of wind blew the rope ladder, and in a panic, Irelynn wound her legs around the rope as she lost her grip.

Dangling upside down, her camera slid, hitting her nose as she grappled with the camera strap to keep it from falling from her neck. She prayed as the jungle below rushed by in a green blur. Closing her eyes, she fought nausea bubbling up her throat. Looking down at the horrified men below, she realized it was the perfect shot. Raising her camera, she snapped a few photos before Jonsie, beneath her, pushed her up so she could grasp the ladder and finish the climb.

Strong arms gripped her by the waist and pulled her into the chopper, with the last two men quickly following her lead.

Leaning against the bulkhead, Irelynn breathed a sigh of relief. Pulling the green towel from around her neck, she wiped the blood dripping from her nose and lifted her camera to capture the scowling faces of the men around her. "Well, that was fun."

"You're one bookoo dinky dau chick," Jonsie replied.

Irelynn gave him a dazzling smile. "I've done worse."

Hefting her rucksack onto her back, she slung her cameras over her shoulder. Irelynn waved at the jeep as it pulled away from the nurse's barracks. Smiling, she made her way inside. A few bottles of shampoo and wine delivered before the mission, guaranteed her twelve hours of sleep and a shower before she headed home. Nodding her head in greeting to some nurses as they prepared for the day ahead, she spotted her friend Rose. Placing her things on the floor by an empty bunk, she was tempted to flop on the bed in exhaustion.

"Hey Rose," Irelynn said.

"You're back. How was your run through the jungle?" Rose replied.

"Exhausting. But I got the story and shots I wanted."

"You're crazy. You know that, right?"

Her eyes danced with mischief. "Crazy, with a splash of sass," Irelynn replied.

Rose shook her blonde head. "You're incorrigible."

"So far, it's worked in my favor."

"Hey. I'm going with a few girls to the officer's club tonight.

Do you want to go?" Rose asked.

"Hmm. I don't know. The last time I went with you, I met that First Lieutenant with all those hands."

Rose smiled. "You need to relax. Have fun."

"Fighting off a man with a thousand hands is not my idea of fun."

"Well. Think about it."

"I will. I need a shower. Then, I'm going to sit in the sun and dry my hair."

"It's one hundred percent humidity out there. Nothing dries in Vietnam," Rose giggled.

Irelynn shrugged her shoulders. "I can try."

The water flowed red as she washed the red dust and dirt from her hair and body. Drying herself off, she dressed in jean cutoffs and a black tank top. Pulling a small mirror from her bag, she gently touched her tender nose.

"I'm damn lucky I didn't break my nose."

"How did you do this?" Rose asked as she poked and prodded Irelynn's nose.

"I got hit in the face by my camera while dangling upside down on a rope ladder swinging from a Huey."

Rose grimaced. "I need to learn *not* to ask how you get your injuries."

"Another item to add to my "do not tell dad list," Irelynn said, stuffing her dirty laundry in her rucksack.

"Are you still wearing those sexy panties and bra when you're out in the bush?" Rose asked.

"Always. It saves my sanity and reminds me that underneath the fatigues and dirt, I'm still a woman," Irelynn replied.

Rose grunted. "It's not like you can hide it. You're every man's wet dream with those curves and that face."

"Hence the baggy fatigues and dirt. I don't want to give anyone ideas."

"I'm off to the hospital. Get some sleep. I'll wake you when I get back."

"I will. First, I need to write down some notes from the mission before I forget them," Irelynn replied.

She was sitting on sandbags piled high around the nurse's barracks; her legs stretched out in front of her to catch some sun. Notepad in hand, Irelynn thoughtfully chewed on the end of her pencil. Writing down her impressions of the mission and the soldiers on the team:

The men, for the most part, accepted my presence. A few, like Sergeant Mallory, had shown outright disdain for a woman amid a man's war. A few could not understand why I would willingly put myself in harm's way when so many had no choice.

She didn't see it creeping along the top of the sandbags until the rat was almost upon her. With a screech, she jumped as the creature scampered across her lap. Losing her balance, she toppled head first into the small space between the metal siding of the barracks and the sandbags. Her legs flaying over the sandbags, her bottom up in the air, she struggled to pull herself upright.

"Great. Just great," Irelynn mumbled. "I seriously need to work on my upper arm strength."

A deep chuckle behind her, and she ceased her struggles.

Who's behind me? Mortified at her predicament, she felt her cheeks burn as she renewed her efforts to free herself.

CHAPTER 2

Captain Brendan Corrington could barely contain his delight. The shapely woman's behind wiggled invitingly as she struggled to pull herself upright.

"Hold. Hold still. I've got you," Brendan commanded.

Shaking his head, placing his hands on her waist, he lifted her. Flipping her over, he set her on the sandbag wall.

The woman swept her thick shoulder length chestnut hair off her face, and he inhaled sharply. Sparks flew from her amber colored eyes. Framed by thick dark eyelashes, they complimented her pert nose and full lips. Her creamy tanned complexion blushed pink at his perusal. His gaze swept her body, pausing momentarily on her heaving chest before coming to rest again in her beautiful eyes.

His hands still rested lightly on her waist. "What's your

name?" he whispered. He paused; his eyes widened, shifting slightly to her left.

"Don't move," he hissed, his hands tightening.

Her eyes slowly moved to where he looked, and the woman inhaled sharply. Her eyes looked into his in horror.

A two-foot snake rose not far from her on the sandbags: hissing, its fangs exposed in an open mouth snarl.

Yanking her off the sandbags, they rolled to the ground. Just as quickly, he rolled from her, pulled his sidearm and shot the snake dead. Turning back to her, he sheathed his weapon.

"Are you hurt? Did it bite you?"

Her eyes were wide; her lips trembled.

"I… I'm fine. Did you just kill my pet snake?"

"What?" He rumbled. "Are you kidding me?"

Looking down at her, he realized her eyes danced with amusement. His eyes narrowed as he offered a hand to her and pulled her to her feet.

"Hmm. Pet snake. You couldn't find a puppy to adopt?"

"I already have one. She's one hundred and twenty pounds. She might get jealous," she replied.

He looked down at her. She was small, fine boned, maybe five foot three at the most. At six foot two, the top of her head hit barely above his shoulder.

"Dog or man. I can't see either wanting to share you," he replied. "Where's the dog?"

"At home with my parents."

"And a man?"

"I'm a little busy. I don't need one of those right now."

"You might if that perfect little ass of yours gets into more trouble."

"My bum is not open for discussion."

"No?"

"No. Now I'm going inside and going to bed."

A wide grin split his handsome face, and he chuckled at her apparent angst. Unable to resist teasing her. "Alone?"

She stomped over to the door. "Yes, alone. And just so you know. I'm not some damsel in distress either."

"Relax, Sparky. Never said you were." His gaze smoldered as it dropped from her face and swept her body.

"Let me know if you change your mind about sleeping alone."

He chuckled as her mouth dropped open and her cheeks flooded a delightful pink.

"Oooh," she yanked the door open and went inside, letting the screen door slam shut with a bang.

"Sweet dreams," he called out. He chuckled again and trotted back to where his tall red headed buddy stood waiting for him.

"Anyone ever tell you that you're supposed to woo the ladies, not piss them off?"

"Not this one, Mac. She's got a wild spark, and stunning to boot."

"She is beautiful. Nice shot on the snake, by the way," Mac replied.

Brendan grinned. "Damn. I never got her name."

Irelynn closed the door and leaned against it. She put her hands to her cheeks to cool them. Using one hand, she fanned herself.

What is wrong with you, girl? You should be offended… but you're not. She climbed into her bunk, pulling the sheet up to cover herself. Her skin still burned where the man's hands had touched her waist.

God. He was so tall. Dark hair and those eyes. So blue. A girl could lose herself in those eyes. She groaned. "How am I supposed to sleep after that?"

A pet snake? For Pete's sake. God, he's infuriating.

CHAPTER 3

Irelynn sat cross legged on the bunk, wearing a sundress of burnt orange with tiny brown and yellow flowers. She applied some clear lipstick to her soft full lips. Her copper-colored chestnut hair fell in waves to softly brush her shoulders. Sighing deeply, she looked into the hand held mirror; her father's eyes stared back at her. After talking about her Saint Bernard, Ralph, earlier, she realized how homesick she was. And after not seeing her family and Ralph for over nine months, it was probably time to schedule a visit home. She looked up as Carole; a sleek brunette settled herself on the bunk across from her.

"Now tell me again about this gorgeous hunk who rescued you from the snake."

Irelynn rolled her eyes. "What's to tell? Tall, dark, and

handsome. Broad shoulders, with an infuriating smile. Oh, and crystal blue eyes."

"Captain Corrington. Army, Green Beret? I can't say I've ever heard of him, but I will be on the lookout for you."

"Don't bother. If I never see him again, it will be too soon," Irelynn replied.

"What is it they say? 'Me thinks she doth protest too much.' William Shakespeare," Carole laughed.

Irelynn paused from applying mascara and lowered the mirror.

"What about the sleeping alone part? I mean. It's obvious he was getting fresh with me."

"God knows, girl. You need it," Carole snickered.

"That's not very helpful," Irelynn replied.

Both women looked up as Rose sat down.

"Look at it this way, Irelynn. You're what, twenty-three? It's past time you lost your virginity."

"I plan to. Eventually."

"Are you saving it for marriage?" Carole asked.

"I don't know. I haven't met anyone who interested me enough," Irelynn said.

"Till now," both Rose and Carole said.

Glaring at them, she set the mascara down and reached for her combat boots.

"You're seriously going to wear those things with a dress again?" Carole said.

"I didn't bring sandals. So. Yes," Irelynn replied.

"Which reminds me. I forgot the red dress and high heels. I'll bring them for you next time."

"Here's some clip-on earrings. We'll plan on piercing your ears tomorrow," Rose said.

Irelynn rolled her eyes.

"We're bringing you into the twentieth century whether you like it or not," Rose said.

"Don't you think that being the most kick ass female war correspondent in the middle of a combat zone would qualify as the twentieth century? That is, without losing my virginity to some G.I. who just wants to get laid."

"The sex is more for blowing off steam," Rose said.

"If I need to blow off steam, I'll run around the block or something," Irelynn grumbled.

The officer's club was an open-air tiki bar with a grass roof covering several tables. Officers seated at the bar and tables enjoyed ice cold cocktails and beer, along with mouthwatering fare guaranteed to fulfill the need for American food. Music blared from the jukebox as Rose, Carole, and Irelynn chose an empty table close to the wood railing surrounding the entire bar. Irelynn slid her rucksack under the table as she sat down. She smiled at the Vietnamese waiter, who stopped to take their order.

"Hey Tran, we'll split a basket of French fries. And I'll have a shot of Tequila and a glass of Sangria," Irelynn said.

"Same here," Carole and Rose both said.

"Did you get the Heinz ketchup yet?" Irelynn asked.

"No Heinz, just ketchup," Tran replied.

Rose giggled. "They don't understand the difference between kinds of ketchup."

"I don't get what the issue is. Every time I'm here, I tell him just order it from the United States, and I'll be happy," Irelynn replied.

"If you want to confuse him, order catsup," Carole said.

"They're the same thing," Irelynn snickered.

An hour later, a few tables had been pulled together to accommodate the arrival of more off duty nurses. Most of the nurses were on the small dance floor wrapped in the arms of Army officers of every rank. Empty cans of beer and wine glasses littered the table as Irelynn sought to push the empties to the edge of the table. Irelynn looked up from her task and froze. *He's here.*

Captivated by his good looks, she watched as the captain and a red headed man sat at a table in the middle of the bar. Giving Rose and Carole a look of sheer panic, she dove under the table.

"What are you doing?" Carole said.

"That's him," Irelynn whispered.

"Where?" Rose whispered back.

"In the middle of the bar. Sitting with a big red headed guy."

"Oh my God. He's gorgeous. They're both gorgeous. Okay.

Now tell me why you're hiding under the table?" Rose said.

Irelynn gave them an exasperated snort, "I don't want him to see me."

"Coward. Get up here," Carole said. "Shit. I lost an earring," Irelynn said.

"You have to find it," Rose cried.

Irelynn lifted her head to peer over the table at the captain. Looking around the floor, she spotted the gold twisted rope earring. "There it is."

Crawling on all fours between the tables, she almost had it in hand when it was kicked away. She crawled after it as it was kicked out of reach by some large boot again. It finally rolled to a stop beneath a table. Looking back at Carole and Rose, they were covering their mouths in embarrassment and shaking hysterically. She glared at them and reached for the earring. With the earring finally in hand, a large combat boot moved and set upon her pinky finger.

Mouthing a silent scream as the bones in her pinky cracked. She squeaked as she tried to pull her finger free, pausing at the conversation she unwittingly overheard.

Brendan entered the bar with his childhood family friend, Mac. Sitting at the empty table in the bar, they ordered beers.

"I'm telling you, Brendan. I just need to talk to the

Montagnard Chieftain and see if Mai Le is there. Maybe he knows where she is or what happened to her."

"Anything to help, bro," Brendan said. "The brass ordered me to host a journalist at my firebase. They want photos and a feel-good article about the Yards and how we're working with them. Not only training their guerrillas, but on a humanitarian basis. You're welcome to tag along."

"I'm sure plenty of good men are willing to brave the bush. You might get lucky and have a woman reporter show up," Mac said, wiggling his eyebrows.

"Lucky? Oh, hell no. Considering Colonel Bragg's thoughts on the matter. My aversion to women in the field is well known. I refuse to have my team and I take responsibility for a woman that deep in the highlands."

They paused as the waiter delivered their beer and a bowl of popcorn.

"There's a lot of outstanding women reporters in Nam," Mac replied, popping a piece of popcorn into his mouth.

"I still don't want to deal with a woman in the bush," Brendan replied.

"Heard a rumor today about some cheeky woman reporter dangling upside down on a rope ladder just to get some photographs," Mac said.

"See. That proves my point on how unpredictable and dangerous women are."

Hearing a squeak under the table, Brendan and Mac paused, looking at each other in a silent language; they looked under the table.

Brendan raised his eyebrows. There she sat, the woman who was on his mind all day. On all fours, her glorious eyes wide open, with the pinkest cheeks he'd ever seen.

"Could you lift your boot? Please," Irelynn whispered.

He looked down at his feet. Seeing her small hand trapped under his foot, he frowned and lifted his boot. She pulled her hand out and waved it a bit.

"What are you doing?" Brendan asked.

"Um. Well." She opened her hand. "My earring was kicked under your table." She took the earring and clipped it to her ear lobe. "I'm just going to crawl away now."

Brendan's face split into a wide grin. "Not so fast, Sparky. Let me look at that finger."

Exchanging an amused glance with Mac, he stood as she crawled from under the table. Taking her other hand, he pulled her to her feet.

They were blocking the path of people trying to get through; he picked her up and set her on an empty barstool.

He lifted her dainty wrist. Her hand was soft and smooth, nails trimmed short. He wiggled her pinky to check for breakage. "It doesn't appear to be broken. Though, you could have a hairline fracture. You should go to the hospital and get it X-rayed."

"No. I'm not going to waste their time. They have enough men to look after," Irelynn said.

Brendan looked over to the bartender. "Mike. You got any tape?"

"Yeah," Mike said as he pulled a roll out of a drawer.

Brendan took the duct tape and pulled off a strip, taping her pinky to her ring finger.

"What's your name?" Brendan said. "Irelynn Cross."

"That's a beautiful name." He smiled at the blush that crept into her cheeks.

"What's yours?"

"Brendan Corrington."

"Nice Irish name," Irelynn said.

"My mother was Irish."

"So is my father," Irelynn replied.

Brendan put the finishing touches on the tape, holding her hand in his. "There you are. It's right as rain."

The sky above them rumbled with thunder in response as sheets of rain poured down around the cozy tiki bar.

Her eyes widened, and he could feel her pulse quicken in excitement.

"You like storms?"

She nodded her head. "I love them. Especially when the air fills with static. I get the shivers when the hair on the back of my neck and arms stands straight up."

"You do realize that means lightning is about to strike?"

She gave him a breathtaking smile. "I love the tingle."

Her eyes sparkled with mischief, and he was momentarily stunned by the beauty of her smile.

"Come. Dance with me," Brendan said, tugging her hand; he led her to the dance floor. Pulling her into his arms, they danced a slow waltz as the overhead lights flickered, and the jukebox stuttered.

She fit perfectly in his arms as he dipped her.

He felt the electric charge in the air as the hair on the back of his neck rose and his skin tingled. He looked into her eyes.

She felt it too.

Lightning struck close by, and she smiled again. Pulling her back up, he held her close.

His mouth hovered over her temple, down to the frantic beat on her slim throat, then over her plump lips as he inhaled her sweet scent.

She pulled away. "I have to go."

"Why?"

"I...I need to go run around the block," Irelynn breathlessly replied.

Brendan's eyebrows arched in amused curiosity.

Rushing from the dance floor, she scooped up her rucksack, and before he could say anything, she disappeared out the exit and into the stormy night.

Mac, who held Rose in his arms on the dance floor, stopped next to Brendan. "I don't know Brendan, you, and women. I may have to have a chat with your brothers about you. What happened?"

"She said she had to run around the block," Brendan replied with a grin.

Rose stifled a giggle.

"Do you know what she meant by that?" Mac asked.

Rose rolled her eyes. "Oh yes," she replied with a snicker.

"I'm going back to my quarters. You two have fun," Brendan said as he clapped Mac on the back.

Mac pulled Rose back into his arms. "So, my wee wild Rose. Tell me everything you know about that pretty girl in combat boots."

"Did you see the steam rolling off the two of them?" Rose said.

"Yeah. We may have to give them a little shove in the right direction. You know. Help them along a wee bit," Mac replied.

Rose raised a delicate eyebrow as a delicious grin lit her pretty face.

Peeling off her soaking wet dress, Irelynn sat and removed her boots. Her thoughts were on the man she had almost kissed. She touched her lips, remembering his scent and the sizzle between them.

Some of it, the storm, the rest was all him. He made her feel like she was on fire and unsettled.

Her only recourse was to get as far away from Captain Brendan Corrington as possible.

Coward. You're running away.

She took a slow deep breath before she grabbed her rucksack and the rest of her things. Tossing them inside the bag, she quickly dressed in clean fatigues and a t shirt. Slinging her cameras and gear over her shoulder, careful not to disturb sleeping nurses, she quietly let herself out.

Out on the main road, she thumbed a jeep ride to the airfield to catch the first flight out to Saigon at dawn.

CHAPTER 4

The city below Irelynn's second floor apartment bustled with life as street vendors hawked their wares, children ran and played, while their mothers called out to each other in mid-day greetings. Irelynn rolled over in bed, stuffing a fluffy pillow over her head to block out the racket. She was not a morning person and tended to be grumpy until at least noon when she started her day. She did her best writing at night while the city slept, pounding away on her typewriter through the wee hours of the morning. Last night was a rough one. Her wastebasket overflowed with crumpled paper as she had to keep starting over. Her mind returned to Brendan. He made her blow hot and cold at the same time.

Hot: She could not forget how his lips had hovered over her own. Her insides had melted, and she felt like mush when he touched her.

Cold: He had infuriated her with his off-hand comments about women reporters in the field.

Rolling over again, she rubbed her hand across her brow. It was a dream of hers to visit a Montagnard village. Deep in the jungle, most along the Cambodian/Laos borders. It was dangerous and terrifying, right up her alley.

She held up her hand and stared at her pinky still taped to her ring finger. "I believe in my dreams," she whispered to herself. "All of them."

Okay, Irelynn. Put your thinking cap on. How will you get them to take you on this mission if they're against women reporters?

She had one thing going in her favor: her birth name. Her parents had named her Irelynn George Cross. A mix up at the hospital put her legal first name as George on her birth certificate. Writing under George I. Cross, in the beginning, most expected a male journalist to show up for missions. Now, a well-respected freelance journalist and photographer, she had made a name for herself with her grit and dedication.

Pulling the mosquito netting aside, she rolled from bed. Sitting on the edge, she spotted a rat scaling the small balcony railing outside. She eyed her slingshot sitting on the nightstand.

Filthy vermin. If the window were open, I'd have a perfect shot.

Padding barefoot to the bathroom that also served as her darkroom, she showered and prepared for the busy day ahead.

An hour later, with a shopping bag in hand, she headed out the door toward a lunch date with her fellow correspondent and friend, Rebecca Ronan. Irelynn strolled down the sidewalk past street stalls and restaurants.

A traffic policeman stood in the middle of the street directing traffic as the delicious smell of pork rolls, and beef Pho drifted with the stench of exhaust fumes of cars, motorcycles, and scooters piled high with families all vying for their place within the chaos of the city.

Irelynn waved as she spotted Rebecca waiting for her outside of the Continental hotel. A key meeting place for war correspondents, the Continental boasted a wide variety of French cuisine, guaranteed to satisfy the pickiest palate. Her mouth watered at the thought of crusty loaves of bread and French Onion soup.

They were seated at their table within the luscious courtyard of the hotel. The table with its crisp, white linen tablecloth, the water, and wine glasses sparkling like diamonds in the sun reminded Irelynn of why she loved this restaurant. Lush Bougainvillea vines with pink flowers overflowed the trellis while bright green Geckos scurried to and fro under the shade of Frangipani trees.

Rebecca swirled her glass of Viognier wine. "How have you been, Irelynn?"

"Good. For the most part. I'm happy to be out of the bush, but it can be hard at times to sit here amongst this beauty when troops are wallowing in the filth and mud," Irelynn replied.

"True, but we all have a job to do here. We report on the war. They fight it."

"I know. Oh, I don't know. Maybe, it's time for a break. I haven't been home in a while. I miss my family and Gramie."

"Maybe, honey, you just need to get laid."

Irelynn grimaced. "Oh god. Here we go again."

"Don't knock it until you've tried it," Rebecca smirked.

"Casual sex is not my thing. Besides, half the guys here are married."

"It doesn't have to be another correspondent. There are tons of diplomats and sexy military guys of all ranks. All single. 'The world is your oyster.'"

"What is it with all the Shakespeare lately? You sound like Rose and Carole."

"How are they? I still owe them a bottle of wine. Next time I'm up that way, I'll stop in Da Nang to say hello," Rebecca said.

"Oh, I'm sure they'd give you an earful," Irelynn replied.

"What happened?"

"Just some embarrassing encounters with an Army Captain," Irelynn replied.

"I'm all ears."

"Well. First, I went ass over teakettle and got myself jammed between the sandbags and the nurse's barracks. He pulled me out. Then, there was this snake he killed. He practically seduced me. Then, a few hours later, when I was under his table looking for my earring, I overheard him talking about taking a journalist out to one of the Montagnard camps, but he won't take a woman. Then he stepped on my finger, darn near breaking it, and he almost kissed me on the dance floor."

Rebecca blinked. "That's an awful lot to decipher. I'm hearing two stories here. You're unusually flustered by this man. Tell me about him."

Irelynn gulped her wine. "He's a Green Beret." She paused as the waiter delivered their soup and bread. "Yes. Not much scares me, but this man does. Not because he's The Boogie Man, but because I knew when he said some wildly inappropriate things, he was teasing me. I was both outraged and thrilled. I am attracted to him, and it unsettles me."

"Hmm. Now the other."

"I heard them talking from under the table. The brass ordered him to take a journalist to one of the Montagnard camps for photos and a feel-good story. You know, it's been my dream to get into one of those camps. But he refuses to take a woman on the mission."

"You need to tread carefully, Irelynn."

"Since when have I ever let men stop me? I intend to find a way to be on that chopper and get that story."

"We've all heard the stories. Special forces men are a whole different breed," Rebecca warned. "What if this captain is on that chopper as well?"

"It sounded like he was the commander of the firebase. Didn't you tell me it's better to beg forgiveness than ask for permission? I need a perfect plan."

Rebecca pulled her sunglasses down. Tossing her blonde hair over her shoulder. "The way I see it. You have two options. Schmooze the brass, which you've always been good at, or disguise yourself as a man."

Irelynn drummed her fingers on the table before taking a sip of wine. "Sweet talking the generals may be easier at this point. I think I'll send a letter to MACV and see if that works."

"There's a ball at the American embassy on Saturday. You're already on the guest list. Do you still have that amber ball gown? It matches your eyes perfectly," Rebecca said.

Irelynn sighed deeply. "Yes. I was thinking about going anyway. That dress, though, as lovely as it is. The neckline is so low."

"Honey. That's exactly what you need."

"Fine. I'll go. Just keep me away from the champagne. The stuff goes right to my head."

"Oh. A word of warning. Edwin Baltini is back in town. Watch your back."

Irelynn hissed. "That's just great."

"On that note. Here, I bought you some mace," Rebecca said.

Irelynn hefted the can before placing it in her shopping bag. "Mace. Why?"

"It might come in handy against douchebags like Baltini. Promise me you'll keep it close."

"I'll keep it in my rucksack," Irelynn replied.

CHAPTER 5

*B*rendan pulled at the neck of his dress blues. "Mac, how I let you talk me into this is beyond me."

"Relax. It's only for a few hours, and you never know who you might run into at these affairs," Mac replied.

Brendan growled. "You just didn't want to suffer through this alone."

Mac grinned, his emerald, green eyes sparkling with amusement. "What else are blood brothers for?"

"We were kids when we did that. I still remember getting ripped a new asshole by father and Aunt Meg," Brendan replied.

"They did have to haul six boys to the infirmary for stitches," Mac said as he looked at the faint scar on the palm of his hand.

Brendan looked at his own scar in the same spot. "Whose bright idea was that anyway?"

"I want to say it was Elijah's, but it could have been any of us."

Brendan looked around the large ballroom. A black-tie affair was celebrating the American Fourth of July, the women dressed in a kaleidoscope of colorful ball gowns. The tinkling of flutes of champagne added to the laughter of the city's elite gathered in mass.

"It's like another world," Brendan said. "Take this elegant ballroom with its crystal chandeliers and gold velvet drapes. Pick it up and drop it into Washington, D.C.; you wouldn't know the difference.

"Yeah. You wouldn't know it's a country at war by all these stuffed shirt diplomats dancing the night away," Mac replied. "I suppose it's time to work the crowd and see if we can find Mai Lei's former employers. See if they know what happened to her."

"I'll work this side of the room," Brendan replied. "Mr. and Mrs. Le, correct?"

"Yes."

"General Smead is heading this way," Rebecca said.

Irelynn nibbled on a fresh strawberry and took a sip of champagne. "Great. Another one that doesn't like women in the field."

"Relax, Irelynn. He's a brilliant military strategist, and he adores you. He might be the one who can help you."

"I went to college with his daughter, Anne. He treats me like I'm his daughter too."

"Smile, kiddo."

Irelynn plastered a smile on her face. Turning to the tall, slender man, who walked toward her with an air of command and authority. "General Smead. It's nice to see you again."

"Irelynn, Rebecca. Lovely as always," General Smead replied. "Irelynn. May I have this dance."

"Of course," Irelynn replied.

He led her to the dance floor, pulling her into his arms in a slow waltz.

"So, how goes the war, General Smead?" Irelynn said.

"Is this on or off the record?"

"Off. After all, this is a party."

"Yes. Seeing you here tells me that you want something."

She smiled up at him. "I come to plenty of these parties."

General Smead grunted. "Only when necessary."

"It's all about contacts. Besides, you wouldn't be here in Saigon unless it was necessary either."

"True," General Smead said. "The war is not going well, Irelynn. As Anne's friend, I'd rather see you back home."

"How's Anne doing? I haven't heard from her lately," Irelynn said.

"Busy chasing after her babies. She's due with her third child soon, which is where you belong. Not in the bush chasing after the troops for your next story."

"Hmm. We've had this discussion before. I'm not ready for marriage or babies."

"What are you looking for this time?"

"I've heard through the grapevine that special forces will allow a reporter into one of the Montagnard camps. I want that gig."

"No."

"No? Why not?" Irelynn cried.

"It's dangerous."

"You know me and how good I am at my job. If I was a man..."

"If you were a man, I wouldn't be dancing with you."

"One way or another, I will find a way to go," Irelynn said.

"What would I say to your father if I had to call him and tell him his little girl had been injured, or worse, killed in Vietnam?"

"My father doesn't know I'm here," Irelynn said. "Don't you tell him either. He'll show up with my brothers in tow."

"I'm surprised you would deceive your father."

"I'm not deceiving him. I'm protecting his sanity."

"Where may I ask, do your parents think you are?"

"Backpacking the Hippy trail through South Asia."

"Green Berets are a different breed. They don't always follow the rules."

"But they get the job done, don't they? I'm well aware there's a disconnect between the regular army and special forces. I think I can handle them."

"I can see you're determined. Colonel Bragg oversees Special forces at Da Nang. I highly doubt he would allow you to go," General Smead said. "My aide is signaling me."

Turning to a tall red headed man standing at the edge of the dance floor.

"Major, would you mind finishing this dance with this lovely young lady for me?"

The man turned a delighted smile to Irelynn. "Of course, sir."

Irelynn sucked in her breath. *Oh shit. Big red headed guy. If he's here, Brendan might be as well.* The man pulled her into his arms and glided around the dance floor.

"Irelynn, right? Pretty name."

She peeked around his shoulders, looking around the ballroom for that one man who never failed to leave her a quivering mess. "Ah. Yes." Looking around his massive shoulders again, she spotted Brendan on the far side of the room. "Damn," she muttered.

"Looking for someone special, darlin'?" The red headed man said.

"What? No. Absolutely not," she said as she hid behind the man.

Irelynn spotted Rebecca standing next to the dance floor, watching her dance. She reached out and grabbed her by the arm.

"Rebecca. Big red headed guy. Big red headed guy, meet Rebecca." Then she scrambled out the open terrace door to the veranda as fast as her feet could carry her.

Mac pulled the tall woman into his arms and maneuvered them around the dance floor so he could get a better view of Brendan. Smiling, he knew Brendan had spotted Irelynn as she hastily exited the ballroom. Brendan's face had split into a grin as he moved through the crowd before disappearing out the terrace door at the opposite end of the ballroom. The woman in his arms tried to peer out the doorway, curiosity, and excitement on her face; her eyes flickered to Brendan going out the other door.

She inhaled sharply. "Is that him?" she breathed.

Mac looked down into the flushed face of his dance partner, then back out the doorway. "So, she is interested in Brendan?"

"Of course, she is. Did you see her reaction to seeing him? I'd give anything to be a little mouse in the corner right now."

"Rebecca, right? I'm Mac, by the way."

Bending over and peeking around the corner of the doorway, Irelynn looked for Brendan, where she had spotted him moments earlier. "Damn. Where is he?" she muttered.

She straightened up, a kerplunk on the ground, and she realized she had lost her earring. Dropping to her knees, she crawled around, looking for the missing earring. "Oh, for the love of God. Again?" she muttered.

Enough of these clip-on earrings. You will bite the bullet and get your ears pierced once and for all.

The dim lighting on the terrace didn't help her search for the earring as she crawled around. Feeling with her hands, she patted the ground as she went until she came to a pair of boots standing in front of her. Looking up, she paled at the image she must present to the man standing above her.

"Brendan," she breathed as she felt the burn of embarrassment from her cheeks to her toes.

CHAPTER 6

Brendan peered down at the woman who tormented his dreams these past few weeks.

The reflection of the lamps around the terrace sparkled like the stars in her luminous eyes. Her chestnut curls were swept up into a chignon bun with soft tendrils escaping to curl around her heart shaped face.

His gaze caressed her flawless skin and the gown's cut against her creamy cleavage.

A large gold nugget on a delicate chain dangled provocatively between her full breasts. Her amber colored ballgown sparkled like a thousand diamonds as she chewed her lower lip in consternation. A sparkle on the ground next to her, and he kneeled and picked up the missing earring.

Holding his hands out to her, she placed hers in his, and they rose to their feet. His long fingers stroked her cheek before clipping the earring on her delicate earlobe. He smiled when she shook with a soft shiver.

"You seem to have issues with your earrings," he breathed.

Reaching up, she slid her hands around his neck. Her lips hovered over his.

He pulled her into his arms; his lips touched hers. He reveled in the touch of her smooth, plump lips.

Her breath was warm and sweet, tasting of champagne and strawberries.

Pulling her closer still, her breasts crushed against his chest, he burned where their bodies touched. The kiss was everything he knew it would be. He deepened the kiss, never wanting it to end.

He finally pulled away from her lips, placing another kiss on her forehead.

"I should probably tell you I've been drinking champagne. I had to kiss you to see what I missed last time," Irelynn said.

His hands cupped her face, and he found her lips again.

She was intoxicating, her confession endearing.

"You've enchanted me, Irelynn. I've been thinking about you," Brendan said, his voice a smooth rumble in his chest.

Her hands felt warm as they rested lightly on his chest. A beautiful smile lit her face. "The same here," she softly replied.

A throat cleared, and they both looked over to see a man standing five feet in front of them. A soft gasp escaped from Irelynn, a slight tremble shook her body, and she shrunk into his side.

"Well. Well. What have we here? Miss Irelynn Cross, sinking her claws into another unwary victim," the man said. The man, in his mid-forties, slightly graying hair, paunchy and on the small side, sneered at Irelynn.

"What do you want, Teeny?" Irelynn asked.

"I told you not to call me that," Edwin Baltini snarled.

"I'm surprised they even let you back in-country," Irelynn said.

"No thanks to you," Edwin snarled.

"That's what happens when you try to steal others hard earned work. Stay away from me. Edwin," Irelynn said.

"You heard the lady. I suggest you leave," Brendan growled.

Edwin looked at Brendan, nodding his head. "Very well. By the way, Captain. Irelynn's best when she's on her knees."

Brendan looked down at Irelynn, the shock, and outrage on her face apparent.

"I'm not going to tell you again. Get the fuck out of here. Now," Brendan barked as he took menacing steps toward Edwin.

Edwin slithered back inside the ballroom, turning around to see Irelynn jump from the first floor terrace wall.

"Oh no you don't. Not this time." He climbed the wall and jumped after her.

Irelynn dipped her hands in the cool water of the massive water fountain, patting her face and neck to cool herself down. Sitting on the edge, she removed her combat boots and socks, setting them aside. She lifted her A line ball gown above her knees and stepped into the knee-deep water.

Deep in thought, she flicked the water with her foot.

Her mind traveled back to the day not long ago when she had fought off Edwin Baltini's sexual advances, leaving her bruised and battered. He had fared much worse, thanks to the defensive training from her brothers. That, and his theft of her work, left a bad taste in her mouth for working with male correspondents.

Sighing deeply, she turned to see Brendan standing next to the fountain.

She inhaled sharply.

The light shone upon his black hair. His broad shoulders, trim waist, and long legs filled out his dress uniform.

She slightly shimmied her shoulders as a delightful shiver slid down her spine, her eyes drawn again to his handsome face; his blue eyes sparkled in the dim light of the tinkling fountain.

He looked down at her combat boots. Raising an amused eyebrow. "Combat boots and ballgowns? You are the most unusual woman I have ever met," he quipped.

She wrinkled up her nose. "I suppose you were expecting glass slippers?" she replied.

"Like Cinderella, you seem to have a penchant for running away."

"I'm sorry. I was embarrassed."

"Don't be. Men like that are scum."

Brendan climbed into the fountain, boots, and all. The water sloshed as he strode toward her. Pulling her into his arms, "I was about to ask you to dance back there before we were so rudely interrupted," Brendan said. "So, Irelynn, will you dance with me?"

"Here? In the fountain?" Irelynn breathed.

"Why not? If you listen closely, you can hear the music floating through the gardens from the ballroom. Breathe in. Do you smell the Jasmine and Dalat roses?"

"It is very romantic," Irelynn said. Dropping the hem of her gown, it floated and swayed in the water as they moved in a slow dance of enchantment.

"You're going to ruin your gown of a thousand stars," Brendan murmured in her ear.

"Said the man in his dress blues," Irelynn whispered back. Behind them, the night sky lit up with fireworks of red, white, and blue.

"Perfect," Brendan breathed as he lowered his lips to taste hers. He didn't stop until he heard another throat clearing. Looking up, he spotted two Marines in fatigues on patrol of the embassy grounds standing in front of them.

"Evening, Sir," said one Marine.

Brendan grinned. "Evening, men."

Irelynn squealed with laughter when he scooped her up in his arms and stepped from the fountain. He grabbed her boots and strode across the garden towards the terrace.

Mac looked down into the brown eyes of his blonde dance partner. She fit into his arms perfectly. Tall or small. He loved women.

"So, tell me, lass. Tell me all about your wee friend Irelynn."

"Why? Are you interested?" Rebecca asked.

"Me? Nah. I'm just watching out for my buddy. Seeing what he's getting himself into."

"She's a sweet girl, but not one to mess with. She can be bold, brash, and gutsy. A top-notch war correspondent."

"So, she's not afraid of much?"

"Just having a love life. Why are you so interested in your friend's affairs?"

Mac grinned down at her. "Natural curiosity. I've never seen him so taken with a woman."

Rebecca paused; her eyes widened. "Shit. Edwin Baltini," she hissed. "What's he doing here?"

Mac stiffened. Looking around the ballroom, "Where?"

"He just came in from the terrace. If Irelynn saw him, damn, this is not good."

Maneuvering Rebecca around the dance floor so he could get a good look at the man.

"So that's what the little prick looks like."

"You've heard of him?"

Mac grunted. "What's he got to do with Irelynn Cross?"

"Earlier this year, they were working together. Irelynn

spent a week in the bush with Baltini and an Army reconnaissance team documenting the Viet Cong's tunnel system. Irelynn convinced them to allow her into the tunnels after they had cleared them. Edwin, the spine-less coward he was, didn't want to enter them. Her photographs alone of the tunnels and chambers were top notch and earned her respect from the troops. Edwin stole her photographs, claiming the story was his alone. Then when confronted by Irelynn, he tried to assault her sexually. Thank God for Irelynn's abilities."

Mac nodded, his face brutal, and unforgiving as stone. "Come on, lass. Let's get some champagne."

They stood by the long table heavily laden with delicacies sipping their champagne, watchful eyes on the terrace doors.

"While we're standing here. Do you know Mr. and Mrs. Le?"

"Yes, I do. I'm not sure if they're here, but I'll keep my eye out for them. Why?"

"Now I can't give away all my secrets, can I?" Mac replied, giving her a wink.

"I can see you're a man of secrets. You're Special Forces, aren't you?"

"Maybe."

"What's a girl got to do to get a gig with Special Forces?"

Mac laughed outright. "I can guarantee you. No woman will ever be allowed on a mission with Special Forces."

"Hmm. Interesting," Rebecca replied. "Look. There they are."

They both looked to the terrace door where Brendan and Irelynn stood holding hands.

"Look at them. They're both glowing," Rebecca said.

"They are glowing," Mac replied.

"Why are they all wet?" Rebecca exclaimed.

Irelynn moved away from Brendan, her fingers trailing through his fingertips as he let her go. She strolled through the crowd toward her table to get her clutch purse and wrap. Spotting Mac, Brendan smiled and strode toward them.

Rebecca inhaled sharply through her teeth. "Oooh. What a man."

Mac raised both eyebrows in amusement.

"What? I like men," Rebecca said.

Making introductions, they chatted for a minute. Excusing herself, Rebecca walked to the table to speak with Irelynn.

"You sneaky bastard. You knew she might be here, didn't you?" Brendan said.

Mac grinned. "Maybe." Sobering, he faced Brendan. "Edwin Baltini is back. I saw him come in from the terrace while you were out there."

"Shit. That was him. Damn it. He was pretty nasty to Irelynn, and she obviously didn't like him."

"He might be trying to dig up more on your sister-in-law, Elyse," Mac said. "It still sticks in my craw that I wasn't working that case."

"You were recovering from a gunshot wound to your ass. Cut yourself some slack. Let's not forget Baltini's connections to General Nguyen. We all believe he was working with the general to kidnap Elyse," Brendan snarled.

"It's too bad we didn't figure it out until after Elyse was rescued," Mac said.

"He slipped out of town shortly after, and we lost track of him. I wonder what he's up to now?"

"What's his connection to Irelynn?"

"According to the lovely Rebecca, he stole some of her work," Mac said.

"What kind of work?" Brendan asked.

A tinkling of whispers and laughter from Rebecca and Irelynn behind him, and he turned, a big smile on his handsome face. He was holding out his hand, a warm gaze on his face as he looked down at Irelynn.

She slipped her hand into his, and he gave her a slight squeeze.

"I'm going to see Irelynn home," Brendan said. "We're both soaking wet."

"Yes. Go get out of those wet clothes," Rebecca said with a snicker.

Irelynn's eyes widened, then narrowed at Rebecca.

Brendan cleared his throat. "I'm only in town through Monday, Irelynn. Would you care to join me for dinner tomorrow?"

"Oh. I'm sorry. I'm leaving at noon tomorrow for Vung Tao. I'm going out on a combat mission."

Brendan drew in a sharp breath and stiffened. "A mission? What kind of a mission?"

Startled by his response, she glared at him. "I'm going out in the bush with the Australians," Irelynn gritted out. "It's my job."

"Your job? I thought you were a nurse," Brendan said.

"A nurse? I can't even put a band aid on straight. I'm a war correspondent."

"A war correspondent. Are you telling me you're one of those women who risk life and limb to get their story?"

"Yes. That's exactly what I do." Jabbing her finger into his chest to enunciate every single word. "I report on the war."

"You don't belong here, Irelynn," Brendan quietly stated.

"Of all the nerve. You have no right to tell me where I belong. Goodnight Captain. I'll see myself home."

Looking at Mac and Rebecca, who stood with slack jaws. "Goodnight." With that, she left. Her ballgown swishing with each angry step, she wound her way toward the exit

"That is one infuriating woman," Brendan seethed before following Irelynn out.

Mac and Rebecca looked at each other.

"Well. That went south fast," Mac said.

"She's a damn good reporter. She deserves respect, not condemnation."

Mac looked over to the exit. "She's got big balls to go toe to toe with a Green Beret."

"Irelynn's not called a scrappy little bruiser for nothing,"

Rebecca replied with a smirk. "Come on. I see Mr. and Mrs. Le over there."

Hailing a rickshaw, Irelynn climbed in. Giving her address to the driver in Vietnamese. Lost in thought, she didn't appear to notice the delay in leaving the embassy grounds.

Brendan stepped up to the rickshaw. Lifting the startled Vietnamese man off his bike. He took off his dress jacket and pulled a few bills out of his pocket, placing them both in the confused man's hands before grabbing the rice hat off his head.

"Wait here. I'll be back in a bit," Brendan said. Climbing aboard the bike, he pushed off and headed toward her address.

Sitting in the seat in front of him, talking to herself, she spoke in French, and he understood every word.

"Asshole. What does he know about me? How hard I've worked. I've crawled in the mud through blood and guts. I slept in the rain. Sheets of it, pouring down, chilling me to the bone. I've been filthy, just like the troops. I've had dysentery and lice. I was there when men lost their lives, and yes, I had close calls myself. I have earned every ounce of respect and damn it; I belong where I say I belong. I thought he might be the one. He made me feel so alive. It's not fair. I believe in my dreams...." she whispered. "It really hurts coming from him."

Brendan pulled up in front of the storefront address.

She climbed out and handed him the fare without looking at him. Walking to a side door, she turned to the light, and he could see the shimmer of tears on her face. Key in hand, she let herself in and quietly shut the door behind her.

A minute later, the lights came on in the apartment above the store.

Brendan sat for a while in quiet reflection before pedaling back to the embassy.

Back at the embassy, Edwin Baltini exited the men's room. Walking down the long hallway toward the ballroom, he paused in front of a large photograph. The woman pictured, a beautiful ballerina in mid leap.

"Ah. Elyse Booker, the one who got away. I would have paid a fortune for her," a man behind him said.

"Unfortunately, the general let her slip away," Baltini replied.

"He paid the ultimate price for his incompetence. I want Irelynn Cross."

Edwin Baltini snickered. "We'll do our best."

"Don't disappoint me again, Baltini."

CHAPTER 7

A thick cigar dangled from Colonel Michael Bragg's mouth. Feet up on his desk, he rifled through a stack of paperwork. Pausing on one telegram, he ran a hand through his gray crew cut in frustration. Slamming his feet on the floor, he bellowed.

"Murphy. Get your ass in here."

Corporal Murphy appeared in the doorway. "Yes. Sir."

"What the fuck do we know about this reporter, George Cross?"

"He's been pretty supportive of the troops. He writes mostly about the troops and what they go through. Photographs are top notch. He's got a huge following back in the world. He comes highly recommended from MACV."

"And this is the bozo they want us to take to Ben Het?"

"Yes, Sir."

"Where the fuck is Corrington?"

"He went back to Ben Het yesterday. He left two men to escort Cross once they had your go ahead. Mac, umm, Major McLoughlin, has arrived back from Saigon."

"Mac is back? Find him. I want to see him before that fucking reporter plops his nosey ass on one of my choppers. God damn reporters. That's the last thing I need. Some pansy-ass distracting my men with their questions. Two days. That's all Cross gets."

"Yes, Sir." Corporal Murphy said as he left the Colonel's office. Sitting back at his desk, he typed up the telegram to send to George I. Cross, located in Saigon.

Be at Da Nang AB on Tuesday, July Thirteenth, Nineteen Sixty-Nine, at twelve hundred hours and ready to leave for two days at Ben Het Special Forces Camp.

Colonel Michael Bragg

Commander, U.S. Special Forces Group/CCN.

Meticulously packing her rucksack, Irelynn could barely contain her excitement. Looking up as Rebecca handed her a cup of coffee.

"I can't believe my letter to MACV worked," Irelynn said. "You're sure about this, kiddo?" Rebecca asked as she settled herself on Irelynn's couch.

"As sure as I'll ever be. As long as I don't get caught, I'll be in and out of that camp before anyone ever figures out I'm a woman."

"I don't doubt your abilities, Irelynn, but Special forces men are different."

"Well, I write as George I. Cross. I guess they haven't figured it out that I'm a woman."

"You've never had to disguise yourself as a man before," Rebecca said. "Thank God, for the most part, that the attitudes toward women war correspondents have changed."

"Except the Green Berets," Irelynn said.

Irelynn held up her newest creation. Tied much like a corset above her waist, the bum was a padded contraption she had invented. It hid her tiny waist and curvy hips, bulking up her ribs. Along with the ace bandage, she would use it to flatten her breasts. It hid her female attributes to perfection.

"This, along with a dark-haired wig, will cover my hair. Before I board the chopper, I'll stop in the village to get dressed in baggy fatigues, dark sunglasses, and camouflage paint on my face to complete my male ensemble."

"Hmm," Rebecca murmured. "It looks hot."

"Nasty, hot, and sweaty. I'm sure not at all fun to wear, but worth it for my needs," Irelynn replied.

"Oh. Don't forget to pack these for Rose," Rebecca said as she handed her a pair of red high heels and a red dress.

Irelynn raised her eyebrows, then frowned. "Never could walk right in these damn things. I'm not sure what possessed me to buy the dress or the shoes."

"Aren't you worried about running into Brendan?"

Irelynn paused, a deep sadness passing over her beautiful face. "No. Remember you told me he's short? He should be back in the world before I arrive at the firebase. I'll never see him again."

"Please be careful. I worry that if they figure it out, there'll be hell to pay," Rebecca warned.

"I'll worry about paying the devil his due if I get caught."

"Okay. Let's practice walking and talking like a man again."

Stepping out of his hut, which was both his office and private quarters, Brendan looked around the camp. Children ran and played outside the massive longhouses that housed the Montagnard's troops and their families. The women preparing a mid-day meal of rice and fish for their men shooed the children away from the campfires. There were times when life in the camp seemed almost idyllic. He couldn't begin to explain how much he admired the Montagnard people. At four hundred plus within the base camp, the men were fearsome fighters, brothers at arms that he would trust with his life and had on many occasions. Twelve special forces personnel, including himself, guided the Montagnard's in a guerrilla capacity in the fight against the NVA and VC, providing training, arms, medicine, and food for the villagers. Brendan looked at his watch, expecting the reporter within the hour. His brow fell in a thunderous frown.

His mind, once again, returned to Irelynn. He had mistreated her. If he could go back in time and re-word what he said. However, he was still firm in his belief about women in the bush. That would never change. It's not like he doubted her abilities, but she scared the hell out of him. When she admitted to working in the bush, his protector mode had roared to life. Was it a chauvinist attitude? Probably. Her rant in French when he pedaled her home in the rickshaw had shaken him to the core. He had wanted nothing more than to climb off that rickshaw, take her in his arms and kiss the tears off her face. He didn't because he knew they would never see eye to eye on this matter. He believed in women and equal rights. Mom before her death and Aunt Meg had seen to that. But this felt different. A tug on his leg and a giggle brought him out of his musings. A little girl of three hung on his leg. Pretending her hands were cat claws, she growled at him, reminding him of Irelynn. "Okay, kitten, you want to play." Holding his own hands up like claws, he roared back as the little one ran screaming in delight while he chased after her. After ten minutes of playing 'Tiger" with the children, laughing, he plopped down next to his second in command, Warrant Officer Rick Morgan, who was taking a much-needed break.

"Not sure where these kids get their energy from," Brendan said.

"They're sure going to miss you when you leave, Skipper," Morg replied.

"I'll miss them too. That reporter, Cross, should be here

soon. I want you to make sure he gets the photos he needs," Brendan said.

"Why didn't they send a Stars and Stripes reporter?"

Brendan rubbed his brow. "The brass wanted someone who had a big following back in the world. It's important to show the good we are doing here."

"I'd be happier not to have to deal with them at all," Morg grumbled.

"I hear you," Brendan replied. "I'll be in my office if you need anything. Ah Morg, don't involve me unless it's necessary."

Peering over the top of her sunglasses, Irelynn, aka George Cross, tried to quell her wildly beating heart. Seated in the chopper, directly across from her, was "Big red headed guy," Mac, as he had introduced himself when they boarded the chopper. He was big, around six four, muscular, and impressive in his combat gear. He peered intently at her for a minute, then, smiling, he leaned back and closed his sparkling green eyes.

Breathing a sigh of relief, Irelynn focused on the breathtaking scenery. Pulling her camera out, she took a few pictures of the countryside below. Rice paddies gave way to plantations of rubber trees, then thick jungle, followed by the mountains of the central highlands. Off in the distance, she could see a formation of Huey choppers as they transported troops into battle. She said a quick prayer for their safety, snapped a few pictures, and re focused her attention below. A river twisted and turned in gentle curves through a lush valley nestled between the emerald mountainous hills. Further north, her eyes caught and followed the vapor trails of two F-4 jets high in the sky above her. Snapping photos, she saw them lowering altitude and dropping ordinance on their target. Napalm. She inhaled sharply, surprised that she had captured the power and fury of the moment on film. Her attention turned to the other occupants of the chopper.

The man sitting next to Mac, Sergeant Nelson, was the name on his shirt. Sandy brown hair cropped short. Just as big as Mac, he grinned at her.

"You're a scrappy little fucker, aren't you?" he shouted over the noise.

Lowering her voice as she had practiced. "Makes for a smaller target."

He leaned back, resting his head against the wall, giving her a quizzical look before looking away, focusing on the scenery below. The man next to her, Staff Sergeant Smith, gave her an amused sideways glance before looking out the doorway.

Irelynn closed her eyes, eventually lulled to sleep by the chopper blades as they rotated in a whoop-whoop sound.

Awakening a short time later, Irelynn's heart quickened as the base camp came into view. The camp cut into the top of a mountain was large but compact. She counted five longhouses, numerous huts with roofs made of vegetation within a village. The military side of the base had many outbuildings, their roofs of tin glistening in the hot sun. The bunkers with machine gun mounts were too numerous to count, spread out around the perimeter of the firebase. Fascinated with the layout of the camp, surrounded by wire and a moat of all things, she raised her camera.

A hand blocked her camera. "No pictures of the perimeter or fortifications," Smith growled.

Irelynn nodded. "Understood."

Whirlwinds of dust swirled around the chopper as it landed on the helipad. Nodding her thanks to the pilots, following her escorts, she jumped off. Ducking low, her hand held her floppy hat in place. Bracing herself against the force of wind, her combat boots dug deep into the muddy soil as the chopper lifted off, heading back to Da Nang. A deep sense of satisfaction enveloped Irelynn as she slung her rucksack over her shoulder. *I made it. So far, so good.*

She got a few shots off her camera before another man approached her.

He looked her up and down. "I'm Warrant Officer Rick Morgan. You can call me Morg."

"George Cross," she replied.

"You're not what I expected."

Irelynn raised her eyebrows. Oh, you have no idea. "What were you expecting?"

"Thought you'd be taller," Morg replied. "Come on. Let's get started."

Irelynn looked around the camp, trying to decide what to

shoot first. "Can I just roam around and see what sparks my interest first?"

"Go ahead. Just stay out of the village until you're invited in by the Chieftain. He knows you'll be here today and has agreed to let you take pictures. Don't talk to or touch the villagers until you have his permission."

"How do I tell where the village proper starts?" Irelynn asked.

"The entrance to the village is marked by bamboo fencing. You need to watch your step here, there's a lot they consider taboo, and you don't want to insult them inadvertently."

"Got it," Irelynn replied.

Strolling away, Irelynn lifted her camera and started documenting the base camp. Pulling out a notebook, she took notes of what she saw and what Morg had told her.

Mac approached Morg. "Hey, Morg. How's it hanging?"

"Mac. Good to see you again," he said as he reached out to bump fists.

They both watched Irelynn for a minute. "I can't put my finger on it, but somethings off," Morg said.

Mac grinned. "Where's Brendan?"

"The Skipper is in his quarters."

"He won't be a Captain after today," Mac said.

"Did his promotion finally go through?"

"Yup. I think they're trying to entice him to stay."

"It won't work. Skipper's ready to go back to the world and start a new life," Morg said.

"He deserves it. Be ready for a brief pinning ceremony if time permits."

"Yes, sir. At least we have a reporter to document it."

Mac looked over to where Irelynn was taking photographs. "Keep an eye on him."

"Yes. Sir," Morg replied.

"George." A peal of deep rumbling laughter rolled in his chest, and Mac hefted his rucksack over his shoulder and headed over to Brendan's office.

CHAPTER 8

Brendan looked up at the knock on his door; Mac filled the doorway. "You made it."

Tossing a few envelopes onto the desk, Mac eased his long frame into a chair in front of Brendan's desk.

"I see the Army has you set up here like a king."

Brendan looked at his desk made of crates and spare wooden planks. "Only the best," he replied with a grin.

"I rode out here with that reporter MACV sent," Mac said.

"And…?"

"Oh, I think you will want to meet him yourself."

Picking up one of the envelopes, he looked inside. "Well, that's a cryptic statement. Heh, it looks like my promotion went through," Brendan said.

"It's about damn time," Mac replied.

"I'm still out of here in seven weeks. I'm tired of war and all that goes with it."

"Well. You've been in for what eight nine years. How many tours of duty have you done?"

"Four, no five," Brendan replied.

"What will you do when you get back to the world?"

"I don't know yet. I've been thinking about Law enforcement."

"CIA?"

Brendan grinned. "I think I'll leave that for you. I'm thinking something more local."

"Street cop?"

"Smaller still," Brendan said.

"Town sheriff?" Mac asked.

"Maybe. I don't know. Like I said. I'm still kicking it around. What's in the other envelope?"

"A little more info about Edwin Baltini."

"So, you're pretty sure he was involved with the plot to kidnap Elyse? Is she safe?"

"Yeah, I think the wee fairy is safe for now. Elijah will see to it. Right now, we are more worried about other women being targeted. Also, we believe he may still be spying for the NVA. Troop movements, things of that nature. He disappeared for a while. We believe he may have been in Hanoi."

"Okay. So why are you telling me this?"

"That envelope contains your new orders," Mac replied.

"New orders. What the fuck does that mean?" Brendan snarled as he tore open the envelope.

Reading through the orders, he exclaimed, "Saigon! Irelynn Cross! What the hell is going on?"

"I've got a tail on Baltini. He's been following Irelynn. What we don't know is if it's personal or if it's related to two missing American women."

"Missing as in MIA?"

"No. Missing as in kidnapped. Both nurses," Mac replied. "What does this have to do with Irelynn?"

"Baltini was seen with both of those women before they disappeared."

"You think Irelynn's a target?"

"Yes. Look at it this way, Brendan. You're almost short. Your replacement is due up here within a few days for some OJT. You've already established a relationship with Irelynn. After seeing you together at the ball, Baltini won't think it's unusual that you're with her in Saigon. Your orders are to work with me to protect her."

"Why do I have visions of Elijah chasing after Elyse running through my head?" Brendan growled. "I'm a Green Beret, not a babysitter."

"It worked out well for them," Mac said.

"After what happened at the embassy ball, I doubt Irelynn would even speak to me."

"That's where I'm counting on that Corrington charm."

"Wait. You left her unprotected to come up here?" Brendan

growled.

Mac grinned. "Oh, I think she's in safe hands right now."

A wave of jealousy hit Brendan as his eyebrows fell in a thunderous scowl. "Whose hands?"

Rising to his feet. "Come on," Mac chuckled. Curiosity moved his feet as he followed Mac outside.

Once outside, he stood with arms crossed over his chest. From his vantage point, Brendan scanned the camp. He saw nothing out of the ordinary. Montagnard troops practiced their drills. The old Chieftain and another group of warriors sat in front of a longhouse; their women served the mid-day meal. Four out of the dozen men he had here were out on missions. The rest either trained the remaining Montagnards or were sleeping after a night on a patrol or guard duty. The smell of rice and chicken floated through the camp as mothers called the children to stop playing and eat. His gaze drifted to a small naked child sitting in the dirt while she fisted rice from her bowl made of leaves into her mouth.

Further away, right outside of the village, the reporter lay on his belly, camera aimed at the child. A belly laugh from the Chieftain and Brendan's gaze landed on the older man's young wife; barely eighteen, her belly swelled to full term as she whispered in the older man's ear. Drifting to Mac, he raised his questioning eyebrows. Mac grinned again. *What does he see that I don't?*

His eyes fell on the reporter again. The man moved to his knee's crawling closer to the fencing to view the child. His eyes flickered to Morg, who stood twenty feet back from the man. Signaling with his hand, he called Morg over while continuing his perusal of the man on the ground.

The man was almost effeminate in the way he crawled. His clothes were baggy, but the rear end. The fabric was stretched tight across his shapely bottom. What the fuck? Brendan's eyebrows shot straight up as he whipped around to stare at Mac. If Mac's grin could have gotten any bigger, his face would have split in two.

Brendan's mind raced as he whipped around again. Short dark hair, black rimmed glasses, but that profile. He knew that delicate profile.

I'm going to kill her.

He whipped back around to face Mac and Morg.

"You keep spinning like that, and I'm going to have to start calling you twister," Mac said.

Brendan opened his mouth and then snapped it shut.

"What's wrong, Skipper?" Morg asked.

"Anything seem off to you, Morg?" Brendan asked.

"Well. Yeah, now that you mention it. That reporter, he's... I don't know what it is," Morg replied.

"That's because he is a she," Brendan growled.

Morg's eyes flickered to the man on the ground. "Holy shit. That's it," he replied as he moved to go confront the person.

Brendan's arm snaked out, stopping him. "No. We'll play along with Irelynn's little charade for now."

"Irelynn? You know this chick?"

"Oh yes," Brendan replied. "Mac, you knew. Why didn't you have the chopper turn around and take her back to Da Nang?"

"Not my call, my friend. Besides, I didn't figure it out until we were almost here," Mac replied.

"So, what are we going to do?" Morg asked.

A devious smile replaced the cool anger shadowing Brendan's face. "Oh, we're going to have a little fun with this. We're going to teach her a lesson she won't soon forget. Then, I'll put her sweet ass on a chopper back to Da Nang."

"What about the rest of the team? Should we tell them?" Morg asked.

"Not yet. Let me come up with a plan first. Meanwhile, we are going to make George Cross as uncomfortable with her deception as possible," Brendan said. "Keep a guard on her at all times, Morg. She can bunk with me."

Both Mac and Morg raised their eyebrows in surprise. "It's not like that," Brendan said.

"Sure, it's not," Mac replied. "Pretty girl. Alone with you in your hut. Imagine the possibilities."

"Why I keep the two of you around is beyond me, "Brendan growled. "This is strictly for her safety."

Mac and Morg nodded, their grins a mile wide. "Whatever you say, Skipper," Morg said.

CHAPTER 9

It was the children who fascinated her the most. They were not at all what Irelynn expected. Used to the children of Saigon, especially the orphans who begged in the streets, she couldn't get over the difference. These children lived behind barbed wire for their protection. They seemed to not have a care in the world as they laughed and played, their eyes shining and bright. They seemed happy. Irelynn knew it might not always be the case in a war-torn country. The threat of attack from the VC and NVA was constant, and their way of life had changed. She wasn't sure if it was for the good, or not. It was one of many questions she had.

Crawling on her knees, eye level with the small child as she sat in the dirt. The child, a little girl of no more than two, rose to her feet and waddled over to another little girl of ten or so. Intent on her task of corralling smaller children, the older child hefted the little one to her hip as she doled out small leaves filled with rice to the other children.

From what she had been able to gather from limited resources on the Montagnard culture. There were twenty or so different tribes within South Vietnam and more in the north. Depending upon customs and culture, each village determined the hierarchy of life for the people who made the mountainous region their home. Men were the hunters, cleared the fields, and provided security. The women were the gatherers, helped plant the fields, and wove baskets and cloth while keeping the home fires burning. Older girls were tasked with watching the younger children while the boys cared for the animals. Everyone seemed to have duties; even the elderly worked to provide for the village.

Irelynn smiled at the beautiful simplicity of the moment. Turning to snap pictures, she spotted a few American soldiers deep in conversation.

Raising her camera, she caught the muscled back of one of the men, with long legs and a magnificent ass. Hands on his hips, he turned his head…

Her heart fluttered and dropped into her stomach.

Brendan. Oh shit. Shit. Shit. Shit. He's not supposed to be here.

Terrified of discovery, her own words came back to haunt her. Dropping her camera to her chest, she ran around the corner to hide behind the outbuilding closest to her. Leaning against the wall, she tried to catch her breath.

I'll pay the devil his due if I get caught.

Heart pounding in her chest, she peaked around the corner.

He still stood with the other two men. Raising her camera, he was a gorgeous man, even with the sweat stains on the back of his shirt; his back muscles rippled as he raised his arms and folded them across his chest. Then clapping Morg on the shoulder, Brendan and Mac went inside the hut. Breathing a sigh of relief, she closed her eyes and leaned back against the wall.

"Okay, girl," she whispered. "You can do this."

Glancing over the bamboo and twig fence, she caught the eyes of the wizened old Chieftain on her. He smiled a toothless grin and turned away.

Lost in thought, she walked back to where she had left her rucksack and the duffel bag containing gifts for the villagers.

None of the men here know I'm a woman. They only know me as a pesky war correspondent.

Sighing deeply, she stiffened her spine, "I'll figure it out." She jumped when Morg came up beside her.

"Come on. You can stow your gear in the Skipper's hut for now," Morg said.

"Oh. Um. That's alright. I can carry it. I don't want to bother him," Irelynn replied.

"Nonsense. You're going to have to meet the Skipper at some point."

"Skipper?"

"Captain Corrington. By the end of the day, he'll be a Major."

"My sources told me his tour was up, and he returned to the United States."

"Your sources were wrong. He's got about seven weeks to go," Morg replied.

"I see that now," Irelynn grumbled.

"Might as well get it over with. Watch your step, though. He eats reporters like you for breakfast."

"I wouldn't worry too much about me. I've been known to chew up and spit out a few nasty captains in my day."

Morg raised both eyebrows and chuckled. "We'll just see about that."

Pulling the screen door open, Morg waved his hand in. "After you."

Stepping inside the hut, Irelynn scanned the small war room. Military maps of the area hung on the walls, and various boxes and crates served as tables for communications equipment. The clock on the wall ticked in a slow, steady beat as she realized she was holding her breath. A sandy haired man of twenty or so sat at a desk, an unlit cigarette dangling from his mouth as he typed with one finger on an old typewriter. He looked up, and his gaze rested on Irelynn and flickered with amused interest before he waved them into the inner office.

Morg nodded to the man, "Corporal Davis."

Pausing in the doorway, her eyes briefly scanned Mac

before coming to rest on Brendan behind the desk. Her heart lurched when he raised his eyes to sweep her from head to toe. She was vaguely aware of music from 'The Doors, Crystal Ship' playing on the radio in the background. Memories of warm kisses the night they danced in the fountain at the ball filled her mind. A deep longing to return to that night filled her. Shaking herself, she pushed her feelings aside.

"Mr. Cross. Come in," Brendan said.

"Please. Call me George," Irelynn replied.

"George. Okay, George. Let's go over a few rules for the duration of your visit here. First, stow your gear on the top bunk in the room through there. Since we don't have a VIP hootch, you'll bunk in here with me."

"In here? With you?" she squeaked.

"Sure. Why not? We're all men here," Brendan said.

"I'd prefer to set my pup tent up outside."

"I insist. There's plenty of room in here. For your own safety and ours, you are to go nowhere without one of my men as an escort. That includes the mess hall, the latrine, and the village. Do not speak to the Montagnards or go into the village until invited by the Chieftain. No photographs of our defense's. Is that clear?"

"Yes."

"If one of my men or I give you an order, you follow it," Brendan said.

"I don't follow orders, but if someone asks me to do something, I will," Irelynn replied.

Brendan narrowed his eyes as he rose from his desk.

Stalking around her like an animal on the prowl, he stood behind her, leaning over her shoulder.

"So, you don't follow orders," he softly snarled in her ear. "I don't give a fuck what you want to call it. When we tell you to do something, you do it without question or argument. Is that clear, George?"

"Yes, Captain," she replied.

"Good to know," he cheerfully replied before smacking her bottom.

She jumped, eyes wide, she turned to him. She opened her mouth.

"Something to say, George?"

"No."

"Good. Keep your gear off the floor. We have issues with snakes and rats. You don't want to find either in your boots in the morning. You're dismissed."

Nodding, she went into the next room. With great effort, she hoisted her gear up on the top bunk. Rubbing her sore bottom before grabbing a small bag holding extra film, she left the hut.

"Oh Morg, tell Jones and Perkins I want to see them," Brendan called out behind them.

"Yes. Sir," Morg replied.

Brendan lost in thought for a moment before turning to Mac. His eyes sparkled with restrained mirth.

"The smack on the ass was a nice touch," Mac chuckled.

"I would have preferred to turn her over my knee."

"You know me, Brendan, how well I can read people. I'm telling you that girl has feelings for you," Mac said.

Swinging his arm wide, Brendan pointed out the door. "That girl. Is trouble with a capital T."

"Best kind to have. You've got to admit she's got big kahunas to think she could pull this off."

"How long should I let this game continue?"

"You'll know when the time is right."

"I should call for a chopper and end this now."

"Tomorrow is soon enough."

"And if we're attacked?"

"Then she goes in the underground bunker with the rest of the women and children."

"She does appear to be a woman used to taking risks."

Mac nodded. "You've got new orders. You could keep her here until you're ready to leave yourself."

Brendan paced back and forth. "Hell, the fuck, no. Davis, get in here," Brendan bellowed.

Davis' chair scraped across the floor as he stood, appearing in the doorway seconds later. "Yes. Sir."

"How long is Cross scheduled to be here?"

"Till Thursday morning. Sir."

"What are the chances of getting a chopper out here tomorrow?"

"Unless we need a dust off, supplies, or we're under attack, none. But you never know with HQ," Davis replied.

"Two nights. Damn it. It galls me to give her the story she wants," Brendan said. "Alright, you're dismissed, Davis. Send Perkins and Jones in when they get here."

"What else gall's you?" Mac asked.

"Don't you have somewhere to be?"

"Yeah. Once the Chieftain invites me into the village. I suppose I'm bunking with the troops," Mac said as he hefted his rucksack over his shoulder. "Might as well get settled in. I will enjoy watching the sparks fly for the next few days."

"Sparks? Yeah. Irelynn definitely has spark, doesn't she?" Brendan murmured.

CHAPTER 10

Shell casings flew furiously in every direction. The sound of gunfire and the smell of earth and gunpowder assaulted Irelynn's senses as she lay in the dirt. The camera aimed toward the line of Montagnard men lying on the ground, their weapons pointed toward the man shaped card- board targets lined up against a wall of sandbags. Pings of dirt and mud flew up, splattering the targets as some bullets missed their mark. The men's guttural shouts mixed with cursing and grunts of the American and Vietnamese soldiers standing behind them.

Everywhere she looked, she saw training in progress. Twelve Green Berets and an equal number of Vietnamese soldiers worked in tandem to train the Montagnard men in the use of firearms. Already fierce jungle fighters and trackers, the Yards, as the Americans called them, were interesting people. The men in loincloths, sweat coated their foreheads and bodies, some with long sleeved Army shirts, others bare chested in the one hundred degrees heat with one hundred percent humidity. It was hot and miserable in the highlands. Irelynn's black glasses slid down her nose as she opened her canteen. Pouring water on the green towel she pulled from her neck; she dabbed at her face and neck, careful not to ruin her camo paint. She glanced over as the largest pair of boots she'd ever seen came up next to her.

"Hold your camera up, dude."

"What?" Irelynn asked.

"Your camera. Hold it up," the man replied.

Coming to her knees, she held up her camera. The man smiled and sloshed a bucket of water in her face. Sputtering with indignation, she jumped to her feet.

"What the hell did you do that for?" she snarled.

"Relax. Can't have you collapsing from heat stroke."

Her hands were clenched in fists as she glared at his six-foot-five frame.

"You're a feisty little shit."

"No shit," Irelynn replied.

The big blonde man grinned at her, "My name is Carlson. I'm the medic."

"You're the medic? Do they call you Doc?"

"Carlson or Doc, it doesn't matter."

Wiping at the water dripping from her nose, Irelynn was grateful that her floppy hat and wig had stayed in place. She looked up to see Carlson peering intently down at her.

"You know you don't need camo paint when we're on base. Right?" Carlson said.

Irelynn sighed impatiently. "I'm a photographer. I use camo paint on my face to reduce sun glare and to help differentiate between light and dark contrasts."

"Hmm. That makes sense. If you're interested, we'll be lining up the villagers for their monthly checkups tomorrow morning."

"I'll be there," Irelynn replied.

"Good," Carlson cheerfully replied; as he turned to walk away, he smacked her bottom.

"Oh, and a reminder. Take your salt tablets and find shade when you can," Carlson called over his shoulder.

Irelynn hissed and glared at his back while rubbing her bruised posterior. "Damn, slap happy bunch of perverts," she grumbled.

Every time I turn around... Sighing again, Irelynn aimed her camera at the group of laughing men standing thirty feet away.

Assholes.

I have to pee.

Irelynn grimaced. "Great. How am I going to pull that off?" *Alright, you've got your rain poncho to cover yourself. You've used that on combat missions before.* She looked longingly over to the far side of the camp where the latrine was located. Half walls enclosed the open-air hut with seating for six.

Maybe I can sneak over there once it's dark.

"Toughen up, buttercup. It's not like you haven't overcome obstacles before."

Turning quickly, she slammed into an immovable brick wall. Strong arms grasped her shoulders to steady her. Looking up, she gasped. *Brendan.*

"Talking to yourself, George?"

"Always," Irelynn replied.

"Do you answer yourself as well?"

"Sometimes."

"That's a good sign of being loco," Brendan said. "We're all a little loco," Irelynn replied.

"Some, more than others. Of course, it's always important to be true to yourself and who you really are."

Irelynn blinked. Her mind raced as she looked down at the ground. Shame filled her. *I never meant to deceive you. You weren't supposed to be here.*

Brendan clapped her on the back, almost knocking her to the ground. Catching her, he set her on her feet.

"Geez, George, you're going to blow away in a strong wind. Maybe some early morning P.T. training would bulk you up a bit. We'll start tomorrow."

Irelynn glared at Brendan. "I assure you I'm physically fit."

Brendan reached out and patted her on the tummy. "I don't know. You're kind of chubby. I'm sure you'll benefit. I'll wake you at O-Four-hundred."

"No. Thank you, I don't do mornings unless absolutely necessary," Irelynn replied.

"I thought you've been out with the troops on combat missions?"

"Many times," Irelynn replied. "But that didn't involve sit-ups at Four O'clock in the morning."

"Good to know. How about lunch? The mess hall is open now."

Brendan could barely contain his laughter. So, she doesn't do mornings. He was going to have fun with that one. He knew she was physically fit. She had the type of body meant to bring a grown man to his knees. If he had a deck of cards filled with every woman he had ever known, Irelynn Cross would be that one wild card in the deck. The unknown. For all that he was still angry with her that she had tried to play him for a fool, she intrigued him. Every time he looked at her when her wig was slightly askew or when she forgot to deepen her voice, she was terrible at deception. Even now, her shirt soaking wet, overly large glasses sliding down her nose, she was adorable, and he couldn't resist teasing her.

"You smell a little ripe."

Irelynn's mouth dropped open and quickly snapped shut. "That's a little like the pot calling the kettle black," Irelynn replied.

"So it is. We all stink, but you more so than others."

Brendan chortled inside as shock played across her face. He didn't make a habit of telling women they stunk, but since she was going to pretend to be a man, he would treat her like one.

Watching her face, he knew she was tempted to raise her arm and take a sniff. She didn't smell, but the prankster long buried deep inside had resurfaced and found delight in making her squirm.

Standing just outside of the fencing separating the village from the military side of the base, they waited for the Chieftain to make his appearance. Irelynn glanced up at Brendan and Mac on either side of her. Reflecting on one of the most trying days that she could remember. Filled with regret, she acknowledged this was the most stupid, hare-brained idea she had ever come up with, and she had come up with some doozies in her past. Peeking over at Brendan, he had showered and smelled faintly of soap. She had taken great pains to avoid the outdoor area while Brendan showered. Rushing inside his quarters to wash up. Using water from the canteen, her precious sliver of soap, and a piece of an old towel as a washcloth, she cleaned up as best she could before donning a clean shirt. Now, standing next to Brendan, she inhaled his clean scent.

"Did you just sniff me?" Brendan asked.

"What? No," Irelynn stuttered, her cheeks on fire.

"You're a little strange, George. Be careful."

"I don't understand. What does that mean?" Irelynn replied.

Brendan raised one eyebrow.

"Never mind," he whispered before exchanging a glance with Mac.

Irelynn turned to Mac. "What's he's talking about?"

Mac shrugged his shoulders. "I'm not going there."

Irelynn rolled her eyes. Turning to face them, she lifted her camera, aiming it at the two men, and snapped a few photos. She continued taking pictures until it was clear on the faces of the two men that they were getting irritated. Looking past them, she paused. Letting her camera fall to her belly, she fished around in her pants pocket, pulling out a round rock. Reaching around, she pulled her slingshot from her back pocket, lifted it, and let the rock fly.

Brendan narrowed his eyes at the cold deadly look on her face as the rock whizzed past his ear. Jumping, he turned to see what she had aimed at; he was shocked at the giant rat that now lay dead next to a pile of sandbags.

Whipping back around, he glared at Irelynn. "You could have warned me," he snarled.

"Sorry. Filthy vermin. Rats spread disease and have fleas. I didn't want it to get away," Irelynn replied.

"You almost hit me."

"If I wanted to hit you, I would have," Irelynn snarled

back. Mac shook with laughter; one arm crossed over his chest, and his other hand rubbed the bridge of his nose. "Ah. Here

comes the Chieftain."

"Behave yourself," Brendan said.

"Behaving is overrated," Irelynn snapped.

"Reporters who don't behave may find themselves locked up in the brig," Brendan replied.

Irelynn inhaled sharply at his threat. "You've heard of freedom of the press, right?"

"Not on my firebase."

Irelynn lifted her chin. "Whatever."

"Uh, guys, the chieftain," Mac said.

Sparks flew from her amber colored eyes; her chin was set in a stubborn tilt as she looked up at him. Her stance practically dared him to follow through with his threat. Momentarily lost in her eyes, he became aware of the Chieftain standing in front of them, looking back and forth between them. A twinkle of amused interest flickered in the older man's eyes. Then the Chieftain reached out, pulled the waistband of her pants out, and peered inside.

CHAPTER 11

*J*relynn's breath caught in her throat as her brain stuttered and her stomach sank to her knees. The Chieftain let go of her waistband, taking the slingshot from her hand; casually, he turned away. Slingshot in hand, he walked away, leaning heavily on his wooden walking stick.

He called over his shoulder in his native tongue to come along. Brendan placed his hand on her back and gently pushed her forward into the village.

She looked between Brendan and Mac's faces. They could have been set in stone. Neither gave away what they were thinking. It was odd that they didn't say a word, not that she would have been able to explain it. *Maybe they didn't see it.*

"Holy cow! The old man knows," she mumbled under her breath. *As long as Brendan doesn't figure it out, I'm good. If anyone else had tried a stunt like that, I would have slapped them.* Now, unsure of how to react, she brought her camera up, retreating into the fascinating life of the Montagnard village.

To Brendan, she never looked more beautiful, the sparkle in her eyes, the smile on her face. He wasn't sure if her passion or natural exuberance for her work shone through the most. He had howled with laughter on the inside when the Chieftain looked inside her pants. Thank God Mac had been able to hold it together, or it would have been his undoing. He gently prodded her toward the Chieftain's longhouse, as she had a habit of stopping every few feet when something caught her eye.

"If you keep dawdling like this, we won't make it to the Chieftain's hut until after the meal," Brendan said.

"Oh, sorry. Childhood habit," Irelynn replied. "By the way. What's for dinner? I mean, is it safe to eat?"

Brendan grinned. "Rice. Maybe some chicken and other delicacies. You never know for sure."

"You'll tell me what I'm eating, right?"

"Oh yeah. Sure," Brendan replied, nodding his head.

If looks could kill, the glare she gave him would have put him in his grave.

"Trust me, George."

The Chieftain stopped in front of his longhouse. He waited for them to catch up before climbing the stairs. The hut was built on stilts, ten feet above the ground, and was at least one hundred feet long, big enough to house a large extended family. A community room ran down the center with private sleeping quarters for each family on either side. In the very back was the cooking area where the women prepared dinner.

Brendan explained each detail of the house as they followed the Chieftain to an area where he waved his arm for them to sit. Irelynn was on one side as a guest of honor, and he sat on the other with Mac next to him.

He watched Irelynn's face as she took in each detail of the Chieftain's home, from the homemade weaved mats lining the rough-hewn wooden floor to the large gourds and weapons hung decoratively upon the walls. Her eyes filled with curiosity and wonder, and she raised her camera again. Reaching across the Chieftain, he pushed her camera down.

"Pictures after we eat," Brendan said.

She nodded in agreement and watched as a young, heavily pregnant woman approached them. The woman offered Irelynn a large leaf filled with plain rice.

"My wife. She will bear this old man many strong children," The Chieftain said, as Brendan translated for him.

Irelynn nodded at the woman. "His wife? She's young enough to be his granddaughter."

"They start young. Harsh conditions limit the average lifespan of the Montagnards. This village is one of the lucky ones. Hunger and disease, not to mention the VC and NVA, have taken their toll. We do what we can for them. In turn, they allow us to train their men to fight the enemy, to protect their people and their way of life," Brendan said. "Their fierce and loyal."

"You speak very fondly of them," Irelynn said.

"They're good people," Brendan said.

Irelynn turned her attention to Mac, who was distracted watching the women at the far end of the house. "He's looking for someone."

Brendan nodded.

"Who?"

"That's Mac's story to tell," Brendan replied.

More women approached with chunks of meat on a large leaf and small bowls of what looked like soup with small pieces of meat floating in the broth. Irelynn hesitantly took the offerings, placing a small chunk of meat on her rice. The Chieftain handed her a bamboo straw and pointed to a large gourd on the floor in front of them, encouraging her to drink.

"What is it?" Irelynn asked.

"Bear paw rice wine," Brendan said.

"Bear paw as in real bears?" Brendan nodded.

"And the meat?"

"Snake."

Irelynn shuddered. "The soup?"

Brendan grinned. "Tiger penis soup."

She looked down in horror at the meal provided. "You're kidding me, right?" she whispered.

The Chieftain smiled, encouraging her to eat.

Brendan grinned as she looked back and forth between him and Mac. She lifted her chin, narrowed her eyes, and picked up the snake meat. Taking a bite, Irelynn grimaced, chewing the tender, pink meat slowly, never taking her eyes off him. Finishing, she picked up the bowl and drank the soup. Taking her bamboo straw, she leaned over and drank some wine from the gourd, an unspoken challenge in her eyes.

"It's quite good. Tastes like chicken," Irelynn said.

Mac, next to him, shook with laughter. "God damn little shit is a snake eater," Mac said under his breath.

Brendan grinned, his white teeth showing his amusement as he tore off a chunk of the snake.

Damn. She's magnificent.

Tearing her eyes away from Brendan, Irelynn locked gazes with the Chieftain.

"Merci. Thank you for the meal," she said.

The old man's eyes lit up. "Parlez vous Francais?" he asked.

"Oui. Yes. How is it you speak French?" Irelynn replied in French.

"French missionaries. From when I was a much younger taught me their language."

Looking over to Brendan and Mac, curiosity on their faces. Irelynn relaxed; they didn't seem to understand the conversation she and the Chieftain were having.

"Why do you pretend to be a man?" he asked.

Irelynn's eyes widened, and she glanced over at Brendan.

"They do not respect my job because I'm a woman. They would not have allowed me to visit this base, or you, if they knew."

"What is it you do?"

"People tell me their stories, and then I tell the world."

"With words and pictures from your little box?"

"Yes. Pictures from my camera."

The Chieftain nodded. "I see. So, this justifies deception?"

"I am sorry. I regret my actions. Please accept my apologies if I have offended you."

"I am not offended, just curious. My people and I live simple lives, but we, too, have those who are not satisfied with their place. One of my daughters suffers from wanderlust. I pray to the spirits of the mountains and streams and the Christian god in the sky that she will come home."

"She must be very special."

"I have many sons and daughters. All are special to me in their own way." His eyes caressed his young pregnant wife. "Even those who are not yet born. But yes, she is special, and I miss her."

"I pray she comes home."

"What about your father? Does he not miss you?"

"Yes, he does, and I will be going home soon," Irelynn replied.

"Where is your home?"

"In America, northern California," Irelynn replied.

"The American Captain. He's a fine man."

"Yes, he is."

"He is going home. You should choose him."

Sadness crept into her, and Irelynn shook her head. "As much as I wish it so, he would never accept me as I truly am."

"I think you are wrong. You are strong and brave. He is a ferocious fighter and an honorable man. Together, you would make a strong alliance with many children. Has he seen you as you truly are?"

"Yes."

"You are attracted to him. Why haven't your parents arranged a marriage?"

"In America, parents do not arrange marriages. Men and women decide for themselves."

Irelynn looked into his kind, old, weathered face. "I'm fine as I am."

"I will think on what I can do to help you," The Chieftain said. "But for now, I am ignoring my other guests."

He turned to Brendan and started conversing with him in his native tongue. Irelynn wasn't sure what was being said, so she sat in quiet contemplation until she was approached by a woman with chunks of something. A slight frown marred her brow until the chief turned back to her.

"It's wild vegetables. Bamboo shoots and sweet potatoes gathered in the forest by the women. Eat."

Irelynn took a bite of the vegetables, eyes on Brendan; she leaned over and took another long draw of the rice wine.

A little sour, but the wine's not bad either.

CHAPTER 12

The night had been long and sleepless. Brendan tossed and turned as much as the tiny temptation that slept three feet above him. He was aware of everything about her. Every breath she took, every soft sigh. When she rolled over pounded her pillow in frustration. And when finally settled, she drifted off. She talked in her sleep and, from the sound of it, cried. Sorrow filled him that she suffered from nightmares. You would have to be a fool not to admit war wouldn't affect you somehow.

Whose bright idea was it to have her bunk in here?

Of course, he had understood every word of Irelynn and the Chieftain's conversation. He could read, write, and converse in French since he was a small boy. His Aunt Meg had taught Mac the language as well. Irelynn's comment about not being respected by him had felt like a sucker punch to his chest.

He did admire her, but the protector in him wanted to shield her from the horrors of war. He had seen enough, and if she had embedded with the troops, she had probably seen a lot as well. Brendan punched his pillow again.

Why the hell would she willingly risk her life?

Sighing deeply, he ran his hand across his brow. Giving up on sleeping, he reached for his boots. Pulling them on, he silently crept from his bunk.

Outside, he nodded to Jenkins, the man he had posted outside his door in case Irelynn took to wandering the base at night.

"All quiet, Skipper," Jenkins said.

"I know. It's too quiet," Brendan replied.

"Three days now. It always leaves me on edge when we don't see any action for so long."

"I'm going to make some rounds of the men on guard duty.

Keep an eye out for George in case she wakes up."

Brendan looked up as red flare streaks flashed through the night sky, lighting the base and perimeter. "Yeah. Too fucking quiet," he muttered.

An hour later, he stood in front of his bunk bed. The glow of the security lights shone through the lone screened in window at the top of the room. Her wig had come off during the night, and her thick hair spread across her pillow. Thick eyelashes rested on her angelic face while one foot hung off the top of the bunk, her pale pink toenails catching the light in the room.

Brendan shook his head as a soft chuckle escaped him. *God, she'd make a terrible spy.*

Crawling back into bed, fully clothed, he left his boots on. He lay there for another hour until, just before dawn, he heard a deep sigh. *She's awake.*

Soft movements above him told him she was putting on her boots and adjusting her clothing. She silently slid off the top bunk, her shirt catching on the edge of the top bunk. The ripe curves of her hips and smooth belly presented themselves as her shirt caught on the bunk and slowly and teasingly scooted up. Her feet hit the floor just as he spotted the bottom of her lush, round breasts.

Holy fucking shit.

She pulled her shirt down, rain poncho in hand; she silently tip toed from the room. Brendan waited a minute before creeping out after her to find Jenkins hiding in the shadows.

"I figured you'd be out here in a second," Jenkins whispered. "Which way did she go?" Brendan asked.

"Toward the shitter."

"Come on. Let's have some fun."

He found her sitting on the toilet. The poncho draped discreetly over her body.

"Good morning, George," Brendan loudly said as he stood on the other side of the half wall.

The look on Irelynn's face was priceless. Shocked, then mortified.

He spotted Morg and Jones making their rounds, and he signaled them over to where they stood.

Irelynn hid her face under the palm of her hand as the men stood in front of her chatting about the war.

"Do you think you can give me some privacy?" Irelynn gritted out.

"There's no such thing as privacy in the Army," Brendan cheerfully replied.

"Why didn't you use the piss tube outside Skipper's quarters?" Morg said.

"I… uh… will you all just leave," Irelynn snarled.

"Come on, men. Don't want to interrupt a man's morning dump," Brendan said as he walked away. Stopping forty feet away, he turned to see her leave the latrine and run toward his quarters.

He chuckled and nodded to Jenkins to follow her.

Morg choked on his laughter. "Damn, Skipper. You're evil."

Brendan flashed him a devilish grin. "Come on. It's almost sun-up. Let's see if the cook has any coffee brewing."

Scrambling up to the top of the bunk bed, Irelynn dove under the blanket. Placing her hands on her cheeks, she could feel the burn of humiliation. Of all the worst possible scenarios, she never would have imagined what just happened. Unbidden tears burnt her eyes, angrily, she brushed them away. "Stop it. You're tougher than this."

Listening for the screen door and possible footsteps, she took her ace bandage and hastily wrapped her breasts. Pulling the bum on, she tied the strings before lowering her shirt. She quickly finished preparing for what was starting to be a rough day. She made her way to the mess hall with a notebook and camera.

Standing in the mess hall, quietly pulling the screen door shut behind her, she spotted Brendan, and a few of his men lingering over coffee, empty trays from breakfast littered the table in front of them. Still steamed, she ignored them and crossed the hall to pour herself a cup of coffee. Taking her cup, she looked around the small mess hall; four or five tables, along with their long benches, were spread out in no order. Choosing a table, she settled herself at the opposite end of the hall from Brendan. Writing down her thoughts about last night's meal with the Chieftain, she felt eyes upon her. Looking up, she caught Brendan peering intently at her over his coffee cup. Refocusing on her notes for a minute, she peeked up again; blue eyes met amber eyes. She gave him a scathing glare before dropping to the notebook in front of her.

Don't look at him. Focus on your work.

She chewed on the end of her pencil before looking up again, only this time, Brendan was sitting across the table from her.

Startled, she jumped, almost falling backward off the

bench. "Holy shit. Don't sneak up on me like that," she cried.

"Nervous, George?"

"No. I've got nothing to be nervous about," she snapped.

"Did you sleep well?"

"No. A word of warning, Captain. It's morning. Don't annoy, bother, harass, tease, or talk to me. Don't even breathe in my direction before I've had my coffee," she snarled.

Brendan gave her a slow, easy smile. "Not a morning person, huh."

"I told you that yesterday."

He gave her a boyish half smile. "So, you did. Do yourself a favor. Instead of eating your pencil, have some breakfast. I find it helps with early morning grumpies."

Irelynn looked down at her chewed up pencil and grimaced. "I don't eat breakfast."

Brendan rose from the bench. "I have a base to run. Enjoy your morning, George."

Her eyes followed him as he walked away; he had a quick word with the cook before dumping his tray and heading out the door. She grinned at his swagger.

Damn. He's cool…and annoying.

Twenty minutes later, breakfast was in full swing as the mess hall filled with hungry men. Mostly American and a few Vietnamese soldiers, they were loud and boisterous. Setting their trays down, a few men sat at her table. She almost made a snarky comment but remembered she was invading their territory, not the other way around. Morg sat across from her, and one man on either side of her. The table quickly filled with American soldiers as some moved from other tables to sit with her.

There was no doubt in her mind that Brendan, knowing she valued peace and quiet, had sic'd them on her. She stewed at his underhanded move.

Trays piled high; she watched in amazement as they wolfed down their food.

"You guys are going to get indigestion eating so fast," she said.

"You have to scarf down your food. You never know if we're going to be under attack and when we'll have the chance to eat again," Perkins, sitting next to her, said before belching loudly. What followed was a chorus of belches as some men moved to go get seconds.

A tray piled high was plopped down in front of her. She looked up in surprise to see the cook standing behind Morg.

"Skipper said to make sure you ate," he said before stomping away.

Irelynn looked down at the tray in front of her overflowing with scrambled eggs and some gray gloppy looking mess over toast. It took all she had not to gag.

"What is that?" she whispered.

"It's S.O.S. Shit on a shingle," Morg said. "It's not bad once you get past how it looks."

"It's got to be better than that cock you ate last night," A man she hadn't met before offered.

A few men at the table guffawed as Irelynn narrowed her eyes. So that's how it's going to be.

"I guess you would know," Irelynn replied.

A hush fell over the table as the man rose. Anger contorted his face as he grabbed his tray and headed toward the door.

"Uh oh, I guess I pissed off the meanest badass one," Irelynn said.

"That would be the Skipper. Michaels comes in second," Morg replied. "Don't worry about him. He just got in from a two-day patrol and doesn't know yet."

"Doesn't know what?" Ireland asked.

"Oh. Um. He didn't know there was a reporter here." Morg quickly replied.

"But he knew I had tiger penis soup for dinner," Irelynn replied.

"Word travels fast. So, tell me. What kind of missions have you been on?"

"All kinds. I've been up to the DMZ. I've been to the Rock with the Marines. That's a harsh place. Khe Sanh, after the siege. The Mekong Delta. I've been on riverboats with the brown water Navy. I've been everywhere."

"Khe Sanh? Did you see her?" Jones asked. "Her?"

"Yeah. A woman, a ballerina."

"A ballerina? At Khe Sanh?" Irelynn asked. "Yeah. I heard she traveled with the Marines."

"That was just some wild story made up by some asshole

jarhead," Morg said.

"I heard she had big tits," Jones said.

"Big tits? Look at this," Carlson said as he pulled a rolled up magazine from his side pocket. Opening the magazine, he showed the picture of a naked woman to Irelynn.

Irelynn's eyes widened; her cheeks burned. "I've got work to do," she stuttered when one man leaned over and lifted his leg, ready to let one rip.

I have five brothers. I don't need that kind of torment.

Irelynn scrambled from the table; howls of laughter followed her hasty retreat out the door.

A table was set up just outside the village, overflowing with the medical supplies necessary for the monthly check-ups of the villagers. The medic, Carlson, picked through his supplies and pulled a tongue depressor out. Next to him, an interpreter translated his questions to a young mother sitting on a chair, her child on her lap.

A few hours into it, they were finally finished with the check-ups. Irelynn looked up to see Brendan standing next to her.

"What do you think?" Brendan asked. "Did you get enough photos?"

"Yes, I did," Irelynn replied. "Everything you've done for these people, it's amazing. I love watching the little ones."

"What about you, George? You got kids at home?"

"Me? No. Someday I will," she replied.

"Why are you here? What makes you tick?"

"What makes me tick? The story. The need to know and share the truth without the sugar coating."

"All while putting your life in danger."

"Isn't that what you do?"

"I'm well trained in the art of warfare. You're not."

"No. I'm not, but I'm a damn good reporter. Not everyone belongs at home, barefoot and pregnant."

"Barefoot and pregnant?"

Irelynn paled. Shit! "I mean with a subservient wife at home."

"You under rate women, George. I've known plenty of strong independent women who had families at home. My mother, my aunt, who helped raise my brothers and me, and even my sister-in-law. No one would ever accuse them of being subservient."

"You can't deny that it's not that way for many women."

"True, but I digress. The Chieftain has invited us for dinner again."

"Good. He still has my slingshot."

"Yeah. About that. He wants lessons."

"Lessons?"

"For the boys. He saw you kill that rat."

She swallowed a lump in her throat. Her stomach flipped and nausea bubbled up her throat. "What's for dinner?" she whispered.

Brendan grinned. "Chicken."

CHAPTER 13

Irelynn rubbed the bridge of her nose before taking another sip of water. Her throat was sore from maintaining the deeper male voice for the past two days. After a morning of photographing the villager's check-ups and training the boys on the fine art of working a slingshot. Now she stood in a circle of men. Two men in the center engaged in hand-to-hand combat training. Brendan and a young Montagnard soldier, the exercise was brutal and vicious. Stripped to the waist, their bodies glistened with sweat. Muscles strained as they grappled with each other.

Brendan had the advantage with his height and weight, while the young soldier was quick and agile, getting his licks in when he could.

Irelynn inhaled sharply as the soldier landed a sharp blow

to Brendan's ribs. Grunts and groans were followed by the shouts and cursing of the men who watched. She couldn't keep her eyes off Brendan. Powerful muscles rippled across his back. Black hair lightly curled across his chest and drew her gaze down his stomach to the V of muscles. Her thoughts wandered to what he might look like below the beltline. Everything about the man oozed sexual magnetism. A warmth spread through her, and she shifted uncomfortably at the sudden ache between her thighs.

Biting her lip, she refocused on taking more pictures of the man she considered a gorgeous man. He was fascinating, a true leader. She watched how he interacted with his men, the Montagnards, and the children. He had a lot more to admire than just a killer body.

Irelynn found herself rudely shoved aside by the same man who had teased her at breakfast.

Losing the shot she wanted, she growled. "Watch it, buddy."

The man snarled and roughly shoved her into the circle. "Asshole. Who the fuck do you think you're talking to?" Michaels said.

Sensing the trouble, Irelynn dangled her camera to the ground and stepped back further into the circle. A hush fell over the men, and the fight behind her stopped.

"Michaels," Brendan shouted.

Michaels didn't stop as he advanced on Irelynn. Anger and rage twisting his features, he kept coming.

"Michaels. Stand down," Brendan yelled again, panic in

his voice. He moved like lightning from across the circle just as Michaels swung his fist at Irelynn. Quick and nimble herself, she ducked. Brendan came up behind her as two other men jumped into the fray to hold Michaels back. He struggled to free himself from their tight grip.

Her heart pounded in her chest. Fear took her breath away as Brendan's arms came around her to pull her back tight against his chest.

Time stood still.

She realized how he held her in his arms, her body crushed intimately into his. She could feel his heart beating frantically, his warm breath against her neck.

This is the way a man holds a woman.

Trembling, inhaling sharply, she struggled for release. "Hold," he snarled a whisper in her ear, and a tingle of fear slid down her back.

He lifted his head and looked out to the circle of men. Holding her still with one arm, he stroked her cheek before removing her glasses. He pulled the hat off her head. Then he lifted the green towel off her neck, wiping the camo paint from her face. Gentle fingers then reached up and pulled the wig off her head, tossing it aside, he quickly pulled the pins from her hair.

Her chestnut hair cascaded down to her shoulders, and sharp gasps filled the air.

"Gentlemen. Meet Miss Irelynn Cross," Brendan said.

He knew.

Memories flooded her mind of the past two days. The

humiliation and embarrassment of trying to use the latrine. The smacks on her bottom, naked pictures at breakfast. Her gaze caught the men in front of her. Most grinned, but a few, like Michaels, were surprised.

They had known of her charade from the beginning. Seething, she raised her chin in defiance. Anger filled her, and the fear he might try to remove the rest of her disguise triggered her need to escape his hold. She pulled her elbow forward and slammed it into his ribs. The air left him with a swoosh and a guttural grunt. Then she bent forward and rolled him over her shoulder. He landed flat on his back. He looked up at her, eyes wide and shocked. His mouth dropped open when he looked at the knife she held in her hand.

"You're armed?" he squeaked.

"No. It's yours," Irelynn snarled, throwing the knife to the ground.

Rolling to his feet, he checked his boot. "Jesus."

"You knew. You all knew." Her accusation hung heavy in the air.

Her rage, barely held in check, bubbled over, and she grabbed the first thing that came to mind. She pulled rocks from her pocket and started throwing them as fast as possible. One rock hit Brendan in the shin, and he hobbled backward with the rest of the men.

"Irelynn, stop it," he yelled.

"You played me for a fool," she growled as she threw another rock.

"Played you for a fool? Exactly what did you try to do to

us, George?" Brendan snarled back as his hand shot down the rock. "Pretending to be a world-renowned journalist, stealing his name. Disguising yourself as a man."

She threw another rock.

"My name. Is. George. Irelynn. Cross.

You sexist, chauvinistic, misogynistic... jerk. I am that world renowned reporter. You just can't accept that one of the best...is a woman."

She looked over to see that the other men, including the Chieftain and Mac, were sitting or leaning against a sandbag wall, watching them with interest. Brendan strode to stand in front of her. Hands on his hips, his stern face giving no quarter.

"Bull shit. Prove it."

"I don't have to prove anything to you, Brendan. I have MACV's authorization to be here. They invited me."

"Do they know you're a woman?"

"It shouldn't matter."

Brendan rolled his eyes. "You know damn well it does. Or you wouldn't have tried to disguise yourself. Which, I might add, you do very poorly."

"Maybe so, but at least it opened my eyes to what kind of man you are."

"Me? This has nothing to do with me."

"Of course, it does. You weren't supposed to be here," Irelynn said. "I wouldn't have done it if I'd known you were here."

"Why not?"

"I'm not answering that."

"Is it because you thought we still had a chance?"

"A chance? Put it this way. If you were the last man on earth, I would still die a virgin."

A look of surprise played across his face, and she groaned at what she had just admitted.

Gasps and soft chuckles from the men, and both turned to glare at them.

"That's enough from the peanut gallery," Irelynn snarled. Anger spent, she reached down, picking up her camera, glasses, and wig. Shaking the dirt off, she gave them all a scathing glare and stomped away.

"Where are you going?" Brendan called out.

"I am going to get ready for dinner." She growled over her shoulder. "Not that it's any of your business."

"Everything you do is my business."

Irelynn loudly snorted over her shoulder.

Rubbing his face in frustration. Brendan watched Irelynn walk away. Mesmerized by the angry swing of her hips, he grinned.

At least she's no longer walking like she has a stick up her ass. Laughter behind him, he swung around to face the men. "Don't you assholes have work to do? Find something, or I will find it for you."

The men scrambled away, leaving Mac, the Chieftain, and Morg grinning at him.

"I wish I had popcorn for that," Mac stated.

"Morg, go find out when that chopper is supposed to arrive," Brendan said.

"Yes, sir," Morg said, and he left the group.

"So, you're giving up. Just like that?" The Chieftain said.

Brendan looked at Mac with a questioning glare.

"I translated the whole argument for him, "Mac said.

"You heard the lady. She doesn't want anything to do with me," Brendan replied in French.

"The smallest of sparks must be fanned before you get the full flame," the Chieftain replied.

"Maybe so, but I'd burn in hell with this one," Brendan replied. Picking up his shirt and weapon from on top of the sandbags, he slowly limped toward his quarters.

CHAPTER 14

In a strange way, Irelynn felt a sense of relief that the gig was up. For crying out loud, she had been so mad she had thrown rocks at them.

What were you thinking, girl?

"They're lucky I left my slingshot on my bunk, and that I can't throw worth a damn."

Feeling a twinge of guilt for hitting Brendan in the shin, she brushed it off, stomping her way into his quarters. "Whatever," she muttered.

The screen door slammed shut behind her as she strode past Morg and the clerk, Davis, barely sparing them a glance as they dived to the floor. Climbing up on her bunk, she angrily pulled off the bum. Unwrapping the ace bandage, she freed her breasts from the confining material. Pulling her shirt out, she fanned it, breathing a sigh of relief as cooler air hit her belly. *Thank God that's over.*

She yanked her rucksack, pulling out a clean pair of fatigues, shirt, and panties. Digging, she sought her bra buried at the bottom of the bag. Her hand brushed against a hard object, pulling it out. Red high heels. She dug further, pulling out her red dress.

I was supposed to drop these off to Rose.

Clutching all to her chest, a wicked idea came to mind. Smiling a grin that was pure mischief. If he can play games, so can I.

Hearing the screen door shut and Brendan's footsteps walking into his office, she quickly stuffed everything into her rucksack.

With the scrape of his chair, Irelynn knew he was sitting on the other side of the thin wall. Whatever chance they may have had was gone, and her heart dully throbbed. Brushing at the tears sliding down her cheek, she jumped down from the bunk and quickly ran out the door heading to the village to find where the women bathed in privacy.

Hobbling over to his desk, yanking out his chair, rubbing his shin, Brendan sat and pulled off his boot, letting it fall to the floor with a thud. Pulling down his sock, he pulled his pant leg up to his knee. Examining the bump on his shin, "Vicious, stubborn, wildcat," he muttered.

Irelynn ran out of the bunkroom, through his office, and out the door in a blur.

Brendan jumped to his feet. "Where do you think you're going?" he bellowed, running out after her.

He caught her right outside his quarters, grasping her by the arm. "Irelynn. Hold," he said.

She stopped and turned to face him. "What do you want?"

"You can't just run around a firebase," Brendan said.

Irelynn rolled her eyes. "I am not running around. I'm going into the village to bathe."

Reaching out, he tilted her chin up in a tender grasp. He was struck by her beauty, residual camo paint, and all. Looking deep into her amber eyes, he held her gaze until her eyes filled with unshed tears, and she tried to pull away.

"Let me go," she whispered.

"Listen to me…"

"Listen to you? Did you listen to me? No. You just called me a liar in front of all those men."

"Irelynn."

"Let me go. We're done here. I have nothing more to say to you."

Irelynn yanked her arm free.

"You're just mad because you got caught," Brendan growled.

"Mad that I… Oh, hell no. I'm mad because instead of stepping up to the plate and confronting me in the beginning. Like a coward, you chose to play games."

"Hell, the fuck, no. Don't turn this back on me. You chose to deceive me."

"Like I said before. You weren't supposed to be here. I had an opportunity. I took it."

"All's fair…"

"Is that it, Brendan? We're at war?"

"We're certainly not in love," Brendan snarled.

"Fine. Bring. It. On."

"I will."

Irelynn glanced behind him. "It looks like your backup has arrived, Captain."

Brendan swiveled around to see Mac and Morg standing behind him. He turned back to see Irelynn walking away. Catching up with the Chieftain who had passed them by, she locked her am in his, laughing at something he said.

His brow dropped into a thunderous frown, swinging back to Mac and Morg. "When the fuck is that chopper coming?"

"A couple of hours, Skipper," Morg replied.

While Morg struggled to keep a grin off his face, Mac's eyes dropped to his feet, his eyes sparkling with amusement. Looking down, Brendan realized he only had one boot on; the other foot was bare, pant leg pulled up.

"This. This is exactly why I didn't want a woman up here." Stomping toward his office, he howled when he stepped on a rock. Hopping and hobbling the rest of way into his office, practically ripping the screen door off, he left it hanging by one hinge. His cursing trailed outside.

"Mother Fucker. She wants a war. I'll give her one."

Mac and Morg looked at each other. "You going in there?" Mac said.

"Nope. He's fucked."

"Yup. Come on, let's go get a cup of coffee."

The village was larger than Irelynn expected as she walked through on the arm of the Chieftain. The old man had explained that while he was the Chieftain, he and the Shaman had been elected to their positions. Theirs was a matriarchal society where women ruled the roost, owned the property, and made the social decisions for the tribe. The missionaries still visited from time to time to check on their progress, but now they had their own ordained minister; the young Shaman performed baptisms and weddings in the Christian faith while being careful to honor the spirits of the forest, mountains, and streams.

Irelynn shook her head, confused by the Chieftain's explanation of their faith. While it was not her place to judge, she realized the missionaries had their work cut out for them in completely converting the tribe to Christianity.

They stopped in front of a longhouse. "The women will help you prepare for the ceremony," the Chieftain said.

"What ceremony?" Irelynn asked.

"A blessing ceremony of sorts."

"Oh, that's so sweet of you. You are too kind."

"The captain. He's a good man."

"He knows how to push my buttons."

At the confusion on the older man's face.

"He knows how to annoy me."

"Ah, then it's meant to be," replied the Chieftain.

"What's meant to be?"

"Ah, the women. We'll see you when it's time for the friendship joining with the captain."

Irelynn looked up to see the women waiting for her. "This should be interesting," she muttered to herself. "Seriously, I just want to clean up and get dressed in privacy."

Joining?

Confusion set her brow into a frown. Turning to ask the Chieftain to clarify his statement, he had already walked away.

Sighing deeply, with a smile for the women, Irelynn climbed the stairs.

Irelynn applied mascara to her lashes. Looking up, six women and some small children watched her in apparent fascination. Twisting their faces, they copied her every facial move in the mirror. They were as curious about her as she was about them. It had been this way for the past few hours as she washed her body and fixed her hair into an updo. The women almost lost it when she pulled her razor out to shave her legs and armpits. They smiled, giggling amongst themselves. She didn't understand them, not one spoke French, English, or even Vietnamese, but they shared the camaraderie of womanhood as she helped them shave their legs.

They were dressed in ceremonial clothes. Long skirts with short tops and beautiful handmade beaded necklaces adorned their chests and wrists. Irelynn knew at one time in their recent past, the women would have been bare breasted. The French missionaries had encouraged the women to wear bras and cover themselves. Looking down at her black lace bra matching her panties, she smiled. It was the one thing they had in common. The women had been excited, oohing when she pulled it from her rucksack.

Irelynn stood, reaching for her dress. A wicked red, it would cling and accentuate every curve on her body. Slipping it over her head, it settled to a few inches above her knees. She pulled a necklace from her bag. The gold nugget dangled from the chain and nestled between her lush breasts. Slipping into the red high heels, other than lipstick, she was ready. The women couldn't take their eyes off the shoes; Irelynn giggled.

"I suppose you've never seen high heels before. Although none of you wear shoes anyway, trust me, my feet will be killing me by the end of the night."

Applying her lipstick, she puckered her lips, glancing at the women who puckered their lips as well.

"Well, come on. You're all wearing mascara, and you shaved your legs. Might as well put some lipstick on too."

Smoothing her dress down over her curves, Irelynn smiled a wicked smile.

"I might burn in hell for wearing this dress, but he outed me as a woman, and that's what he's going to get."

Glancing at his watch, Brendan muttered, "She's late."

"Women are always late," Mac replied.

"Aunt Meg was never late."

Mac chuckled. "Aunt Meg was military. She was ten minutes early for everything."

"Did you get the answers you needed from the chieftain?" Brendan said.

"Yeah. Mai Le's his daughter. The only thing I know for sure is that she was dismissed by the Le's. And…"

"And what?"

"She was dismissed because she was pregnant."

Brendan let out a slow whistle. "Your baby?"

"Yes. Now I'm searching for a woman near full term. I can't just walk away. I can't leave her or a child of mine in the middle of this war. I have to find her," Mac said.

"Let me know if I can help."

"I will."

Brendan looked at his watch again. "How long could it possibly take to wash up and throw on clean fatigues?" he growled.

Mac looked down the path as Irelynn approached. "There's your answer right there."

Turning around, Brendan sucked in his breath.

"The red heels are a nice touch," Mac said. "Not something you normally see on a firebase."

"Wouldn't be a damn bit surprised if she sprouted horns to match," Brendan murmured.

"Well, it certainly looks like she brought out the big guns," Mac snickered as he clapped him on the shoulder. "I'll let you fight your little war and wait inside with the chieftain."

Brendan never took his eyes off her as she walked through the village. Past the single men's longhouse, up to the pens holding the pigs and other livestock. To the bullpen, where they kept their prize bull destined for sacred sacrifice at some point. A young boy within the pen fed and watered the bull. Tethered to a pole, the bull stomped and snorted its impatience as it was known to occasionally escape the pen.

Brendan's eyes caressed the red dress hugging each mound of her breasts, dropping to the curve of her waist and hips. Camera in hand, the skirt floating around her thighs in a delicate swish as she walked toward him. Behind her walked the women with whom she had spent the afternoon.

The bull bucked and snorted, pulling on the tether; it broke the rope holding it in place. The bull broke through the pen, running wild; it ran up the road behind Irelynn and the women. The women dispersed, screaming as the entire village erupted into chaos.

Brendan screamed, "Irelynn. Run."

Irelynn turned, spotting the bull; she ran with the bull hot on her tail. She kicked off her shoes, scooped them up and ran toward Brendan as fast as she could. Running toward her, adrenaline pumping, his vision tunneled as he grabbed her hand and pulled her along, the bull quickly gaining on them. Reaching the side of the Chieftains longhouse, they were trapped. Brendan cupped his hands, Irelynn climbed up, and he hefted her up to the roof made of bamboo logs, palm fronds, and thatch. Jumping, he swung himself up as the bull rammed into the stilts under the house.

Brendan landed next to Irelynn on the roof with a woof. He could hear the laughter of the villagers and the bull stomping and snorting below. Gripping her in his arms, he looked into Irelynn's wide eyes; they both held their breath at the cracking and creaking of the roof beneath them.

Irelynn squealed as the roof gave way, and they went crashing through the canopy of fronds and thatch, landing with a thud in front of Mac and the Chieftain.

Lying on his back, he clutched her tightly to his chest. She sat up, straddling his waist, and his hands slid to her hips. His eyes held hers in a heated exchange before dipping to her full breasts. Her thighs still gripping his body, her eyes crinkled, and she burst out laughing with deep belly chuckles. Brendan grinned, and they roared with laughter.

Rolling off his body, she tried to catch her breath. "Well, at least we know what it's like to run with the bulls."

Brendan chuckled. "Yes, we do. Are you alright?"

"Yes. You?"

He nodded before looking over to Mac and the Chieftain, their mouths hanging open. Mac and the Chieftain looked up to the hole in the roof and back to Brendan and Irelynn with a questioning look. Mac, for once in his life, was speechless.

Brendan cleared his throat. "The bull escaped and chased us through the village."

Mac started laughing. "Well, you certainly know how to make a grand entrance."

"They'll be laughing about this one for years," Brendan said.

"So will we," Irelynn replied.

A blush stained her pale cheeks as she slipped her shoes back on. The Chieftain's eyes went immediately to her red shoes, looking up at him with questioning eyes.

"I have no idea how to explain those," Brendan said in fluent French.

Irelynn hissed, and he realized his mistake. "You speak French?" she said.

"Oui."

"You understood my entire conversation with the chieftain last night," she stated.

"Yes."

"Why, you sneaky, lowlife…The only reason I'm going through this 'Friendship joining' with you is that the Chieftain is a sweet old man. Once this is over, I don't ever want to see you again."

"You may not have a choice in that," Brendan sneered back.

"What is that supposed to mean?"

"You'll find out," Brendan said.

Standing outside the longhouse, a great fire roared in the pit. The Montagnard's and half of his men encircled Irelynn and Brendan, standing side by side. The atmosphere was one of gaiety and joy as the villagers imbibed in large gourds of rice wine. Irelynn was still seething as she watched the Shaman intone some ritualistic prayer in front of them. He bound their wrists and hands with vines decorated with delicate pale white flowers; then, he handed them straws. Kneeling, they drank from a small gourd of wine. She glared at Brendan over the gourd, he glared right back at her.

Staring into the most beautiful blue eyes she had ever seen on a man, she snarled, "You're an ass, Brendan."

"And you're a deceitful liar," he snarled back.

The Shaman asked Brendan a question and he snarled back to the man. "Yeah, whatever."

Asking the same question to Irelynn, she looked to him for translation. "He wants to know if you agree," Brendan said.

"Sure. Why not," Irelynn sneered back.

A woman tied twine bracelets decorated with tiny beads around their wrists as the Shamon intoned another prayer.

Her eyes narrowed as he looked down at her cleavage. "My eyes are up here. Quit looking down my dress." Sucking up wine, she hiccupped.

"I'm a man. It's all right there," Brendan replied, sucking on his straw.

"That doesn't mean you have to look."

"If you didn't want me looking down that evil red dress at your spectacular tits, you wouldn't have worn it," he snapped.

Irelynn opened her mouth to refute but snapped it shut. With the devil in her eye, a quiver shot through her, and she pulled the bodice down a bit further to show more cleavage and then plumped up her breasts.

"There, now they're spectacular," she snapped back.

Brendan groaned, his body reacting with a will of its own at her display. Desire shot through him, and he sucked harder on his straw. His eyes narrowed as she gave him a wide-eyed innocent look, sucking wine through her straw until they emptied the gourd with a gurgling slurp.

The sound of a chopper coming in for a landing filled the air around them as the Shamon ended with final amen. The villagers shouted a joyous, "Amen."

Brendan looked over his shoulder at the chopper; turning back to her, he gave her a devilish grin. "Party's over, George."

Scooping her up, he slung her over his shoulder; he started shouting orders to his men in attendance.

"Morg, grab her bags and boots. Perkins, go check her bunk for anything left behind and grab the handcuffs from my desk." The men scrambled into action, and he ran to the helipad with Irelynn screaming and pounding him on his back.

Setting her in the chopper, he ducked to avoid a blow from her fist.

"You're not even going to let me finish the job? "Irelynn cried.

"Oh, you're done."

Morg handed him Irelynn's rucksack and boots, setting them on the floor in front of her. Brendan looked to the pilots, who leered at Irelynn's attire. Snarling, Brendan took off his shirt and placed it around her shoulders. Perkins approached him and handed him her camera bag and the handcuffs. Placing the bag on her lap, he snapped the handcuffs on one wrist, clipping the other side to the hand bar next to her.

"What the hell," Irelynn said.

Turning to the pilot, "Have the MP's meet you at Da Nang. I want her in the brig until I can identify who she really is."

"The brig?" Irelynn shouted. "You can't do this."

"Watch me," Brendan said. He wrapped his hands in her hair, crushing her body to his chest; he claimed her lips. He cruelly ravished her mouth in a dark, hungry kiss that melted his toes, leaving him aching for more.

"See you in a few days, George."

"I won't be there," she snarled in his face.

He stepped back, running for cover as the chopper lifted off. Irelynn threw her red high heels out the chopper door, and he ducked as one sailed by while the other hit him in the chest.

Grinning, Mac came up next to him as he watched the chopper fly away and handed him a form.

"Eh, what's this?" Brendan said, rubbing his chest and taking the form from him.

"The Chieftain said it's your marriage certificate."

"What?"

"I kind of looked it over. It's written in Vietnamese. I'm no expert, but it looks legit. That wasn't just a friendship joining ceremony. You just got married, dude," Mac said with a grin.

Dumfounded, Brendan opened his mouth, looking at the chopper flying away. "Are you fucking kidding me?"

"I'd kiss the bride, but you know, you did just send her away."

"Shut up, Mac," Brendan growled.

He was startled at the sound of gunfire, and mortar rounds filled the air around him.

Terror shot through him at the thought the chopper could be shot down, and he screamed. "Irelynn."

He watched in a panic as the chopper made evasive maneuvers to avoid small arms fire and rockets flying through the air—the gunner sprayed the jungle with return fire as the helicopter sped away. Shaken to the core, he breathed a sigh of relief that the helicopter wasn't hit as it continued toward Da Nang.

Explosions went off near the perimeter; they were under

attack. Springing into action, shouting orders at his men, he sprinted toward the perimeter where the firefight was underway. Leaping over sandbags with Mac right behind him, he landed in a deep mud filled trench. His boots sloshed in puddles before he fell to his knees and crawled to where Perkins lay wounded.

"Medic," Brendan screamed.

CHAPTER 15

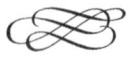

Yanking on the handcuffs as explosions sounded behind them, Irelynn looked out the door in horror.

"Brendan," she whispered.

"Take me back," she pleaded with the pilots. "Please."

The chopper shuddered at the pings from bullets hit against the hull. Irelynn felt a burning sensation in her shoulder. She looked down in shock at the blood seeping through Brendan's shirt.

"I'm hit!"

Shock filled her as she lifted her head and watched explosion after explosion around the base.

Tears rolled down her cheeks. "No. Brendan. No, please God, keep him safe."

Reaching up to her hair, she pulled out a bobby pin,

keeping an eye on the pilots and the gunner who focused on the flight as she worked on the lock until she was free. Rubbing her wrist, she tossed the handcuffs out the door. She looked down at her shoulder again; digging through her rucksack, she pulled out a silk scarf and wrapped it around her wound. Then, she buttoned Brendan's shirt before pulling on socks and her boots.

Leaning back against the seat, her tears continued to roll down her cheeks. "I'm so sorry, Brendan. I'm so sorry for everything I've done. I want to see you again. To taste your kisses and feel your arms around me. Please, survive this." She closed her eyes to calm her nerves. Lulled by the hum of the chopper and blood loss, she fell into an exhausted sleep. Waking right before they landed at Da Nang, she readied herself. Two feet off the ground, with the gunners back to her. Irelynn made her getaway, jumping from the chopper; she ran across the airfield, disappearing into the night.

Their defenses had held. The pounding guns had fallen silent as the NVA slunk away in defeat at dawn. Brendan was grateful that between the bamboo fencing, spikes, and the poisonous bushes of the Montagnard's, along with the moat and barbed wire, they hadn't been overrun. It had been a long bloody night. He had fourteen injured, including two of his own, and six of the Montagnard warriors were dead. The dust-off choppers sounded in the distance. They would transport any wounded men to the hospital at Da Nang.

He rubbed his face, Irelynn. Just the thought of her chopper almost being shot down filled him with a sick feeling that sat like a stone in his stomach. He was still waiting for HQ to call and confirm she was sitting in the brig, steaming mad, he assumed. It was the plan he and Mac had come up with late the night before last. Punish her for her daring charade, while keeping her safe for a few days while he tied up loose ends. His eye caught and lingered on her red high heels sitting on his desk. Next to them lay her gold nugget, the delicate gold chain broken. He wondered if she was aware she had lost it. He pulled the so-called marriage certificate from his pocket. He didn't read Vietnamese or the Montagnard's written language; he could not decipher the form letter. Sighing deeply, the Chieftain and Shaman had a lot to answer for, but he heard a while ago the Shaman had been wounded during the attack and didn't survive.

He looked up to see Davis standing in the doorway. The look on his face didn't bode well.

"What is it?" Brendan barked.

"HQ is on the line. I think you're going to want to talk to them yourself," Davis replied.

"Tell me."

"The MP's had a flat tire, so they weren't there when the chopper arrived. Irelynn jumped off the chopper as it landed and took off. They haven't found her yet. And…"

"And what?" Brendan snarled.

"There was blood all over her seat. She must have been wounded when the chopper was hit."

Brendan felt his face drain of color. "Patch the call through to me and find Mac."

"Oh, and Captain Pierce has arrived," Davis said.

"My replacement. Good."

The dreadful sinking feeling filled him again. Blood all over her seat? Wounded? Where?

His phone rang, and he picked it up. "Where is she?"

Burning with fever, Irelynn lay on a woven mat on the dirt floor. Opening her eyes, an old Vietnamese woman poked and prodded her wound. Then, helping her lift her head, she gave her sips of water through a bamboo straw. Shards of pain ripped through her shoulder. She couldn't go to the hospital. Brendan would find her there, and she didn't relish sitting in the brig. Unable to go to the nurse's barracks either, the last thing she wanted was her friends getting in trouble because of her. In dire straits after three days, as infection and fever had set in, she had finally sent a note to Rose to see if she could secretly come to her aid.

Now she lay in a hut in a village south of Da Nang. Worried sick about Brendan, her life as she knew it was in shambles. She could see no way past her mistakes; guilt and misery plagued her, and she deserved it. Brendan. She couldn't even think about him. She had lost him before they ever had a chance. If he was even still alive. Looking up through a hazy fever fog, she spotted Rose and Carole standing in the doorway. Tears rolled down her cheeks as they rushed forward; her vision tunneled and went black.

"Irelynn. Drink some water for me," Rose said.

Raising her head, Irelynn blinked. "You're here," she croaked.

"Drink," Rose ordered.

"Of course, we're here," Carole replied. "You're a very lucky girl. The bullet entered and exited through the fleshy part of your arm, missing the bone."

"We gave you a shot of penicillin, cleaned, and dressed the wound," Rose said, placing her hand on her forehead. "You're still feverish."

"What happened? The MP's are crawling all over the base looking for you," Carole said.

"I made the mistake of messing with the Green Berets. One Captain Brendan Corrington in particular," Irelynn replied.

"He's at Da Nang and a Major now," Rose said. "He's leading the search for you. He already questioned us once."

Relief washed over her. "Brendan's there?" Irelynn whispered. "The firebase was attacked as I was leaving. I took a bullet in the arm. Shit. Were you followed?"

Rose and Carole looked at each other. "No. We don't think so," they replied.

"I need to leave. I'll have to avoid military transport and hitchhike to...." Irelynn paused, "I'm not going to tell you where I'm going. He might question you again."

"Irelynn. You belong in the hospital where we can take care of your wound, not running off to hide from Brendan," Rose said.

"You don't understand how much he hates me. He wants to destroy my career, throw me in the brig and throw away the key." Irelynn cried.

"Irelynn. You're wrong. That is not the impression we got from him. He's worried sick," Carole said.

"Maybe so, but I can't go to the hospital or risk him finding me here. I'm slightly feverish and in pain, but I will be okay."

"We need to leave. We have to be back before curfew," Rose said.

"Promise us you'll check in and let us know how you're doing," Carole said.

"I will. Now get out of here before you get in trouble. I'll be fine now, thanks to both of you," Irelynn replied, giving them both a one armed hug as they left.

Giving them a weak smile, she waved as they pulled away in their jeep. Getting dressed, she grabbed her rucksack and camera bag. Spotting the bloody red dress lying on the floor, she picked it up. Anguish filled her as she remembered Brendan's eyes on her before the bull chased her down. He had made her feel beautiful. It would be nice to pretend, even for a moment, that he really wanted her for more than just sex. Though that last kiss. That kiss was angry, even harsh, but then it changed to something deeper, more meaningful. Sighing at her mixed feelings. *I shouldn't want him, but I do. He would never want me now anyway.* Dropping the dress, bloody rags, and used medical supplies into the cold firepit outside, she quietly left the village.

Sitting in Colonel Bragg's office, Brendan eyed the young private standing at attention in front of them. He couldn't be more than eighteen, nineteen at most, his hair so blond; it reminded him of corn silk. The poor kid was practically shaking in his boots.

"Okay, Private Nielsen. Start from the beginning," Brendan said.

"Yes, Sir. I was driving near the airfield when I spotted an American woman hitchhiking. I picked her up and gave her a ride to the village just south of here."

"Can you describe her?"

"It was dark out, sir. She looked to have reddish brown hair and was very pretty. She wore a long Army shirt with Green Beret patches over something red. A dress, I think, and combat boots."

"That's her," Brendan stated. "Was she injured?"

"Yes, Sir. The left side of her shirt was all bloody. I don't know the extent of her injuries. Sir."

"Soldier. Why the hell didn't you take an injured woman to the hospital?" Colonel Bragg bellowed.

"Sir. I offered more than once. She was skittish and refused. She threatened to get out and walk. I figured she'd be safer if I drove her where she wanted to go," Private Nielsen said.

"Show me on the map over there on the wall exactly where this village is located," Brendan said.

"I know the elders of that village pretty well," Mac said as Private Nielsen pointed the village out.

"Thank you, Private. You're dismissed," Colonel Bragg said.

Once the door closed, "Now the other two items. Who exactly is this girl? And her press credentials, are they fake? Then, there's the matter of your surprise wedding," Colonel Bragg said. "I've requested that the Chaplain, Father Andrews, review the whole issue."

"Father Andrews?" Brendan and Mac both sputtered.

"Is that a problem?"

"If he's the same one, we knew him growing up," Brendan said.

"I'm surprised he's still alive and serving," Mac chuckled.

Colonel Bragg nodded his head. "That's right. You two grew up together. I've heard his stories about your family."

Brendan and Mac both grinned. "I'm sure his stories were greatly embellished," Brendan said.

Colonel Bragg laughed, "I'm sure they weren't."

"Back to the matter at hand. My contacts are checking Irelynn's identity and credentials. I'll let you know what I find out," Mac said as they stood to leave.

An hour later, Brendan stood in the middle of the village in front of the fire pit. Spotting the dress, bloody scarf, and bandages, he pulled the dress from the pit. Holding the bloody dress up, he inhaled sharply. Worry creased his brow, and he rubbed his face. *Where are you, Sparky? How badly are you hurt?*

A shadow crossed in front of him, and he looked up to see Mac standing on the other side of the pit.

"I talked to the elders and the old mamasan that took care of Irelynn. The old woman said Irelynn had a bullet wound in the shoulder. She took care of Irelynn for a few days until two American women showed up this morning."

"Nurses, I'm assuming," Brendan said.

"Yeah. They were here for a few hours. Irelynn left shortly after they did."

"That means she's on the road somewhere. Probably heading to Saigon."

"It's getting dark. This area is crawling with VC at night.

We need to get back to the base," Mac replied.

Brendan sighed. "I suppose your right. I wanted to talk to

Father Andrews anyway. If I can't find a military transport out tonight, I'll leave for Saigon at first light."

The small chapel on the base was empty. Brendan genuflected and made the sign of the cross before sliding into the front pew. He sat for a while in silent prayer before quiet footsteps came up the aisle. He looked up as Father Andrew's slid into the pew next to him.

"Father Andrew's," Brendan said.

"Brendan, my son, how are you?" Father Andrews replied. "I've been better."

"I spoke with Mac earlier. He hasn't changed one bit."

"Mac is Mac. He's a good man," Brendan replied.

"I never could decide who was the biggest mischief maker out of the six of you boys."

Brendan grinned. "Five Corrington boys and Mac. I think each of us played the ringleader at one time or another."

"Your father and aunt stepped right up to the plate after Mac's mother ran off with another man, and his father was KIA."

"There was no way my father, or Aunt Meg, would have let him go into the foster care system."

"How's your father and brothers?"

"Father is good. According to his letters, he's enjoying his retirement and spending time with the baby."

"Ah, yes. Elijah and Elyse. I suppose they're busy with

their little one. And Donall? How's he doing? I had heard about him being captured after his plane was shot down. My prayers were answered when he escaped."

"Mine too. Last I heard, no one has seen him yet. They're giving him time to process all of it. I assume he'll contact them when he's ready."

"Perfectly normal. What about Aiden and Collin?"

"Aiden is still at An Khe. Collin is somewhere in the Mekong Delta. Belinda, his wife, is still in Taiwan as far as I know."

"Tell me about this girl and what happened," Father Andrews said.

Brendan smiled. "She's full of spark and fire. I don't think I've ever met anyone quite like her before. She's a war correspondent, passionate about her work, and very independent. Also, the most infuriating woman I've ever met."

"I see. Go on," Father Andrews replied with a hint of a smile.

"I had danced with her at the embassy in Saigon. She showed up at the firebase with a fake name, disguised as a man for a piece she's writing about the Montagnard's for MACV. Awful disguise. I saw right through it. We gave her hell for a day or so before I exposed her as a woman. The old Chieftain, the wily fox that he is, must have seen the attraction between us. He decided that he should join us in a friendship ceremony. It turned out to be a wedding instead."

"So, you were deceived by the Chieftain. Was this woman also part of the deception?"

"Irelynn? No. I don't think she even knows we're married."

"Irelynn. I know a young reporter named Irelynn. She stops in from time to time."

"Father Andrews, do you know her real name?" Brendan asked.

"George. George Irelynn Cross."

Brendan felt like someone had gut punched him. "She didn't lie about her name. Maybe she wasn't lying when she said I wasn't supposed to be on base."

"Brendan, the sacrament of marriage requires consent. Did you and Irelynn provide any type of consent?"

"I have no idea. It's possible. We were in the middle of a fight. I was not paying any attention to the Shaman."

"One question of a personal nature. Did you consummate the marriage?"

Brendan shook his head. "I kissed my bride after I put her on a chopper, then watched in horror as the NVA tried to shoot it down."

"Let me see the marriage certificate."

Reaching into a side pocket of his fatigues, Brendan pulled out the paper and handed it over. Father Andrews looked it over before handing it back.

"Brendan. It's possible in the eyes of God, you and Irelynn are married."

Brendan sputtered.

"Before you say any more. Let me explain. The certificate appears to be a valid document, though unsigned by you or

Irelynn. I'm not sure it's legal. You most likely have grounds for an annulment if that is your wish. Irelynn has a say in this as well. But, let me leave you with these parting words. God works in mysterious ways. Sometimes our path and who we walk that path with are chosen for us. It's possible this was meant to be. I need to think on this, talk to a few other chaplains, and pray for guidance," Father Andrews said. "I'll do what I can in my time left here. I'm retiring from the military and will return stateside to a new flock soon."

"I wish you well," Brendan replied.

"Thank you. I'm looking forward to peace and tranquility."

CHAPTER 16

The troop transport truck bumped and swayed along the rut filled highway. The four Vietnamese guards played a game of dice as the truck bed swayed back and forth with each bump in the road. Hidden in the back under filthy blankets lay two American women. Tied up and drugged, the women were unaware they were heading north to an unnamed buyer.

Edwin Baltini sitting in the front passenger seat, snarled as the truck hit another pothole. The driver ground the gears as he maneuvered the truck through the muck and mud.

"You, fucking moron, watch for the potholes," he snarled at the Vietnamese driver as he pulled a flask from his shirt pocket.

Taking a swig of whiskey, Baltini's face twisted and contorted in anger. Irelynn Cross. He had lost track of her, again. He had spies crawling over Saigon searching for her to no avail, making it necessary for him and his men to make the trip north to search for her at Da Nang. His employer was still angry about the loss of Elyse Booker, prima ballerina and daughter of the former ambassador. Now the man wanted Irelynn Cross just as badly. Edwin hoped the two women he held in the back of the truck would appease him for the time being.

Spotting two American nurses, changing a tire on a broken-down jeep on the side of the road further ahead. Edwin smiled, rubbing his hands in glee.

Four is always better than two.

"Pull up behind that jeep," he ordered. "Get the men from the back."

Putting a charming smile on his face, he climbed out of the truck. "Ladies. May I be of some assistance," he purred.

Fumbling with her keys, Rebecca set her bag of groceries down in front of her door. She jumped as someone stepped from the shadows.

"Rebecca."

Peering into the shadows, she stopped cold. "Irelynn? Is that you?" she squealed.

"Keep your voice down. I need your help," Irelynn whispered. "I'm wounded."

"Oh my God, Irelynn. Come in."

Irelynn stumbled into Rebecca's arms, leaning heavily on her. The two made it slowly up the stairs.

"You're burning up with fever," Rebecca said.

"I know. I was feeling better after Rose and Carole gave me a shot of penicillin, but now, I'm tired and feverish again after traveling down from Da Nang."

"Why did they let you leave? How did you get here?"

"They had no choice. I hitchhiked here."

"It's a two-day drive from Da Nang to Saigon under good conditions. You must be exhausted. Here, lie down on my bed. I'll start some tea," Rebecca said.

Irelynn sank onto the bed, "I just need to rest for a minute," she mumbled. Closing her eyes, she was out like a light.

Opening her eyes, Irelynn lay in bed for a few minutes watching dust particles float in the sunbeams shining through the window. Looking around the room in confusion, it took her a minute to remember where she was. Black and white photographs of long forgotten actresses were framed and hung on one wall. Frilly floor to ceiling drapes decorated the windows, and a dressing table with a white lace skirt adorned with vintage perfume bottles sat beneath an enormous gilded mirror. Pink satin sheets and a matching coverlet adorned the bed where she lay.

Rebecca's. I'm at Rebecca's.

The sound of pots and pans clinking came from the small kitchen. The aroma of chicken soup drifted in the air, and her stomach growled in response. Sitting up, she pulled the sheet over her chest. Her arm ached; looking down, she noted fresh bandages around her wound.

"You're awake," Rebecca said. "And starving," Irelynn replied.

Rebecca handed her a cup of soup. "Here. Drink this."

Taking the offered cup, Irelynn slowly sipped the flavorful broth. "Hmm. It's good."

"I went to the market this morning. My mom always said chicken soup heals the mind, body, and soul."

"Thank you. How long did I sleep?"

"About twelve hours. I took the liberty of putting a clean nightgown on you. I also contacted a doctor friend who hooked me up with some penicillin and clean bandages. Let me tell you, I've never given anyone a shot before or cleaned a wound. It was a little scary."

"I'm sorry."

Rebecca waved her hand. "Think nothing of it. You'd do the same for me. What happened? How were you wounded?"

"My trip to Ben Het was a disaster. You were right. Green Berets are nothing to mess with," Irelynn said.

"Did they shoot you?"

"Of course not. I got shot when the NVA tried to shoot down the chopper. Brendan was there," Irelynn whispered.

"What! Oh no. I thought…"

"We thought wrong. Our relationship was over before it

started. I can't go back to my apartment. Brendan's searching for me," Irelynn cried. Tears rolled down her face as Rebecca wrapped her in a warm embrace. Everything that had happened over the past few days came pouring out in a tear filled rant.

"Go ahead and cry, kiddo. We'll figure this out. I have to leave. If I don't show for the Five O'clock follies, they may figure out you're here."

"Irelynn nodded. You're right. You need to go. If anything, maybe you can find out what's going on."

The press room at the Rex hotel was loud and boisterous as reporters jostled each other for a seat before the podium. A ceiling fan hummed from above, drowned out by the noise of the bustling city below. A broken air conditioner sat below a row of open windows as the occupants fanned themselves in the stiflingly hot room. Brendan leaned against the wall in the far corner. His brawny arms crossed over his chest, his eyes on the street below. Mac stood across the street in the shadows of a doorway, watching for Irelynn, Rebecca, or both. A blonde woman crossed the street, walking at a fast clip; she pulled open the door to the Rex hotel and slipped inside. *Rebecca, perfect.* Brendan leaned out the window in a signal to Mac. Mac, at a discreet distance, followed the woman inside.

A man stepped up to the podium, papers in hand; he began the military's daily press briefing. Brendan slipped from the room to meet Rebecca as she stepped from the elevator. The doors closed, and another elevator dinged as Mac stepped out. Flanking Rebecca on both sides, Brendan pushed the button to call the elevator back.

"Hello, lass," Mac said.

"Mac," Rebecca said in surprise.

"We've got a few questions," Brendan said as they took her by the arms and guided her back into the elevator, pushing the button for the rooftop bar.

"Now, wait a minute. I'm missing the Five O'clock follies," Rebecca replied.

"You're not missing anything more than a sugar coating of the war," Mac replied.

The doors opened, and they escorted her past the swimming pool to a table under the shade of an umbrella.

"Sit," Brendan said.

Rebecca opened her mouth to argue the point; thinking better of it, she slid into the chair. A waiter appeared to take their order.

"What will you have?" Mac said.

"A Martini, straight up," Rebecca replied. "Whiskey, for me," Mac said.

"Same," Brendan said.

"Where is she?" Brendan said, his voice a low growl.

"Who?" Rebecca replied.

"Don't play games, Rebecca. Irelynn. Where is Irelynn?"

They paused as the waiter delivered their drinks. Rebecca picked up her Martini and gave them a silent toast.

"I have no idea," she replied.

"I said, don't play games. She's injured, and her life is in danger," Brendan said.

"How?" Rebecca asked.

"How well do you know her nurse friends as Da Nang?" Mac asked.

"Quite well. She introduced me to them," Rebecca replied. "We know that Rose and Carole visited Irelynn at a village where she was sheltering after she was wounded," Brendan said, downing his drink.

"Maybe she's with them," Rebecca said.

"No. Irelynn left on foot shortly after," Mac said. According to the villagers, they left in their jeep.

"Rose and Carole's jeep was found with a flat tire by the side of the road. They never made it back to the base. They're missing," Brendan said.

Rebecca inhaled sharply before downing the rest of her drink. "Carole and Rose? Interesting."

"Along with two other nurses from different bases," Mac said.

"Okay. Back up. What does this have to do with Irelynn? And what will you do about finding Rose, Carole, and the other women?"

Mac raised his hand to have another round of drinks delivered. "How well do you know Edwin Baltini?"

"I already told you at the embassy party what he did to Irelynn. He's a scumbag," Rebecca said with a slight shudder of her shoulders.

"We believe Baltini is behind the kidnapping of these women," Brendan said. "And he wants Irelynn. He followed her before she made the foolhardy mistake of pretending to be a man to access my firebase."

"You shouldn't have been so cruel to her," Rebecca snapped.

Brendan raised his eyebrows. "So, you have spoken to her? Where is she?"

"All I'm going to say is that she is safe," Rebecca replied.

"She's not safe as long as Baltini is after her," Brendan said.

"And just so you know. I was never cruel to her. I merely treated her like a man."

Brendan handed Rebecca a bag. "Open it," he demanded.

Rebecca opened the bag and pulled out red high heels. She raised one eyebrow and gave Brendan a questioning look.

"Irelynn and I need to talk. Tell her I thought she might want her wedding shoes back," Brendan said.

"Wedding shoes?" Rebecca asked.

"I'll be here on the roof every night at eighteen hundred hours if she wants to talk. Oh, and here's her gold nugget and chain," Brendan said. Then with a nod to Mac, they got up and left.

Pushing the button for the elevator, "Everyone's in place?" Brendan asked.

"Yup. We'll be following Rebecca. See where she goes,

who she talks to," Mac replied. "Do you think Irelynn will show?"

"We'll see. Something is off, Mac. I don't know what it is, but I can feel it in my bones."

Steam rose, filling the bathroom and fogging the mirror as Irelynn stepped into the shower. She breathed a deep sigh of relief as the hot water hit her body, trailing in soothing rivets down her neck and shoulders. One handed, she glided the soapy washcloth over the hills and valleys of her body, washing away the filth and dried blood of the past few days.

"I can't believe Rebecca put me in her nice clean bed. I can't tell the difference between dirt and blood," Irelynn mumbled.

Gently washing around the wound. "I shouldn't be washing this, but it's so gross."

A knock sounded on the door, and Rebecca stuck her head inside. "How are you doing, kiddo?"

"Oh, good. I'm glad your back. Here. Open the shampoo for me," Irelynn said, handing the bottle to Rebecca.

"Give me your hand," Rebecca said, squirting a good portion into her hand.

"This shampoo smells fantastic. How did you find it here?" Irelynn said as the breeze of flowers and bergamot, warmed with notes of iris, jasmine and rose that made up the scent of Shalimar drifted through the steam.

"VO5. The black market," Rebecca replied.

"My Gramie used to ship me a bottle from time to time," Irelynn replied.

"That's right; your grandmother sent you care packages. It's too bad she stopped sending them."

"Yeah, no mail or packages anymore. It's odd. You sent the last postcard, right?"

"Of course. From Kathmandu. Have you tried calling them again?"

"The last time I tried, my three-year-old niece answered the phone. She set it down, and no adult ever picked up the phone."

"When's the last time you attended a wedding?"

"My brother Matthew, a few years ago. Why?"

"Have you ever worn red shoes to a wedding?" Rebecca asked.

The shower shut off, and Rebecca handed in a clean towel. "No. The only time I have ever worn red shoes was the other day in the village," Irelynn said.

"I have your red heels. He called them your wedding shoes."

Irelynn's mind raced, and her heart beat frantically in her chest. "Who?" she whispered.

"Brendan. He's here in Saigon. Finish up and get dressed. We need to talk."

"Oh. Hey Rebecca. Have you seen my gold nugget necklace? I seem to have lost it somewhere?"

"Haven't seen it, kiddo."

She'd give anything to be wearing her combat boots right now. Irelynn's feet hurt as her heels clicked in a staccato beat down the sidewalk. A long blonde wig and floppy straw hat hid her chestnut curls. Using a small purse hanging diagonally across her chest as a rest for her injured arm, she walked past the street vendors and beggars. Catcalls and whistles from American troops followed her to the post office next to the Rex hotel. Tucked under her arm was a package containing the article and negatives of the life of the Montagnard's. The photographs she had taken had been developed at a steep price by another contact of Rebecca's. She gritted her teeth at the thought of paying for something she usually did herself, but it was too risky to sneak into her apartment to develop the film.

Taking turns, Rebecca was at home now while she ventured out. She glanced over her shoulder and spotted the two Vietnamese men who followed her. Though a good six inches shorter than Rebecca, between the blonde wig, shared hat and sunglasses, and dressed similar to Rebecca's style, Irelynn felt pretty confident they had fooled the men who trailed them. Not knowing if they worked for Brendan or Baltini, just that she had to make them think she was Rebecca.

Her thoughts returned to Rose and Carole. She felt helpless as a baby. All her contacts had been of no help. She felt well enough to make the dangerous trip to Da Nang. It was either that or risk jail and meet Brendan at the rooftop bar. Or both.

Grumbling to herself, "Wedding shoes. What the hell does that mean?"

The following day, before sunrise, Brendan peered over to Rebecca's apartment. Adjusting the telescope, he couldn't see anything. The drapes were drawn shut, the apartment dark. Rebecca had a prime location, right across the street from the Rex hotel. It hadn't taken him long to figure out that Irelynn was hiding there.

Quite a few American officers had their quarters located at the Rex Hotel, Brendan's room was on the second floor, and Mac's room was next door. Mac had pulled some strings to get these rooms. The two Army officers who had to vacate grumbled and complained but capitulated to orders to move across the hall.

A knock sounded at the door, and Brendan got up to let Mac in. "Morning Mac," Brendan said.

"Morning," Mac grumbled.

Throwing a towel around his shoulders, Brendan slipped into his flip flops. "I won't be more than an hour or so."

"Get out of here. Go enjoy your swim," Mac replied. "I'll keep an eye on the ladies."

Brendan sidestepped a few officers as they stumbled from the elevator after a night of hard drinking. One Lieutenant gave him a drunken salute, mumbling something incoherent as he leaned against his buddy. Brendan smiled, remembering his bygone days of revelry.

The doors opened, and Brendan walked to the pool. Dropping his towel, he slipped the flip flops off his feet and dove into the pool. Not at all big, it served his purposes as he completed forty laps across the pool. Comfortably tired now, he rested in the corner of the pool. Lost in thought, he returned to Irelynn.

The elevator dinged, and the doors opened. Out stepped the woman of his dreams. Irelynn. She walked toward the pool, shedding her robe as she went.

Brendan inhaled sharply. Even in the dark, he could see her lush curves. Her breasts pushed invitingly against a thin t-shirt; skimpy white panties barely covered her womanhood.

He didn't move or make a sound as she padded up to the pool and jumped in.

Mac leaned forward as a small light appeared in the apartment across the street. A few minutes later, a small figure opened the door and dashed across the street. Scrambling from his seat by the window, Mac ran into the hallway and down the stairs. Pausing at the landing, he peeked around the corner. Leaning over the wood banister, he watched as Irelynn crossed the lobby and entered the elevator. Looking over to the clerk at the desk, the old Vietnamese man was leaning back in his chair, mouth wide open, the man was sound asleep. Creeping down the stairs, Mac watched what floor the elevator stopped on.

Rooftop. He chuckled, *Perfect.*

Sighing deeply, he made his way down to the lobby. Settling himself into a comfortable chair, he looked at his watch before picking up the newspaper.

CHAPTER 17

Surfacing, Irelynn brushed the wet hair from her face before slowly and painfully side paddling across the pool's shallow end. Leaning back to float, she willed the ache in her arm to stop. Soft clouds floated through the sky. A few stars not drowned out by the city lights sparkled in the night sky. Across the western horizon, the lights of Tan Son Nhut Airbase shone in the distance.

Her thoughts returned as they often did of late to Brendan.

Why? It's so unlike me to fall head over heels so fast for a man. A man who probably doesn't want anything to do with me. Damn, I really screwed things up. I'm not good enough for someone like him anyway.

Rolling to her stomach, she came face to face with a man who surfaced from the water behind her—screaming in fright, unable to swim away; as the man's arms wrapped around her waist and he pulled her close.

"Good morning, George," Brendan breathed.

"Brendan," Irelynn whispered. "What? What are you doing here?" she stuttered as she tried to shove off his body.

"Don't you think it's reckless to swim with one arm injured? Not to mention the germs in the pool."

"I… Oh my God. Brendan." Something snapped inside, and she flung her arms around his neck. He pulled her trembling body tighter to his chest, and her legs wrapped around his hips.

"Shh. It's alright."

"I was scared. So scared when I saw the explosions near the base. I thought that I could lose you," she sobbed.

"I'm okay, George. Let me see your arm," Brendan said.

His fingers gently stroked her injured arm, turning it so he could get a better look at the wound.

"The light is so poor. I can't see how bad it is," Brendan said.

"The bullet passed clean through. It's already starting to heal," Irelynn said.

Brendan released her arm, pulling her back in; his hands wrapped around her head and his lips found hers. Tasting her, he reeled as her light touch roamed his body. Lost in his kiss, he plundered her mouth, groaning when she melted against him.

His hands explored her body in turn. The ache and the need inside him grew with each stroke of his hands. His senses were on fire. She was on fire.

Arching her back, she grasped his shoulders as Brendan left a trail of kisses from the hollow of her neck to her breasts. She cried out when he suckled one, then the other. His hand slipped between her thighs, and her cries filled the night. His lips found hers again, leaving her panting and moaning into his mouth before her body exploded, her cries of passion echoing his own.

Dawn was breaking; the sun peaked over the horizon. Her body quaking, she wrapped her arms around his neck and laid her head on his strong shoulder. He moved to set her on the shallow end stairs. Her body shook with the sudden chill in the air. Lifting her head and he looked into her eyes; her cheeks flamed.

"No. Don't be embarrassed. It's natural and beautiful. You're beautiful," Brendan whispered in her ear.

"Brendan. I… I've never…I mean. I had no idea."

"You don't have to say it. I already know."

"That was amazing," Irelynn breathed.

Brendan smiled, cupping her face. "There's so much more, my love." He placed kisses and nibbles along her jawline. "So much more," he breathed.

"Will you show me?"

"Not here or now, but I will," Brendan said.

"Brendan. What did you mean by wedding shoes?"

"It's going to come as a shock to you. We're married."

Irelynn blinked. "Married? You're kidding, right?"

"No. I'm not. The chieftain. It wasn't a friendship joining ceremony. It was a wedding ceremony."

"You can't be serious," Irelynn cried.

"It's true. I don't know if it's legal yet. But, according to Father Andrews, we may be married in the eyes of the church," Brendan said.

"Father Andrews. At Da Nang?"

"Yes."

"How is this possible?"

"The shaman was an ordained priest."

"Impossible. That was a pagan ceremony. I've been to enough weddings to know the sacraments of marriage. I didn't hear them. You understand their language. What did the shaman say?"

"I don't know. I was focused on you."

"You have to have consent. Did we consent to a marriage?" Irelynn's mind raced back to the joining ceremony. "He did ask us questions. What did we say?"

She looked into Brendan's horror filled face.

"I said, 'Yeah, whatever.'" Brendan growled.

"And I said, 'Sure, why not,'" Irelynn cried. "Rings. We don't have rings."

Brendan lifted her delicate wrist. "Yes, we do," he replied, pointing out the bracelet on her wrist and the one on his own.

They looked into each other's shock filled eyes. "We're married!"

"I would have liked to of had a choice," she whispered. "I barely know you."

"Don't you think I would have wanted the same?" Brendan snarled. "Don't worry, George. There's always divorce."

"Why do you only call me George when you're mad at me? I didn't do this. As for a divorce. I'll be excommunicated from the church."

"Then an annulment," Brendan snapped.

"I see you've already given this a great deal of thought. So, what about what we just did? Is that what you want? Benefits without the commitment."

Climbing from the pool, she grabbed her robe, angrily jerking it on; she tied the belt around her waist. "Don't worry, Brendan. I'm not going to hold you to this marriage sham, but I'm not your plaything either. What we just did was a mistake. It won't happen again."

Turning, she ran to the elevator. Jamming the button multiple times, the doors opened, and she slipped inside but not before she saw Brendan running after her.

"Irelynn. Stop. That's not what I meant," he called out as the elevator doors slammed shut.

Deep down, leaning her head against the doors, she knew there could never be anyone but Brendan.

The doors opened, and she raced through the lobby past a man with a newspaper sitting in a chair.

Irelynn raced into the apartment. Rebecca still slept, a sleep mask covering her eyes, her blonde hair spread across her satin pillow.

"Rebecca. Wake up. I need to leave. Now." Irelynn said as she pulled her rucksack out from under the bed. Slamming it on the bed, she ran to the dresser, pulling her clothes from the bottom drawer.

Rebecca sat up. "Wait. What happened?"

"He's here. I went for a swim at the Rex like I always do when I stay overnight."

"Brendan?"

"He must be staying there. I need to leave. He told me the wedding shoes were mine. We got married when we were at the firebase," Irelynn said, pulling on her fatigues.

Rebecca shook her head to clear the confusion. "Slow down. That doesn't even make sense."

"Tell me about it."

"What are you going to do? Where will you go?" Rebecca asked, stuffing her feet into fluffy high heeled slippers.

"The marriage. I'll think about that later. For now, I've got good investigative skills. I'm going to see if I can find Rose and Carole."

"Not without me, you're not."

"Then you'd better get dressed and packed. I'll explain everything once we're on the road," Irelynn said.

Rebecca went to open the drapes.

"No. Leave them shut. He might be watching," Irelynn said.

"How will we get out of here without him seeing us?" Rebecca asked.

"The bathroom window faces the back of the building."

They went to the bathroom window to peer out onto a narrow, filthy alleyway.

"It's not that big of a drop," Irelynn said. "We can make it. We can make a rope out of sheets."

"It might be difficult with your injury," Rebecca said.

"I'll be fine."

Rebecca pulled her hair into a ponytail and pulled on her fatigues and boots. "You're right. I've been sedentary for too long. Let's do this."

Once they had everything together, they opened the window, tossing the makeshift rope; Rebecca went first. Irelynn tossed down the rucksacks, and with her cameras securely over her shoulder, she followed. Pushing through the pain in her arm, she made it to the ground. Turning around, a Vietnamese man smiled as he held a knife to Rebecca's throat.

"Oh shit," Irelynn breathed as she looked around at his

two grinning friends. One of the men grabbed Irelynn by the hair, pushing her and Rebecca down the alley toward a waiting truck, passing by the body of a Vietnamese man lying on the ground. Irelynn was sure he was one of the men who often followed them.

He must have been working for Brendan. She struggled against her captor as the man raised his fist, striking her chin; all went black.

Pacing back and forth in front of the window. Brendan looked across the street to Rebecca's apartment.

"Why the fuck are the drapes still closed?" he growled. Anguish gripped his heart at how he had left things with Irelynn. He knew he had screwed up. She had taken what he said the wrong way. Even after such a short time, he did have feelings for her. Confusion rolled through his brain like a train wreck. Rubbing a hand across his stubbled chin in frustration. Something wasn't sitting right.

"Something's wrong," Brendan snarled.

Mac looked up from cleaning his gun. "Yeah, I'm feeling uneasy too."

"I'm going over there," Brendan said. Grabbing his sidearm, he tucked it in his waistband before running out the door. Not waiting for the elevator, they practically flew down the stairs and through the lobby. Narrowly missing getting hit by a rickshaw, Brendan held up his hand to stop traffic as they ran across the street. The door was locked, but Mac quickly picked the lock. Slipping inside, they took the steps two at a time to the second floor apartment. Picking the second door lock, Mac smiled as Brendan pulled his gun and inched open the door. A quick scan of the silent apartment told them the women weren't there. Mac put his ear to the bathroom door before opening it, spotting the open window and the rope of pink satin sheets tied to the claw foot bathtub. "Shit," Mac said. "Damn it—sneaky little shit. I'm going to turn her over my knee when I catch her," Brendan snarled as he leaned out the window.

Street orphans roamed below, one picking up a rucksack covered with travel patches and peace signs. Brendan recognized the bag as Irelynn's. "Drop it," he yelled out the window. The child took off with the rucksack in hand.

"I'll get the front," Mac yelled as Brendan jumped out the window; using the sheets, he rappelled down the building. Landing like a cat, Brendan chased the child around the building into Mac's waiting arms. Mac picked the child up and set him to sit on a barrel.

"Where is the woman who had this rucksack?" Mac demanded.

The terrified child started to cry, "Men took the women," he said. "They beat one of them and put them both in the truck."

"Baltini," Brendan whispered.

"Soldiers?" Mac asked the child.

"No. Just Vietnamese men," the child replied. "I heard them say they were going to Da Nang."

Exchanging glances with Mac, Brendan pulled a dollar bill from his pocket. Giving it to the kid. "Here, go get something to eat," he said.

Brendan and Mac watched the child run up the street. Hefting Irelynn's rucksack over his shoulder. "I'm surprised the scrawny kid could even lift this. What do you think? VC or hired henchmen?" Brendan asked.

"Maybe both. I'll get a jeep and contact the authorities.

The man we had in the back alley is dead," Mac replied.

"Six American women. What could Baltini possibly want with them?" Brendan asked.

"I don't know."

"You got pictures of any of these women?"

"I'll get them from HQ when we arrive in Da Nang," Mac said.

CHAPTER 18

Groaning, Irelynn lifted her head as waves of nausea swept over her. *How long have I been out?* She tried to roll to her side and bumped into Rebecca. With her hands tied in front of her, she gently prodded her. "Rebecca. Rebecca, wake up," she whispered. Moaning, Rebecca opened her eyes. "Hey, kiddo. You okay?"

"My head is pounding, and my arm is on fire."

"It's bleeding again," Rebecca whispered.

"How about you? Are you okay?"

"My jaw is sore. Those assholes sure know how to wallop a girl. Where are we?"

"We're in the back of an Army truck stopped somewhere. Exactly where? I have no idea," Irelynn replied.

"I'm assuming Baltini is behind this," Rebecca said.

"I'm a little scared. I've got the feeling we'll find out exactly what happened to Rose and Carole."

"I'm scared too."

Voices filled the air as a jeep pulled up next to the truck. "Shhh. Someone's coming," Rebecca said.

"Listen. I hear English mixed in with the Vietnamese," Irelynn whispered, closing her eyes.

The tailgate dropped, and a man jumped onto the bed of the truck. He poked Irelynn and then Rebecca. He grunted at their lack of response. He stroked Irelynn's cheek, then ran his hand down the contours of her body. He grunted again at her lack of response before jumping out of the truck.

"Good job. That's her," Baltini said. "I'm not sure he'll want the other one, but we'll see. It works in our favor. Correspondents disappear all the time. Bring the other two. Eight women now. That ought to make the bastard happy."

Two more unconscious women were loaded into the truck. A minute later, the truck pulled onto a bumpy road. Irelynn lifted her head to peer over Rebecca's shoulder at the other women. She didn't recognize either one. Spotting the two guards sitting close by, she laid her head back down. She shuddered at the thought of Edwin Baltini's hands touching her.

What could they possibly want with us?

Lieutenant Colonel Martha Boise pushed her way past Murphy into Colonel Bragg's office. Barely nodding at Brendan and Mac, who jumped to their feet to stand at attention. She was a force to be reckoned with as her gaze narrowed in on Colonel Bragg.

"Two more. I'm missing two more of my nurses," she hissed. "Where are they, Colonel?"

"Colonel Bragg paled before barking. "Two more? You're sure?"

"Of course, I'm sure. They were working at a public clinic this morning giving immunizations, and they did not return. This makes six. Who is kidnapping my nurses? I want answers, and I want them now."

"Calm down, Martha. We're doing everything we can. We've also got two civilian female correspondents missing, "Colonel Bragg said.

"Reporters?" Who?"

"Irelynn Cross and Rebecca Ronan," Brendan said.

Martha inhaled sharply. "I know both of those women. Irelynn's a fearless reporter, and Rebecca is well... let's just say she's lucky she has Irelynn. Just last summer, they co-wrote a wonderful piece about my nurses."

"Are you aware if Irelynn writes under any other names?" Colonel Bragg asked.

"George I. Cross. Everyone knows that's her real name," Martha said.

"Does MACV know?" Brendan asked. "They sent Irelynn

to us for a story about my firebase, but she was disguised as a man."

"Oh, they know. I'm not defending her behavior, but if Irelynn felt the need to disguise herself, it's because she cares very deeply about the subjects she writes about. If anything, we all know there's no love lost between the regular army and special forces. They knew they were pulling a fast one on you."

"I'll deal with those assholes later. Let's get back to the problem at hand. Eight American women are missing," Colonel Bragg growled.

"Do you have photographs of the last two nurses?" Mac asked.

Martha handed the files to Mac and followed the men into the conference room next door. The pictures and files for each missing woman were spread across the table. Laying the pictures side by side, the foursome looked at the pictures.

"Look at these women. They're all beautiful," Brendan said.

"Stunning. All of them," Martha said.

"Look at this. A black woman, a Hispanic woman, two blondes, two redheads, two brunettes, Mac said.

Brendan took the pictures and laid them in the order Mac specified.

"A blue eyed blonde, a green eyed blonde. The redheads, blue and hazel. The brunette, blue, Irelynn's chestnut hair with amber eyes. A stunning black woman with dark brown eyes, and a Puerto Rican beauty with chocolate brown eyes," Brendan said.

"A veritable smorgasbord of womanhood," Colonel Bragg said.

Martha raised one eyebrow. "No. Not a smorgasbord. A stable," she cried.

The foursome looked at each other in horror. "My God. Is someone creating an American whore house with our women?" Mac whispered.

Colonel Bragg went to the door and flung it open. "Murphy. Get me General Smead, on the line. On the double," he bellowed.

"Martha. Your nurses are confined to quarters. They'll be escorted to and from the hospital for their shifts and the mess hall. And I want the guards doubled around the nurse's barracks. I'll be in touch."

Martha nodded. "Yes. Sir." She saluted and left the room.

Colonel Bragg turned to Brendan and Mac. "This is the last fucking thing I need. I want your sorry asses on the road hunting down whoever thinks they can profit off American women."

"We're pretty sure it's Baltini," Mac said.

"Edwin Baltini? We'll revoke his press credentials and bar him from stepping foot on this base or any other base in-country. You bring me his head on a platter if you have to. And I want our women back. All of them. I'll have the MP's set up check-points from here to the DMZ." Coronel Bragg left the room and stomped next door, leaving a trail of colorful profanity.

Brendan and Mac cringed as the Colonel's door slammed shut. Mac picked up the women's files while Brendan looked at the photographs on the table.

"Mac. If what we suspect is true. It wouldn't be just any brothel. It would have to be high-end. American women would be considered rare. I can think of only two cities where something like this would be profitable. Saigon, and…"

"Hue city," Mac said.

"When's the last time you were in Hue?" Brendan asked.

"I haven't been that far north since before the Tet offensive. The city was nearly destroyed."

"We have to consider that the women may have been taken into North Vietnam," Brendan said. He looked down at the picture he held of Irelynn in his hand. His thumb gently stroked the picture as he remembered how good she had felt in his arms. He looked up to see Mac watching him.

"How do you feel about Irelynn?" Mac asked.

"There are times when anything is possible, but then again, impossible. Irelynn is somewhere in the middle. I want to know if there is really something between us."

"There's a name for a woman when you can't decide if you want to kiss her or throttle her," Mac said.

Brendan smiled. A soft chuckle escaped him. "Yeah. A pepper pot."

Chilled by the breeze as welcome as it was from the sultry heat of the day, Irelynn stood at the window, peering through the bars at the city spread out before her. Pulling the sheer robe closed for warmth, Irelynn sneered at the ridiculous outfit and shoes she was forced to wear. She felt like a Forties pin-up girl. The revealing nightgown and robe, along with the high heeled slippers with tufts of white feathers, felt more appropriate for a wedding night in years long past. Her benefactor, or pimp as she called him. Whomever he was, preferred that the women held captive in his brothel be dressed in the same manner.

The city below drew her attention again. The citadel, with its high walls and moat in the distance, sat next to the Perfume River winding its way through Hue city. It was beautiful. She had always wanted to visit in the autumn when the orchards to the north dropped their blooms into the river. Their pungent smell gave the river its name as it lazily flowed into the South China Sea. Though the city had suffered through the month-long Tet offensive the year before, the architecture of the imperial city with the backdrop of the mountains to the west was breathtaking. The rubble of once grand pagodas and palaces littered the view, and Irelynn sighed deeply. Never in a million years would she have thought she'd end up held captive in a place like this. Tonight, the high-end brothel would open its doors for the first time. Scores of wealthy men and high ranking officials would pour through the doors, all vying to be the first of many clients.

Guilt riddled her for not fighting harder. Anger burned

beneath an outwardly calm demeanor at the thought of the opening night auction. She wouldn't make it easy on any of them, and God help the man who thought she would capitulate to forced prostitution. The sting of the welts on her back spoke of the past week with her captors, but she had left more than one of the guards bruised and bloody. Her thoughts floated to Rebecca, Rose, Carole, and the other girls. There was also a young Montagnard woman held captive. The woman had recently given birth. Irelynn could still hear the woman's cries and pleadings through the thin walls daily since her child was ripped from her arms and taken away.

Locked inside the room, Irelynn looked at the large bed with its tufted headboard and yards of silk decorating the wall behind it. It was a bit gauche, right down to the chaise lounge chair in front of the window. It reminded her of a Hollywood boudoir from a B rated film and fit in with the outfit she was wearing. The room meant for a starlet to entertain men was outright disturbing.

Irelynn shuddered and rubbed her arms. "I think the guy's got a Hollywood fetish," she muttered as she paced about her room. A gilded cage was still a cage, and she wasn't taking what they had planned for her laying down. She had a plan, now, if she could speak with the other women.

A knock sounded on the door, and a key was turned in the lock. Anh, a young Vietnamese girl of fifteen or so, stood in the doorway; behind her stood a burly guard, a thick belt dangling from his meaty fist. Irelynn gave the guard a look of contempt as he held his belt up in a threatening move.

Anh moved to a small table to pick up the un-eaten tray from lunch.

"Thank you. Anh," Irelynn said.

Picking up the tray, Anh exchanged a knowing glance with Irelynn. Under the plate sat a note for Rebecca. For all her innocence, Anh had been a key player in delivering the secret messages between Irelynn and Rebecca. Irelynn still seethed at Anh's treatment. She was kidnapped from her village, forced to serve as a maid here, and eventually on her back in a brothel. Irelynn swore she'd see her returned to her family.

Once Anh left the room, the guard motioned for Irelynn to follow her to the common area. Irelynn sneered at the other Vietnamese guards as she passed them. She was surprised to see the other women lined up in front of the large sitting area. Mai Le, the Montagnard woman, could barely stand on her own. She was supported by Mary, a tall willowy redhead, one of the first nurses kidnapped, and Irelynn. Irelynn glanced at the other women, all dressed in the same manner as her, right down to the silly high heels on their feet.

A door opened at the far end of the room, and Edwin Baltini strode into the room. Stopping in front of the women, he sneered, showing his contempt for them.

"Ah, the ladies. Never was there a finer display of American pussy. All primed and ready to spread your legs for any man that can afford what your benefactor charges. You'll be well used, and when you no longer please the clients. Your throats will be cut, and your bodies thrown in the river." He stopped in front of Mai Le and lifted her chin. "The Montagnard. Another beauty. Too bad, from the looks of you. You won't last the night," he said.

"Leave her alone, Baltini. She just gave birth a few weeks ago. Can't you see she's sick?" Irelynn said.

Baltini turned to Irelynn. "And the great George Irelynn Cross. Famous writer and photojournalist. So nice to see you brought so low, Irelynn. I might even watch as your chained to your bed, and your first client slides between your thighs."

"Enough, Edwin," A man called from the doorway.

Irelynn and Rebecca exchanged shocked glances. "Mr. Le. You've got to be kidding me," Irelynn breathed. "He's the benefactor?"

"Hardly," Mr. Le replied. He raised his hand, "My dear." Rebecca stepped forward, taking Mr. Le's hand; she turned to smile at the women.

"My mistress and your new owner," Mr. Le said.

CHAPTER 19

*G*asps of dismay from the other women filled the air. The shock hit Irelynn full force as her head reeled.

"Rebecca. No," she whispered, fighting back nausea.

"Oh, come now, Irelynn. Don't be so naïve. Surely, you realize I couldn't continue to hang onto your coattails for the rest of my career. With you out of the way, I can return to Saigon and take my place as the top female journalist in country. All while knowing that the high and mighty Irelynn Cross is here in Hue City servicing men on her knees. Bringing me a hefty profit, I might add," Rebecca smirked. "And, of course, I'll be the one to console that handsome husband of yours." Rebecca fingered the gold nugget hanging from her slim throat.

"My gold nugget," Irelynn said.

"Brendan gave it to me to return to you. I rather fancied it and decided to keep it for now. It's too bad…" Rebecca sneered.

"You bitch," Irelynn said. "Stay away from Brendan and give me back my necklace."

"I was going to say; it's too bad that I must give it up. Since Anh is the same size as you, we'll strategically place the necklace near her burnt body. Brendan will never know the difference."

"You're evil. I hope you burn in hell," Irelynn snarled. Rebecca gave her a small smile and looked over to where Anh stood, terrified and shaking. Rebecca nodded to a guard who took his belt and started beating the girl. Irelynn jumped to go to the girl's defense. She was held in place by a guard behind her and Baltini in front of her.

The smile on Baltini's face faded when Irelynn head butted him, breaking his nose and knocking him to the floor. Then Irelynn rammed her elbow into the guard's ribs and flipped him over her shoulder to land on top of Baltini with a grunt. Edwin shoved the guard aside, pulled a gun from his waistband, aimed it at Irelynn, and fired. Mai Le jumped in front of Irelynn at the last moment and took the bullet meant for Irelynn.

Irelynn looked down in slow motion horror as Mai Le crumpled at her feet. More guards poured into the room, and hand-to-hand combat ensued as nurses remembered their basic training. The fighting was vicious and intense; Irelynn looked over to see Georgia, the beautiful black nurse, take off her high heeled slipper and throw it across the room to hit a guard right between the eyes, knocking him out. Following her lead, she took her slipper with its four-inch spike and hit Baltini in the head.

Baltini's gun skidded across the floor, and Irelynn and Rebecca both jumped for it. Irelynn landed on it first. Then she balled her fist and punched Rebecca in the face knocking her flat on her back. Picking up the gun, Irelynn waved back the remaining guards and anyone else who wasn't unconscious. Forcing them into one of the bedrooms, Rose locked the door.

Carmen and Carole knelt in front of Mai Le on the floor.

Irelynn handed Rose the gun and dropped to Mai Le's side. "Hey, Mai Le. It's going to be okay. We're going to get you to the hospital now. You've got six nurses here. Hang in there," she crooned in French.

"No. I'm dying. Find Seamus. Tell him…tell him. Our baby girl is out there somewhere. She has his eyes. Please. Find Seamus. He'll find her. I know he will…" Her voice trailed off; then she was gone. "No. Mai Le. No," Irelynn cried. "Seamus. Who is Seamus?"

"She's gone. Irelynn," Carmen said, closing Mai Le's eyes.

Irelynn looked up to see Anh standing in front of her. The poor girl shook like a leaf; tears ran down her sweet face.

"We have to get out of here," Irelynn said, wiping her

tears from her face. Rising to her feet, she gripped Anh in a tight hug until her shaking stopped.

She took the gun back from Rose. "I had no idea nurses could fight like that."

"For the most part, we can do whatever is necessary to protect ourselves," Carole replied. "I can't say I saw Rebecca's betrayal coming."

Irelynn gritted her teeth. Rebecca's treachery cutting deep. "Forget her. She's not worth it. Do you know how to use a weapon?"

"Yes."

"Maybe they have a stash of guns somewhere in this house," Irelynn said. "Anh. Where's that closet you said they stowed our gear? Do they have weapons? And outside of this room, do they have more guards?"

"They have guards outside. I know where the closet is. I think they have guns in there," Anh replied.

Irelynn glanced over at Rose checking the pulse of Rebecca, then Baltini.

"They're both alive," Rose said.

"Leave them. Someone, please help me. Let's take Mai Le into her room," Irelynn said, walking over to Rebecca. She reached down and yanked her gold nugget and chain from Rebecca's throat.

Five minutes later, they stood in front of a closet; Irelynn used the key taken from an unconscious guard. Opening the door, inside, they found a cache of weapons, ammo, and their gear.

"Damn. Where's my rucksack?" Irelynn said, pulling the straps of her cameras over her shoulder. She looked over her shoulder to see Angie pulling a rifle from the rack.

"Look at the markings. These are Chinese rifles," Angie said.

"That proves that Rebecca and Baltini were working with the VC," Irelynn replied. "Damn, now where're my boots?"

Angie pointed to the other side of the closet. "They're lined up over there. It looks like they were saving them."

"There's no time to put them on or find clothes. We'll have to go as we are," Irelynn said.

Carole pulled at the translucent material of the nightgown clinging to her curves. "We're half naked."

"It's not like we can wrap ourselves in sheets for this," Rose said.

Irelynn pulled a rucksack from the shelf. "This is Rebecca's. Here, someone take it. It might have something useful to us." When they were ready, and everyone was armed. Mary and

Georgia reported that several troop transport trucks were parked next to the house.

"Ready, ladies? Let's get the hell out of here," Irelynn said. "What is it the troops say out in the bush?"

"Saddle up," Rose replied.

"Seriously, every time I hear that, I'm looking around for a horse," Irelynn replied.

Pinching the bridge of his nose, Brendan let out a deep sigh. It was a sheer stroke of luck that they had found the house where the women were held captive in Hue City after a week of searching. Now they were on standby, a block and a half away with a clear view into the compound. Four troop transport trucks and about fifty troops, a mix of special forces and PAVN, the South Vietnamese troops, stood ready to storm the compound and rescue the women. Brendan lifted his binoculars to scan the house and grounds for movement. A groan from beneath his heavy boot reminded him that his foot rested on the back of a trussed-up businessman. The man had made the mistake of drunken bragging to an informant about a brothel full of American women. It had taken everything in him not to beat the hell out of the man after he had led them to the compound.

"You going to let Major Nguyen get that asshole out of here?" Mac asked.

"What? Oh yeah. Get him out of here," Brendan replied. He watched as the man was pulled to his feet and led away to one of the trucks.

"We'll let the Vietnamese authorities handle the men that show up for the auction," Mac said.

"Sends a clear message, doesn't it? Mess with our women, and you'll end up rotting in prison," Brendan said.

"Somethings going on at the house," Mac said, raising his binoculars.

Brendan raised his, lowered them, rubbed his eyes, and raised them again. "That's our women. What the fuck are they doing?" he yelled.

"They're breaking out," Mac shouted.

The sound of gunfire filled the air; all hell broke loose as a truck raced through the compound. Half-naked women in the back of the truck were shooting at armed guards who ran for their truck. The first truck crashed through the gate, followed by the second truck filled with screaming guards, and raced up the street toward them.

"Are you fucking seeing this, Brendan?" Mac yelled.

"Jesus Christ," Brendan bellowed, throwing the binoculars; he raced for a jeep parked nearby. He slid over the hood screaming at the driver to go. Mac landed in the back seat just as the trucks raced past them. The rat a tat tat of small arms fire echoed back and forth between the two trucks as people on the streets ran in terror.

The men ducked as bullets pinged the jeep. Sitting up, eyes wide, the driver, a blonde kid of no more than nineteen, turned to Brendan. "That truck…is filled with chicks," he said.

"I know. My wife is driving," Brendan screamed. "Go." Someone tossed Mac two M-16's, and he threw one to Brendan. Behind them, the troops scrambled for their trucks, and the chase was on.

The jeep raced up behind the second truck. Brendan raised his rifle and started shooting at the men in the back. The men in the back of the truck split, half shooting at the truck in front of them, the rest, shooting at the jeep and the trucks behind them. Brendan broke the windshield out with the butt of his rifle; leaning through the broken frame, he spread himself halfway out to lay on the hood. The jeep wove back and forth, avoiding gunfire as Brendan started picking off the men in the truck. Mac stood up, bracing his feet wide; he sprayed the truck with small arms fire.

The kid driver drove the jeep up onto the sidewalk hitting vendor stalls. Fruit, vegetables, and dry goods flew in every direction as screaming people dove out of the way. Passing the second truck, Brendan rolled to his back, shooting at the truck driver while Mac continued spraying the truck. Brendan's gun jammed, and he tossed it away. Pulling his sidearm, he put a bullet into the man hanging out the passenger window. The man slumped over and dangled from the truck before falling out. The kid pulled alongside the truck with the women, and Brendan and Mac jumped, landing in the truck bed.

Up ahead, Brendan could see the Perfume river; the bridge was out, destroyed months ago during the Tet offensive. Brendan crawled to the front of the bed and banged on the window while Mac and the nurses continued shooting at the other truck. Brendan climbed onto the running board alongside the truck and slid into the passenger seat to come face to face with a handgun. Irelynn dropped the gun when she saw it was him.

"The bridge is out," Brendan screamed.

"I know," Irelynn yelled back. "The brakes are gone. I can't stop."

Brendan whipped around and broke the back window out with his elbow. Yelling to Mac, "The bridge is out. Brace yourselves."

Mac scooped eight women into his arms, pushing them to the floor. Locking his feet and arms around the bars under the seats to keep the women beneath him pinned in place.

Irelynn hit the gas, and the truck sailed over the open expanse of the bridge, landing on the other side with a boom as all four tires blew, the truck sliding to a screeching sideways stop. Behind them, the second truck tried to make the jump, its occupants screaming all the way down before landing upside down in the river.

Brendan still braced himself, his legs on the dashboard, his hands gripping the back of the seat and door frame. Adrenaline rushed through his body as he sat staring at Irelynn in shock.

"What?" Irelynn said.

He opened his mouth while he struggled for words. "Where the fuck... did you learn to drive like that?"

Irelynn gave him a wide smile. "My family owns a logging company. Sometimes things got a little wild."

Brendan nodded his head. "That explains a lot. Come here."

He pulled Irelynn into his lap, facing him, she straddled his thighs. He ran his hands over her shoulders and arms. "Are you hurt?"

"I'm fine. I'm so happy to see you," Irelynn said, wrapping her arms around his neck. "Did I ruin your knight in shining armor, rescuing the damsel in distress moment?"

He pulled her tight to his chest. "Fuck no. Sparky, you drive me crazy."

Looking out the back window, Brendan could see Mac laying spread eagle on top of a pile of women, his face still buried between the breasts of… someone.

Brendan shook his head, *Typical Mac* then he pulled Irelynn in for a long kiss.

Behind him, Mac came to his knees, raised his arms in victory, and whooped. "Hot damn. What a ride."

The jeep and trucks filled with soldiers pulled up next to them. The troops jumped out, scrambling down the riverbank searching for survivors while Mac helped the nurses.

Mac gushed over the women as he lifted them down from the truck. "Mary, sweet Mary. The lovely Carole, my wild Rose, Angie, looking good, ah…Georgia and Carmen, beautiful. And who might you be, sweetheart? Anh, welcome, Anh," He spotted Brendan and Irelynn coming around the back of the truck and pulled her into a bear hug. "And you. You're crazy, but damn, woman, you can drive. Now, where's that kid driver? Fucking stock car racing at its finest." Mac found the kid, wrapped him in his embrace, and rubbed his knuckles on the top of his head.

The women stood lined up in their skimpy attire. Chinese automatic rifles held high in their hands, fluffy high heels on their feet, ammo belts slung precariously between their breasts. Happy smiles lit their faces as they whooped, laughed, and hugged, celebrating their harrowing escape.

The special forces Captain Clark approached Brendan, unable to take his eyes off the women. "Valkyries. Now I've fucking seen it all," he said.

Brendan turned to look at the women. "Ah yeah. We need something to cover them up with." He paused. "Shirts. We need seven shirts."

The captain frowned. "There are eight women."

Unbuttoning his shirt, "One of them will wear mine," Brendan said.

"Which one?"

"My wife," Brendan replied. "How'd you get over here, anyway?"

"There's another bridge half a click to the south," Captain Clark replied.

Taking off his shirt, Brendan strode over and placed it over Irelynn's shoulders.

"Thank you," she said. Sniffing the shirt, she rolled her eyes and slipped her arms into the sleeves.

"It's that or nothing," Brendan said with a chuckle before looking at Mac with a grin.

Mac had a look of consternation on his face. "Where's Rebecca?"

Irelynn's eyes narrowed, her anger palpable. "We left her unconscious on the floor after I knocked her traitorous ass out."

"What?" Brendan said.

"Rebecca, Baltini, and Mr. Le were behind this," Irelynn snarled. Her eyes softened and filled with tears. "Oh, Brendan. We had to leave a Montagnard woman, Mai Le, behind. Baltini killed her. She deserves a decent burial."

Turning in horror to look into his friend's pain filled eyes. "Mac. I…" Brendan said.

"Where is she?" Mac whispered.

"We carried her into her room and put her on the bed," Irelynn whispered back.

Mac took off, jumping into the jeep; he pulled away with the tires screeching.

Irelynn plucked at Brendan's arm. "What's Mac's real name?"

Brendan's heart ached for his friend. "Seamus," he replied.

"Oh my God. She's the one he's been searching for."

"Captain Clark. Let's get these women back to the base," Brendan said. "They need a shower, clothes, and to be debriefed."

The following day, the sun was rising as the chopper lifted off. Mai Le's body lay before Mac, wrapped in a body bag. He was on his way to return her to her father as promised. The Chieftain would see that she was laid to rest with her ancestors.

"I'll find our little one, Mai Le. By all that's holy. I will find her," Mac whispered.

CHAPTER 20

Tossing back another shot, Irelynn felt the tequila burning down her throat. Tipping the glass upside down, she slammed it onto the bar. Raw pain and anger filled her. "Rebecca. How could I have been so blind?" she mumbled. She looked up as Mac slid into a stool next to her. "Hey Mac," she said.

"I've been looking for you," Mac said.

"Yeah, after leaving Anh at the orphanage here in Da Nang, I needed a drink."

"She'll be okay there until we find her family. The nuns are kind. They'll take good care of her. She'll help them out too. Anh loves kids."

"So many babies. So many American babies," Irelynn said. "Lonely soldiers and beautiful women. It's bound to happen."

"I don't understand how they can give them up," Irelynn said.

"Life is hard here. Harder yet if you have a mixed-race child. If you were one of those children's mothers, you would understand that they had to choose between food and shelter for their child or death on the street. Vietnamese society doesn't look kindly on these kids."

"It's sad," Irelynn replied.

"That's why I have to find Molly. Well, that, and because she's mine."

"Molly? You named the baby?"

"Yeah, a version of Mai Le," Mac said.

"Anh told me what happened after the baby was born. That bitch told her to throw her in the river. Anh couldn't do it. She ran into an elderly couple from her old village. They were on their way to a refugee camp. She gave them the baby," Irelynn said.

"I know. I'll find Molly."

"Anh should've escaped right then and there with the old couple."

Mac tossed back a shot of whiskey. "Then we would have never known what happened with the baby."

"The nurses were amazing. All of them. So strong and admirable. I'm surprised they put them back to work," Irelynn said.

"They are strong, and their angels. They desperately needed their help. It might not seem fair that they weren't given a rest, especially after everything they already deal with.

Twelve hour plus days, knee deep in death, and caring for the wounded. Got shot in the ass last year. Met the prettiest little nurse."

Irelynn rolled her eyes. "I thought you had Mai Le?"

"I did. Mai Le was a free spirit. I rented a little villa in Saigon to keep her safe. I adored her, but I never loved her. She lived her life, and I lived mine. I'd see her when I could. I was gone for a few months on a mission. That's why I didn't know she was pregnant. In our own way, we were happy. Some of this is my fault. She got bored, so I had contacts that found her the job with the Le's. I never personally met the Le's until the party at the embassy. By then, it was too late. Maybe if I had taken the time, I would have known what kind of people they were."

"Did she see other men?"

"Nah, she would have told me if she did," Mac said. "As I said, she was a free spirit. She was a lot like you."

"In what way?" Irelynn asked.

"She was never content living in that village. She wanted to travel and see the world."

"I'm sorry she never made it any further than Saigon. How did the Chieftain take it?'

"I think he always knew her life would be short lived." Brendan slid onto a stool on the other side of her, and Irelynn gave him a sad smile.

"Did you find them yet?" Irelynn said.

"No. Rebecca and Baltini escaped. We're watching for them," Brendan said.

"I should have killed them when they were lying there. I should have known or at least seen the signs that Rebecca was involved," Irelynn said, tossing back another shot. "Maybe then I could have prevented it. Saved the nurses from being kidnapped, Mai Le from dying, and Mac's baby…"

"You can't hold yourself responsible for their actions, Irelynn," Brendan said.

"None of us saw it coming," Mac said.

"And Mr. Le?" Irelynn asked.

"Singing like a bird," Mac said. "We know a whole lot more about their operation. Rebecca and Baltini were running drugs on her supposed business trips. Bringing heroin back from other countries. Selling it to our troops. They were also somehow involved with a spy ring.

Anything to make a buck and support their lifestyle."

"Which brings us to another issue," Brendan said as he pulled some postcards and letters from his side pocket. Placing them on the bar in front of Irelynn.

"We found these in Rebecca's rucksack and thought you would want to see them."

Irelynn picked up the stack, inhaling sharply. "These are for my family." Irelynn started to shake. "Do you know what this means? There are eight postcards here and all my letters home. Thailand, Singapore, everywhere that she went. Once per month, Rebecca was supposed to mail these. This means my family hasn't heard from me in over eight months. Oh my God. They might think I'm dead or missing. I have to go home. Now. Right now."

Irelynn reached down, pulling her rucksack onto her lap; she stuffed the postcards and letters inside.

Outside, the sky rumbled, and the rain came down in sheets. Brendan placed a light hand on her arm.

"Irelynn. You're not thinking clearly. You can make a phone call later," Brendan said.

"Why not now?" Irelynn cried.

"It's the middle of the night back in the world. And you've been drinking," Brendan gently said.

Irelynn looked up into Brendan's eyes. They were so blue. So beautiful, calming, and full of…love. Never had a man looked at her like this before. Time stood still. She no longer heard the pounding rain on the roof or the music. Everyone and everything around them ceased to exist. Only the look in his eyes that she knew was mirrored in her own.

Lifting her rucksack, Brendan slung it over his shoulder; then, sliding his arms underneath, he lifted her in his arms.

"Sir."

Brendan swung around with Irelynn still in his arms. Two MP's stood behind him.

"Sir," The young MP said again.

Brendan snapped. "What is it?" Irelynn slid to her feet.

"Sorry to interrupt. Sir. We have orders to take Miss. Cross into custody."

Holding Irelynn close, she hissed in his arms. "By whose orders?" Brendan snarled.

"Colonel Bragg's," the MP replied.

Mac stood up. "What's this all about?"

"I'm sorry, Sir. You'll have to speak to Colonel Bragg."

Brendan looked down into Irelynn's shocked face. "Irelynn. I…"

"You planned this. You've always wanted me in the brig. You bastard," she hissed, yanking herself out of his arms, clenching and unclenching her fists.

"No. I have nothing to do with this," Brendan said.

"Come along, Miss," the MP said; taking her by the arms, he turned her around, pulling her arms behind her and placing handcuffs on her wrists before leading her away.

Brendan and Mac watched in shock as she was placed in the back of a jeep, and the jeep pulled away.

"What the fuck is going on, Mac?"

"I don't know, my friend, but let's find out."

Brendan and Mac angrily strode down the hallway toward Colonel Bragg's office. Their broad shoulders and set of their jaws gave no quarter as others scrambled out of their way. Brendan burst through the door of the office; not bothering to wait for permission, he barged his way past Murphy, who tried to block his way into Colonel Bragg's office.

"You can't go in there, Major," Murphy said, trying to hold him back.

"The hell I can't," Brendan snarled, pushing him out of the way.

"It's alright, Murphy. Let him in," Colonel Bragg said.

Brendan crossed the room, reached across the desk, and pulled the Colonel out of his chair, slamming him up against the wall.

"What the fuck are you doing to my wife?" Brendan snarled in his face.

Mac scrambled behind Brendan, pulling him off the Colonel. "Let him go, Brendan."

"Stand down, Corrington," Colonel Bragg said.

Brendan gave him one more shove before letting go of his collar. Colonel Bragg stepped around Brendan, straightening his shirt and tie as he went back to sit at his desk.

"I'm surprised you call this woman your wife," came an unfamiliar voice.

Brendan and Mac whipped around to look at the man they hadn't noticed before.

"Who the fuck are you?" Brendan said.

"Marchetti? What are you doing here?" Mac asked.

"Mark Marchetti, CIA. I'm here running an investigation."

"An investigation into what?" Mac said.

"The woman in the brig," Marchetti said. "We don't really know who she is."

"Irelynn?" Brendan asked. "Her name is George Irelynn Cross."

"We don't know that. George Irelynn Cross disappeared eight months ago, backpacking along the Hippy trail. According to the State Department, her family lost contact with her in Istanbul."

"There's an explanation for that," Brendan said. "Rebecca was supposed to mail her postcards and didn't."

"Is there? The real journalist Rebecca Ronan's body was found in Istanbul. The woman who stole her identity was Sandra Saunders. It's possible they just haven't found Cross' body yet, and the woman we are holding is also an imposter."

"What about her work? All of her articles and photo-journalism."

"She could be a wanna be journalist, just like Sandra was," Marchetti said. "If you think about it, it's a great cover."

"I know beyond the shadow of a doubt that she is George Irelynn Cross," Brendan bellowed.

"You don't know shit," Marchetti yelled back.

"Pictures. Do you have pictures from her life back in the world?" Mac asked.

"Not yet. I have FBI agents at her parent's house right now picking them up."

"Let us talk to her. We'll figure this out," Mac said.

"No. You're both too close to this. Listen. She may be the real thing, but until we know for sure and figure out if she was working with Sandra Saunders and Edwin Baltini. She stays in the brig. In fact, I'm going to transfer her down to LBJ."

"Are you fucking crazy? LBJ? Do you realize what could happen to a woman at Long Binh Jail?" Colonel Bragg snarled. "She stays here until this is resolved."

"You have no authority on this, Colonel Bragg," Marchetti said.

"I've got friends in high places, Marchetti," Brendan said. "She. Stays. Here."

"Fine. For now. And Bragg, I want the brig off limits to both of these men," Marchetti said, leaving the office.

"Who do you know in high places?" Colonel Bragg asked.

"The Chairman of the Joint Chief of Staff is one of my father's best friends," Brendan said. "Along with former Ambassador Booker."

Colonel Bragg whistled. "Listen, you two assholes. Stay the fuck away from that brig."

"Or what, you'll throw us in the brig as well?" Brendan said.

"Don't fucking push me, Corrington. I can get pretty fucking creative with jail cells, and it won't be anywhere near one George Irelynn Cross.

I'll find some woman to guard Irelynn, ensure she has privacy, and all that. I'll have Father Andrews check in on her a few times daily. We'll get to the bottom of this and keep her safe."

"Who the fuck is that asshole Marchetti?" Brendan asked.

"Technically, our boss. All the way from the good ole

U.S.of A. It's unusual that a paper pusher is here in Vietnam and taken such an interest in this case," Mac replied.

Brendan rubbed the bridge of his nose. "God. She's never going to forgive me for this."

"You called her your wife. We don't even know if the marriage is legit yet," Colonel Bragg said.

Brendan looked down at the bracelet on his wrist. "I spoke with Father Andrews again this morning. In the eyes of the church, it is."

"I hope this works out for you, Brendan," Colonel Bragg said.

"It will. You see, I'm already hopelessly in love with her."

Brendan looked up to see both Mac and Colonel Bragg grinning at him.

"Well, that was fucking mushy," Colonel Bragg said. "Get the fuck out of here. Oh, and Corrington."

"Yes, Sir."

"You may temporarily work for the CIA, but your sorry ass is still mine. If you ever come into my office like that again, I will find a special place in hell for you."

"I thought I was already here. Sir."

"Not even close," Colonel Bragg said. "You're dismissed."

CHAPTER 21

*P*acing back and forth in her cell, Irelynn looked at her watch again, only to see a slim bare wrist.

"Damn it. I keep forgetting they took my watch," she said after two days of being stuck in this hellhole jail with moaning and groaning men in the other cells. Some big fight between Marines and Army had filled the cells overnight. She felt sorry for them last night at the sounds of heaving from over-indulgence and now as they woke up with hangovers. She sighed deeply, then brightened at the sound of the door opening and high heels clicking down the hallway. *Sierra. At last.*

Irelynn could hear wolf whistles and cat calls following Sierra Byrne as she passed by the other cells. Stopping in front of her, Sierra shook her curly black hair and rolled her beautiful blue eyes.

"Animals," she said with a giggle. "I brought yer

breakfast and supplies." She waited while the MP who followed her unlocked the cell, and she set the tray on a small table. "Here, I know how important it is ta be prepared." She opened her purse dangling from her shoulder and handed Irelynn a small handful of tampons and pads.

"I pooled the girls in the office, and all contributed," Sierra said.

"Oh, thank God. Kiss them all for me," Irelynn said. Settling herself on the bunk, she patted a spot for Sierra to sit down.

Nibbling on a piece of toast, "I'm expecting the curse any day now. They should be selling tampons at the PX."

"We've been begging them forever," Sierra sighed. "Mind you, they'll sssell all sorts of things for the men ta buy for their girlfriends at home, but nothing for a girl stationed here might need."

"When I get back to Saigon, I'll send you a care package with a few boxes of tampons, shampoo, and whatever else I can find on the black market."

"That would be nice." She looked up to the blankets hanging on the front bars of the cell for privacy.

"This will be over soon, and ye should be able ta leave."

"I can't wait," Irelynn replied.

"What are ye going ta do?"

"I'm going home."

"What about yer handsome Major?"

Irelynn shrugged her shoulders.

"Well, I can tell you this, he's over at Colonel Braggs still trying ta move heaven and earth ta free you."

Irelynn worried her lower lip. "He hasn't come to see me."

"Didn't anyone tell ye the brig is off limits to both him and that big gorgeous redhead?"

"Watch your step with Mac," Irelynn said.

"Why?"

"Well, he's a good man, but he really....I mean really likes women."

"I think I'm okay. Men like him rarely notice girls like me," Sierra said. With my lisp and all, well, you know."

"Have you looked in the mirror lately? You're stunning," Irelynn said. "Don't sell yourself short."

"I am short," Sierra giggled.

"That's not what I meant. And lots of men like small women. I only come up to Brendan's shoulder."

Sierra leaned in and whispered. "We've been friends for a while now. Right? SSo, tell me, how does that work?"

"How does what work?'

"You know...when he..." Sierra's cheeks flamed. "When he makes love ta you? My Grand Da wasn't happy about it, but I saw plenty back home on the farm, but I don't think it's the same."

Irelynn's eyebrows rose straight up. "Well...I don't know. I mean, we never. Other than that time in the pool, well, he said there was more. I have no idea."

"But...I heard yer married ta him." Sierra said.

"Well. I guess we are, but we haven't… Who did you hear that from?"

"Ye forget I'm a secretary for the brass. I hear things," Sierra said. "Ye guess? How can ye not know?"

"It's a long story," Irelynn said.

"You're a little crazy. Ye know that."

"Oh, you have no idea," Irelynn replied.

"Are ye in love with him?"

Irelynn chewed her lower lip. "I'm not sure how or when it happened. But yes. He consumes my thoughts and my dreams. I'm in love with him."

Sierra stood and smoothed out her service skirt. "I have to go now. Come on; Father Andrews is waiting to speak to you. I'll escort you to the biffy first."

Pacing back and forth, Brendan stopped to glare at the smile on Mac's face.

"You're going to wear a hole in the floor," Mac said.

"How would you feel if that was your woman in the brig?" Brendan snarled.

"I seem to recall that was your original intention," Mac replied.

"That was only to keep her in place until I arrived," Brendan growled.

The door opened. Colonel Braggs strode in, pointing at a chair. "Sit," he ordered.

"God damned VC, two firebases nearly overrun last night. How the fuck do they expect me to run a war and deal with this shit too," Colonel Bragg said.

Pulling a cigar from his drawer, he flipped his lighter open. Lighting the cigar, swirls of smoke filled the room as the Colonel leaned back in his chair. A knock sounded on the door. "What the fuck do you want now?" Colonel Bragg bellowed.

A harried looking Murphy opened the door. "Sorry to disturb you, Sir. Father Andrews and others are here to see you."

"Others? What others?"

Father Andrews pushed his way inside. "Colonel Bragg, I must protest. You simply cannot jail a woman with the men," he said.

Lieutenant Colonel Boise pushed her way past Murphy, fanning the air of cigar smoke. "Colonel Bragg, I must insist you release Irelynn. We know who she is."

A man strode past Murphy and stomped to the desk. "Colonel Bragg, I'm sure you've heard of Freedom of the Press. You can't jail correspondents."

"Who the fuck are you?" Colonel Bragg demanded.

"Myron Culp. Editor in Chief, Saigon press corps. You have one of my people incarcerated."

Murphy threw up his hands in defeat as six nurses poured into the office, loudly protesting Irelynn's treatment. Mark Marchetti stepped into the room. "What's going on?"

Brendan and Mac exchanged amused glances; together,

they rose to lean against the far wall to watch the circus unfold.

"Marchetti, you'd better have good news for me," Colonel Bragg bellowed over the din of voices, all calling to be heard.

"I…" Marchetti stuttered.

Behind him, a loud "Ten Hut" rang out. All Army personnel snapped to attention when General Smead and two of his aides entered the room.

"Bragg. What kind of a circus are you running here?" General Smead demanded.

Colonel Bragg opened his mouth and snapped it shut. His angry glare landed on Marchetti.

"I got a call this morning from one furious grandmother. Said she chased two FBI agents demanding photographs of her granddaughter off her family's property. Do you have any idea what it's like to be reamed a new asshole by an eighty-seven-year old woman? A woman that I wouldn't mess with under normal circumstances. Why the hell didn't you call me? Irelynn went to college with my daughter, Anne. I know her family." General Smead said. "I've ordered Irelynn to be escorted here." A sound behind them, and General Smead whipped around. Irelynn stood in the doorway with Sierra and two MP's.

"You talked to Gramie?" Irelynn squeaked.

All eyes turned to Irelynn, and everyone spoke at once. "Irelynn."

"Clear the room, Colonel Bragg," General Smead said.

Turning to the MP. "Get those handcuffs off her and wait outside."

The MP stepped forward and removed the cuffs. Irelynn rubbed her wrists, "Thank you," she whispered.

"Murphy. Escort this fucking… circus next door to the conference room," Colonel Bragg said.

"Colonel Bragg," Father Andrews admonished.

"Sorry, Father," Colonel Bragg said.

"Brendan, you, Mac, and Irelynn stay behind," General Smead said. "And you as well, Marchetti."

Murphy shooed the remaining chattering group out of Colonel Bragg's office, pulling the door shut behind him.

"Irelynn. We owe you an apology," General Smead said.

"My Grandmother and parents, they must be worried sick," Irelynn said.

"They'll be fine. Your grandmother was grateful your parents weren't home when the FBI showed up at the door. I guess your father and brothers were out clearing Sugar Mountain. Your mother had taken lunch up to them. She'll explain everything to them."

Irelynn nodded her head.

"So, your parents didn't know you're here in Vietnam, in the middle of a war?" Brendan said.

"I never meant to deceive my parents. They're overprotective. I was their change of life baby. I didn't want to worry them. I'm a bit of a wild child."

"No shit," Brendan replied.

Irelynn narrowed her eyes at Brendan. "I still don't know what's going on here," Irelynn said.

Mark Marchetti stepped forward. "Tell us how you met Rebecca Ronan."

"I had been backpacking on the Hippy Trail. It was in Istanbul. I was having a cup of Turkish coffee in this cool outdoor café on the Sea of Marmara when Rebecca and Baltini approached me. They were interested in my work. As a freelance journalist, I was documenting my journey and selling my articles and photographs."

"How did you end up in Vietnam?" Mac asked.

"They convinced me to abandon the Hippy Trail and fly with them here to document the war," Irelynn said. "I thought it was an exciting challenge and jumped at the opportunity. I've never regretted coming here. I thought I could make a difference in some small way."

"As foolhardy as your decision was, you have made a difference," Brendan said.

"Are you seriously going to go there again?" Irelynn said.

"It's possible they were using you to gain credibility with the press corps. Now that we have verified your identity, I think I will take this opportunity and speak with the bureau chief. Oh, one more question. Did Rebecca ever give you anything to hold onto for her?" Marchetti asked.

"She's given me lots of things," Irelynn replied.

"Specifically, something she wanted back?"

"Not that I'm aware of," Irelynn replied.

"Very well, for now," Marchetti said before slipping out the door.

"I'll take my leave as well," General Smead said. "Anything else comes up. You contact me."

"Yes, Sir," Colonel Bragg replied. "Mac, let's um… give them a few minutes of privacy."

She warily moved to the other side of the Colonel's desk without taking her eyes off Brendan.

"So, other than asking how I met Rebecca, no one has told me why I was jailed," Irelynn said.

"Marchetti wanted to verify you are who you say you are," Brendan replied.

"My identity? Why didn't he just ask to see my passport?"

"Those can be forged."

"That isn't possible."

"Tell that to the real Rebecca Ronin. Her body was found in Istanbul, beaten and strangled, her identity stolen."

"That's awful, but I had nothing to do with the poor woman's murder."

"You don't realize how close you came to it being you lying on that slab in the morgue. You're incredibly naïve and reckless."

"Naïve and reckless? I assure you. I am neither," Irelynn said.

"You don't consider backpacking across the Middle East

and South Asia by yourself as reckless? Not to mention landing in the middle of a war."

"No. It was an education. I visited exotic locations and met many amazing people." Irelynn realized they had been slowly circling the gray metal desk. Leaning on the desk, she looked into his intense blue eyes. "I don't owe you an explanation, nor do I need your permission to be here."

His appreciative gaze dropped to her exposed cleavage; his eyes sparked and burned with a heat she felt down to the tips of her toes.

"Quit undressing me with your eyes," Irelynn snapped.

"Then I'll use my hands."

"Focus, Brendan. We're in the middle of a discussion."

"I am focused," he replied.

"Not on my breasts."

"They're still spectacular."

"You should know. You had your mouth all over them." Irelynn felt the burn on her cheeks. *Oh my God, what did I just say?*

The heat in his eyes intensified, and her eyes flickered to the door.

Run. Now.

"No. No more running from me," Brendan whispered. He reached out for her, squealing in protest she scooted around the desk before sprinting for the door. Brendan was up and over the desk in a heartbeat. She made it out the door and through the anteroom before spilling into the hallway, coming to a screeching halt in front of Colonel Bragg and Father

Andrews. Mac, leaning on the door jam of the conference room, looked on as Brendan came roaring out of the room. Running straight into Irelynn, he wrapped his arms around her to keep her from falling. She slapped his hands down and glared at him.

"Irelynn. Damn it. Listen to me." Brendan said.

She nodded her head toward Colonel Bragg. Brendan cleared his throat. "Sir."

Irelynn could feel the burn on her cheeks, looking up at the Colonel, and she lifted her chin in defiance.

The Colonel looked to the MP. "Corporal, take Irelynn back to the brig." The MP stepped forward, pulling her arms in front of her; he slapped the cuff 's back on her wrists.

"Wait. What?" Irelynn blustered.

Colonel Bragg smiled as Brendan stepped forward. "Sir. Permission to detain Mrs. Corrington in a place of my choosing."

The Colonel's smile widened. "What say you, Father Andrews, are they married?"

"Well, yes. I believe so," Father Andrews replied. "Permission granted, Major Corrington."

Brendan grinned, picking the key to the handcuffs from the MP's hands. "Thank you, Sir."

He turned and lifted Irelynn over his shoulder and trotted down the hall.

"Put me down. Damn it, Brendan. You slimy toad. Who the hell do you think you are?"

Brendan answered with a swat on her bottom. Her howl of outrage and his laughter filtered down the hallway.

Mac grinned as he watched them make their way down the hall. Irelynn slung over Brendan's shoulder, her eyes spitting fire, hand's cuffed together in front of her; using both hands, she gave them the finger.

Colonel Bragg chuckled and walked back into his office. Mac heard him bellow.

"Why the fuck is there boot prints on top of my desk. God Damn little piss ant. Chasing women around my desk. Fuck. I don't even get to chase women around my desk. Murphy. Get your ass in here."

Murphy rushed past him, and Mac heard a deep sigh next to him, "That was ssso romantic. Ye know she loves him," Sierra said.

Mac looked down into the prettiest midnight blue eyes he'd ever seen. Creamy alabaster skin, a pert little nose. and luscious full lips smiled up at him.

"Hello, love. You're a bonny wee lass." Mac said.

She wagged her finger under his nose before primly stating. "I'm not having any of yer Don Juan funny business." She nodded goodbye to the nurses making their way out of the conference room before heading down the hallway.

Mac watched the swing of her curvy hips. Smiling, he

could have sworn he heard a slight lisp and an Irish brogue in that sweet little voice.

"Don Juan, funny business," he chuckled.

Intrigued, he was tempted to go after her. Instead, he looked at Rose and Carole. "Rose. Who is that tiny temptation?"

Rose laughed. "That's Sierra Byrne. She's a secretary for the brass. You stay away from her. She's a sweet girl and much too innocent for the likes of you."

Mac gave her a wounded look. "Hey."

Carole giggled. "Oh, don't look so sad. You do have a reputation, you know. Let's go have a drink. We just found out that Irelynn and Brendan are married. You can tell us all about it."

"All that time in Rebecca's Hollywood house of horror and Irelynn never told you?"

"She was locked up. We didn't see her much," Carmen replied.

Mac locked arms with the nurses, three on each side of him. "Come, my lovelies. I've got a reputation to uphold here." Grinning like the cat who got the cream. He and the ladies made their way down the hallway to glares from other envious men. Once at the exit, he looked back down the hall hoping for one more glimpse of the bouncing black curls that went with the slight lisp and Irish brogue.

CHAPTER 22

MID AUGUST 1969

Tossing Irelynn on the bed, Brendan locked the door. Dropping her rucksack, he unbuttoned his shirt before emptying his pockets and dumping the contents into a small bowl on the table next to a bottle of whiskey. Irelynn eyed him warily before she scrambled to the stand on the other side of the bed. Sighing, he sat and removed his boots. Irelynn jumped with each thump as he dropped his boots. Stripping off his socks, he sighed with relief, wiggling his toes before rising to open the curtains on the lone window. He stared out the window for a moment taking in the picturesque view of the Port of Da Nang and, further out, the

South China Sea. Turning around, his eyes swept over Irelynn.

Her chestnut curls swept down to fall at her shoulders; her eyes were wide, and she followed his movements around the room. She was breathing shallowly, and he could see the frantic beat of her heart on her neck. The cute little purple sundress swirled around her thighs, and her ever present combat boots shuffled nervously. She held her hands in front; her wrists still shackled. He strode over and picked up the handcuffs key from the bowl.

"Come here," he said.

Her eyes still wary, she moved to stand in front of him. He unlocked one wrist. Taking her by the hand, he led her to the bed.

"Sit," he ordered.

Narrowing her eyes at him, she sat in a huff on the edge of the bed. He locked the handcuff to the brass headboard. She was silent as he knelt at her feet and removed her boots and socks.

"So, this is how it's going to be," she whispered.

"No. I thought you'd like to be comfortable. I need to take a shower. I want to make sure you're still here when I come out," Brendan said.

Lifting her chin with a gentle hand, he looked deep into her eyes. "Do you really think that's the kind of man I am? The kind that takes advantage of a vulnerable woman. Answer me."

She shook her head, "No. You're not."

"Alright then. I'll make it quick."

Ten minutes later, Brendan reaching for the towel to dry off, heard a banging on the wall. Little shit. Grinning at his reflection in the mirror before wrapping the towel around his lean waist, he peeked out the bathroom door. Irelynn had her back to him, both feet between the bars braced against the wall; she yanked on the handcuffs. The headboard rattled and banged against the wall.

"You're going to injure your wrist, and the neighbors might think we're doing something else," Brendan said.

She dropped her head back and glared at him upside down. "Like what?"

Brendan grinned and shook his head." Never mind."

Her eyes widened when she noticed the towel wrapped around his waist. She scrambled to sit upright, grabbing a pillow she clutched it to her chest.

"Are you going to put some clothes on?"

Brendan looked down and grinned. "I will while you're in the shower."

"What if I don't want to take a shower?"

"That's fine. I'll get dressed." Slowly moving to unwrap the towel, he stopped when she squealed.

"Fine. I'll take a shower."

"I thought you'd say that." Picking the key up, he strode to the bed; taking her hand, he unlocked the cuff leaving the other side attached to the headboard. She gave him a questioning look.

"In case you misbehave, and I have to lock you up again,"

he said, pointing toward the corner. "Your rucksack is over there."

She scrunched up her nose and stomped over to pick up her rucksack.

"Nope. Leave it here. Pick out the clothes you need."

Glaring at him, she picked out shorts and a shirt before stomping into the bathroom and slamming the door shut.

Brendan breathed a sigh of relief when he heard the shower start. No windows in the bathroom; he could relax for a few minutes. Dressing first, he picked up the phone, dialing room service, he ordered dinner. Twenty minutes later, the shower stopped, and after a minute, she peeked out the door.

"Um. I know this is weird, but I forgot my bra and panties. Will you give me my rucksack?"

Brendan laughed. "No."

He heard a snort of disgust. "Fine. Will you please pick out something that matches? They're at the bottom of the rucksack."

"That I can do," Brendan said.

Hefting the bag onto the bed, he first checked a side pocket and found a canister of mace. Would she use it on him? He didn't know, but he wasn't taking any chances. Shaking his head, he stuffed it in his pocket before reaching inside and pulling out a few cameras, two pairs of fatigues, t shirts, sundresses, and other clothing, all neatly rolled. Then two cans of C-rations, pound cake, and other various items. Pulling out a pair of red high heel shoes, he grinned. Finally, finding a small pile of panties and bras wrapped in plastic.

Laying the delicate items on the bed, he rolled his eyes. Picking up a pair of sheer pale pink panties. "She's trying to kill me," he muttered, laying them back on the bed. "Fuck me. Pink or black? Which torment do you prefer?" Chuckling, he scooped up the pink. Knocking on the door, he couldn't help but groan as her slim hand reached out and tugged on the silky panties and matching bra as they slid from his grasp.

"Thank you," she said.

Inhaling sharply, he stared out the window. Fighting for control, want and need raged through his body, and his heart pounded in his chest. An ache grew and he tamped it down by sheer willpower. The door clicked and she stood in the doorway, towel in hand she fluffed her hair. His gaze swept her body, she looked sexy and comfortable in her cutoffs and white tank top.

"Do you wear those lacy little things under your fatigues?" he asked, smiling at the flush of pink on her cheeks.

"Always. Just because I'm crawling through mud and filth doesn't mean I can't be all girl underneath."

Nodding his head, he was saved from responding by a knock at the door. Pointing to the table and chairs in front of the window. "Sit."

She narrowed her eyes and raised her chin a notch.

Brendan raised an eyebrow at her defiance. "Or I can chain you back up to the headboard."

Walking over, she sat on a chair, crossing her arms; she glared her displeasure. Brendan opened the door and pulled a dinner cart into the room. Tipping the man, he shut the door.

"I took the liberty of ordering dinner for us," Brendan said, smiling as she perked up at the aroma of Italian food. Jumping to her feet, she strolled over and lifted the silver lid from the plate. She inhaled deeply, "Spaghetti and meatballs. My favorite. How did you know?"

"It's my favorite as well," Brendan replied.

"I didn't know you could get spaghetti in country."

"Every once in a while, a gem of a restaurant pops up in hotels that cater to Americans," Brendan said as he set the plates and wine glasses on the table. Handing her silverware, he opened a bottle of red wine. Pouring a small amount into both glasses, he gave her a glass.

"What shall we toast to?" Brendan said.

"Spaghetti," Irelynn said, raising her glass.

"Spaghetti," Brendan replied. Lifting his glass, he stared into Irelynn's eyes as she took a sip.

Blushing under his intense stare, Irelynn picked up her fork and swirled the pasta in the thick red sauce.

"Why am I here?"

"To talk. To get to know each other better. Would you prefer to be in the brig?"

Stabbing her meatball, "No. I guess I can add that to the list of things I won't tell my father."

"Sounds like an ogre?"

"Far from it. I was his little princess and a disappointment."

"Disappointment? How so?"

"He wanted me to be more traditional. I have five older

brothers. I was always trying to keep up with them. You know, this sauce is good, but it has a funny aftertaste I can't quite identify," Irelynn said.

Brendan set his fork down, throwing his napkin on the plate; he leaned back in his chair, swirling his wine glass. "Yeah. I thought so too."

"What about your family?" Irelynn asked.

"My father, four brothers, and Mac. Two of my brothers are married, and I have one nephew."

"Where are they?"

"Aiden, Army, is at An Khe. Collin, a Marine, is in the Mekong Delta. My father, a Colonel, recently retired from the Marine Corps, and the twins are now back in the world. And, of course, Mac is here."

"They all served?"

"Yeah."

"Are they all as annoying as you?"

"Yes. And then some."

"Why isn't Mac out looking for his baby?"

"He's got people looking for Molly. We're still working on this case. Baltini and Rebecca, or whatever her name is, are still out there.

"This is about more than drugs and kidnapping women, isn't it?"

Brendan grinned. "You scrunch your nose when the reporter in you gets a scoop."

"That's patronizing," Irelynn replied. "You didn't answer my question."

"And I'm not going to."

"I'm guessing you're a CIA operative, just like Mac."

"I can neither confirm nor deny for either of us," Brendan replied.

Irelynn snorted and gave him a look of pure exasperation before turning to look out the window.

Watching her stare out the window he could see the questions forming in her head as emotions played across her face. "What are you thinking?"

"I'm thinking that somehow, I ended up embroiled in a "Secret Agent Man" type spy plot, and your job is to protect me. Is that right?"

"I like that song."

"Me too. But that's the second question you didn't answer. It puts a whole new light on being married to your work."

"You're my wife, Irelynn. I want you safe."

"Your wife? I thought you didn't want the commitment?"

"I never said that. I only told you that there were options."

"You don't even know if it's legal or…"

"I know Father Andrews spoke to you this morning." Irelynn jumped to her feet. She paced back and forth, wringing her hands.

"You don't want me as a wife, Brendan. I need more. I could never be satisfied with the white picket fence and everything that goes with it. You would end up hating me."

Brendan stood and pulled her into his arms. He lifted her chin, so she looked up into his eyes. "That's not true. I believe it's possible to have it all. I believe in my dreams, and I believe in yours as well," he whispered.

Irelynn sucked in her breath. "What about love? I can't have you tied to me out of honor or duty."

"Can you not hear what I'm trying to tell you? I'm in love with you."

"Brendan. I…" her eyes widened and filled with confusion and hope.

His mouth came crashing down on hers. His hands dropped to her waist, and he pulled her closer. His mouth ravaged hers, exploring and devouring the recesses of her mouth until she moaned with need. His hands settled on her hips, tugging her shirt he pulled it over her head. He traced a finger over her full lips, down her slim throat to her collarbone, then down along the curve of her cleavage before cupping her breasts in his large hands. Reaching behind her, he unhooked her bra, dropping it to the floor. Her body quivered under his touch as he lightly trailed his hands up her smooth back and over her shoulders, pausing briefly on the puckered red scar left by an NVA bullet. He stroked the spot with his thumb before placing a gentle kiss on her wound.

"I've wanted to do that for a while," he whispered. "And this." Capturing a pink crest with his mouth before moving to its twin. She arched her back and mewled in his arms. Pulling his shirt off, he pulled her tight against him before lifting her in his arms and carrying her to the bed. Laying her down, he stripped off his clothes and joined her on the bed. She shivered with need as he found her pliant, sweet lips again and pulled her panties off her slim hips. She returned his kisses with a fiery passion that matched his own.

He nibbled on her chin, "God. I could never get enough of you," Brendan breathed.

"I love you," Irelynn cried.

Her arms wrapped around his waist; he kneaded her breasts and continued to plunder her lips and neck with kisses and whispers of love. Her arms slid off his shoulders, and she lay still. Brendan raised his head in alarm. "Irelynn?" Touching her face, he tried to rouse her. He moved to sit up before falling limply to lie on her chest. "Drugged. We've been..." his vision blurred, and all went dark.

CHAPTER 22

Opening her eyes, Irelynn's head was groggy, and her mouth felt like dry cotton. Warm breath tickled her neck, a large hand rested familiarly on her breast, something hard pushed against her backside. Eyes wide, she turned her head to see Brendan snuggled into her. Still deep in sleep, she smiled at the boyish charm and masculinity he exuded as effortlessly as he breathed. Her gaze rested on his dark wavy hair and handsome face before drifting down to his chest and muscular arms. On a whim, she lifted the blanket to peer below. Inhaling sharply, she remembered seeing that thing coming at her last night. Confusion filled her. *What happened? I don't remember anything after his kisses and...* Horror filled her. *Oh my God. Did I fall asleep in the middle of it?* The slow burn of embarrassment rose from the tips of her toes to the top of her head. Mortified, she slid from under his arm and off the bed.

Sliding her pillow next to him, she breathed a sigh of relief that he didn't stir.

Staring down at him, she couldn't love him more. "I have to be true to myself," she whispered. "I love you. I want to be with you, but I'm scared I'll end up breaking your heart." Then she clipped the handcuff around his wrist.

When he wakes up, this should buy me some time. It's kind of strange that he hasn't woken up.

She quickly dressed in her jeans and a tank top; she pulled her hair up into a ponytail and repacked her rucksack. Spotting Brendan's shorts and boxers on the floor, she picked them up. Her can of mace and the key to the handcuffs fell to the floor, the can of mace rolling silently under the bed; picking up the key, she looked to Brendan, still peacefully slumbering.

Shit. *What do I do with this key? I don't want him getting loose too quickly.*

Moving to the bureau, she stopped in confusion at the sketchbook and the ball of yarn and knitting needles. With no time to investigate further, she emptied the drawers of his clothes, leaving his socks. Grabbing the last long-sleeved shirt in the drawer, she slipped it on. She lovingly caressed the name patch before removing the gold oak leaf insignia pins and setting them on the dresser. He earned these. He should have them. Pinning on his old Captain's pin she found in the drawer on the lapel before pulling on her rucksack and cameras. She picked up the neatly folded stack of fatigues and boxers.

Is that all of his clothes? Remembering the shirt hanging

on a hook on the back of the bathroom door, she grabbed it. Stopping by the bed, she looked at Brendan peacefully slumbering. "Please forgive me, but I need to go home. I need time to sort this out," she whispered.

Peeking out the peephole on the door, she could see the back of a soldier standing guard. *Damn. Why is there a guard outside the door?* She watched as the man moved from his post. She could hear his footsteps going down the hallway. Breathing a sigh of relief, she opened the door. The guard was down the hall, looking out the window. Quietly pulling the door shut behind her, she snuck the opposite way down the hall to the stairwell. Going down the stairs, she noted the blood stains on the floor and bullet holes in the walls, before stopping on the second floor when she spotted a maid's cart in the hallway. Lifting the towels on the cart she slid Brendan's clothes beneath them.

Scooting back down the stairwell, she peered around the corner of the stairs that emptied into the lobby. The lobby was in a shamble's; Mac and a group of officers sat at a table playing poker. Irelynn leaned back against the wall. "Damn." her heart pounded in her chest as she peeked back around the corner. Mac faced the stairs. A cigar dangled between his teeth as he dealt the cards. Beer bottles littered the table, and smoke hung thick in the air, the men laughing at some joke Mac told.

There is no way I can get across the lobby with Mac sitting there. "Where's the kitchen?" she whispered to herself. A commotion in the street, and all the men pulled their weapons and crawled to look out the windows. *Perfect. Now's my chance.* Taking a deep breath, she ran down the stairs and edged around the lobby to the kitchen door. Stopping with a quick hello to the startled cook, she handed him the key to the handcuffs before slipping out the back door.

The sun was just rising as she hailed a rickshaw. Taking in the sights and sounds of the city, she wondered if she would miss Da Nang. Home was calling to her, and she was tired of war and all that went with it. She longed for the scent of pine trees and how the sun set over Sugar Mountain.

"You're going to miss your friends and the people you've met along the way," she whispered. "Brendan. I'll miss you the most."

Lost in her thoughts, guilt riddled her. *What were you thinking? You left a naked man handcuffed to the bed and stole his clothes.* "It was just to buy myself time," Irelynn rationalized. "Besides, he's not in any danger. There is a guard outside his door, and Mac is downstairs. He has all the help he needs." *He's going to kill you when he catches you.* "Catch me if you can. Major Corrington. Catch me if you can."

The Rickshaw pulled up at the Da Nang Base main gate. Flashing a smile to the guard, she showed her press credentials,

"Good morning, Rusty," Irelynn said.

"Morning sunshine. Where are you off to today?" Rusty replied.

"Saigon first to collect my things, then I'm going home," Irelynn replied.

"Aw, man, I'm jealous. I've got four months to go. So, you're done here? Lucky you."

"Yeah. I miss my family, and I'm sick of dodging bullets."

"I hear you."

"You take care, Rusty."

"You too, sunshine. Watch the north side of the airbase. We got hit pretty hard last night."

"I must have slept through it. Of course, it's not the only thing I slept through."

Rusty raised a curious eyebrow, and Irelynn felt the burn of embarrassment on her cheeks.

"If you hurry, you can catch the first transport plane to Saigon," Rusty said.

"Thanks, Rusty. Goodbye."

"Goodbye, sunshine."

Catching a ride to the airfield, she was dropped off in front of the terminal. She was tempted to grab a direct flight home, but she had to return to Saigon to put her affairs in order and pack her things before heading home.

"Irelynn."

Irelynn turned to see Sierra jogging up the sidewalk. "Hey, Sierra. You're out jogging early."

"Where ye going? Where's Brendan?"

"Um... he's back at the hotel," Irelynn said.

"He let ye go?"

"Well. Not exactly."

"What does *not exactly* mean?"

Irelynn stifled a giggle. "I sort of left him naked and chained to the bed. I hid his clothes too. You know, to slow him down a bit."

Sierra's mouth dropped open. "Are ye insane? Do ye realize what he's going ta do when he catches ye?"

"If, not when."

"No. I think it's definitely when."

"I have to go now, Sierra."

"Irelynn, you've been my friend since day one. It was ye who sat with me, a perfect stranger, in the mess hall for lunch. I was alone and scared, questioning my wisdom in joining the Army. I can't let ye make this mistake."

"I value your friendship Sierra, but I need to go home. Now," Irelynn said as she turned and walked away.

Sierra ran after her, grabbing her arm. "No. Ye can't."

Shrugging off her hand, "Yes, I can," Irelynn said, walking away again. She let out an oof when Sierra tackled her from behind.

"What the hell, Sierra."

Sierra sat on her chest, pinning her arms down. "He loves ye."

"Get off of me. Do you think I don't know that? I love him too, but I need to get home."

"Why can't ye wait? He only has a few weeks left on his tour of duty."

Irelynn bucked Sierra off her and rose to her feet. 'I can't wait. Besides, I need time to think, and I'm so embarrassed that I fell asleep while we were making love last night."

"How do ye fall asleep in the middle of something like that?" Sierra asked.

"Well, I don't know. I was so ready for it to happen. The kissing and touching, it was beautiful. And then…poof…I woke up this morning. What kind of woman falls asleep during that?"

"I'm sorry to hear that happened, but ye need to stay here."

"No."

She was tackled to the ground again. They rolled around, each fighting for dominance until they were pulled apart by two MP's.

"Not that I don't enjoy a good cat fight, but you can't brawl in the street here," the first MP said.

Held back by the other MP, Irelynn snarled. "It was not a catfight. We were merely having a discussion."

"It looked like a cat fight to me," said the MP. You're both under arrest."

"I'm a civilian and a member of the Press Corps," Irelynn replied, showing her press badge.

"Let her go," he replied while placing handcuffs on Sierra.

"Wait. Can't you let her go too?" Irelynn cried.

"Nope. Orders are orders. If you're in the military and you brawl in the street, you go to the brig."

"I'm sorry, Sierra. I hate leaving you like this. Call Mac.

He was in the lobby of the hotel playing cards. He'll get you out of this mess."

"Mac?"

"Yeah. You know. The big red-headed guy."

"Oh. Ye mean Don Juan."

Irelynn grinned. "Don Juan. I suppose it's fitting."

"Irelynn. Please… ssstay."

"My family thought I was missing for the past eight months. Please understand, I must go home. Please let Rose and Carole know. I'll write as soon as I can."

"I do understand," Sierra said as she was led away to a waiting jeep."

Irelynn turned back to the building and went inside to secure a seat on the next transport flight to Saigon.

After sweet cajoling and a winsome smile to the company clerk, she sat in the front seat of the plane.

"Is this seat taken?"

Irelynn looked up to see Myron Culp, the Saigon editor-in-chief.

"Myron. Yes. Please sit. I never did get a chance to thank you for coming to my aid."

"It's the least I could do for you, kid. Not that I did much. Though I did have an interesting conversation with Marchetti."

Irelynn leaned over and whispered. "I think he's CIA

too."

"Most likely. The funny thing about Rebecca, all she ever wrote was fluff. She never got into the nitty gritty like you did. I always thought she was trying to learn from you. You're a damn good reporter, and your photos are top notch, even if you are a freelancer."

"Thank you."

"Where you off to?"

"I have to get my stuff out of my apartment, and then I'm going home."

They paused as troops made their way on board and moved to the back of the plane. Many of the men paused to flirt or wink at the unexpected beautiful woman on board.

"I'll never get used to being the center of attention," Irelynn said.

"You can't blame them. Some of these kids haven't seen an American woman since they left home."

Last on board was a man with a straw hat, long shoulder length brown hair, and sunglasses. He moved quickly to the back of the plane.

"How about I save you some time? I'll take a crew over and pack up your stuff. That way, you can catch a flight to the U.S. right away," Myron said.

"That's not necessary. For the most part, it's a furnished apartment. I can pack my things myself."

"Nonsense. It's the least I can do. You just make me a list of what you want, and I'll have it shipped."

"That's very kind of you. I am anxious to see my family."

"Where's home?"

"North of San Francisco."

"Beautiful part of the country," Myron said. "I take it that you're not coming back to Saigon?"

"Never say never. Plenty is going on with civil rights, women's rights, and war protests to spark my interest at home," Irelynn said.

"If you're interested in a job, I've got some contacts at the San Francisco Chronicle."

"It's not a bad idea. I can find a job and an apartment in the Bay area and go home to see the family on the weekends," Irelynn replied.

"What does your husband think?"

Irelynn worried her lip. "He believes we can have it all."

"He's right. You can."

Irelynn looked to the window as anguish overtook her. The rest of the hour long flight passed in silence.

Standing at the Pan Am counter, Myron stood at Irelynn's side, intent on making sure she secured a seat on a flight leaving within the hour for Treasure Island Naval Base in San Fran- cisco. Further down the counter, the same long-haired man was also booking a flight. Myron watched the man, something about him tugged at his subconscious. A sense of familiarity and unease settled over him. He smiled and waved as Irelynn climbed the metal stairs to the plane, turned, and waved. Breathing a sigh of relief, he felt he had done his duty making sure she was safely on board and heading home. Making his way to the street, he hailed a taxi to take him the five miles from Tan Son Nhut Air Base to his office in Saigon. Settled in the cab, he bolted upright, realizing what was so familiar about the long-haired man. "It's Edwin Baltini," he whispered in horror. In a panic, he pulled his handkerchief from his pocket, wiping the sweat from his brow. He urged the driver to drive faster. "I have to call Colonel Bragg."

Edwin Baltini sat in the back of the plane and snickered. He could hardly believe his good luck. Not only had he successfully made it out of South Vietnam without being captured, but Irelynn Cross was on the same plane. He had plans for the slut. First, he had to get that can of mace from her. He cursed Rebecca for giving it to Irelynn in the first place. It had seemed like a good idea at the time to hide it once they had become embroiled in running drugs and secrets across borders for profit. But Rebecca was greedy, holding out for more money, withholding from both him and the boss exactly where and with whom she had hidden the can. Once she had confessed Irelynn had it, they had failed twice to secure her rucksack. The first time, the idiots he had hired had left it behind in the alley behind Rebecca's apartment. Last night's failed attempt to kidnap her was the second time they didn't find the can in her rucksack. Edwin sneered. They had barely escaped that fiasco with their lives.

Edwin closed his eyes. The memory of the boss holding the gun to his forehead as he gave him one more chance to secure his property turned his stomach. Fear of what would happen if he failed again strengthened his resolve. Irelynn Cross had ruined him; this time, he would make her pay with her life.

The plane taxied down the runway, then lifted off to cheers from the troops. Irelynn's stomach felt queasy, and her ears popped as the light as air feeling overtook her. She looked out the window to the South China sea as the plane climbed higher into the sky. Her heart thudded in her chest, and she choked on a sob.

"God. I miss him already," Irelynn whispered. *Sierra was right. I'm making a mistake. Oh, Brendan, I'm so sorry.*

Looking around the plane at the happy faces surrounding her, their tours of duty complete, these troops were going home. To what? Irelynn wasn't sure, but she wished them the best that life had to offer. Closing her eyes, she leaned back in the seat.

"He's going to kill me."

CHAPTER 23

Mac threw down his losing hand and glared at the captain sitting across from him. The dark-haired man gave him a wicked grin as he scooped his winnings from the center of the table.

"Thanks, Mac, it's been a pleasure beating your ass."

Mac grunted. "Contrary to your belief Angelo, you're not the best poker player I've ever crossed."

"No kidding. So, who was the best?" Angelo asked.

"One hundred pounds of pure trouble named Elyse Booker," Mac said.

"Booker. The daughter of the former ambassador. I saw her at Chu Lei; she was up dancing on the roof of the mess hall before it caved in. Rumor had it she was under the protection of the Marine Corps," Angelo said.

Mac chuckled. "That sounds like Elyse."

"I can't believe they'd put a bunch of jarheads in charge of a woman," Captain Faust said.

"The Marine who looked after Elyse, and married her, also happens to be one of my best friends. The whole family are like brothers to me. One of them is upstairs drugged. Speaking of: How are they doing?" Mac said.

"I checked their vitals about two hours ago. They'll both be fine," Angelo said.

"You're the doctor," Mac said.

"What a fucking night," Captain Mitchell said. "I'm surprised they slept through it."

"I'm going to have a lot to explain once they wake up," Mac replied.

A telephone rang at the front desk and the Vietnamese clerk picked it up. "Hey Mac, a call for you."

Mac looked at his watch, "Pretty early for a damn phone call."

Taking the call, perplexed, Mac returned to the table. "I have to run over to the brig. I'll be back soon."

"I'll wait till then to check in on my patients upstairs," Angelo replied.

Mac parked his jeep in front of MP headquarters. A heavy frown creased his brow; he wondered at the early morning call from the MP's. Something about bailing out a soldier for brawling in the street. "Why the fuck does it concern me?" He growled. Running a hand over his day-old beard, he stomped into the MP headquarters.

He was unable to believe his eyes. Hands on his hips, he stared down at the woman behind bars, who, surprisingly, filled his dreams. Pale blue running shorts and a matching shirt. White tennis shoes on her tiny feet, her knees were skinned, bloody, and covered with dirt. Grass and twigs were stuck in her silky black hair. Midnight blue eyes looked imploringly up at him while a slow blush spread across her fair skin.

"Brawling. You…were brawling in the street?" Mac said.

"We weren't brawling," Sierra replied.

"Okay. So, you weren't brawling, but you were arrested for brawling."

"Yes."

"Okay, my wee brawler. What does this have to do with me?"

"She told me ta call ye."

"Who?"

"Irelynn."

"Irelynn? Irelynn is back at the hotel, drugged from an attempted kidnapping last night."

"No, she's not."

"Yes, she is," Mac said.

Sierra reached through the bars and thumped him on the

forehead. "Ye big lug. Do ye have bricks for brains? Yer not listening ta me. I was trying ta stop her."

Mac raised his eyebrows at her insubordination. "You're a sassy wee lass, aren't you? Okay, Sierra, what are you trying to tell me?"

"Irelynn is on a plane heading ta Saigon…Sir."

Mac turned and bellowed for the guard. "Unlock this fucking door." Once the guard unlocked the door, he reached in and pulled her from the cell, practically carrying her to his jeep.

After a harrowing ride through the city, Mac pulled up in front of the hotel with screeching tires. Jumping out of the jeep, he pulled Sierra into his arms and stormed through the door. Brushing the glass off a chair, he set her at the table. Her eyes were wide; she looked around at the curious faces of the men at the table and then at the destroyed lobby before looking to him for an explanation.

"So, this is what a den of iniquity looks like," Sierra whispered.

Mac opened his mouth to explain when from two floors above, a banging noise started. The crystal chandelier shook with each slam against the wall. The plaster fell from the ceiling as everyone in the room looked up.

Mac winked at Sierra. "Lass, are you sure about that

airplane? It sure sounds like they're having a good time upstairs."

Dark red crept into her cheeks as she looked up at him with confusion. "Irelynn is probably already in Saigon," Sierra said.

The banging noise continued until it sounded as if it was moving down the hallway. The stairwell echoed with foul cursing with more thumping and banging. Brendan appeared on the landing, hitting a full-size brass headboard against the wood railing as he struggled down the final flight of stairs. He stood at the bottom, his wrist shackled to the headboard, a sheet gripped tightly by his other hand dangled precariously low around his hips.

"I'm going to fucking kill her," Brendan snarled. "Then I'm going to throttle her. Then…then, I'm going to chain her to my bed and…"

Mac's jaw dropped as he took in the sight standing in front of him. "Bro. Didn't realize you were into kink."

"I am not into kink," Brendan snarled.

He looked around the lobby. "Where is she?" he growled, kicking a bullet casing away with his foot; he took in the shattered windows and the bullet holes everywhere. Shards of glass and bullet casings littered the floor. Tran, the hotel clerk with a broom in hand, worked to return order to the lobby.

"And what the hell is going on here?"

"Um. Well. Long story short. The VC tried to kidnap Irelynn last night. They attacked the hotel, and there was a big street battle after a few of them were caught trying to carry Irelynn out of your room," Mac said.

Brendan's mind raced as he recalled the previous night. Luscious warm lips that tasted of red wine, the hollow of her neck, the frantic beat of her heart against his chest, and the curve of full breasts in his hands. Panic when she fell limp in his arms.

Worry creased his brow. "We were drugged. We passed out right in the middle of... Where is Irelynn? Is she alright?" Brendan said.

Angelo spoke up. "I'm Dr. Morelli. I've been monitoring you and Irelynn all night. She's fine."

"There's more. Baltini and Rebecca or Sandra, whatever her name is, were spotted here last night. They escaped again," Mac said.

"Damn it. Answer my question. Where. Is. Irelynn?"

Brendan looked down to see a dark-haired beauty step up next to Mac. Wringing her hands, she looked up to him with a sheen of tears in her eyes.

"She caught a plane to Saigon earlier," Mac said.

"You let her go?" Brendan bellowed.

"I didn't let her do anything. She snuck out," Mac replied.

"I tried ta stop her. Really, I did. She loves you. She was mortified and humiliated thinking she fell asleep in your arms," Sierra said.

Anguish and disappointment filled his chest as he turned to look out the window. "She was drugged."

Looking down at the brass headboard, his wrist was still shackled too.

"Mac. Find me a key to these handcuffs. I'm going to Saigon."

"Irelynn didn't leave you. She had ta go home." Sierra pointed to his wrist. "She told me she did that ta slow you down. Amongst other things."

"Amongst what other things?" Brendan growled.

Sierra clapped her hand over her mouth. "You're a bonny man and all, but yer going ta have ta find some clothes."

A cook stepped from the kitchen, bowing to Mac; he handed him the key to the handcuffs.

"A woman ran through the kitchen earlier and gave me this," he said.

"Ask, and you shall receive," Mac said, laughing as he unlocked the handcuffs and handed them to Brendan. "You might want to keep these if you catch her."

Brendan rubbed his wrist to ease the ache. "When not if," he growled.

"That's exactly what I ssaid," Sierra said.

Brendan started back up the stairs. "Bring her. I'm sure she knows more."

Sierra dragged her feet when Mac tugged on her arm. "Come on, love. You heard the man."

"Upstairs? That's where the officers ssleep. I can't go up there with a naked man."

"Sure, you can. Plenty of ladies go upstairs," Mac said.

"Are you daft? That's what I'm talking about," Sierra replied.

"That sassy mouth is going to land you back in the brig. You're safe with us. Now move. And that's an order," Mac said.

Brendan climbed the stairs with his sheet dragging behind; he was held up once when Sierra stepped on the sheet pulling it from his hips.

"SSorry. Didn't mean ta step on yer toga," Sierra said.

Brendan gripped the sheet pulling it tighter around his waist and turned to look at Mac. "Why is it always the little ones?"

"Wee troublemakers," Mac replied with a chuckle.

Sierra rolled her eyes. "Like I want ta walk up the stairs staring at a man's hairy arse and dangling willy," she mumbled.

Brendan glared at Sierra as Mac's laughter rang out.

Striding down the hallway with as much dignity as he could muster, Brendan stopped in front of the soldier guarding his room.

Pointing at the guard, "Mac. I'm getting dressed. Find out how Irelynn slipped past him and why he didn't come to my aid."

Slamming the door behind him, Brendan went to the

bureau; yanking the drawer open, he cursed loudly. He yanked open another drawer, then the last. Pulling out a couple of pairs of neatly rolled socks. He spotted his combat boots right where he left them and his gold oak leaf pins and green beret sitting on top of the bureau.

Grabbing a pair of socks, he went to the door and yanked it open. "She stole my fucking clothes. All she left me was my socks, boots, and my clusters."

"It kind of puts a new light on "out of uniform", doesn't it?" Sierra quipped.

"What do you know about my missing clothes?" Brendan growled.

"Irelynn said she hid them ta slow you down, Sir," Sierra whispered.

They looked to see an old Vietnamese woman waiting patiently to speak with them. She handed Brendan his stack of clothes.

"I found these on my cart. Tran said they were yours," she said before walking away.

Brendan flipped through the stack. "No shirts. Just t-shirts. She stole my last long-sleeved shirt."

Pulling Sierra by the arm, Mac followed Brendan into the room. "Um. Private Monroe said he only stepped away for a minute to look out the window after hearing gunfire outside. He heard the bed banging against the wall, but he thought you had the Mrs. in here."

"I'm still confused about the bed banging against the wall thing," Sierra said.

Brendan and Mac exchanged amused glances. "I'll let you explain that one, Mac?" Brendan snickered.

"Never mind, love," Mac said.

The telephone in the room rang. "Mac, get that for me," Brendan said. "I'm going to get dressed, and then I'm going to go get my shirt back."

Dressing quickly, Brendan opened the bathroom door to see Sierra sitting at the table and Mac, still on the phone, his back to him. Mac hung up the phone and turned around. A pained expression on his face.

"What's wrong?" Brendan said.

Mac looked over at Sierra, sitting quietly in her chair. "That was Colonel Bragg's office. We have to get over to grave services. MP's found the body of an American woman by the airfield."

Feeling like someone gut punched him in the heart, Brendan inhaled sharply, his knees almost buckling under him.

"No. It's not her. I just know it's not Irelynn," Sierra sobbed.

Mac placed his hand on Brendan's shoulder before kneeling in front of Sierra.

"Tell me, love. Did you see Irelynn get on the airplane?"

"No. I last saw her going inside the building."

Without a word, Brendan pulled on his socks and boots and grabbed his Green Beret before rushing out the door.

Brendan and Mac stood on either side of the slab. Looking at the body bag in front of them. With a few deep breaths, Brendan nodded to the mortician; the man unzipped the bag.

After more deep breaths, Brendan looked down at the woman's body. His knees went weak with relief.

"It's Rebecca," Mac said.

"It appears she was badly beaten and strangled. We would need an autopsy to know for sure," The mortician said.

"You'll be hearing from Colonel Bragg's office on how to proceed," Mac said.

"We have to notify Marchetti as well," Brendan said.

Brendan and Mac approached the jeep; a tearful Sierra sat in the back seat. Her arms were tightly wrapped around herself.

Mac gently raised her chin and looked into her eyes. "It's not Irelynn."

Sierra broke into sobs and threw herself into Mac's arms. Brendan smiled when he realized there was something between Mac and Sierra.

Dragging Sierra behind, striding into Colonel Braggs office, Brendan and Mac stopped cold when Colonel Bragg bellowed at them, "Well? Who's the woman at the morgue?"

"It's Rebecca, uh Sandra," Brendan replied.

"At least we know. We've got more trouble. Myron Culp just called. He thought he had put Irelynn safely on a flight back to the world. Edwin Baltini is on that same flight in disguise."

"He probably killed Rebecca before getting on the plane," Mac said.

Brendan rubbed his brow in frustration. "How quickly can you get me on a flight home?"

"You've got a few weeks left in your tour. There's bullshit government bureaucracy. I don't know, but we'll get on it," Colonel Bragg said.

"Let me help. I'm pretty good at cutting through the red tape," Sierra said.

"Who are you, kitten?" Colonel Bragg said.

"Private Sierra Byrne. And don't call me kitten…Sir."

Mac snorted, "More like a wee feral cat," he murmured under his breath.

Sierra glared at Mac. "Say it again, and I'll box your ears."

"Kind of proves my point," Mac snickered.

CHAPTER 24

After twenty hours of flight time and a layover in Singapore, touchdown on American soil, Irelynn breathed a sigh of relief. Climbing to her knees, she peered over the back of her seat; lifting her camera, she took pictures of the men. Their faces registered a wide range of emotions. Some laughed and smiled; others were stoic, and the rest had old eyes in the bodies of young men. They told the tale of horror as they looked at her with the thousand-mile stare she had witnessed on so many occasions. Still, they were home; she was home. Wiping the tears from her eyes, she had seen so much, but it was nothing compared to what these men had lived through. Looking out the window at the bright California sunshine as the airplane taxied over to the terminal. She snapped a photo of the stewardess, who gave her a stern look for unbuckling her seatbelt before the plane came to a complete stop. Feeling anxious, she wanted to get off the plane before the men to capture on film the final leg of their journey home.

Hefting her rucksack over her shoulder, she adjusted her camera and rose from her seat when the door was opened. Standing at the top of the stairs, she breathed in the cool, dry air. Shivering slightly in the cooler temperature, she ran down the stairs past the MP's standing at the bottom. Turning to the men exiting the plane, her camera beat out a steady staccato of clicks. Turning back toward the chain link fence, crowds of people stood chanting. A frown marred her brow as she read the signs with foul messages of "Baby killers. End the war" waved in time to the anti-war chants from the protesting crowd. Feeling a slow-motion horror, she turned to capture the shocking pain that replaced the happiness on the returning soldiers' faces.

"No," she whispered. "Don't do this. You have no idea what they've been through for you." Tears ran down her face as rotten fruit and vegetables were thrown at the returning troops, some landing square on the chest of one young soldier. Pulling her slingshot from her back pocket, she picked up a tomato and shot it back into the crowd. She felt a gentle hand on her elbow. She looked up into the sad face of a sandy-haired Marine.

"No. Leave them be. They're exercising their first amendment right. Freedom of Speech. It's what we fought for," he said.

"But…" Irelynn stuttered.

"It's alright. Come on. I'll escort you to customs," he said.

California map in hand. Irelynn dropped her rucksack to the ground. Sitting on a bench, she took a sip of the ice-cold bottle of Coke while she stared at the map. With the bus terminal right outside the base, she could buy a ticket heading north to the last stop on the route, hitchhike to Cross Point logging camp. Then, catch a ride up Sugar Mountain to her parent's place. Ripping the wrapper off the Seven-Up candy bar, she chewed thoughtfully on the treat she hadn't tasted since she left home. Brushing at the green grass stains on her knees, she plotted her route home.

She spotted two men, twins, on the other side of a wide sidewalk, one in jeans and one in a naval uniform. They ducked behind the bench they had been sitting on. Her curiosity piqued, she picked up her camera and started shooting photos of the men's odd behavior. Abandoning her Coke and candy bar on the bench, she followed them across the base as they followed another man, an admiral. Moving with a familiarity that brought an ache to her heart. She had fought to hold back burning tears every time he had slid into her thoughts over the past twenty-four hours. Pushing Brendan from her mind, she raised her camera, capturing the essence of the identical sleuthing twins.

They were peering out from the side of a building when

she snuck up behind them. She peeked around them to see the admiral approaching a row of outdoor telephones.

"He's making a phone call," the uniform clad twin said.

"Who is he calling that he has to come over here to use the phone?" said the jeans clad twin.

"I can find out for you," Irelynn said.

Both men jumped in surprise before turning to look at her.

She gave them a delicious conspiratorial smile and winked.

Standing two phones down from the admiral; Irelynn fingered the slim dime in her hand before sliding it into the coin slot. She had offered to listen in on the man's phone conversation. Pretending to dial a phone number, she listened to the man on the phone next to her. He was rude and foul mouthed, speaking to someone named Gary. The admiral glanced over at her; she shivered in disgust as his lust filled eyes insolently swept her body. He hung up and walked away.

"Perverted old lecher," Irelynn mumbled as she returned to the twins. Relaying the telephone conversation to the men, she handed the uniformed twin her business card. Glancing at his name tag, she froze. *Corrington.*

She looked between the two men—warm brown eyes, not blue. Everything else was so similar, height, the breadth of their broad shoulders, black wavy hair, and even their posture was the same. *Shit. Shit. Shit. They're related to Brendan.*

"That's why you look so familiar. Oh shit. I have to go."

She snatched her business card from his hand. "You never saw me." She stopped, "No. Actually. Give him a message for me. "Catch me if you can."

Catching the amused grins of the twins, she took off across the grass like a bat out of hell, not stopping until she found the bench she had been sitting on. Snatching up her Coke and candy bar, she made a beeline to the front gate and the bus terminal across the street.

Curled up in her seat, Irelynn rubbed the goosebumps on her arms and draped herself with Brendan's shirt. After so long in the heat and humidity of Vietnam, she had forgotten the cool breeze of the San Francisco Bay area.

Catch me if you can. How stupid was that to throw out a direct challenge to Brendan? Sierra was right, when not if. Truly, if you're honest with yourself, you want him to catch you.

The bus traveled up the pacific coastal highway snaking through redwood forests. Breathtaking views of blue green surf crashing into jagged outcrops of rock and foamy sea spray. The rocky beaches were heavily populated with Sea lions and harbor seals at rest. Beach towns popped up along the way with lighthouses and gift shops to lure in delighted tourists.

At some point, the bus veered northeast, heading toward the mountain range. Irelynn leaned back against the seat. Closing her eyes, she fell into a deep slumber.

A gentle shake on her shoulder and Irelynn woke to see the smiling face of the elderly bus driver.

"End of the line, sweetheart," he said.

Irelynn stared at him in confusion, rubbing the sleep from her eyes. "What day is it?"

"Sunday," he replied.

"I just might make it home in time for supper," Irelynn said. "Well, if you're hungry now, the Redwood Café here has some pretty good food."

"Thank you. I might just do that," Irelynn replied.

Stepping off the bus, Irelynn looked around. A few cars and semi-trucks were parked outside of the lone café located in the middle of nowhere. The two-lane highway disappeared into a point on the horizon as the wind whipped at her face. Rolling green hills filled with lush forests, the mountain range further north called to her in a comforting call to home. Removing Brendan's shirt, she folded it over her arm and went inside. Choosing a stool at the far end of the counter, she pulled the menu from behind the napkin holder.

French fries or onion rings? Both sound good. She hadn't had either in quite some time.

"What'll it be, honey?"

Irelynn looked up to see a woman in her mid-forties, blonde hair piled high in a beehive hairdo, her bright blue eyes smiling at her.

"Hi. I'm trying to decide between some fries or the onion rings," Irelynn said.

"How about I save you the time? You can have a half order of each."

"That would be cool. Not too many, though. I don't want anything to go to waste."

"Anything else?"

"A tall glass of lemonade sounds delightful. I'm parched."

"Coming right up, honey."

"What kind of ketchup do you have?"

The woman reached under the counter and set a bottle of Heinz in front of her. Irelynn smiled; *God, it's good to be home.*

Slurping her lemonade, Irelynn sucked every last drop through her straw. It was time to move on. Her wedding bracelet caught her eye, and she delicately stroked it. Brendan. It seemed to her the closer she got to home, the more she missed him. She couldn't forget how safe she had felt in his arms or how she had left him soundly sleeping, and now,

Irelynn had to figure out how to explain Brendan to her family.

"That's a lovely little bracelet," the waitress said as she handed her the bill.

"Thank you. It's my wedding bracelet."

"A bracelet. That's a little nontraditional."

"You should have seen the wedding," Irelynn replied, jumping down from the stool; she hefted her rucksack onto her back and placed a five dollar bill on the counter to cover her tab.

"Keep the change."

"Are you sure? That's a hefty tip. Where are you heading, honey?"

"Cross Point. Home."

The waitress looked out the window to the now empty parking lot. "You got a car?"

"Nah. I'm hitchhiking the rest of the way."

"A pretty girl like you out there alone. You be careful. There are a lot of nuts out there. Especially with that serial killer lose in San Francisco this summer."

Irelynn smiled. "Don't you worry about me; I can take care of myself. "

Ryan Cross smiled at his large family gathered around a large circular dining room table. His five sons were seated at the table, along with three lovely spouses. Besides the new baby who napped in the guest nursery, six grandchildren sat around the kitchen table arguing over the best cartoons on Saturday morning. His eyes passed proudly over each of his sons before pausing on the lone empty chair. His heart skipped a beat.

Where are you, baby girl? His eyes moved on to meet the concerned eyes of his mother, who the family affectionately called Gramie.

The old Saint Bernard, Ralph, slept soundly in the doorway to the kitchen. He smiled as his wife, Rachel, hands full with a basket of homemade biscuits, stepped over the lazy dog.

"Ugh, this old dog. She's going to be the death of me. She won't move for nothing," Rachel said, setting the biscuits on the table before sitting down.

"Ralph won't move from that spot unless it's to eat, do her business, or if Irelynn was home. Then, she follows her around like a puppy," Ryan said.

The table fell quiet for a few minutes.

"Enough. She'll come home when she's good and ready," Gramie said.

"I hope you're right, Gramie," Rachel whispered, passing a big bowl of mashed potatoes to her youngest son, Sean.

"I wish I would have been here when the FBI showed up at the door," Rachel said.

"I told you. At first, I thought they were after my moonshine. Then they wanted pictures of Irelynn. I told them that all they had to do was call General Smead to verify it was her, then I called him myself."

"Mom, I keep telling you. Prohibition ended in the thirties. You have a permit. Your still is safe from the feds. If I had known that Irelynn was in Vietnam, I could have had Smead keeping me posted all along," Ryan said.

"She's alive. We have that much information," RJ, the eldest son, said. "Please pass the biscuits."

"Irelynn always had wanderlust. As to how she ended up in South Vietnam is beyond me," Matthew replied, giving his wife Amy's hand a squeeze.

"It's all a bit confusing to me. It's too bad Smead couldn't explain everything in detail. Rachel said. "I feel we only know bits and pieces of the story."

The old dog lifted her head and sniffed the air. Standing up, the dog looked to the front door before taking off like a bat out of hell, running straight through the screen door.

"What the hell is wrong with Ralph," Ryan growled.

Everyone fell silent, jumping at the female squeal of delight outside. "Irelynn," Rachel sobbed. "She's home."

Chairs scraped back as everyone scrambled from the table to run outside. In the driveway, Irelynn lay spread out with Ralph lying on top of her, the dog whimpering and licking her face.

"Oh my god, Ralph. Yes, I'm happy to see you too," Irelynn cried. Kissing the dog on her snout, she pushed the dog, who outweighed her by twenty pounds, off her chest. Irelynn rose to her feet, wringing her hands. Tears ran down her face as she faced her family.

"I'm so sorry. I had no idea what was going on. I never

meant to bring pain to you. It was cruel and selfish of me. Please forgive me."

They stepped off the long lazy porch in mass. Tears and laughter followed as Irelynn was crushed in one embrace after another, landing in her parents' arms, who cried tears of joy.

"Welcome home, baby girl," Ryan said, wrapping his tiny daughter in a bear hug.

"Thank you, Daddy. It's good to be home. Is that pot roast I smell?"

CHAPTER 25

Throwing the file on the conference room table, Brendan stood to stretch his arms. Walking over to the wall, Brendan stood looking at Sierra's creation. A timeline map spread across the length of the wall. It was a brilliant idea, and he appreciated the visuals the map provided. The beginning of the map started in Istanbul when the real Rebecca Ronin was murdered, and Irelynn met Baltini and Rebecca/Sandra.

His gaze fell on the photos of the nurses and Irelynn. Shaking his head, he recalled their wild truck ride to freedom. He looked up when Marchetti opened the door.

"Corrington, glad you're here. Here are Rebecca Ronin's and Sandra Saunder's autopsy reports and photos. It looks like the same M.O. to me."

Flipping through the folders, Brendan paused at the

pictures of both women. "Similar height, weight, and long blonde hair. Looks like Sandra was a shoo-in for Rebecca."

"Beaten and strangled. We can place Baltini with both women."

"He killed Mai Le as well," Brendan said.

"We pretty much know the motives for the real Rebecca and Mai Le, but why did he kill Sandra?" Marchetti asked.

"No idea. Did we get Baltini's file yet? At this point, who's to say that's his real identity."

Tossing the files on top of the others, "Where's Mac?" Marchetti asked.

The door opened, and Mac came in with a package in his hands. "Mail call," Mac said.

"Ah. A care package from Elyse and Elijah," Brendan said.

"Maybe she's got news on Donall and his situation," Mac said.

"Last I heard, the Navy reassigned him to Edwards. And there's a girl involved," Brendan said. Opening the box, he tucked an enclosed letter into his pocket and pulled out a jar of peanuts.

"Donall's got a girl in every port," Mac said. Sitting down, he stretched his long legs out on top of the table; he grabbed the jar and opened it with a pop before popping a few nuts in his mouth.

Brendan grinned. "Said the man with a girl in every nook and cranny in South Vietnam."

Mac's face split into a wide grin.

"Better watch out, Mac. One of these days, you're going to be blindsided by a woman."

"I've gotten pretty good at dodging cupid's arrow," Mac replied.

Brendan laughed. "For you, it's going to be a two-by-four. And you won't see it coming."

The door opened again. Sierra bustled in with a tray teeming with steaming cups of coffee and cookies. She placed a cup in front of Brendan,

"Here's the file ye requested," she said, placing it and a plate of chocolate chip cookies on the far end of the table between Marchetti and Brendan. She handed a coffee cup to Marchetti.

Walking past Mac, she knocked his feet off the table. "We're ye brought up in a barn?" she asked before picking up the tray and rushing out of the room, mumbling about giving his lord- ship next door his coffee.

Brendan picked up a cookie; taking a bite, he grinned at Mac. "Kind of looks like you're in deep shit."

Mac glared at Brendan before the door opened back up. Sierra bustled back in, placing a cup in front of Mac. She reached into her pocket and tossed some dried cream and sugar packets on the table in front of him. "Here ye go. What was it ye said last time? Ye only like blonde and sweet. I've taken the liberty and ordered a locking file cabinet for yer files, along with a telephone line. Both should be here this afternoon. If ye need anything else, I'll be at my desk," she said before rushing out of the room.

"Quick and efficient," Marchetti said.

"Like a whirlwind," Brendan said with a laugh. "We should steal her from the brass."

"Blonde and sweet. I was talking about my fucking coffee. Never saw a woman get so worked up about cream and sugar," Mac grumbled. "Damn. She's cute."

Brendan laughed before his own arguments with Irelynn entered his mind and crushing anguish filled his chest.

Toughen up. She's home. You'll be out of here soon.

Rubbing his forehead. "Let's see what's in that file."

A few hours later, Brendan sighed deeply. Rising to his feet, he faced the timeline map. "Why? Why did they try to kidnap her again? We shut down the brothel. They had a chance to escape the country but didn't. Instead, they came back. They took a big risk and failed to kidnap her from the hotel."

"Maybe Irelynn has something they want," Mac said.

Brendan's brow slid into a deep frown. "Possible."

"She has no idea that Baltini tried again. And we have no idea why Baltini got off during the layover in Singapore and didn't get back on the plane."

"Any news from Singapore yet? I'm thinking something spooked him, or he's covering his tracks and took another flight to San Francisco," Brendan thoughtfully replied.

"We've got people working on it. It's been hard to track

where Baltini and Rebecca have been since they use so many alias' and fake passports."

"He could've gotten off the plane under one name, bought another ticket under a different name, and still been on the same plane as Irelynn," Mac replied.

"Nope. Not quite like that," Marchetti said, rising from his seat. "Other than flight crew and military personnel. There were only two civilians on that flight. Irelynn and one John Erickson. Erickson never got back on that plane. I've got a report right here. A soldier mugged in the men's room in Singapore's airport. Knocked out, only thing stolen was his uniform."

"Baltini got back on the plane, taking that soldier's seat," Mac said. "That's how he evaded the MPs at Treasure Island."

Brendan slammed his hand down on the table. "That means Irelynn is still in danger. Marchetti, when the fuck am I getting out of here?"

"Let me make some calls," Marchetti replied.

"Let's go find Sierra and see how far she's gotten," Mac said.

Pausing the Dictaphone recording, Sierra delicately dabbed her spelling error with the tiny white out brush. Sighing deeply before gently blowing on the paper, she hit the back button on her typewriter to correct her error.

"Jesus, Mary, and Joseph. Could the day get any worse?" she mumbled under her breath. Glancing up she could see her direct superior, Lieutenant Garris, glaring at her over the top of her glasses, the woman's face stuck in a perpetual frown. Hitting the start button on the Dictaphone machine, she hadn't typed three words when long shadows fell across her desk, and someone hit the pause button on the machine.

Looking up, Sierra rolled her eyes. "Oh, look. It's Satan and his evil twin." She looked around the office as other secretaries paused their work to stare at her visitors before her gaze landed back on Lieutenant Garris, whose frown had deepened to a frightening scowl.

"Are ye crazy? I'm already in trouble after running for ye two and his lordship," she whispered.

Mac and Brendan grinned down at her. "His lordship?" Mac asked.

"Colonel Bragg," Sierra replied. Sierra's eyes widened as Lieutenant Garris rose from her desk. "Shite. The dragon lady is on her way over here. Ye two, need ta leave."

Mac pivoted to look at the formidable woman. "I'll handle this." Mac moved away to meet the woman.

Peeking up through her eyelashes, Sierra could see Brendan staring down at her. He looked tired, and his eyes held a hint of sadness.

"Do you have any news for me, Sierra?" he gently prodded.

"I do. Oh my god. Look at that. He's got the dragon lady giggling and blushing," Sierra said.

"Mac has a way with... words," Brendan replied.

Sierra snorted.

"Do you like this job?"

"Not particularly. I like ta do things for the brass. But sitting here typing all day gets old."

"It sounds like you need some adventure," Brendan said.

Sierra snorted again. "If ye listen ta the Army, I'm living that adventure now. I was always a wee bit envious of Irelynn. She had freedom and an exciting job. She's sso sweet and caring. She could talk ta anybody. Always showed up right when I needed her the most. Even though I didn't get ta see her that often, I miss her."

"She sounds like a good friend to have."

"She is. I'm going ta box her ears when I ssee her next."

"How long do you have left on your tour?"

"A little under three months," Sierra replied.

They both looked at Mac as he approached. "Grab your things, love, and anything you have for us. You're ours for the rest of the day," Mac said.

"Why does that ssscare me," Sierra whispered.

An hour later, Sierra, Brendan, and Mac stood outside the officer's club. "Are the two of ye daft?" Sierra grumbled.

Mac gave her a look of bewilderment. "What?"

"Yer both officers. I'm enlisted. I can't go in there," Sierra said.

"I'm sorry, love. I completely forgot you were enlisted," Mac said.

"I'll get us a beer. What will you have, Sierra?" Brendan said.

"I'll go out on a limb here and have a Coke," Sierra replied.

Brendan nodding his amusement, stepped inside the outdoor tiki bar to order drinks.

"Hmm, Coke. Living on the wild side, are we?" Mac murmured."

"Not with the Coke. With being in the same proximity as the two of ye outside of work," Sierra said. "You know. Fraternizing with officers."

"Consider this a work meeting. We'll go sit at the picnic table over there, love. Then you can tell us all about Irelynn and how far you're getting in cutting through that red tape for Brendan."

"How's he doing?" Sierra said.

"He's managing."

Brendan returned, setting the beers and coke down on the table.

"I worry about Irelynn. Now that Baltini is back in the world. I don't think it's right that she has no one ta protect her. I don't understand why ye don't have that creepy fancy pants CIA man, Marchetti, reassign both of ye to work in California. I mean, I know about the CIA working on American soil stuff, but I think it's manageable if you have the FBI do the dirty work. Be much easier than trying ta get the Army to give up one of its own and let ye out early. Sir."

Brendan grinned. "You've been reading the reports."

Sierra blushed. "According to Miss. Smith, a good secretary figures out the nitty gritty so she can anticipate yer needs and offer fresh solutions."

"Whose Miss. Smith?" Mac asked.

"My high school typing teacher," Sierra replied.

"Did Miss. Smith instruct you on international espionage?" Mac teased.

Sierra rolled her eyes. "She never mentioned it."

"What other solutions have you come up with?" Brendan asked

"I grew up not too far from Irelynn. My Uncle Barney is the sheriff for Cross Point, the town Irelynn's family lives in. Ye both need jobs or yer going ta stick out like sore thumbs in a lumber town."

"Baltini can I.D both of us," Mac murmured.

"What I mean to say is, yer going to have ta go undercover if ye want to catch Baltini," Sierra said.

"It's not a bad idea," Brendan said. "Let's have another beer, then get back to the office and talk to Marchetti."

"My turn. I'll go get this round," Mac said.

"There is one thing I wanted to say to ye, Brendan. Mac said he wanted me ta tell ye more about Irelynn. Ye need to be asking your questions ta Irelynn. Face to face. I know she said she needed time to sort her feelings out. But ye have ta understand how she feels. She barely knew ye before she found herself married ta ye. Ye didn't really date or get to know each other. Ye didn't propose or have the wedding I'm sure both of ye would have envisioned. Were ye planning on just barreling in ta town on yer white steed? Ye need to woo her."

"I need a plan," Brendan said.

"The last thing ye want is for Irelynn ta think yer staying married ta her out of a sense of duty. I know she loves ye, but I also know she thinks she doesn't deserve ye."

"Why would she think she doesn't deserve me?"

"She deceived ye by going incognito to yer firebase, but truthfully, I think Rebecca, I mean Sandra, may have pushed her in that direction."

"You didn't like Rebecca, did you?"

"I know we shouldn't speak ill of the dead. I only met her once, sitting right here at this table. Something was off and I wish I would have listened ta my gut instincts and spoken up at the time," Sierra said.

"What's your gut telling you now?"

"Irelynn is in grave danger," Sierra whispered.

CHAPTER 26

Rolling to her knees, Irelynn launched herself at her opponent, her brother Jamie. Knocking him on his back, he rolled to his feet and knocked her back to land on her bottom. "Come on, Irelynn. You can do better than that," Jamie said as Irelynn rolled into him, knocking his feet out from under him. A crowd of onlookers hooted and howled at her sudden move. Jamie rose and offered his hand, pulling Irelynn to her feet.

"Damn, little sis. You're better than you were but not good enough yet."

"I can hold my own," Irelynn said. Pulling her flannel shirt off her shoulder, she put her finger through the rip in the sleeve. "Damn. A hole in my shirt, and I lost half my buttons."

"Just like old times," Jamie said.

"Mom's going to have a fit that I'm adding to her mending pile again," Irelynn said.

"She'd rather be doing your mending than wondering where you are."

"Don't go there, Jamie. It's hard enough."

Looking out to the crowd of lumberjacks, Irelynn smiled at the familiar faces of the men gathered around them. Some she had known forever, and they treated her like a sister; others were new to the company. Those men stared at her, unsure what to make of the beautiful woman who fought like a man.

"I know… What the fuck is that?" Jamie snarled.

"What?" Irelynn said. Looking to where his eyes rested. *Oh shit! My wound.*

Irelynn nervously flipped her shirt up to cover her shoulder. "Ah. Jamie."

"Don't ah Jamie me. I know a fucking bullet wound when I see one. Does dad know?"

"No. And I don't want you to tell him or mom either."

"Tell mom or dad what?"

Irelynn whipped around to see her other four brothers standing behind her, Ryan Jr, fraternal twins Matthew and Michael, and the youngest, Sean.

"Um, RJ. I…"

Jamie stepped up and flipped her shirt over her shoulder to show his brothers her bullet wound.

"Christ, Irelynn. You got shot?" RJ said.

"Leaving a firebase near the Cambodian/Laos border.

The chopper I was on took fire from the NVA."

"You could have been killed," Sean said.

"But I wasn't. Listen, guys, I get you're not happy I was in South Vietnam, but it's my job."

"It's not the place for a woman," Matthew said.

"Oh my God. Now you sound just like…" *Brendan.*

"Just like who?" Michael said.

"Never mind," Irelynn replied.

"What else are you not telling us?" RJ said.

Irelynn shook her head. "I'm not a little girl anymore. The five of you need to back off." Irelynn looked from brother to brother, all big men at six foot one, with copper curls and amber eyes to match her own. They towered over her small frame.

"Please."

RJ nodded. "Mom's looking for you. She wants you to take something up to Gramie's cabin."

"Okay," Irelynn said.

"Ah, Irelynn. It's Saturday," Sean said.

Irelynn grimaced. "Oh no. No. No. No." She looked at her brothers' grinning faces. "She's still teaching?"

"Yup. There isn't a man on this mountain who will go near Gramie's on Saturdays," RJ said.

"Where's she getting her victims?" Irelynn asked.

"From town. Mostly newbies to the area," Michael said with a wide grin. "We like to send the new hires up there."

"Kind of an initiation to the job," Matthew snickered. "We time them. It's fun to watch them come screaming back."

"Mom's busy in the front office. Someone has to do it," Jamie said.

"Fine. I'll do it," Irelynn ground out. "Come on, Ralph. Let's go make a delivery." The old dog stood, shook its mane, and followed Irelynn to the main house.

Keys in hand, Irelynn pulled the double garage doors open. Climbing in her truck after helping Ralph up, she lovingly wiped the dust off the dashboard before pulling out of the garage. Irelynn was grateful that Sean had kept the old fifty two Chevy running for her, taking it out at least once a month to run it through its gears. Driving the mile up the road to Gramie's cabin, she stopped to watch a mama black bear and her two cubs cross the road in front of her. Pulling into Gramie's driveway, a couple of cars were parked in front of the large cabin. Grabbing the basket from the front seat, Irelynn slid from the truck, the dog jumping out after her.

Sniffing the air, she could detect the tangy, pungent odor of corn, yeast, and alcohol. Shaking her head, *Gramie's still making moonshine.* Moving up the steps, she crossed the large porch with its welcoming porch swing and opened the front screen door. Following the giggling from the back of the house, she walked into the kitchen, setting the basket on the table, she moved to the large sunroom off the kitchen.

Irelynn's hands flew up to cover her eyes.

Peeking between her fingers, A naked man knelt on a platform in the middle of the room in an atlas type pose. Six little old ladies, not a one under eighty, sat at their easel's drawing. Sipping their moonshine, they giggled and called out lewd comments.

Oh, Gramie. You and the ladies are incorrigible.

Slowly she inched backward out of the room. *They haven't seen me yet. Out.*

"George. Come in and say hello," Gramie called out.

"Damn," Irelynn muttered before plastering a smile on her face.

Waving her arm toward the naked man. "Please, cover him up," Irelynn said.

"Don't be such a prude, sweetheart," Gracie, well into her nineties replied.

"Oh, God. Are you still a virgin?" Gramie called out.

"Gramie!" Irelynn sharply replied as the pink rose on her cheeks.

"You're blushing, my dear," Agnes said.

"Oh, fine. We're done for the day anyway. Brian, my love, cover up," Gramie said.

Peeking out her eyes, Irelynn watched the young man slip into his jeans and pull on a gray t shirt. *Okay, so he has a nice bum.*

Gramie kissed him on the cheek and handed him a twenty dollar bill. "See you next week, sweet cheeks."

Irelynn rolled her eyes, watching as he let himself out. "Seriously, Gramie. They're getting younger and younger."

"College student. Perfectly legal," Gramie replied.

"Irelynn dear. Did you get a chance to practice what we showed you with the banana?" Alice asked.

"I'm not answering that," Irelynn grumbled.

"Isn't it the summer of love? Weren't there men on your trip?" Agnes asked.

"Quite a few," Irelynn replied.

Collecting purses and canes, Irelynn helped the ladies out the door and to their vehicle.

"Whose driving?"

"I am," Gracie replied.

"Do you even have a driver's license?" Irelynn replied.

"Never did," Gracie giggled.

"How much moonshine did you drink?"

"Not nearly enough, my dear," Gracie said, patting her arm.

Irelynn watched the car pull away and head down the winding road toward town like a bat out of hell.

Gramie patted the empty spot on the swing next to her. "Come sit with me."

Settling herself into the porch swing, "How can you let Gracie drink when she has to drive?"

"Gracie." Gramie waved her hand. "Pshaw. I give her and the ladies watered down moonshine. They don't know the difference."

"Good."

"What's going on, George? You seem so sad, not at all yourself. You know you can always talk to me."

"He calls me George sometimes too. Though, it's usually

when I'm in trouble," Irelynn said.

"Hmm. So, there is a man involved."

"Yes."

"Tell me about him."

"Tall. Handsome. He's the type of man who makes you shiver when you're not cold. He's intense, kind, and annoying. I'm not even sure where to start," Irelynn said, running her fingers along the edge of her wedding bracelet.

"Where to start? At the beginning, of course."

Smiling, she leaned on Gramie's shoulder and launched into her tale.

An hour later, Irelynn wiped at the tears on her face. "So, we're married, but it's all a mess, and I'm confused."

"That's quite the adventure. Has no one told you that it's possible to have it all? However, you're a coward for running away from love. You're afraid of the commitment, not your young man."

"You don't pull your punches, do you?"

Gramie waved her hands. "Of course, I understand the shock of a surprise marriage, but you must give him a chance."

"Oh, Gramie. You're right. I used my excuse to come home as a reason to run from him. I should have stayed."

"I understand why you wanted to come home. I also know you'll leave again,' Gramie said.

"It's not what you think. I will find a job in San Francisco, but I plan to come home a few times a month. I have no desire to be so far from home again."

"That's good to hear. You need to tell your parents about your husband and your bullet wound. And how do you fall asleep your first time in bed with a man? Perhaps, the ladies and I should instruct him on how to please a woman?"

"Gramie!"

Rachel Cross stood on her front porch, looking up the hill toward Gramie's cabin. Ryan came up behind her and wrapped his arms around her waist.

"Irelynn's still up there?" Ryan said.

"Yes. I'm hoping she's letting it all out to Gramie. She's been so quiet and withdrawn."

"It doesn't bother you that she confides in Gramie?"

"Of course not. I've always been grateful she had another set of loving arms to hold her and ears to listen. She'll come to us when she's ready."

"Before I forget. Barney asked if he could rent out Irelynn's cabin for a new deputy starting in a few days."

"I don't see why not. The cabin is sitting empty since she's staying down here with us. I'll freshen it up tomorrow." She opened the screen door. "Suppers ready. I'm sure Irelynn will be back soon," Rachel said.

"I'll be right in," Ryan replied.

Ryan rubbed his forehead. *Oh, baby girl. What have you gotten yourself into this time?*

CHAPTER 27

Sierra pulled the jeep up in front of the admin building with a screech of tires. Brendan grinned down at Sierra before pivoting to Mac.

"I'm surprised she can reach the pedals," he said.

Mac grinned as he hefted his duffel bag into the back seat. "Probably has wooden blocks tied to her wee feet," he murmured.

"I heard that," Sierra said.

Brendan hefted his bag into the back and hopped in, leaving the front seat for Mac.

Taking in the sights and sounds of the city for the last time, Brendan breathed a sigh of relief. Home, he was finally on his way home, with time to spend a few days with his family before heading north to find his runaway bride. He smiled; speaking of brides, Elyse's letter contained a surprise.

Donall had discovered his own pepper pot and was getting married. *Hell. I'm married.* Sighing deeply. *How do I explain a Montagnard wedding to a she-devil in a red dress?*

"Sir. Sir," Sierra said. "We're here."

Jarred from his musings, Brendan looked up to see they had parked in front of the Pan Am airplane. Standing by the jeep, Sierra handed him a stack of envelopes. Here's yer itinerary, plane tickets, a map to Cross Point from Treasure Island, Uncle Barney, uh…Sherriff Griffith's address, and a private letter for my aunt."

Brendan leaned in and kissed Sierra on the cheek. "Thanks for your help, munchkin. I hope to see you again."

Sierra smiled. "I'm out of here in a few months. Ye just might."

With a nod to Mac, Brendan hefted his duffel bag over his shoulder and walked away.

"Oh, Sir. Go easy on Irelynn for the handcuff 's thing," Sierra called out.

Brendan stopped and turned around. He started laughing. "Not a chance."

Throwing his duffel bag on a luggage train, he watched as Sierra offered a handshake to Mac. Mac, being Mac, pulled her into his arms, giving her a long lingering kiss. Brendan grinned. "Every nook and cranny."

Mac ended the kiss and strode over to dump his duffel bag. Together they walked up the stairs to the plane. Pausing at the top, Brendan looked around for one last time.

"You ever coming back?" Mac asked.

"Nope. You?" Brendan said.

Mac's gaze lingered on Sierra, still standing by the jeep with a shocked expression on her sweet face, her fingers tracing her swollen lips. "I'll be back for Molly, and… though she doesn't know it yet, that wee lass interests me. Though she might not be speaking to me by then."

Brendan looked at him in confusion. "Why not?"

"You know the kid Murphy, Colonel Bragg's assistant?"

"Yeah."

"His tour is up. The kid's going home. I pulled some strings and had Sierra permanently reassigned as Bragg's new assistant."

Brendan guffawed, "They'll kill each other."

"Nah, I look at it more like keeping each other in line. Besides, Special Forces take care of their own. He'll keep her safe."

Brendan chuckled, clapping Mac on the back. "Let's go home, bro."

Brushing her wind-swept hair from her eyes, Irelynn looked up to the tall buildings surrounding her. Overwhelmed by the size and pulse of the city, she pulled her jean jacket closer. "Wow. San Francisco. This is going to take some getting used to again."

Fresh from Vietnam, her experience, journalism work, and Myron Culp had come through for her, and she had a new job at the San Francisco Chronicle. Just the other day, she had taken a photograph of two stunning women at the women's march, and it had made the front page. Pulling a folded newspaper and a city map from her purse, pencil in hand, she circled the advertisements for apartments she was interested in.

"Now to find a place to live. Can't stay in a hotel forever," she murmured. "Average rent is one hundred dollars a month…ouch."

Much cheaper to stay at home with her parents, but it was too far from work. They weren't happy she would be so far from home, but she agreed to come home every weekend.

"Ooh. Here's one. A boarding house, rent, sixty per month." Irelynn spotted a phone booth at the end of the crowded street. An hour later, she stood outside a beautiful Victorian home; the front door was painted red, and the neighborhood was quaint and well kept.

Mom and Dad would approve.

Ringing the doorbell, she waited a minute before an elderly Chinese woman opened the door. "Hello, Mrs. Wang. I'm Irelynn. We spoke on the phone earlier. I'm here about the room for rent."

"Please come in," Mrs. Wang said.

Irelynn stepped into the large foyer; her eyes were drawn to the wide staircase. Wow. I would love to slide down that banister. Irelynn looked around the home. It was clean and homey. Mrs. Wang waved her into the sitting room. "Please sit."

"You have a lovely home," Irelynn said.

An older man entered the room with a tray filled with a steaming pot of tea and cups. He set the tray on the table and bowed before shuffling out of the room.

"My husband. Mr. Wang. A good man, he spends his time in the garden. So, Irelynn, tell me about yourself."

Irelynn spun around the large room. It was fantastic. Located on the fourth floor of the rooming house. Bright and sunny, the round room was surrounded by windows. A beautiful oriental rug lay on hardwood floors shining from a recent coat of wax. French doors led to a widow's walk surrounding the room with a sitting area with stunning view's overlooking the city and bay. The four-poster brass bed looked clean and comfortable. A slate blue stuffed chair and table created the perfect sitting area for reading or writing.

Pinching her arm, Irelynn couldn't believe her luck securing such a beautiful place to live. Her gaze fell on the bed. *Brendan.*

She wrapped her arms around herself and looked down at the floor. Questions flowed through her mind like a raging river. *How is he? His tour should be up. When does he come home? How long before he finds me? Should I look for him first? Where?*

Does he still love me?

Shaking herself out of her humdrum mood. *What's done is done. You're crying over spilled milk.*

"God. Now I sound like my mother," she mumbled.

You'll be paying the devil his due soon. A delicate shiver ran down her spine.

And then some.

Brendan shook his head in amusement. Besides the fact that they had temporarily lost the bride, Donall and Anablue's wedding was a smashing success. The wedding was over. He was ready to deal with his own bride. Pulling out of Elijah's driveway, Brendan was still chuckling at the look on his family's face's when he dropped his bombshell news. He had a wife, and he was going to find her. Of course, he knew exactly where she was.

He was wearing his old blue jeans and a black t shirt, with black leather boots and his old black leather jacket. All pulled from his father's storage locker. The old Harley he had bought a few days ago rumbled between his thighs. Smiling, he headed north on the Pacific Coast Highway One, his only goal. Irelynn. Two hours later, he pulled into Cross Point. Rumbling down the street he pulled into a parking spot in front of the sheriff's office. Climbing off his bike, he caught the wide eyes of two gawking high school girls. He nodded his head in greeting before entering the office. Once inside, he told the receptionist, a forty-ish blonde, he wanted to see Sheriff Griffith.

Sheriff Griffith was short, portly, in his mid-sixties with a shock of thick gray hair. Shaking hands with Brendan, he smiled at the receptionist.

"Missy. Would you mind running across the street to Nan's? I believe I saw Ryan Cross having coffee earlier. Tell him I'd like to see him. Oh, and you might as well take a break."

He winked at Brendan as the woman grabbed her purse and left the office. "Town gossip. Lovely lady, but, well, you know."

"Thank you. I appreciate that. We must keep this between the three of us for now," Brendan said as he took a seat in the sheriff's office.

"Before I forget. Here's a letter from Sierra."

"Thanks. The wife will appreciate it. How is Sierra?"

"She's got a good job as a secretary for a colonel. She's safe."

"Can't say I understand. With the number of boys from this area going to Vietnam, now we have girls to worry about as well. Though after everything she went through I guess I do understand."

Brendan looked up as a man filled the doorway. His eyes widened at the massive size of the man. Six four, burly chested, his hair the same chestnut copper brown as Irelynn's, streaked with gray. Intelligent amber eyes looked him over before he thrust a callused hand out in greeting.

"Ryan Cross. Irelynn's father. What's going on with my little girl?"

Brendan rose and shook his hand. "Brendan Corrington. We have a lot to discuss. Sir."

Brendan drove past the lumber mill that employed town folk, winding his way up the mountain road—passing the road to the lumber camp, its twenty or so loggers also employed by Ryan Cross to harvest the redwood pines on the mountains. The main house with the front office and various cabins owned and occupied by the Cross family were further up the road. Each cabin built a mile or so apart offered privacy for each family. Irelynn's cabin was the last cabin on the right. Why they called them cabins was beyond him. Some were large to accommodate growing families, and the largest was the parent's house. Finally, pulling up in front of Irelynn's cabin. A cabin in the woods didn't begin to describe the place. The oldest cabin on the property was built by Irelynn's grandfather before he had married and started a family. It was small and comfortable, six hundred square feet of rustic beauty, recently updated with modern conveniences. All meant to lure Irelynn home and keep her there.

The scent of fresh pine hung heavy in a soft breeze; Brendan watched a mama deer and her fawn cross the road. A skunk trekked through the brush on the other side of the driveway, harkening to a long-ago memory of his brothers and him getting sprayed. He could still smell the tomato juice bath they took afterward.

I'll have to ask if anyone remembers that.

Shaking his head at the memory, Brendan walked up the steps and crossed the porch; unlocking the front door, he stepped inside. A couch and two chairs sat on an oval wool rug in front of a large stone fireplace. A small kitchen was off to the left, with an updated bathroom in the far corner of the cabin. A double bed with a vibrant multicolored bedspread graced the back wall. The timbers of the walls were stained and varnished to match the high polished wood flooring. It was small, comfortable, and Brendan fell instantly in love.

He had to call Mac. Irelynn, as usual, didn't stay put. She had found a job and a place in San Francisco and was supposed to return on the weekends. She had thrown a wrench into their carefully laid plans, and he wasn't surprised.

Picking up the telephone, Brendan called the hotel Mac was staying at. Incognito as bums, Mac and his team were staking out the newspapers and places they thought Baltini would show. He was the new deputy sheriff Carson, supposedly hired to keep an eye on the mountains for someone who had been breaking into rental cabins further north. In reality, to keep an eye on Irelynn, he would do his best to stay hidden from her until the time was ripe. Sighing deeply, he knelt in front of the fireplace, intent on starting a fire to remove the chill in the air. His thoughts on amber-colored eyes looking trustingly up at him and whispers of love. Lighting the kindling, he leaned over to gently blow on the sparks. Flames greedily rose to consume the wood, reminding him of the chieftain's words.

The smallest sparks need to be fanned before you get the full flame.

"Give us a chance, Sparky."

CHAPTER 28

⁂

Stopping in town on her way up from San Francisco, Irelynn bought the necessary chemicals to set her dark room up again. Now, fresh from spending the morning playing with the littles, her nieces, and nephews. Her boxes mailed by Myron had arrived from Saigon. Irelynn opened them to see what should go to her bedroom or the darkroom. Picking up a box, she carried it to the darkroom to unpack and get to work.

After a few hours of developing the film from the plane ride home from Vietnam, Irelynn hung the last roll of negatives up to dry. Cleaning up her space first, she took a few dried photos from another line down to take a closer look at the smiling faces of returning troops. There, further back in the plane, sat a scowling soldier. Looking closer at the man,

Irelynn stumbled back and gripped the countertop behind her. Edwin Baltini. He was on that flight from Vietnam.

Shock and terror reverberated through her body, shaking her to her very core. Memories flooded her mind, and she panicked.

Gripping the doorknob and stumbling from the room, she ran through the house and out the back door. Finding a familiar path, she ran through the forest. Tripping over fallen branches, she snagged her shirt on the thick undergrowth of the pathway. Breaking into a clearing, she ran for the other side to her tree. Wide as a car, more than a hundred feet tall, it was her special place. Built into the side of the large tree was a tiny tree house with an old swing hanging from ropes below.

Sitting on the swing, she worked to slow her breathing. Pulling her feet back, she began to swing to and fro. Thoughts filled her mind about everything she had lived through since she met Rebecca and Baltini. Flying to Vietnam with them, bedding down with the troops as they fought a gruesome war. The odd feeling of sitting in a restaurant sipping wine with someone she thought was a dear friend while the war raged around them. Then finding out the woman was not who she said she was—the brothel in Hue city. And the death of a woman who sacrificed herself to save Irelynn's life. The same woman whose newborn was torn from her arms. Young Anh was ripped from her family and forced into slavery. Brendan, the man she loved and married.

It all came crashing in. Everything that she had held

inside for so long came out in deep anguished sobs. Now, Baltini was here. She knew beyond the shadow of a doubt that he would come for her, and she feared for her family and herself.

The swing creaked and groaned as she pumped her legs, arcing high into the sky. She looked up just as the old and frayed rope snapped, sending her flying out into the meadow. Landing on her bum, she flopped back to lie in the sweet grass. Looking up at the blue sky, Ralph came and laid her massive head on Irelynn's chest.

"There you are. I suppose it's a little harder to keep up with me nowadays."

She kissed the old dog's face, and Ralph licked the tears from hers in return.

That's right, girl. You've had your cry. Now you pick yourself up, and you fight.

Rising slowly, she rubbed her bruised posterior. "I've had better landings," she grumbled.

"Come on, Ralph. Let's go see if we can figure out how to find Brendan."

Brendan followed a deer path from the back of Irelynn's cabin past the grandmother's place and further down behind the parent's house to where it emptied into a large meadow. Standing in the shadows of a giant redwood, he watched Irelynn sobbing her heart out. The forest quieted as if to listen to her cries echoing across the meadow. Time seemed to stand still.

An eight-point black tailed buck on the far side lifted its majestic head and paused before sprinting and leaping across the forest floor. Brendan looked down when something nudged his hand. A large Saint Bernard, almost waist high, circled his legs, greeting him and begging for pets and belly rubs. Quietly petting the dog, he watched as Irelynn, pumping her legs, began to swing higher and higher. When the rope broke, and she sailed out into the meadow, landing in a heap of arms and legs, he started forward to see if she was injured. The dog took off from his side and went to her. Brendan breathed a sigh of relief when she reached up to pet the dog, and he stepped back into the shadows. She rose with the dog and crossed the meadow with the dog at her side.

Brendan slipped through the forest to the old tree house. As far as tree houses and swings went, it was like what he and his brothers had built as kids—an A frame roof with a platform. The only difference was the massive tree it was built into the side of, with steps up to the fort built into the tree itself. He could picture Irelynn playing as a child, far enough away from the house to give a sense of adventure, close enough to go home for lunch; looking at the swing; he gave a tug on the remaining rope with its dangling seat. It snapped and fell to the ground to thump at his feet. Shaking his head, he returned to the deer path to return to his cabin, intent on finding new rope to fix her swing before heading into town for a meeting.

Irelynn sat on her front porch next to Gramie, a stack of phone books piled between them. Brendan had once told her that he had family in the San Francisco area. Paging through the phone books for anyone with the last name of Corrington, she sighed deeply as she came up empty handed again.

Gramie took a puff of her cigar and blew a smoke ring. "Any luck getting through to your little friend?"

"Sierra." Irelynn threw her hands up in defeat. "No. Trying to get through to enlisted personnel is like swimming upstream. I'm still waiting to hear back from the Red Cross. And the phone books. Maybe once I get back to work on Monday, they will have more books for the areas surrounding San Francisco," Irelynn said.

"I'm sure he knows where you are," Gramie said.

Irelynn looked up to see a sheriff's car pass by the house, heading toward town. The man driving pulled his cowboy hat down over his face and waved as he drove by.

"Who was that driving the deputy sheriff's car? I didn't get a good look at him."

"New deputy sheriff. He's staying in your cabin," Gramie replied.

"My cabin? Why?"

"Your mother said it was to keep a closer eye on the mountain. There's been some trouble lately."

"Trouble. Here? That seems odd to me," Irelynn replied.

"Agnes saw him in town the other day. I guess he's quite the hunk of man."

Irelynn rolled her eyes. "No luring the new deputy sheriff to your cabin. He might end up throwing you and the ladies into the brig."

"Hmmm. Maybe I should make him a pie," Gramie said. "I know. It's Saturday. Let's go to town tonight. Then, maybe I can see him for myself."

"Oh no. Saturday night in a lumber town can get wild."

"Surely you've been to wilder places?"

"What about the boys? You do remember last time we went out?" Irelynn asked.

"Your brothers tend to make your social life difficult," Gramie replied.

"No kidding."

"They don't get out much anymore. Jamie and Sean, possibly. There are only Blackies and Dukes. We'll go to whichever bar they aren't at."

"Okay fine. I guess you do need a chaperone. When are you going to settle down?"

"I'll settle down when I'm dead. Until then. I'm living every day to its fullest."

Irelynn gave her an indulgent smile. "I love you, Gramie."

"I love you too, George."

Tucked into the far corner of the crowded bar, Brendan smiled at the two men waiting for him before sliding into the booth.

"Hey, Brendan. Do you want a beer?" Collin said.

"Nah. Thanks. I'm on duty," Brendan replied. "Thanks for coming. Almost didn't recognize you two with the scruffy beards."

"Itches like hell," Collin replied, scratching his black beard.

Aiden ran a hand through his beard. "My first beard. I thought it would come in thicker. Get a load of these," he said, slipping on a pair of military black rimmed eyeglasses.

Collin guffawed. "There's a reason they call those birth control."

"They aren't wrong," Aiden chuckled.

"Sorry, dude. We need to hide the family resemblance," Brendan replied. "Since Irelynn met Donall and Elijah at Treasure Island, we can't use them up here."

"Irelynn? I thought her name was George?" Collin said.

"George Irelynn Cross. Uh…Corrington," Brendan said.

"Father said we needed to look like lumberjacks. Elyse and Anablue had more fun coming up with outfits," Collin said. "It's kind of cliché. Flannel shirts and stocking caps."

Aiden snapped the straps on his shoulders. "I'm digging the suspenders."

"We met with Mac, along with Father, Elijah, Donall, Max, and the Ambassador," Aiden said.

"Capt. Jack was there too," Collin said. "Mac explained everything."

"We need lumberjacks to blend in with the crews working here. Baltini may show up here pretending to look for work," Brendan said. "We needed an additional layer of protection for Irelynn since I can't show myself yet."

"Why the deception, man? It's not like you to hide in the shadows," Aiden said.

Brendan grimaced and ran a finger along the edge of his wedding bracelet. "I'm sure Mac explained the circumstances of our wedding. I'm not trying to be a stalker here. Eventually, I'll let her know I'm here and then start slowly. I know she needs time. I want her to have a choice and protect her simultaneously."

"How will you manage her returning to San Francisco during the week?" Collin asked.

"Between the two of you to keep an eye on things here. I can follow her back and forth," Brendan replied.

"What about her brothers?" Aiden asked.

"For now, Ryan Cross Senior has asked that his sons not be involved. Good men, all of them. I guess they tend to be over protective of their baby sister," Brendan replied.

"They're going to be watching over her no matter what. Is that going to cause issues for you down the road?" Collin asked.

"Maybe. We'll see," Brendan replied.

Looking up, Brendan caught his breath. Irelynn stood in the doorway with a tiny older woman in tow. His gaze slowly slid from her shoulder length hair down to her full breasts, partially hidden by a short jean jacket, to the delicate swirl of her floral dress and combat boots.

Brendan grinned. "She's still wearing her combat boots."

Collin and Aiden gave him a questioning look, and he nodded toward the front door.

"There she is," Brendan said. "By the way. She likes tequila."

They turned to look at the beautiful woman making her way toward their side of the bar.

"She's stunning," Collin said, turning back to see Brendan was gone.

"Sneaky bastard slipped out the back door," Collin breathed.

"Drink your beer. Then we can check out our newest sister-in-law," Aiden replied, signaling for the waitress.

Nodding in greeting a few people she knew; Irelynn rolled her eyes at the outright ogling from men in the bar. Sliding into the booth, she caught her grandmother's eye.

"How I let you talk me into this is beyond me," Irelynn said.

"Nonsense. You're young and beautiful. How did you manage with all those men in Vietnam?"

"I was working. I didn't encourage it. And the one time I played with fire in a red dress, I ended up married."

"That must have been some dress," Gramie snickered.

"Oh, it was."

"You've made memories my dear. Cherish them."

"Some of them I prefer to forget."

Irelynn looked up at the waitress, who stopped to drop off two tequila shots.

"We didn't order these."

"This is why I like going out with you. Free drinks," Gramie chortled before downing her shot.

The waitress nodded toward two men sitting a few booths down from them.

"Compliments of the gentlemen."

Irelynn caught the grins of two men. *Lumberjacks. They probably work for dad.* They lifted their beers in a silent toast.

Irelynn lifted her glass to toast them back; pausing, she held her breath. Stocking caps, black beards. Broad shoulders and they appeared to be tall.

They remind me of…Brendan.

Her eyes narrowed, "Who are these guys?"

"Why don't you go find out, dear," Gramie said.

"You're right."

Setting the shot down on the table, she rose and strode over to their table.

"I don't mean to be rude, but who are you?" Irelynn demanded.

The men's eyes sparkled with amusement. "Who are you?" Aiden said.

"I asked you first," Irelynn said.

"I'm Aiden Yarusso, and this is my brother Collin."

Both men slid from the booth and stood. Irelynn's eyes widened, tilting her head back to look into their eyes. *Big. Like Brendan.*

"Are you sure? Prove it."

Aiden pulled out his wallet. "Here. Take a look at my driver's license."

Taking the offered license. In the dim light of the bar, Irelynn read his name.

"Aiden Samuel Yarusso."

Embarrassment burned her cheeks. "I'm.. um…sorry. You remind me of someone. I thought for sure you were related."

"Helluva pick up line," Aiden replied.

The other man, Collin, stifled a laugh as Irelynn glared at Aiden. "I am not trying to pick you up."

"No?"

"No," Irelynn replied. "Oh my god. You sound just like…"

"Like who?" Aiden asked.

"Never mind. I'm seeing him in every tall, dark man," Irelynn grumbled.

"Well. As long as I'm up, dance with me," Aiden said.

Irelynn looked out to the dance floor. A lively two step was in progress.

"I have no idea if my husband would approve or not," she said.

"You're married?" Aiden asked.

"Yes."

Aiden smiled. "I'm sure your husband would approve of you dancing with Collin or me."

"Fine. But your brother has to dance with Gramie."

Collin grinned. "I'd be honored." Stepping over to Gramie, he offered her his hand and escorted her to the dance floor.

"Damn. I should have warned him," Irelynn said.

"Warned him about what?"

"Gramie."

"Collin can handle one little old lady."

Irelynn's face lit up in a mischievous grin. "We'll see."

"Hmmm. Okay. Well, the Two step. Let's see if I remember my footwork. Two quick steps, two slow, lead with my left," Aiden said.

Irelynn giggled. "High school square dancing?"

"My Aunt Meg. Ruthless taskmaster," Aiden replied.

Moving to the dance floor, they blended in with other dancers.

Aiden twirled the woman in his arms before falling back into the two-step dance. He could understand Brendan's fascination with the woman despite Mac's vague explanation of the unusual circumstances of their marriage. Both he and Collin were looking forward to sitting down and hearing the whole story from Brendan.

"Why the combat boots?" Aiden asked.

"In case I need to run," Irelynn replied. "It's kind of a left-over from my work in Vietnam."

Another twirl, and they were back in step. "Vietnam. What were you doing there?"

"I'm a war correspondent. Well, I was."

"Ah, yes. I see the need for the boots."

"You would. You've got military written all over you. Your brother too."

Aiden smiled. "It's that obvious? Your right. I've been home for a few weeks."

"Where were you stationed?"

"An Khe," Brendan replied.

"Camp Radcliff. AKA, The Golf Course. I never had the pleasure of visiting," Irelynn said.

"Trust me. I would have known if you had."

Aiden looked up in time to see two large men moving through the bar heading their way.

"Oh shit!" Irelynn breathed. "Incoming."

"Who are they?"

"Two of my brothers," Irelynn said. "How many you got?"

"Five."

"Only girl?"

"Yes," Irelynn replied.

"So, you're saying this might get ugly?"

"Possibly. You and your brother are more than welcome to sneak out the back. I can handle these two."

Aiden looked her up and down in surprise. "What? You

want to protect me? You can't be more than one hundred and ten pounds soaking wet?"

Irelynn grinned. "Give or take a few," she said as she whipped around to face her brothers as Collin and Gramie came up behind them.

"Sean, Jamie. What's up?" Irelynn said. "What are you doing in here?" Sean said.

"I'm twenty-three, not sixteen. I can be in here if I want, Irelynn replied.

Sean brushed Irelynn aside, stepping in front of Aiden. "Who the fuck are you, and what are you doing dancing with my sister?" Sean said.

Collin stepped up to stand by his side and Aiden sighed deeply. *Brendan. You owe me for this.*

"Relax. It's just a dance."

"Stay away from my sister," Sean said.

Irelynn pushed her way between the men. "Back off, Sean."

Gramie slipped in front of Irelynn; reaching up, she grabbed each of Irelynn's brothers by the ear.

"What have you been told? You'll drive her away again," Gramie said, leading her grandsons away by the ears.

Irelynn turned to Aiden and Collin. "I'm sorry. They mean well."

"Does your husband know your brothers behave like this?" Collin said.

"I have no idea why I'm telling perfect strangers any of

this. Other than Gramie, no one here knows I'm married. How could I possibly subject him to this...mess?"

"I think you're not giving him enough credit," Aiden softly replied.

"I don't even know where he is or if he's forgiven me for what I did," Irelynn cried.

"What did you do?" Collin gently asked.

"I ran away from him," Irelynn whispered. "I have to go. Again, I'm sorry," she said before disappearing into the crowd.

Aiden and Collin exchanged glances.

"We've got to find Brendan. He should know about this," Aiden said.

"Yeah," Collin replied. "Nice save with the driver's license thing. I thought for sure we were busted. I'm glad you have a different last name for the first time ever."

"Yeah. Me too."

"Oh, word of warning. If you ever dance with the old lady. She's all hands."

CHAPTER 29

*L*ifting her rucksack from the front seat of her old pick-up truck, Irelynn was happy to be back in the city after her long drive from her parent's house. Smiling at Mrs. Wang's red front door, it was a welcoming sight, and Irelynn felt safe and comfortable in the big rooming house. The door opened as she reached for the doorknob. A beautiful red-headed woman stood in the doorway. "Hello. You must be Irelynn."

"Hello," Irelynn replied.

"Irelynn. Come in. We were just talking about you," Mrs. Wang called from the sitting room. Stepping into the sitting room, Mrs. Wang pointed to the beautiful blonde sitting in a chair.

"This is Anablue, and Elyse, her sister-in-law. Both, my unofficial adopted daughters."

Squeals of baby laughter echoed down the hallway from the kitchen into the foyer. A baby with thick black curls covering his head crawled into the sitting room while Mr. Wang chuckling behind him gave chase. The baby squealed again, crawling as fast as he could before climbing to stand by Mrs. Wang. Mr. Wang nodded to the women before leaving the room.

"And that little scamp is my son, Bunker," Elyse said.

"He's adorable," Irelynn said. "I'm digging the curls."

"My husband thinks it's time for a haircut," Elyse replied. "I'm not ready yet."

"We were discussing how you and I might be related," Anablue said.

"How so?" Irelynn asked.

"My paternal grandmother's maiden name was Cross. Mrs. Wang recalled that my grandmother had distant relatives near Cross Point. I'll have to run it by my dad to see if he remembers anything. His middle name is Cross," Anablue said.

"What are your paternal grandparents' names?" Mrs. Wang asked.

"Amelia and George Cross. He died young. Gramie is still with us," Irelynn said.

"If we are related, I'll call you my cousin. I've never been able to figure out that cousin's removed thing," Anablue said with a giggle.

"Wouldn't that be cool to find a long lost relative," Elyse

said. "I'm jealous. It's just my dad and me. An only son of an only son thing. Then me and Bunker."

"Bunker's an only son," Mrs. Wang said.

"Not for long," Elyse said, standing up to show her belly. "We're expecting again."

"Me too," Anablue said, standing to show her own belly bubble.

Irelynn breathed in. "I sure hope there's nothing in the water here. I'm not ready for babies."

"I understand you're a journalist," Elyse said.

"Yes. I'm currently working for the San Francisco Chronicle. I've only been back in the world for a month or so," Irelynn said.

Elyse gave her a smile. "The world. I haven't heard that term in a while."

"I'm sorry. The United States," Irelynn said.

"Oh. I know what it means," Elyse replied. "Both my husband and Anablue's are Vietnam veterans. Anablue herself is a Navy veteran."

"Being a woman, I never made it past Hawaii," Anablue said.

"I know plenty of women serving in Vietnam," Irelynn said.

"I was a mechanic working on fighter jets," Anablue replied.

"Wow. That's cool. My friends are nurses and secretaries," Irelynn said.

"It's not an easy place to live. I lived in Saigon... Bunker. Get out of Grandma Wang's yarn," Elyse cried.

Jumping to her feet, she pulled the baby away from the basket of yarn balls.

"He's always getting into his daddy's yarn, too," Elyse said. Irelynn's eyebrows shot up. "Your husband knits?"

"Elijah and all his brothers knit. They were taught by their Aunt Meg," Elyse said.

"Donall said it's calming. He just finished a beautiful blue scarf for me," Anablue said.

Irelynn's mind flashed back to the yarn in Brendan's hotel room. *Could Brendan possibly knit?* "Nah," she muttered.

"It's Bunker's naptime. I'm going to lay him down so we can leave," Elyse said. "It's Jane's, my nanny's day off, so Mrs. Wang graciously agreed to babysit."

"Irelynn. Why don't you come with us? We're going to do a little shopping and then have dinner," Anablue said.

"Yes. That's a fantastic idea," Elyse said.

"Are you sure I wouldn't be imposing?" Irelynn said.

"That's codswallop," Anablue replied.

Irelynn gave her a look of confusion. "Say what?"

"Errr... nonsense," Anablue replied.

Irelynn looked at the two excited faces in front of her. "I guess some girl time wouldn't hurt. You know you two look familiar."

Anablue rolled her eyes. "Probably because our faces were plastered all over the newspaper's front page a few weeks ago."

Irelynn chewed her lip. "Women's march. Yeah. Sorry. I took that photograph. I must say, you two were stunning."

Looking at each other, Elyse and Anablue laughed.

"I still have that photo clipping on my fridge. Elijah growls every time he looks at it. Mind you; he loves it. He just doesn't like anyone else looking at it," Elyse said, picking up the baby, she headed out to the foyer.

Irelynn watched her climb the stairs. "Let me take my things to my room."

"I can help. These stairs are cumbersome," Anablue said.

"Yeah. Four flights up. I thought I was in shape, but these stairs are something else."

"If you ever have the chance, slide down the banister. It's a blast," Anablue replied.

Mrs. Wang came out to the front foyer. "Irelynn. Before I forget again, here's a roll of film you must have dropped."

"Why, thank you," Irelynn said, dropping the film into the front pocket of her rucksack.

Twenty minutes later, purses in hand, the threesome walked out the door. Anablue paused to admire Irelynn's old truck. "Yours?"

"As long as I can keep the old girl on the road," Irelynn replied.

"She's a beauty. Treasure her," Anablue replied as they climbed into her car.

Brendan backed his bike up next to Donall's motorcycle in front of Two Belly Jack's bar. He had followed Irelynn from Cross Point and had lost her once they hit the city limits. He had no idea where she was staying within the city, and she hadn't given her parents her new address yet.

Lifting his arm to look at his watch, Mac, Donall, and Elijah were supposed to meet him at the bar. Donall and Anablue had an apartment upstairs, and he shared one across the hall with Aiden and Collin. Anablue's father, Capt. Jack owned the building and the bar below.

Pushing the heavy door to the bar open, Brendan slipped inside. Waiting for his eyes to adjust to the dim light, he spotted Mac, the twins: Elijah and Donall, and Max, another family friend sitting at the bar.

"Hey, Brendan," Elijah called out in greeting.

"Hey guys," Brendan said, sliding onto a bar stool. "Mac. Tell me some good news."

"Nothing good to share," Mac replied. "Baltini seems to have disappeared, but we believe he's now working with a few men watching Irelynn's movements."

"Irelynn? I thought her name was George?" Elijah said. "George Irelynn," Brendan replied.

Mac leaned in and whispered, "He only calls her George when she's in trouble."

"How often is she in trouble?" Donall smirked as he took a sip of his beer.

"Every day since I met her," Brendan replied, nodding his

head in thanks as Capt. Jack slid a cold beer to him. "Tell me about these men following her."

"Russians," Mac said.

"What? How do you know their Russian?" Brendan snarled.

"We have our ways. We know the Soviet Union is supplying arms, amongst other things, to North Vietnam. It's not beyond the scope that they would be involved," Mac replied. "This is way bigger than Rebecca and her bullshit. Possibly bigger than Baltini, and I still have my doubts he is who we think he is."

"Stands to reason that Irelynn has something they want," Max said.

Capt. Jack lifted a small package behind the bar and handed it to Brendan. "This arrived for you yesterday."

Brendan frowned. "A care package, here? It's from Sierra."

"Sierra? Open it," Mac said.

Brendan opened the package and pulled out a canister of mace and an envelope. Inside was his extra set of gold clusters and a note.

I thought maybe you might want your clusters. Found these in your hotel room when they swept the room clean. The mace was under the bed. It looks like the one Rebecca gave to Irelynn.

Sierra.

P.S. Tell Don Juan I will get even with him.

Mac grinned. "Ah. The wee lass misses me."

Brendan set the can of mace on the bar and handed the note to Mac.

Max reached over and picked up the can of mace. "I'm surprised civilians would have access to mace," he said.

Brendan and Mac exchanged glances. "I guess you can get anything on the black market.

Sierra said Rebecca gave it to Irelynn," Brendan replied. "I remember pulling it from Irelynn's rucksack."

"Let me see that can," Mac replied as Max handed it over.

Holding his breath as Mac examined the can, Brendan watched in fascination as he twisted the top and the can separated in two.

"Holy shit," Elijah exclaimed. "What's inside?" Donall asked.

Mac tipped the upside down and emptied the can. Holding up a reel of film, "Microfilm," he replied.

Standing abruptly, Mac strode behind the bar to hold the film up under the bar light.

"Un-fucking-believable. It's an encrypted list of some kind," Mac said.

"They're probably spies, and that can of mace is what they're looking for," Capt. Jack said.

"I could kiss Sierra for sending this. I wonder how long Irelynn carried this around for?" Brendan said.

"I'm betting it was getting too hot for Rebecca, so she gave it to Irelynn," Mac said.

"And once she was no longer useful, Baltini killed her," Brendan replied.

"These people aren't going to stop. They're desperate. None of you or your families are safe if they figure out your involvement," Max said.

Brendan rubbed his aching brow. "Okay, we have Aiden and Collin watching the lumber camp in case Baltini shows up there. The sheriff in town, Irelynn's father, and myself keeping an eye on her when she's up there. Mac and the FBI are watching her while she's working. The only thing we haven't figured out yet is where she's living."

"I'm betting she knows someone is following her," Mac said.

This back and forth between here and Cross Point is killing me. We need to keep Irelynn in one place," Brendan replied.

"It might be time to show yourself. I know from experience the more you keep from her, the madder she's going to get," Elijah said.

"I had hoped to give her the time she needed while keeping her safe," Brendan said.

"Ah, women. Can't live with them and can't handcuff them to the bed. Oh, wait. That was you," Mac snickered.

Brendan glared at Mac and growled. "Shut up, Mac."

Looking back and forth between Brendan and Mac, Donall chuckled. "Handcuffed to the bed? Oh, this we've got to hear."

"Let me make a phone call. Marchetti is back in the states. I'll have him come and pick up the microfilm," Mac replied."

"I wouldn't tell anyone what you found yet. You might

have more rats coming out of the woodwork," Capt. Jack said.

"I think you're right. I'll wait," Mac replied. "Now, I've got a doozie of a story to tell you."

"Mac, a word of warning. Remember what I said about that two-by-four? Your day is coming," Brendan hissed. "I will get even with you."

Mac grinned from ear to ear.

CHAPTER 30

San Francisco was a hotbed of activity, and Irelynn had seen it all this past week. Women's marches, civil rights, and anti-war marches. Walking backward, Irelynn lifted her camera to get a shot of the woman marching in the anti-war protest. A few thousand strong, the protesters filled Lombard Street, blocking traffic for blocks on end. Signs danced above their heads, shouting their anti-war slogans, some singing as they moved along the route. Police cars blocked intersections guiding the protestors on their way to the park, where speakers with their bullhorns would lead the people in chants against the Vietnam war.

Finding herself a little tired of the hustle and bustle of the crowd, she was jarred by an elbow to her ribs. Stepping back to stand on the sidewalk as people from all walks of life passed her by, her camera didn't stop until she ran out of film.

Turning around, she stood in front of a small café. Pulling the door open, she made her way inside to a booth. Thirsty, she needed a break and wanted to switch out the film and take a few notes. Ordering iced tea, she pulled her notebook out of her backpack. Not willing to call attention to herself, she wanted to blend in and report on the protests. She had switched to the smaller pack after being accosted for using military supplies at the last rally she had attended. A man had snarled in her face, calling her filthy names merely because she was wearing camouflage pants and carrying a rucksack. She had left him on his knees, rocking back and forth, cradling his bruised balls.

Since it was Friday, she relished the thought of spending the weekend sitting on the front porch, listening to the soul soothing quiet of the mountains. Finishing her drink, she looked up when the waitress approached the table.

"Would you like another iced tea?" the woman asked.

Glancing out the large window framed by yellow frilly café curtains. Irelynn froze. Baltini and another man stood with their backs to her scanning the crowd. Slouching down in the booth, her heart beat in a frantic staccato of terror.

Eyeing the man Baltini was with, average height, bald. She had seen him before. But where?

Damn. They've been following me. Shit. I have to get out of here.

Looking up at the waitress. "Um. No more for me. Thank you. Do you have a back door?"

"Through the kitchen," the waitress replied.

She set a ten-dollar bill on the table. "You haven't seen me," Irelynn said.

Pulling her backpack out, she crept through the restaurant and kitchen and out the back door. Running the four blocks to her truck, she chucked her bag into the front seat. Eyeing her rucksack on the floor of the cab. "I should have enough stuff for the weekend," she said. Turning the key, the grinding gears refused to turn over. Pumping the gas pedal, she prayed. "Oh, please, God, please start. Come on, baby; you can do it."

Careful not to flood the engine with gas, the engine finally turned over. With a silent prayer of thanks, she headed out of the city.

Snarling his displeasure in the face of Sergio Ivanov, Edwin Baltini shoved the man back.

"How the fuck did you lose her again?" Baltini growled.

"There're thousands of people here. The woman is puny and blends into the crowd," Sergio mumbled back. "It's how it's been all week. We lose her once the protests are over."

"The three of you are incompetent. Find Andrei and Krill. Meet me at that shit-hole hotel in an hour. I need to go check in with the boss."

"What about Vlad, Igor, and Ivan?"

"Idiot. Don't you listen to anything? I already sent them to Cross Point."

Pulling back his fist, Brendan slammed it into the face of the man shattering his nose. Blood spewed in all directions as the man flew back, landing on his back in a pile of trash. When the man didn't move, Brendan turned his attention to Mac. Making short work of the task, Mac sent the other man to land on top of the first man.

Breathing heavily, both men leaned against a car. "Damn, Brendan. It's just like the bar fights when we were younger," Mac said.

Brendan rubbed his sore jaw. "Much younger," he replied.

Shaking off the pain of his scuffed knuckles. "You're right. I'm getting too old for this shit," Mac said.

"We got lucky finding these two," Brendan replied, rolling one of the men over to retrieve his wallet before moving to the next unconscious man and opening the wallets to look at their identification. "You were right. Russians."

"You've got to admit, Donall was right. We blended right in with the protesters in these hippy clothes."

Brendan grimaced, looking down at the stars and stripes pants he was wearing. "I can't believe Donall, Elijah, and Max wore these outfits at some music festival. What was it called again?"

"Woodstock," Mac replied.

"If I wouldn't have seen Elyse's pictures. I wouldn't have believed it."

Mac grimaced. "It was funny at the time. Not so funny when I'm the one stuck wearing flower power pants."

"It's better than dressing as a dirty bum," Brendan replied. "Where's your FBI people? I want to get out of these ridiculous clothes and head north. If Irelynn is true to form, she's heading to her parents by now."

Mac waved his arm toward the two men running down the dark alley. "Here they come now. I'll go with them to haul these two dirtballs into headquarters. See if we can find out where Baltini is hiding out. Then, I'm going back to your place for a shower. After that, if you need me, I'll be at Elijah's place."

Her stomach growled in protest as Irelynn pulled into the parking lot of the Redwood Café.

"I wouldn't be stopping, but I haven't eaten all day," she growled.

Making her way inside, she sat at the counter, nodding a hello to another patron.

"Welcome back. I see you've got your own wheels," the waitress, Mona, said as she gestured out the window toward Irelynn's old truck.

"Yes. If I can keep it going," Irelynn replied.

"It's got to be better than hitchhiking."

"True."

Twenty minutes later, Irelynn bit into a juicy hamburger, dipping her fries into ketchup; she moaned in satisfaction.

"How is everything?" Mona asked.

"Wonderful. You have no idea how much I appreciate Heinz ketchup," Irelynn replied.

"Isn't it everywhere?"

"Not in Vietnam."

Finishing her meal, Irelynn paid her bill. "I'm sure I'll be back some time."

"Drive safe, sweetie," Mona replied.

Outside in her truck, Irelynn rested her head against the steering wheel in frustration. The old truck wouldn't start, and she was stuck in the middle of nowhere.

"Damn."

Walking back inside, she called to Mona. "My truck won't start. I'm going to have to hitchhike home unless you know a mechanic."

"Old Bob is the only mechanic in these parts, and he's gone to visit his daughter," Mona replied.

"Okay. I'll send a tow truck once I get home. Is it okay if I leave my keys with you?"

"Sure. You be safe out there," Mona replied.

Back at her truck, she took what she needed out of the backpack and put it in her rucksack. Hefting her rucksack over her shoulder, she started walking up the road.

His Harley ate up the miles as Brendan enjoyed the scenery along the way. The coastline faded away as he headed through the redwood forest toward the mountains. Riding along, he spotted the café where he often stopped at. Parked right out front was Irelynn's truck.

Pulling into the parking lot, he parked next to her truck. Climbing off his bike, he looked in the passenger window and spotted the backpack on the cab floor. He looked in the window of the café and didn't see her sitting inside. With a deep breath, he pulled open the door and strode inside.

Spotting the waitress, "The woman driving that truck. Where is she?"

"She left about an hour ago. The truck wouldn't start. She said she was going to hitchhike the rest of the way home," Mona replied.

"Damn it. Doesn't she realize how dangerous that is?"

"She doesn't seem to worry about it. She's going to send a tow truck when she gets home. I have her keys."

"Hmm. Do you have a telephone?"

"The payphone is right outside," Mona replied.

"I'm going to call a tow truck now and have it hauled to my brothers. I know a good mechanic," Brendan replied.

"Okay, mister. The only reason I'm agreeing is because of your bracelet. It matches the one she wears."

Brendan smiled. "She's still wearing it?"

"Yeah. You're her husband?"

"Yes."

"If you hurry, you might catch her on the road before someone else picks her up."

"That's what I'm afraid of," Brendan replied.

Back outside, he made a call to Elijah to arrange the tow truck; jumping on his bike, he headed north.

Passing the occasional car, he slowed to look the passengers over to ensure she wasn't in the car. The semi-trucks were a little more challenging. He passed one on the soft right shoulder of the road in a dangerous move. The passenger turned out to be a big shaggy dog. He throttled up to pass the truck, and the wide-open road was ahead. Cresting a hill, he rode until he spotted her walking on the side of the road. Icey rage at her recklessness slid into pleasure at finding her on the lonely windswept road. He smiled as a shiver ran down his spine.

Consider yourself caught, George.

CHAPTER 31

She heard the rumbling of the motorcycle before she saw it. Turning, Irelynn walked backward, sticking her thumb out, smiling from ear to ear when the motorcycle pulled over. Running up to where the motorcycle waited for her. She paused to look at the biker, A big man, dressed in black from his boots to the leather jacket. A black helmet covered his head, the visor hiding his facial features.

"Thanks for stopping," Irelynn said. "I'm heading to Cross Point."

The man merely nodded and handed her a spare helmet to put on. Strapping the helmet on, making sure the rucksack was snug on her back, she climbed on the bike. The man pointed to the muffler, indicating it was hot.

Nodding at the man. He held her gaze in the mirror for a minute before she shyly wrapped her arms around his waist.

A semi passed them with a haunting wail of its horn, and the bike pulled out onto the open road heading toward the snowcapped mountains in the distance.

Thrilling, exhilarating. Irelynn had never experienced a motorcycle ride, and she loved the wind on her face through the thick pine forest on the long winding road. She held tightly to the dark stranger; his aftershave of woodsy spice and warm earth drifted back, reminding her of Brendan. Tears filled her eyes as she leaned into the man.

Where are you, my love? Do you still think of me?

Clearing her throat and blushing profusely, she leaned back to allow the man his personal space.

Looking down at the arms wrapped around his waist, Brendan smiled at the wedding bracelet visible on her tiny wrist; her fingernails trimmed short, painted a pale pink.

A glance in the rear-view mirror, and from one angle, he could see her leg, the wind from the highway blowing her dress in a teasing show of creamy thigh. Sighing deeply, he tried to remain focused on the road with an occasional glance in the mirror.

Leaning into the final switchback before the town. The sun was setting, the road curvy and dangerous, just like Irelynn. She snuggled into his back, and he realized she had to be cold. That sweet little sundress and thin jean jacket were not enough to keep her warm on a cold mountain. Brendan grinned as Irelynn gripped her thighs against his, raised her arms, and whooped.

He had to agree with her; the switchbacks were his favorite part of the ride. Rumbling into town, they passed a couple of lumberjacks leaning on their car in front of the pizza parlor.

Brendan nodded at Aiden and Collin, their curious eyes taking in the woman on the back of his bike as he slowly passed them. A few minutes later, they pulled up in front of her parent's house.

Irelynn climbed off her bike and removed her helmet. "Thank you for the…" She stopped as he paused before pulling his helmet off.

Her eyes widened, and she jumped back. "Brendan," she whispered.

"George. You've got a lot to answer for," Brendan said, climbing off the bike. Standing in front of her, he reached out to stroke her cheek.

Irelynn stuttered, "I…um… well," she said, her eyes closing; she leaned into his hand, feeling his touch.

Her mother's voice came from inside the house, "Irelynn, is that you?"

She slapped his hand down and scrambled away from him; panic filled her eyes. "They don't know about you," she whispered. "I mean, Gramie does, but no one else."

"Still the coward. Very well. I'll keep your little secret. For now," Brendan whispered back.

The screen door opened, and Rachel and Gramie stepped out on the porch.

"Thank goodness your home. I was getting worried," Rachel said. "Oh, Deputy Carson, how nice to see you again."

"Mrs. Cross. Gramie. The pleasure is all mine. By the way, thank you for the apple pie Gramie."

The older woman's keen eyes flickered back and forth between him and Irelynn with interest.

"You're welcome, deputy," Gramie replied.

Brendan eyed Irelynn as dawning at Gramie's familiarity entered her eyes. Her eyes narrowed, and she glared at him.

"What's going on?" Rachel said.

"Oh. My truck broke down. *Deputy Carson* was kind enough to bring me home," Irelynn gritted out.

"How nice. Thank you for that," Rachel said.

"Yes. Thank you, Deputy Carson," Irelynn said.

"It was my pleasure, Miss Cross," Brendan replied.

He nodded to Rachel and Gramie, "Ladies. Goodnight."

Pulling his helmet on, he climbed on his bike. Chuckling to himself, he pulled away and headed up the road to his cabin.

Irelynn watched for a minute as he made his way up the mountain road before he disappeared around a curve in the road. Whipping around.

"Mom, where is he staying?"

"I thought Gramie told you. He's staying in your cabin."

"How long has he been in my cabin?"

"Since a couple of weeks after you came home from Vietnam," Rachel replied.

"He's been here pretty much the whole time," Irelynn muttered.

"I'm sorry; what did you say?" Rachel said.

"Nothing, mom."

"Come inside, Irelynn. It's getting cold. I've got a nice plate of meatloaf warming in the oven for you."

Irelynn smiled, "Heinz ketchup?"

"It's the only ketchup you let me buy. It's baked in on the top. Just the way you like it."

"Sounds good to me. I had a burger, but I can eat again," Irelynn said as she turned to look back up the road.

"Hurry up. Lawrence Welk is starting soon," Gramie said.

Grinning, Irelynn looped her arms through Gramie's and her mom's.

"Have I told you two lately how much I love you?"

Exhausted after her long day, Irelynn had abandoned a night of television in favor of a good night's sleep. Her body flushed with need; memories of her last night in Da Nang filled her with longing for the touch of his hands, whispered kisses, and the way he tasted when his mouth consumed hers. Sleep was impossible.

She pulled Brendan's shirt out from under her pillow. Hugging it to her breast, she inhaled the faint smell of him. The same scent she smelled on the back of his bike. She should have known it was him.

"This is ridiculous. He's right up the road." Feeling foolish, she stuffed the shirt back under the pillow.

"I wonder what he would say if I showed up at his door. Just to talk, of course."

Throwing the covers back, she threw a flannel shirt on over her nightgown and slipped into her combat boots. Tiptoeing to the door, she opened it a crack. The television blared a performance on the Lawrence Welk show, and Ralph slept on the floor in front of her door. "Damn," she muttered. Silently shuting the door, she opened a dresser drawer pulling out a flash- light. Turning it on, she smacked the bottom several times to ensure it worked. Creeping to the window, she lifted the sash and slid out the window. Landing on her feet, she crept past open windows to the pathway behind the house.

The darkness and shadows of the forest surrounded her. The meager light of the flashlight lit her way as she ran up the familiar path. Coming to a fork in the path, one way led to her tree house swing in the meadow, the other to Grammie's place and her cabin beyond. The brush moved with all manners of nightlife. Climbing over fallen trees, the forest echoed with the hoot of an owl.

She was transported back to Vietnam for a moment as memories of long dark nights bedded down with the troops froze her in place. A small fox scampered across the path, reminding her she was on her beloved mountain.

There's no VC or troops here, just the forest creatures.

The dried pine needles and cones crackled beneath the weight of a larger animal. Spinning around, her flashlight stopped on the dog, Ralph. "You snuck out too? Okay, girl, come on."

She made it to the back of her cabin in ten minutes. She slipped around the front, climbing the steps to the front porch. She signaled to the dog to stay on the porch.

Raising her hand to knock on the door, Irelynn questioned her sanity. Taking a deep breath, she lightly knocked. "It's just to talk," she said.

CHAPTER 32

Relaxed after a hot shower, Brendan rubbed the towel over his hair one last time before pulling on pajama bottoms. A knock sounded at the door, and he threw the towel on the bed before padding softly to the door. Expecting it to be Aiden and Collin, he was surprised to see Irelynn standing in the meager light on the front porch.

"Irelynn."

He looked out to the gravel driveway and only saw his Harley and the police car. His brow lowered, "How did you get here?"

"I came through the woods. I...wanted to talk," Irelynn replied.

Brendan pulled the door open more. "Come in."

She held his gaze as she slipped inside. Wrapping her arms around herself, she looked around the room. "I see they made a few improvements," she said. Her eyes were on him as he strode over to the kitchen table. Picking up a bottle of brandy, he poured a finger full into two glasses. Handing her a glass, "It's a nice little cabin," Brendan replied.

"Why are you here, Irelynn?"

"Why am I here." She turned and ran her hand over an Afghan blanket folded over the back of the couch. "I crocheted this blanket. It was my first and only attempt. I'm here because I wanted to apologize."

"For?"

"Everything. For forcing myself onto your firebase, for running away from you. The last time, I wanted to return as soon as the plane took off. And for…falling asleep in your arms."

"You didn't fall asleep. You were drugged. We both were."

"Drugged? How?"

"The spaghetti."

"The strange aftertaste. I only had a few bites," Irelynn said. "It was enough," Brendan replied. "Did it not occur to you why I didn't wake up? I'm a Green Beret. I should have woken

up the second you moved from the bed."

"I did think it was odd. Who and why did they drug me?"

"Baltini and Rebecca, along with the VC. They tried to kidnap you. Mac stopped them. You had something they wanted."

"Had?"

Brendan's eyes never left her as she moved about the

cabin. Her eyes caught and held his before a deep blush stained her cheeks. She stopped in front of the bed before sharply turning away.

"You're not going to tell me what I had. Are you?" Irelynn said.

"It's no longer important. You don't have it anymore."

"Baltini is here. He was on the plane. I didn't know it until I processed the film from photos I took on the plane. And he and some men were following me in San Francisco."

"I know," Brendan replied.

"Is that why you're here?"

"Part of it."

"And the other?"

"You."

"Me?"

Brendan strode over to stand in front of her. Looking down into her shining amber eyes, he reached out to stroke the smooth skin of her cheek. "Yes. It's all about you, George." She closed her eyes and leaned into his hand. His thumb stroked her full lips before trailing down her shoulder.

"George? So, I'm still in trouble?" she murmured.

"There's still the little matter of handcuffing me to the bed and stealing my last shirt."

A soft chuckle escaped her lips. "Oops."

His finger moved down her chest to the curve of her full breast. With a groan, he pulled her into his arms. His mouth came crashing down on hers as he devoured her lips like a man long denied. His hands gripped the curve of her bottom, and he pulled her tight to his groin. She mewled like a kitten in his arms, her soft moans fueling the fire burning in his blood.

Pushing the flannel shirt and spaghetti straps of her nightgown down her shoulders. His hands caressed the swell of her breasts, placing gentle kisses in the hollow of her throat. His tongue followed, dipping and swirling around each curve until he captured a pink crest in his mouth. His lips never left hers as he lifted her in his arms, carrying her to his bed.

A knock sounded at his door, and he groaned; she cursed softly as he lifted his head at the insistent knocking. Flinging himself from the bed, Irelynn scrambled from the other side.

Striding to the door, he flung it open. "What?"

Seeing Aiden and Collin standing at the door, pizza boxes in hand. He snatched the pizza from Collin's hands and slammed the door shut. Through the door, he heard Collin exclaim.

"Did that bastard just steal my pizza's?"

Turning around, the window on the back of the cabin was wide open, and Irelynn was gone. Sighing deeply, he opened the door to see his brothers still standing there.

"Was wondering if I had to break down the door to get my pizza back," Collin snarled.

Aiden nodded his head toward the dog lying on the porch. "Whose dog is that?"

Brendan looked at the Saint Bernard, who lifted her head at a soft whistle from the woods and took off into the forest.

"Irelynn's," Brendan replied.

Aiden and Collin exchanged amused glances. "Sorry, dude."

Brendan grunted, opening the door further. "You assholes might as well come in now."

Aiden and Collin grinned. "Ah. Brotherly love," Aiden said. Brenden set the pizza on the table before going to the open window. Leaning out the window, he peered into the dark forest, looking for Irelynn.

Behind him, Aiden and Collin made themselves at home at the table; opening the pizza box, they argued about the difference between the pizza cut into triangles or squares.

"You two have piss poor timing," Brendan growled.

"We thought you'd be hungry, and we have news for you," Aiden replied.

"Two men rolled into town this morning. Applied for jobs as lumberjacks, then disappeared into the mountain," Collin said.

"Mac and I made short work of two men in San Francisco today. That makes four plus Baltini," Brendan said.

Another knock sounded at the door. "What the hell is this, Grand Central Station?" Brendan growled before opening the door. Sheriff Griffith and Ryan Cross stood on his porch.

"Sir. Barney. Come in," Brendan said.

"Evening. I thought you should know. Just had two more men roll through town," Barney said.

"We followed them but lost them in the dark on the mountain," Ryan said.

"Shit," Brendan growled. "That makes four up here, possibly more that we don't know about."

"We need more men," Aiden said.

"Mac's going to want to leave his men in San Francisco to hunt for Baltini," Collin said.

"We can bring up Elijah, Donall, Max, and Mac to hunt for the men up here, one of which may be Baltini," Brendan said.

"I think it's time to involve my boys," Ryan said. "Any city boy you bring up here will get lost on the mountain. My boys can act as guides."

Brendan grinned. "City boys. We're all Vietnam veterans. But having guides is a great idea."

"We'll leave you boys to enjoy your pizza now. Let me know when your men arrive," Sheriff Griffith said.

"I'll call them in the morning and have everyone here by afternoon, Brendan said.

"Good enough. Goodnight, boys," Ryan replied as they left.

"What are you going to be doing during all of this?" Collin asked.

"I'm going to be sticking to Irelynn like glue," Brendan replied.

"In more ways than one," Aiden snickered.

Brendan looked at the near empty pizza box and glared at his brothers. "Did you assholes leave me any?"

Collin grinned and turned the box to Brendan. "You know us, Corrington boys. We live off of pizza."

Standing below the window listening to the conversation in the cabin. Irelynn inhaled sharply. *Corrington boys. I knew it. Dad and the sheriff too. What the hell is going on?* Petting Ralph's massive head, the dog licked her hand. Kissing the dog on top of her head. Deep in thought, she moved down the path, turning the flashlight to light the way; she came across a big pile of bear scat. Knowing it was better to know what was in the forest with you, she took a stick and poked at the scat. The smell of pepper wafted up. Grizzly bear. *Damn. Big Ben is back.* On the alert, she shivered in fear and looked around the forest. "Come on, Ralph, it's not safe out here. Let's get home," she whispered, grateful for the tinkling bell on the dog's collar.

CHAPTER 33

*E*lyse Corrington scowled up at her husband. "Seriously, Elijah. Tell me again why I have to stay here?"

"Don't argue with me, Elyse. You and Anablue are both pregnant. You will be fine here with Jane and Bunker. Father and your dad should be back from their vacation tomorrow night. Capt. Jack is picking them up at the airport and bringing them here," Elijah said, pulling his pouting wife into his arms.

Donall hefted his bag into the trunk of Elijah's Camaro. "He's right. I see no reason for you or Anablue to take any risks. I can't think of how either of you would be of any help to Brendan or George." Stroking Anablue's soft cheek. "George's truck will be delivered here this afternoon. Other than it won't start, I'm not sure what's wrong with it, but I'm sure you want to get right on it."

Anablue made a face, "But..."

"No buts. You stay here," Donall warned.

"Can't we at least toss the coin?"

"No."

"Bumfuzzle," Anablue said as she turned around to look at Mac and Max loading their bags into the car.

Mac grinned down at Anablue. "Another wee one. It's nice to meet you, Anablue."

Anablue's brow dropped, and she narrowed her gaze at him. "Weren't you the bum who showed up at our wedding?"

Mac chuckled. "You shouldn't have been able to recognize me."

"That's codswallop. Who could miss those green eyes?" Anablue replied.

"What the hell does codswallop mean?"

"I'm not telling you," Anablue replied.

Max chuckled and leaned into Mac. "Nonsense."

Mac let out a chuckle. "Brendan is right. It's the wee ones who are the most trouble."

"We hardly know anything about George. What's she like?" Anablue asked.

"She keeps Brendan on his toes. She's tenacious, and not much scares her," Mac replied.

"Is she tall or short?" Elyse said. "Blonde or brunette. Is she nice?"

"Maybe a couple of inches taller than you. She's a bit of a spitfire, like you," Mac said.

"Brendan said your Sierra is small too," Donall said.

"Who's Sierra?" Elyse and Anablue said at once.

Mac held his hands up. "Whoa. Stop right there. You two are like dogs going after meat. I'm not telling you a damn thing. Before I know it, you'd have me trussed up and delivered to the altar. I'm never falling in love and never getting married."

"Never say never," Anablue replied.

Elyse giggled. "The bigger they are, the harder they fall. I look forward to dancing at your wedding."

"Quit jinxing me," Mac growled.

"Jinxing you? Yes, I'm guilty of wanting you to find toe curling, gut wrenching, love so deep you can't sleep and wonder how you'd survive without that person. In turn, she would feel just as intensely about you," Elyse replied. "Oh, and at least a dozen little gingers at your feet."

"A dozen? Argh," Mac groaned.

"Quit picking on Mac. We need to leave," Elijah chuckled.

"Okay. Half dozen," Elyse whispered.

Max yelled up the stairs to the apartment above the garage. "Hey, legs. I'm leaving."

"Legs?" Donall asked.

Max grinned. "New nickname for Jane. Sinful. Wicked long legs," he said, his face flushed with pleasure as he watched Jane rushing down the stairs to kiss him.

Mac and Max climbed into the car as Donall and Elijah pulled their wives into their arms and kissed them goodbye.

"Kiss Bunker for me when he wakes from his nap," Elijah said. "Behave and stay put."

Elyse grunted in response. "No promises."

Elyse, Anablue, and Jane frowned as the car pulled out of the driveway.

"I don't like this one bit," Anablue said.

"Stay put, my ass," Elyse said. "Since when have I ever stayed put?"

"I made brownies to cheer us up," Jane said.

"Brownies. God, I love you," Elyse replied. "Come on. Let's have some lemonade to go with those brownies. There's nothing we can do until the baby wakes up."

An hour later, a tow truck pulled into the driveway with an old truck in tow. Anablue, Jane, and Elyse went out to greet the driver. Once the driver dropped the truck and left, Anablue walked around the truck in confusion.

"Elyse. This truck. I've seen it before."

"Where?"

Anablue's big blue eyes widened. "Mrs. Wang's driveway. This is Irelynn's truck. I'm sure of it."

"Irelynn. Isn't that your new friend?" Jane said.

"Yes. She's renting my old room at Mrs. Wangs," Anablue

replied. "We've been out to dinner and shopping with her a few times."

"She's a lovely girl," Elyse replied.

"Elijah and Donall both said the truck belonged to George, Brendan's wife," Anablue said.

"Elijah hasn't shared much about what's going on, but I know Brendan's been trying to figure out where George was living in the city," Elyse said.

"I guess she works at a newspaper," Anablue said. "Irelynn said she took that newspaper photograph of us."

The three women ran toward the house; they scrambled into the kitchen and pulled the newspaper photo off the fridge.

"There, bottom right. Photograph by George I. Cross," Elyse cried.

"I feel like a nincompoop. Irelynn is George," Anablue replied.

Elyse tapped a finger on her cheek. "Hmmm. How can we use this to justify heading up north?"

"Get that idea out of your head. It's not enough to defy the men and head up to Cross Point," Jane said.

"Bumfuzzle. I suppose it's nice to know information, but not need to know. I mean, we could share it in a phone call," Anablue said.

"Damn. Why do you have to be so levelheaded?" Elyse replied.

"I'd rather not worry about being able to sit down for a week," Anablue said.

"True," Elyse giggled, "but I bet the sex afterward is fantastic."

Jane rolled her eyes. "I'm going to start dinner. Hamburgers okay with you?"

Elyse sighed deeply, "I guess we're stuck here. Yeah, hamburgers are fine."

Later that evening, Elyse yawned and stood up. "I'm going to bed."

"Yeah, I might as well head to bed too. Goodnight," Jane said, letting herself out.

Elyse pulled a blanket from the back of the couch and covered Anablue up before heading to the bathroom. When she came out, she saw that Anablue had moved to the bedroom. A light knock sounded at the front door.

Elyse opened the door. "What did you forget?" She jumped back in fright. A bald man held a gun to Jane's head.

"Oh shit," Elyse said as the man signaled for her to back up.

Elyse narrowed her eyes and raised her chin. "What do you want? We don't have any money."

"We're not interested in your money. We're looking for a friend of yours," he replied.

"Who?"

"Irelynn Cross," the man replied.

"Irelynn's not here," Elyse replied, eyeing the man; she moved back to give herself room.

"No. But you're going to help us find her and return what belongs to us."

"I don't know where she is," Elyse said.

"Let me correct myself. We know where she is. We're going to make a little trade. You ladies for Irelynn and our property," he said.

Elyse had maneuvered herself in a half circle, the man now standing in the kitchen.

"I don't fucking think so," Elyse snarled. A nod to Jane, and Jane pulled her elbow back and into the man's stomach. The gun clattered across the floor, and the man backhanded Jane and sent her flying to land on the table. Elyse, a blackbelt in karate, made short work of him as another man burst through the back door. The second man hit Elyse with a meaty fist; turning, he punched Anablue in the face as she came out of the bedroom. She flew backward into the sink and counter. Anablue picked up a cast iron frying pan soaking in the sink. Soup, the dog, jumped, sinking his teeth into the man's balls. The man screamed as Anablue swung as hard as she could, hitting the man across his head with the pan; he crumpled to the floor with a groan.

Anablue dropped the pan and went to the floor to clutch at Elyse and Jane. "Oh my God," she cried. "Elyse, Jane, are you alright?"

Elyse sat up and winced at her sore jaw. "I think so." Soup crawled into her lap and licked her face. "Good boy. You did exactly as I trained you." The baby wailed from the bedroom. "Oh, God. The baby." Elyse scrambled to her feet and ran to the bedroom. Bunker sat in the crib crying with tears rolling down his face. Elyse snatched him from the crib, clutching him to her breast; she cried. "We need to get out of here. Jane, pack what you can for the baby. Anablue, find purses and keys. We're leaving before those men wake up."

Five minutes later, Jane clutched the baby, Elyse with a gun in hand, Anablue with the frying pan, and Soup all crept to Anablue's car. Climbing in, they silently rolled out of the drive-way, not turning on headlights until they were well past the property.

Anablue flipped down the visor and looked at her face in the mirror. "Great. My right eye is swollen shut, and my face looks like…ugh."

Elyse looked in her mirror. "What a pair we are. My left eye is not good."

"You should let me drive," Jane urged from the backseat.

"Not with those ribs. Between our two good eyes, we should make it to Cross Point in no time," Anablue replied.

"What are we going to do when we get there?" Jane asked.

"Find a motel, I suppose. We've got time to devise a plan," Elyse replied as she tucked the blanket around the baby nestled to her breast.

CHAPTER 34

*B*rendan parked his police car in front of Ryan's open garage. Turning at approaching footsteps, Brendan watched as Ryan Cross entered the garage. His eyes fell on maps of Europe, the Middle East, and Asia pinned side by side on the far wall. Green, Red, and yellow stick pins dotted the maps, and postcards from exotic destinations were strategically placed, showing a trail of travel across the world.

"Good morning," Brendan said.

"Morning," Ryan replied. "I see you found Irelynn's wanderlust map."

"Wanderlust."

"She had an itch to see the world."

Ryan stepped up to the map. "The green pins are from her first backpacking trip across Europe. She went with a college friend the summer between her junior and senior years. She saw it all—Spain, France, Italy, etc. The red pins are from her solo trip on the hippy trail after she graduated. They end in Istanbul when she went missing. The yellow pins are where she was supposed to go after Istanbul. I recently added a map of Vietnam to figure out where she was when she was there."

"I can add a few pins there," Brendan said. "Saigon." Brendan pushed a red pin into place. "She had an apartment above a family run grocery store. Da Nang, she had lots of friends there. The Rock, up by the DMZ. Hue city, Vung Tao. Here," he pushed another red pin into place, "My firebase in the central highlands. Everywhere she went, she proved her mettle under the most difficult of circumstances. I think you'd be amazed at her drive and tenacity."

"I suppose it's my fault in a way. I always had wanderlust. I talked about places I wanted to see and experience. But because of responsibilities, I never left Cross Point other than..."

Brendan raised a brow. "Other than?"

"Never mind. It's not important. I had always hoped one of my boys would get out there and see the world. I never expected it from my little girl. I was probably a bit sexist in my attitude. Though, I should've known better. Irelynn comes from a long line of strong independent women."

"I'm probably as guilty as you are," Brendan said. "I've learned a lot about women lately."

"I worry about what she's seen."

"I'm not going to lie to you. She's seen plenty. It's one of the reasons I objected to a woman in the field."

"What are you to Irelynn?"

"I think that Irelynn would want..."

"I can answer that." Both men turned to see Irelynn standing in the garage. She walked in and stood in front of Brendan.

"Brendan's last name isn't Carson. It's Corrington, and so is mine. Brendan is my... husband."

Ryan looked back and forth between the two of them. "You're married? Your mother was right. She said there was something between you two."

"Um. I have some wedding pictures here. I was coming to talk to you." Irelynn said, handing a few pictures to Ryan.

Brendan smiled as she looked up at him. "Mac must have grabbed my camera and snapped a few shots. I didn't know we had pictures until I developed the roll this morning."

Reaching down, Brendan squeezed her hand. "I'm glad you're here," she whispered.

"Me too," Brendan replied.

Ryan looked at the pictures, opened his mouth, and then snapped it shut. "These are the strangest wedding pictures I've ever seen."

"There's a problem with the legality of the marriage since we both thought it was a friendship ceremony, not a wedding. Though, it is recognized by the church," Brendan said.

"Maybe we can sit down with Father Jacobs," Irelynn said.

"He retired. We have a new priest. A former Marine

Chaplain, newly retired from the military. I think he just returned from Vietnam. Father Andrews," Ryan said.

Brendan grimaced, "Oh shit."

"Is that the same Father Andrews we know?" Irelynn asked.

"Possibly. If it is… he's not too happy with the Corrington's right now."

"Why?" Ryan said.

"He was my boyhood priest. He recently officiated at my brother's wedding. He wasn't too thrilled when he ended up knocked into the San Francisco Bay with the rest of us," Brendan replied.

"Who would knock a priest into the bay?" Ryan asked.

"A sea lion."

"I think there's a whole lot more to that story," Ryan said.

Brendan grinned. "Oh yeah."

Rachel opened the door into the garage. "Irelynn. There you are. You have a phone call."

"Please don't tell mom about Brendan. I want to tell her myself," Irelynn said as she went inside.

"I stopped by to tell you all of my brothers are at the lumber camp. They arrived last night," Brendan said.

"My wife will be gone all day. We can have Irelynn spend the day with Gramie. Sheriff Griffith can keep an eye on them. You should spend some time on the mountain today to see what we're up against."

Brendan sighed deeply, "As much as I don't like it, you're right."

"Okay, let's find my boys and get started. Find those men hiding in my mountains," Ryan replied.

Irelynn chewed her lip as she pulled Gramie's Fifty-Seven Fairlane convertible behind the motel outside town. Lifting the bag of medical supplies from the backseat, she looked around to see if anyone was watching before she ran around to knock on the motel door. The door crept open an inch, and Irelynn found herself yanked into the room and pulled into a warm embrace.

"Irelynn. Thank God you're alright," Elyse said.

"Yeah. I'm okay. What happened to you?" She looked at Anablue standing nearby and the woman sitting on the bed playing with the baby and a small dog. "You all look worse than my brothers after a bar fight."

Irelynn pulled Anablue into a hug. "What's going on?"

Elyse went to the windows, lifted the blinds, she peeked outside.

"We were attacked in my home by two men looking for you.

Oh, this is Jane," Elyse said.

"Hi, Jane. It's nice to meet you. Looking for me?"

"Yes. You have something of theirs, and they want you."

"Baltini and his men," Irelynn said. "They were following me yesterday while I was working an anti-war march. I'm confused. How would they know anything about you or where you live?"

"We were discussing that on our drive up. We think they followed Mac," Anablue said.

"Mac? My friend Mac? Big red-head, fake Irish brogue, a girl in every port, Mac?"

Elyse grinned. "Yup. That's our Mac. Sit down, George."

"How do you know my name is George?"

Anablue and Elyse smiled. "Welcome to the family. George. Irelynn. Corrington."

Irelynn's mouth dropped open. "How do you know about Brendan?" she whispered.

Elyse picked through the paper bag and pulled out the ace bandages. "Come on. Help me wrap Jane's ribs; she's in a lot of pain. We'll explain everything we know. Which, thanks to the men. Isn't much."

An hour later, Irelynn peeked out the window. "I should find Brendan; let him know what happened."

"Uh, no. We don't want the men to know we're here. Please don't judge us. It's not like we're setting out to deceive our husbands. They would agree that we're right to leave the house, but if they saw the condition we're in," Elyse's voice trailed off.

"They would be distraught and distracted from finding the bad guys. And above all else, we want them caught and for you to be safe," Anablue said.

"But wouldn't Brendan keep your secret?" Irelynn asked. "You tell one, you tell all. Brendan would never keep it from his family," Elyse said. "Besides all that, I don't relish being confined to quarters. We can help them; they will never even know we're here."

"We have to hide you. This is a small town. It's probably already going around that three beat up women, a baby, and a dog are staying here. We need help, and Jane needs a doctor. Irelynn said. "Where's your car?"

"Behind the motel," Anablue said.

"Gramie's waiting for me at Nan's café. I'll be back in an hour. The sheriff has been following us, so we'll have to be careful," Irelynn said.

"I'm sure we can sneak past him," Elyse replied.

"We'll come down after dark and move your car behind Gramie's cabin," Irelynn said.

"It's a good plan. Seriously. What could go wrong?" Elyse said.

Jane chuckled from the bed. "Ah. Everything."

"Then what?" Irelynn asked.

Elyse shrugged her shoulders.

"He's going to kill me," Irelynn whispered.

Elyse rolled her eyes. "That's my line, and it's only if we get caught."

Late September was chilly on the mountain; the thin nightgowns the women escaped with their lives in weren't enough to keep them warm. Other than the bag packed for the baby, they had no clothes. With Gramie's help, she found a few things for Anablue and Elyse at home. But they needed pants for their growing bellies, and Jane was tall, slender, and another story altogether.

Irelynn looked around the small clothing store, looking for something for all three to wear. Flipping through the maternity pants on the rack, she pulled out two pairs of jeans. Bra's, panties, packs of warm socks, tee shirts. Jeans and new boots for Jane were piled high in the cart. She had soft, barely worn flannel shirts, sweaters, and hiking boots plucked from the goodwill bag in the car.

Standing in the check-out line while the clerk rang up her purchases, Irelynn inwardly seethed at the nosy curiosity of the clerk. The woman eyed her empty ring finger and the maternity pants.

"News to share, Irelynn?"

She gave the woman a tight smile. "Nope. They're for a friend. I'm not expecting."

Paying for her purchases, she scrambled from the store. Throwing her bags in the back seat, she backed out of the parking spot with a squeal of tires. *Damn. Guaranteed, mom will know about this by the time I sit down for dinner.*

By late afternoon the women were settled at Gramie's. The doctor, one of Gramie's former lovers, had gone. The baby played with blocks while Soup and Ralph were deep in the throes of love. Ralph licked Soup's face while the women looked on.

"I think it's cute the way you named her Ralph," Elyse said.

Irelynn giggled, "At the time, I figured as long as I had a boy's name, my puppy could too."

"There's that new song by Johnny Cash, "A boy named Sue." I don't see anything wrong with a girl named George," Anablue said.

"Soup doesn't seem to mind her name is Ralph," Jane said.

"Now, Soup. That's a strange name for a dog," Gramie said. "Arnold named him after he rescued him from the cooking pot," Elyse replied.

"Eww," Gramie said.

"You'd be surprised what people will eat when they're hungry," Elyse said.

"Yeah. Thanks to the Chieftain, I've eaten my share of snake and tiger penis soup," Irelynn said.

Elyse's eyes widened, "Did you just say The Chieftain?"

"Yeah, why?"

"The old Montagnard Chieftain that fought the VC and NVA with Brendan?" Elyse asked. "Looks like he's one hundred years old?"

Irelynn nodded her head.

"That old man wanted Brendan and Elijah to trade me for goats and chickens."

"No way," Irelynn replied.

"Not they would have. But they thought it was pretty

funny. I was outraged at the thought of it," Elyse said, raising her chin a notch.

"It's the bride price," Irelynn said. "That Chieftain was responsible for marrying us."

"Wait. You didn't have a traditional wedding?" Anablue asked.

Irelynn shook her head and reached for her backpack; pulling out her wedding photographs, she handed them to Anablue and Elyse. "I probably should explain this whole part," Irelynn said. "Wow. These pictures are cool. And that red dress…killer," Anablue said, handing the pictures to Jane and Gramie.

"We're listening," Elyse said.

With dinner out of the way and the baby soundly sleeping, Elyse crept from the guest bedroom; quietly pulling the door shut, she crossed the spacious living room to stand before the giant picture window. She gasped at the breathtaking view of the mountain as the sun set behind it.

"It's beautiful, isn't it," Irelynn said behind her.

"I've never seen so many colors in the sky at once. And the snow-peaks are stunning.

"That's Sugar Mountain in front of you. Behind us is Spice Mountain."

"Sugar and Spice?"

"I'm not supposed to know it, but my grandfather named them after Gramie's breasts."

"That's romantic to have mountains named after your breasts," Elyse said.

"Some people would say it's sexist. But it still makes her smile, so who gives a damn what they think."

"I agree. Life is what you make of it. Both you and Brendan deserve to be happy."

"He does make me happy. We still have a lot to learn about each other. I figure it doesn't matter if you're with someone for ten years or ten weeks. You're still going to have to work together," Irelynn said.

"It's hard work. I've only been married for a year, Anablue, for a few weeks. And Jane, her marriage was a disaster. What I'm trying to say is that it doesn't matter the circumstances of how you ended up married. It's what you put into it. Besides, if you and Brendan are still worried about the legality of your marriage, do it again. Nothing is saying you can't still have the wedding of your dreams, whatever that may be."

"That's a good idea. I planned on sitting down and spending time with my mom tomorrow. I think she would enjoy planning a wedding. I told my dad about Brendan today. He was surprisingly calm about it. I'm not sure why I was so afraid to tell him. I think it was easier because Brendan was at my side."

"That's the way it's supposed to be."

"It was you at Khe Sahn. Wasn't it?" Irelynn said.

Elyse gave her a small smile. "Yes. One of many base camps. We kind of zigzagged across Vietnam."

"They still talk about you."

"Let me guess which body parts were mentioned."

Irelynn grinned. "Well. They're men."

"I'm not exactly proud of my time in Vietnam with the Marines. I made life difficult for Elijah and the team. At times, I was reckless and selfish."

"I hope someday you'll let me tell your story."

"I'd love to, but I'm not sure how Elijah would feel about it."

"Do you need his permission?"

"No. But he has a say in it. He lived it too."

"Hmm. Would you say you have it all?"

"Yes. Whose truck is that pulling in the driveway?"

"Shit. It's my dad. You need to hide."

"Damn. Its good Bunker is out cold. Let me get Anablue and Jane," Elyse said, rushing from the room.

Gramie jumped from her chair as Elyse and Irelynn rushed into the den.

"Dad's here," Irelynn said.

Jane was asleep on the couch as Elyse gently touched her shoulder.

"Jane, wake up; we need to hide."

Anablue, half asleep herself, shook her head. "She took one of those sleeping pills the doctor gave her."

Gramie shook out a blanket and covered Jane up head to toe. "For now, she's you. Quickly, all three of you hide in my room. Ralph, you stay with Jane," she whispered.

The front door opened, and Ryan called out, "Mom?"

"I'm in the den, dear," Gramie replied while pushing them down the hallway toward her bedroom suite. Scrambling back to sit in her chair, Gramie threw a blanket on her lap and grabbed a bowl of popcorn from the table.

Ryan strode into the room.

"You're right on time. The Englebert Humperdinck show is about to start," Gramie said.

Ryan shook his head, "I can't stay to visit tonight. I wanted to stop and check on you and Irelynn."

"As you can see, we're both fine."

"You forgot to lock the door again. You need to remember as long as we have strangers on the mountain."

"I have my shotgun."

"Mom. Please."

"Okay, fine."

"Whose dog is that?"

"What dog?"

"The little black and white chihuahua sleeping with Ralph."

"Oh. That dog. You know Irelynn. Always finding creatures and bringing them home."

"He's got a collar. Let's see what his name is." He picked up the dog and looked at his tag.

"Soup. Odd name for a dog. I know just about every dog in town. Never seen this one before. I'll let Barney know so he can find his owner."

Ruffling the dog's head, he set him down. Spotting a pacifier on the floor, he picked it up.

"Who does this belong to?"

Gramie paled, then quickly responded. "The dog, of course."

Ryan's eyebrows shot straight up. "There are only two people in this world I know of who can make the most absurd seem perfectly normal."

"I know, Irelynn and myself. I keep telling you, Ryan, normal doesn't cover real life."

"Okay then. I'm meeting the men at Nan's. I take it Irelynn's spending the night."

"She'll be fine right where she is," Gramie replied.

"I'm leaving now. Come lock up behind me."

Gramie followed Ryan to the front door. "Be careful getting home. Give my love to Rachel."

"Mom, are you sure you're alright? You're jumpy tonight." Ryan eyed his mother suspiciously.

"Nonsense. I'm going to watch my shows, then go to bed."

"By the way. Here's a walkie talkie in case you need to get a hold of me while I'm on the mountain. And Irelynn was right. Big Ben is back."

"I don't want him destroyed. He's the last Grizzly in these

parts. We'll capture him again and take him further out into the Sierra's."

"We'll do our best. Goodnight, mom," Ryan said, leaning down to place a kiss on her weathered cheek before pulling the door shut behind him.

Gramie breathed a sigh of relief as Ryan climbed into his truck.

Smiling indulgently, she knew exactly what room the young women were hiding in her bedroom suite.

Irelynn's eyes danced with excitement. Gramie's glamor room. A crystal chandelier hung from the ceiling, and shelves filled with shoes, hats, and wigs filled one wall. Racks with scores of beautiful dresses and other clothing filled the other wall. A large dressing table with delicate perfume bottles placed in front of a large oval mirror leaned against one wall.

Irelynn had spent many a day in the room playing dress up. She grinned as Elyse and Anablue squealed in delight at the discovery of costume jewelry and multitudes of colorful scarves and accessories of every kind imaginable. It was a little girl's dream come true.

"Are you sure it's okay for us to be here?" Elyse asked.

"Of course. Here. Sit down. Let's try this wig on you," Irelynn said as she put a blonde wig on Elyse's head.

"Ooh. Elijah would love this," Elyse giggled.

"It's like you could pretend to be a different woman every day," Anablue said, putting on a red wig over her blonde curls.

Irelynn rolled her eyes. "You do realize the two of you just exchanged hair color."

Elyse picked up the hairbrush and brushed the hairpiece. "I would kill to have a room like this in my new house."

"Ask Elijah to expand your closet," Anablue said, pulling off the red wig and putting on a brunette wig. "Aren't they still working on the framing?"

"Yes. Oh my god. You look amazing as a brunette," Elyse said.

Irelynn put on a wig with the hair black as night. "Wow. This is a different look."

The women looked up as the door opened, and Gramie stood in the doorway.

"I knew the three of you would be in here," Gramie said.

"It's too bad Jane's asleep. She would love this," Anablue said.

"There's always tomorrow," Gramie replied. She moved across the room to the evening gowns and party dresses. "Here. All of you should try on my flapper dresses." She delicately ran her hand over the sassy fringe on the bottom of a dress. "The first night I wore this one, I met a young pilot. He was quite the lover for all his youth. It ended tragically."

"What happened to him?" Anablue asked.

"He died in WW1, The Great War," Grammy replied.

"I have clothes in here from the roaring twenties and prohibition. The feds never caught me, and I still have my moonshine still. The great depression, WW2. My flour sack dresses. This room is full of memories, passages in time from bygone eras. They speak of a well lived life, pain, sorrow, and great joy. I had a wonderful husband I was madly in love with, and after George died, eventually, many thoughtful lovers," Gramie said.

"You never remarried?" Anablue said, tears shimmering in her eyes.

"I met Irelynn's grandfather when I was sixteen, only a month before the wedding. I had no choice in an arranged marriage. I came to love him deeply; we had Ryan, and I was a widow by nineteen. He left me all of this. I truly believe that against all the odds, I've been a very successful business-woman and still raised my son to be a good man. I never remarried because no one could fill his boots. That, and I didn't want to give up my independence or my business. When you find love, my dear child, hold it close. Nothing lasts forever and there are no guarantees. I've waited a lifetime to be with him again and someday soon, I will be."

"Oh, Gramie," Irelynn said as she pulled her near for a hug.

"Before I forget. Your father saw the little dog. We forgot he was sleeping with Ralph. I told him you brought home a stray."

"Damn. It should be okay. I don't think dad would mention Soup to anyone," Irelynn said.

Elyse nervously wrung her hands. "I hope you're right. I feel like there's something else I'm forgetting." She paced back and forth, the blonde wig dancing against her shoulders with each step.

"Daddy. Oh shit. They're due back tonight. Capt. Jack is supposed to bring him and Elijah's father to my house. If they see my house as we left it. They're going to think the worst."

Anablue paled, her voice shook with concern. "They're going to be worried sick. I know; I'll call my dad right now, tell him what happened and where we are."

"He might have already left to pick them up. Daddy's got one of those new answering machines. I can leave a message and hope he stops at his apartment first, but you know damn well they are going to come up here anyway," Elyse replied.

"We are so screwed," Anablue said.

"Is it okay if we make some long-distance calls?" Elyse said. "You go right ahead honey. There's a telephone on my nightstand," Gramie said.

"Maybe you should just come clean. Let your husbands know you're here and why," Irelynn urged.

"You're right," Elyse and Anablue both agreed.

"It might be valuable information they need to catch these men," Gramie said.

"Alright, first thing in the morning, we'll track them down and let them know what happened," Elyse said.

"I'm sure Jane would agree with us," Anablue said. "I should check on Jane, and I need to go get my car."

CHAPTER 35

Stirring a teaspoon of sugar into his third cup of coffee before taking a sip of the hot brew, Brendan sighed in appreciation. The warmth of the coffee relaxed him and seeped into his cold, aching muscles. It had been a grueling day on the mountain. Twelve men, six on each mountain, searched the forest and the occasional cabin without one sign of Baltini and his men. Ryan Cross was right; the mountain was cold and unforgiving, no place for those unfamiliar with the terrain.

Fourteen men now sat at tables pulled together in Nan's café. Stomachs now full, they reviewed maps of where they would concentrate their efforts the next day. Ryan and Max had spent their day at the temporary command post set up at the lumber camp directing the two six-man teams. Much like when an inexperienced hiker got lost on the mountain, search teams reported in once an area was searched and cleared. Except in this case these teams were armed and deadly. Irelynn's brothers were protective and angry, they ranted that Baltini, and his men were targeting her.

Brendan couldn't imagine what it would have been like if he and his brothers had a baby sister. His reaction to the situation probably would have been similar. At the same time, knowing Irelynn the way he did, he understood more clearly why she was so independent and stubborn. He thought she was trying to prove herself to the men in her family.

The conversation between Sean and Elijah at the far end of the table caught his attention.

"I'm telling you, if Irelynn had stayed home and accepted her lot in life, none of this would have happened. It's best to keep the women home, barefoot, and pregnant," Sean said.

Elijah cleared his throat. "While I admit my wife is pregnant with our second child, and most likely barefoot since she dislikes shoes. She also works full time and teaches on Saturday mornings."

Sean laughed, "What does she teach…piano?"

"No. My wife teaches self-defense classes to disadvantaged women. During the week, she's the Prima ballerina at the Bay Area Ballet Company in San Francisco, though she's now on sabbatical." Elijah pointed at Donall.

"Donall's wife is a Navy veteran. She was a mechanic who worked on fighter jets. She's in the process of buying her own garage, and she's also expecting a child. Collin's wife is an Army nurse currently serving in Taiwan. All strong women.

All are more than capable of doing what they want to do. Unless it's what she wants, it's unfair to expect a woman to stay home, keep a house, and raise children merely because she's female. And I'm the one who gives back to my community by teaching piano."

"What about Brendan?"

"Aiden and Mac are unmarried," Elijah replied.

"And Brendan?" Sean asked.

"Brendan, who?"

"Your brother."

Taking a long sip of water, Elijah looked at Brendan with panic.

After hearing the conversation, Ryan called Sheriff Griffith, sitting next to Max.

"By the way, Barney. Irelynn found a stray I didn't recognize. A little black and white Chihuahua by the name of Soup."

Elijah choked and spat his water out.

Jamie sitting next to Elijah, pounded him on the back. "You alright, dude?"

"I'm going to kill her," Elijah stated.

"Maybe he got into the car, and we didn't notice," Max said.

"No. He likes to sit on my lap and drive," Elijah said. "Where is he?"

"At my mother's," Ryan replied.

"Was there a baby?" Elijah snarled.

"No, but I did find a pacifier. My mother said it was the dogs," Ryan replied.

Donall slammed his fist on the table. "They're here."

As Aiden and Mac burst into laughter, Ryan, the sheriff, and Irelynn's five brothers looked on in confusion.

"I am never getting married," Mac said as Aiden howled.

"Keep laughing, assholes. You're up next," Elijah growled.

A thick fog rolled in as Anablue started her car. Irelynn sat beside her and Elyse in the backseat, leaned over the front seat.

"I hate to tell you this, but I really need to find a powder room," Elyse said.

"Now?" Irelynn replied.

"Yeah. As soon as possible," Elyse replied.

"I have to go too," Anablue said.

Irelynn sighed, "Okay. Um, everything is closed except the bars. Unless you're willing to pee behind a bush?"

"Ah, no. In this fog, I'd be afraid a ghost would sneak up behind me," Elyse said.

"Vampires or werewolves," Anablue replied.

"That's silly," Irelynn replied.

"Maybe so, but it's spooky out here," Elyse replied. "We should have changed back into our clothes. I'm freezing in this dress. I hope no one sees us."

"No one is going to recognize us with these wigs on," Irelynn replied.

"True. I kind of like this dangly beaded headpiece thing," Anablue giggled.

"If we park behind the bar, the bathrooms are in the back. We can sneak in and back out again without anyone seeing us," Irelynn said.

"Let's do it," Elyse replied. "I'd rather not have anyone see my face like this."

Anablue pulled up to the stop sign on Main Street; looking both ways, she rumbled through the intersection and pulled into the alley.

Parking behind the bar, they pulled open the door and quickly moved down the small hallway to the single stall women's bathroom. All three piled in the room. Irelynn twiddled her thumbs while looking at the ceiling waiting for the other two to finish their business.

"Great. Now I've got to go too, "Irelynn groaned.

Once they finished, they opened the door to find a woman waiting her turn. The woman went in and locked the door behind her. With Anablue in the lead, they moved down the hallway. Anablue stopped in a panic. "The men. They're in the bar and coming this way. Back, back."

The women scrambled back to the women's restroom. With the door locked, they looked at the men's room.

"No way," Elyse said.

Irelynn looked around. "The supply closet." They scrambled to the closet and piled in.

Saying goodnight to Irelynn's family, the light from Nan's café faded as the restaurant closed for the night. They strode down the sidewalk to their cars parked at the end of the block. Donall grabbed Brendan from behind, pulling him against the building wall. The men watched as Anablue's car slowly rumbled through the intersection. The men quietly followed the car, watching as it pulled into the alley, and three women entered the bar's back door. Aiden, Collin, and Max slipped up the alley as Brendan, Elijah, Donall, and Mac ran around the building to the front door.

Making their way through the bar, they stood in the hallway as Aiden, Collin, and Max came through the rear door.

"They didn't come back out," Aiden said. "They're not in the bar," Brendan said.

All eyes turned to the bathrooms as a woman emerged from the women's restroom.

"Anyone else in there?" Elijah asked. "No," the woman replied.

Elijah opened the door to double check. A man came out of the men's room.

"Any women in there?" Donall asked.

"I wish," the man replied before making his way past them. Brendan turned, his eyes landing on the supply closet door.

He grinned at Elijah and Donall, pointing at the door before turning the knob.

Three women huddled in the closet, jammed together; the three looked up into the stern visage of their husband's faces.

"Oh fuck," Elyse breathed. "You can't beat me. I'm pregnant."

"Me too," Anablue cried.

"Not me. I'm still a virgin," Irelynn said.

Eyes wide, Elyse and Anablue looked at Irelynn in shock as Irelynn realized what she had said. She looked up into Brendan's stunned face as a blush crept into his cheeks; his brothers looked at him like he had grown horns on his head.

"Oh shit," Irelynn groaned.

"I intend to rectify that real soon," Brendan growled, pulling her from the closet.

Donall reached in and helped Anablue out. "What the hell are you doing … What happened to your face?"

"I…" Anablue looked to Elyse as Elijah helped her from the closet.

"My God, Elyse. Your face," Elijah bellowed.

"They were attacked at home by two men. They came up here for safety," Irelynn said.

Max pushed his way to the front of the pack. "Where's Jane?"

"Jane and Bunker are at Gramie's. Her ribs are badly bruised; I'm afraid she got the worst of it," Elyse said.

"We all got checked out by a doctor this afternoon. Other than bumps and bruises, we're fine," Anablue said.

"What kind of man beats up pregnant women? Or any woman," Elijah snarled.

"A monster," Brendan replied.

Donall put his hand on Anablue's growing bump. "The baby?"

"He's fine," Anablue said.

"Mine too," Elyse said. "It's Jane we're worried about."

"I think we should leave before the fog gets too thick and we can't find our way home," Irelynn said.

Irelynn turned around and spotted Mac, "Hey Mac, I hope you were able to help Sierra?'

Mac grinned. "Never met a more stubborn cantankerous bit of fluff in my life."

Irelynn raised her eyebrows.

Brendan came up behind her and wrapped his arms around her waist. "That means he left her with tender bruised lips and spitting nails."

"You kissed Sierra? I didn't see that coming."

"Neither did she," Mac replied.

"How's the hunt for Molly going?" Irelynn asked.

"I've got people working on that right now," Mac replied.

Irelynn blinked back sudden tears. "I should be there helping them."

"No. You're right where you belong," Mac said.

Irelynn looked over to Elijah and Donall and rolled her eyes. "You're the two I met at Treasure Island."

Elijah and Donall chuckled. "It sure looks like you got caught, George," Donall said.

Irelynn looked at Elyse and Anablue. "These men are your husbands?"

Elyse and Anablue nodded. "Wow," Irelynn said.

Max stepped up and shook her hand. "I'm Max Cohen, a friend of the family."

"Jane belongs to you?"

"Jane belongs to herself. I'm just the man in love with her," Max replied.

Then she looked at Aiden and Collin. "At least your beards don't look so scruffy now."

"It still itches," Collin said.

"All of you are here because of me?"

"Not because of you…for you," Aiden replied.

Pivoting in Brendan's arms. "It's obvious now that you're all brothers. I need a full explanation of what's going on."

Brendan reached out and tugged on her wig. "Nice wig. Let's get out of here. I'll explain everything when we get back to Gramie's."

"Saddle up," Elijah called out.

Elyse snickered. "Where's the horses."

CHAPTER 36

Padding barefoot down the long hall to the kitchen, Irelynn pulled her flannel shirt tighter over her borrowed floor length granny nightgown. Not yet awake, she grumbled a "good morning." before pouring herself a cup of strong coffee. Looking over the edge of her cup, she practically snarled at Brendan's: "Good morning, sunshine."

"Please, don't talk to me yet," Irelynn grumbled into her cup.

Gramie patted Brendan on the arm. "Pay her no mind. We don't talk to George until that first cup of coffee is gone."

Brendan, Mac, and Aiden poured over maps spread across the kitchen table as Elyse and Anablue cheerfully chatted while washing the breakfast dishes. Max and Jane snuggled on the couch watching morning cartoons while

Bunker crawled all over Elijah lying on the floor. Donall and Collin were out on the back deck watching the deer frolicking in the misty morning fog in the meadow in the distance.

Irelynn listened to the men discussing the cabins and where they had been the previous day.

"Have you been to the hippy commune yet?" Irelynn asked.

"What hippy commune?" Brendan replied.

"Here." Irelynn pointed at the map. "This fork in the road. If you head east, you'll find the commune. West goes to Timber Cove, another small town on the other side of Sugar Mountain. That valley is where Sierra's family owns a small vineyard and a farm."

Anablue and Elyse pivoted from the sink at the mention of Sierra's name. Mac glared at the two before refocusing his attention on the map.

"Tell us about the commune," Mac said.

"There's not much to tell. From what I remember, they're nice people and self sufficient. You'd have to ask my mother for more details," Irelynn said.

The front door slammed open, and Rachel called out. "George Irelynn Cross. Where are you? I need an explanation right now."

Irelynn looked up as her mother, and five brothers rushed into the kitchen.

Oh shit. Here we go.

"What's going on here? Why are you buying maternity clothes?" Rachel cried.

"Mom. I'm not pregnant. I bought the clothes for them," Irelynn said, nodding toward Elyse and Anablue.

The front door opened again, and Ryan, Barney, and three other men entered the house.

"Where is everyone?" Ryan called out.

Irelynn didn't recognize the three men who filled the doorway. Feeling overwhelmed, a wave of panic hit her as one of the men stepped forward. There was no doubt in her mind that this was Brendan's father. Her eyes flew to Brendan's. Jumping to her feet, her chair skidded backward across the floor as she made a beeline to the back door. She was out the door and running down the steps. Pulling her nightgown up to her knees, she sprinted across the meadow.

When Brendan moved to follow her, Sean jumped in his way. "What is it you want with my sister?" Sean growled.

"Get out of my way. You stand between my wife and me," Brendan snarled.

"Wife?" Rachel whispered. "What's going on?"

"Back off, Sean. Brendan is Irelynn's husband," Ryan said.

Brendan pushed past Sean and raced out the door and across the meadow.

Back in the kitchen, stunned silence shattered when Elyse said. "I guess this means we're all family."

Everyone started talking at once as Aiden held his hands

up for quiet and pointed toward the baby. In the background, Bunker had pulled himself to his feet at the coffee table. Taking a few teetering steps, he fell to his knees and crawled to where the dogs were sleeping. Laying his head on Ralph's stomach, he stuck his thumb in his mouth and stroked Soup's ears with the other hand.

"Gramie snorted. "Now you're in for it."

Ralph gently came to her feet. Licking the baby's face, she sniffed at Soup before bounding toward the door. RJ opened the screen door, and the dog flew down the steps and across the meadow disappearing into the wispy fog with Soup hot on her trail.

Grateful for the years of training with the Montagnard's, the best trackers in Vietnam. Eyes on the ground, Brendan trotted along, following Irelynn's path through the long grass. He had the feeling she was heading toward her swing. His ears tuned to the sound of nature around him, songbirds called to each other high above while a woodpecker's rata tat tat echoed across the meadow. He looked down as Ralph found him, encircling his legs; the dog panted and pawed at him. Elijah's little dog Soup caught up with them a minute later.

Brendan bent down to scratch Soup's ears. "A little rough keeping up with your sweetheart, buddy? I feel yah."

The threesome followed her path, with Ralph running ahead. Her trail took him from the meadow to the edge of the forest. Ralph came to a spot where the area was trampled by multiple large human footprints. Sniffing, the dog whimpered as Brendan knelt. Brendan abruptly stood, and his vision tunneled. He scanned the ground, looking for her footprints. *She's gone. They have her.* Brendan threw back his head and howled his rage.

CHAPTER 37

Dropping to his knees, Brendan pulled Soup into his arms. "Soup, buddy. I know you're pretty smart. Find your master. Find Elijah and bring him to me. Go." The little dog took off, retracing the path behind them. "Ralph. Find Irelynn." Ralph took off into the forest with Brendan hot on her tail. The dog occasionally stopped to sniff the trail left by the men. With no sign of Irelynn's footprints, Brendan assumed she was being carried. Coming to a small stream, Ralph splashed through the water to the other side. Sniffing around, she picked up the trail and bound up the embankment. Through the forest, they ran. Stopping at a clump of bushes, Brendan plucked a small piece of lace from a branch. Her nightgown. Showing it to the dog, they took off again until they reached a gravel road. Whimpering, nose to the ground, Ralph circled a spot.

Bending down, Brendan looked at the tire tracks in the gravel. *They put her into a car here.* Brendan looked up as Soup led Elijah, Donall, Mac, and RJ through the brush.

"They've got her," Brendan cried.

Mac pulled his walkie talkie, speaking into it. "They've got Irelynn. We're about two clicks behind Gramie's house on a gravel road."

Max's voice came over the speaker. "Roger that. We'll grab the gear and meet you over there."

"This is Old Log Road," RJ said. "We use it for the horses hauling the logs to the pond."

"Where does it lead?" Brendan asked.

"North. It splits off; one way leads up to the Mountains, the other to the main road. If you go south, to the log holding pond by the mill," RJ replied.

"The tire tracks head north, but they may circle back," Brendan said.

"I want half the men to head north, the other half south," Mac said. "Have Barney block the main road from town. No one gets through in either direction."

"Roger that," Max replied over the walkie talkie.

Brendan and the men formed a straight line across the road and headed north on foot, following Ralph, Soup, and the tire tracks. Their ghostly forms disappearing like mist bound spirits into the deep dark forest.

Irelynn opened her eyes. Shards of sunlight slipped through a hole in a dirty window. Closing her eyes, she groaned as drums started pounding in her head.

"Shhh. It's alright," A sweet woman's voice said.

A shadowy figure leaned over her. "Where am I?" Irelynn croaked.

"My name is Rainbow. You're at "Our Happy Place" commune, locked inside the greenhouse with the women. Our men are in the other greenhouse."

"Here. Drink some water," another voice said. "I'm Sunny, and over there is Rain."

Struggling to sit up, Irelynn nodded at the women. "Whose holding us captive?" she said, gently prodding her aching jaw before taking a sip of water.

"Three men. They only let us out of here when they want us to cook for them," Rainbow said.

"No, it's five. It might be six now. They've been coming and going so much I'm not sure. Two more arrived in the middle of the night," Rain said.

"Sometimes they speak in a foreign language. The one they call Baltini is the leader," Sunny said.

Irelynn hissed, "Baltini. This is bad."

Sunny tossed her long blonde hair in aggravation. "I heard him talking. He intends to kill you and throw you in the river."

"Hush, Sunny. Don't scare her like that. What's your name?" Rainbow asked.

"Irelynn Cross."

"You're Rachel's daughter. She's so nice. Sometimes she gives us extra food and clothes," Rainbow said.

"That sounds like something she would do," Irelynn replied.

Crawling to the window, Irelynn peeked out the window. Spotting two men standing guard outside the greenhouse, she sat back. "Those bastards are the ones who caught me in the forest and hit me," she said, rubbing her jaw.

"I know," Rain said. "All I did was offer a flower of peace, and bam, I got socked in the mouth."

Irelynn looked at the fading bruises on the woman's face. "How long have they been here?"

"Two of them have been here for two weeks," Rainbow replied. "They eat like pigs, and we're running out of food again."

Irelynn's mind raced. "Again? Have they taken you to town before?"

"Yes, they're supposed to take us to town today," Sunny replied.

"My mother normally bakes when she's upset. I'm sure she'll need groceries." Irelynn grabbed Sunny's arm. "Listen to me. When you get to town, find my mother if you can. She sticks to her schedule like clockwork. She's always at the grocery store by eleven o'clock. I know. Tell her you need Heinz ketchup. It's a bit cryptic, but my mom should be able to figure out that it refers to me. Hearing it from you should tell them I'm being held here at the hippy commune. Remember, it must be Heinz ketchup. If that doesn't work, you could always ask for goats and chickens."

"She might think it odd. She might be so upset that you're missing that she doesn't shop today. If not, we have a plan B," Rainbow replied.

"What's plan B?" Irelynn asked. "We have Shrooms," Sunny replied. "Shrooms?"

"Magic mushrooms. Natural hallucinogens," Sunny said. "And Blotter Acid, that's LSD. And we have Pot. We figured we'd add it to the chicken stew," Rain said.

"We plan to escape while they're tripping," Rainbow said. "You want to make them a psychedelic stew and hope for a bad trip? That's brilliant," Irelynn said. "I've seen enough drug use in Vietnam. They're either going to be mellow or freaking out. Let's implement both plans and hope for the best."

"Go get the bitch from the greenhouse. I've waited long enough. It's time to start interrogating Irelynn," Edwin Baltini snarled. "I need that can of mace, or I'm dead."

"What if she's still passed out?" Sergio asked. "Awake, or not. Bring her here."

"What about the boss? Shouldn't we wait until he gets here?"

"We'll give him until this afternoon. If the asshole doesn't show, we go ahead without him," Baltini said.

"We still need to take a few hippy skanks to town. We're out of food," Sergio said.

"What happened to hippy communes being self sufficient and stocking supplies?"

"We ate all of it."

"Take them to town, but only let them buy a day's worth of food. I plan on finishing the job and leaving by morning."

"What about the hippies?"

"We don't leave anyone behind who can talk."

At sixty-four, Rachel Cross was still a striking woman. Gray hair tinged her copper tresses as she smoothed her hand over her hair and forehead. Rubbing at eyes, she gripped her hands together in silent prayer. Weary to the bone, her thoughts on her only daughter. She had to stay busy. If she stopped, she'd crumble into a miserable heap until her child was found safe and brought home.

A gentle hand lay on her arm; she turned to the concerned face of Elyse peeking over the front seat.

"She's going to be okay," Elyse said. "They're doing everything they can to find Irelynn."

"I know," Rachel replied.

"Are you sure you want to go to the grocery store?"

"I can take you back to Gramie's, and we can shop for you," Anablue said.

"No. I'm alright. I need to stay busy," Rachel replied.

"You bake when you're upset. Jane does that too," Elyse said.

"I'm surprised the men let us come to town alone," Rachel said.

"I'm more than capable of protecting all of us," Elyse replied.

Pulling into a parking spot, the women walked the half block to the grocery store. Outside of the grocery store, two young women stood panhandling.

Rachel frowned at the women. "That's odd."

"Do you know them?" Elyse asked.

"They're from the commune. So carefree and spirited, they remind me of Irelynn." Rachel inhaled sharply, the ache of worry growing in her chest. She walked up to the women. "What's going on, girls? You know it's illegal to beg in town."

Both women nervously glanced up the street. "Rachel. It's cool to see you. We need money to buy chicken and Heinz ketchup," Sunny said.

"Yes. Heinz ketchup, goats, and chickens," Rainbow said.

"You won't find goats here, but I can buy your chicken andketchup. Wait here; I'll be right back," Rachel said.

Rachel went inside the butcher counter, picked out a whole chicken, grabbed a bag of potatoes and some carrots and handed them to Elyse. Then she marched to the condiments aisle and grabbed a ketchup bottle. Shaking her head, she headed for the checkout counter with Elyse and Anablue in tow.

"What a ninny I am. I need eggs and flour. Might as well get what we came for," Rachel said.

Once outside, she handed the grocery bags to Sunny and Rainbow. "Now you two get home. Make yourselves a nice stew," Rachel said as she gave Anablue a pile of S & H green stamps. "Here. You can have these."

"No thanks. I have thousands," Anablue said, handing them off to Elyse, who rolled her eyes and stuffed them in her purse.

With that, Rachel headed up the sidewalk; she had prescriptions to pick up and needed thread from the Five and Dime.

After an hour or so, Elyse whispered to Anablue. "Not only does she stress bake, but she shops as well."

"I should find a pay phone and check in with Max," Anablue said.

"I saw one over by the ice cream counter," Elyse replied.

Five minutes later, Anablue returned. "The baby and Jane are fine. No news yet."

"I can't stop thinking about Heinz ketchup. Just like Irelynn. I had to buy a couple of bottles for Irelynn to take on her last trip, and I always sent some in Care packages too. She refuses to eat anything but Heinz," Rachel said.

Elyse looked at her, perplexed. "Rachel. Have those hippies ever asked for something so strange before?"

"No. They've never asked for anything. This is a message. I can feel it in my bones," Rachel said.

"The ketchup. That's Irelynn. We've witnessed Irelynn

dumping half a bottle on her fries. Goats and chickens are for a bride. Brendan's bride," Elyse said.

Covering her mouth with her hand, "How could I have been so stupid? They were trying to tell me that Irelynn is at the hippy commune," Rachel replied as tears rolled down her cheeks.

"Come on. Let's get out of here," Anablue cried.

"Damn, I just realized I'm so frazzled I gave the girls my baking supplies. Sunny and Rainbow were nervous too. Someone was watching them," Rachel said. "I'm not sure I understand the goats and chicken's part. But the ketchup… is all Irelynn."

"I'll explain the bride price on the way home," Elyse said. "You know, we could pass as hippies," Anablue said. "You're right. All we would need is to find some accessories," Elyse replied.

"Scarves, jewelry, things like that," Anablue said.

"For what purpose?" Rachel asked.

"We could sneak into the commune. Better yet, walk right in. Find a way to distract those men and get Irelynn out," Elyse said.

"While we're there, you can let our men know where we are. They could surround the place or something," Anablue said.

"Absolutely not. It's dangerous. I may be desperate to get my daughter back, but the two of you will do no such thing," Rachel sternly replied before she turned and walked away.

"Was that a mom voice?" Elyse whispered.

"Yeah, that was a mom voice," Anablue replied.

"I've never heard it before. My mom died when I was three. It's a little scary."

"I'm pretty sure it's meant to be," Anablue said.

Once they were outside, anger rolled off the women in waves as they walked around the car.

"Shi…ooot. Someone slashed my tires," Anablue said.

Rachel snorted with disgust. "I'm sure it was whoever brought Sunny and Rainbow to town."

"We have to find a way home," Elyse replied.

Rachel looked up and down the street. "There, parked in front of the gas station."

"All I see is a logging truck," Anablue replied.

"You're not serious, are you?" Elyse said.

"Get what you need from the car. We're going for a ride," Rachel replied.

Elyse and Anablue followed Rachel as she crept up the passenger side of the logging truck. The truck was filled with a dozen twenty-four-inch-wide logs meant for the mill.

"Are we seriously stealing a truck filled with trees?" Elyse said.

Climbing up into the truck. "We're not stealing it. We're borrowing it," Rachel replied.

Elyse hesitated. "Why can't we just steal a car or get a ride from someone?"

"Now, what would my neighbors think if I stole their car? I don't want to trouble them."

Elyse rolled her eyes. "What about the driver?"

"He's probably in Nan's café. He'll be compensated for his time," Rachel replied.

"Isn't this like... grand theft auto?" Anablue said.

"Technically, no. Did you see the name on the door? Cross lumber. We are borrowing a truck Gramie owns. She'll understand," Rachel replied.

"Gramie? I thought your husband owned the company."

"Gramie owns it, and Ryan runs it. Don't worry so much. We're only taking it to Gramie's house. I'll have one of the boys return it later."

Rachel lifted the visor, searching for the key. "Damn. No keys."

"Anablue, can you hot wire this?" Elyse said.

"Of course. I'm a mechanic," Anablue snorted. "Just give me a minute."

The truck roared to life. Anablue gave them a mischievous grin. "I've never hot-wired a semi before. It's kind of fun."

Heading toward the mountain, Rachel went through the gears to get the truck moving. "Since the sheriff blocked the main road, we'll take an old backroad."

"Are you sure about this?" Anablue said.

"Come on, girls. Where's your sense of adventure?"

"I'm starting to understand Irelynn a little more," Elyse said.

"Who did you think taught her to drive logging trucks,"

Rachel replied. "And Gramie taught me. Back in our day, between the two of us, we had to keep the business running when most of the men went off to war. The women of this town banded together. Everyone had something to offer. Whether it was working at the mill, felling trees, or childcare. We made our soap and grew our victory gardens. No one went hungry. We did what we had to do. Just like right now."

Pinching the bridge of his nose, Brendan groaned in frustration. The trail on the gravel road had run cold at the paved main road winding its way up the mountain. Kneeling on one knee, he picked up some gravel from the main road.

"At least we can see they headed north toward the mountains," RJ said.

"Those are big fucking mountains," Brendan replied.

"Cold and unforgiving. Common sense tells me that they aren't going to take Irelynn too far up in the mountains. The higher in elevation you go, the more you have to deal with the snow and cold," RJ said.

Brendan shuddered, "Christ. All she's wearing is a nightgown and flannel shirt."

"How long have you been married to my sister?"

"A couple of months," Brendan replied.

"You got married in Vietnam?"

Brendan nodded, "Yeah."

"I never understood Irelynn. My dad and I were wounded

in the Battle of the Bulge. After that winter, I never wanted to go further than my backyard. Then along comes my little sister nine months after my dad got home. My dad and I were both drafted, and there she is, this tiny baby girl who grows into a woman. A woman who willingly goes into a combat zone to take pictures to tell the story. I was one scared kid, both then and now. I still can't get those images out of my head. Just knowing that my baby sister has seen the same doesn't sit right with me."

"Your dad didn't mention that you were veterans," Brendan said.

"Nah. He's not going to. In his mind, some things are better left unsaid."

"Helluva backyard you've got here."

RJ grinned. "It's peaceful. Except when Irelynn is home, then all bets are off. We'll find her. Keep in mind, Irelynn's no shrinking Violet. She knows these mountains as well as I do. She's sharp. She'll figure out a way to tell us where she is."

Mac strode up to them, "I wish we had a chopper. We need eyes in the sky."

"How about a plane? We've got a crop duster at the airfield," RJ said.

"You've got a pilot too?"

RJ grinned, "Oh yeah."

"How far away?" Mac said.

"About fifteen miles," RJ said.

"We need a man on that plane. Is it a two-seater?" Brendan asked.

"I think so."

"Who's at Gramie's?" Brendan asked.

"Max is running the show from the house. My dad just dropped Donall off to pick up Michael's truck," Mac replied.

"Send Donall to drop Max off at the airfield," Brendan replied. "Where's father?"

"Gramp's, Pop's, and Capt. Jack are with Collin. I believe they're in Sean's truck about two miles south. Aiden, Matthew, and Michael are with Jamie checking out the log pond," Mac said.

"That leaves you, me, RJ, and Elijah here. Ryan's on his way back with his truck," Brendan said.

Ryan's pickup pulled in front of them. "There's my dad now," RJ said.

"Get the men up here," Brendan said. "The car with Irelynn is already north of us."

Parking the logging truck on the main road in front of Gramie's driveway, Rachel left the beast running since they wanted to return it later. Scrambling from the truck, they ran into the house to find Gramie in the kitchen, preparing tea for Jane, who rested on the couch with the baby. Elyse picked up her sleepy baby; sitting in a rocker, she gently rocked him until he fell asleep.

"How are you feeling, Jane?" Elyse whispered.

"Pretty good, but Max and the dragon lady in the kitchen won't let me move from the couch," Jane replied.

"Where's Max?"

"Donall picked him up," Jane replied. Cries of "Oh no," came from the kitchen.

"Gramie knocked her walkie-talkie into the sink. Help me find Max's," Anablue said. "If we can't find it, there's no way to let them know where Irelynn is."

Elyse carried the baby into the guest bedroom and placed him in the crib. Running to the kitchen, they searched for another walkie-talkie.

Lifting Maps and pushing things out of the way while they searched. "Obviously, Max took it with him," Elyse cried.

"I overheard Rachel and Gramie talking. They intend to drive to the commune to rescue Irelynn if we can't get ahold of the men," Anablue whispered.

"What! They're old ladies. They'll get themselves killed."

"I'm finding old or female doesn't stop this family," Anablue said.

"Ditto," Elyse replied.

The logging truck moving through its gears sounded from the main road.

"They snuck out. Bumfuzzle. They're heading to the commune."

"Not if we beat them there," Anablue cried. "Grab something that looks like hippy clothes and meet me outside."

Anablue and Elyse sprang into action. Elyse ran to grab

wigs and accessories from the glamor room while Anablue ran down to find an available car.

Elyse stopped to check on Jane. "Will you be okay?"

"I'm cool. I think the daughters-in -aw are on their way over anyway. Go. Now."

Elyse grabbed a map from the table and ran outside; she pulled up short in surprise. Opening the car door, she jumped in. "Seriously. Did you hot-wire Elijah's car? He's going to kill us."

"All the other cars were locked. It's this or nothing," Anablue said. "Besides, I've always wanted to take Elijah's shiny red Camaro for a joy ride."

"And there it is. The stinker I always knew you were hiding," Elyse giggled.

CHAPTER 38

After making a wrong turn, Donall pulled up in front of the hanger, and Max jumped out of the car. Donall honked the car horn as an elderly woman walked out of the hangar.

"What took you?" she asked.

"Wrong turn. I'm Max, and this is Donall."

"I'm Agnes; nice to meet you both."

"Is the pilot here yet?" Max asked.

Agnes cackled. "You're looking at her."

Max's jaw dropped, "You've got to be kidding me."

Donall looked down at the woman. For all her tiny size, she stood tall. A few gray curls escaped from her leather bomber hat with fleece lining. Bright blue eyes sparkling with amusement reminded him of his blue-eyed wife.

"Can you give us five minutes?"

"Anything you need, sweet cheeks," Agnes replied. Max and Donall stepped away from Agnes.

"Not to be rude, but do you think she can even see where she's going?" Max said.

" You can do this, Max."

"I don't know. She's got to be one hundred years old," Max whispered.

"Ninety-two. Sight and hearing are perfectly fine," Agnes said. "Come on. I'm going to need both of you."

The hair raised on the back of Donall's neck. "Why?"

"Balance. You both appear the same size," Agnes said, leading the way into the hangar to stand in front of the crop duster plane.

Donall whistled, "She's a beauty. A one-seater?"

"Where am I supposed to sit?" Max asked.

Agnes tossed them each a bomber hat. "On the wings, of course."

"Wait…what?" Donall said.

"Don't be scared. It's my version of wing walkers. The high school kids do it all the time."

"Oh no. No, no, no," Max said, backing away.

"I'm a seasoned fighter pilot, but this is insane," Donall said.

Agnes snorted. "A real fly boy. You'll both be fine. I'll strap you down. Times a wasting, boys. Didn't you need eyes in the sky to find Irelynn?"

Max yanked on his bomber hat. "I can't believe I'm doing this. You Corrington's…are crazy."

Donall lifted his walkie-talkie to his mouth and snarled. "Brendan. You owe me…big time." Brendan's voice came over the walkie-talkie, "Roger, that."

For the better part of the afternoon, Irelynn sat tied to the chair, watching the women as they worked preparing a meal. While the smell was tantalizing and her stomach rumbled with hunger, there was no way in hell she would take a single bite of that stew.

The men guarding them were sadistic in their treatment of the hippies, often raising a heavy fist in a threatening manner they sometimes carried out. Irelynn flinched with every blow delivered and was secretly delighted when one of the men pushed Sunny aside to grab a handful of dried mushrooms to nibble on.

Shivering with cold, her shoulders ached, her feet numb. Cursing Baltini under her breath, she wondered why he had yet to come out of the shack the hippies called home.

They're waiting for someone.

Dinner was ready, and Sunny served bowls of stew, handing them to the guards. Baltini made his appearance; the screen door slammed behind him as he crossed the compound to shove the guards out of his way. Taking a bowl of stew, he shoveled mouthfuls while the women backed away in disgust.

Baltini sneered at the women. "You and your men will eat if there's anything left."

Irelynn watched as the men ate. *Rainbow was right. You're disgusting pigs.*

Baltini's eyes fell on her, and Irelynn shuddered in disgust. Setting his bowl down, he strode over to her chair. Reaching out his hand, he stroked her cheek.

"Ah, the lovely Irelynn. Rebecca was right. We would have made so much money from selling your sweet body."

Irelynn tried to pull back in revulsion. "Don't even talk to me about Rebecca. Brendan told me. She didn't deserve what you did to her as nasty as she was."

Baltini ran his finger down her throat and across her chest to circle her nipple.

"Get your hands off me, asshole," Irelynn sneered.

"Always so high and mighty. After the boss is done with you, it's my turn. And I assure you, you will beg for death when I'm done with you. As to Rebecca, I don't know what you're talking about; she should be here shortly."

Irelynn hissed. *He doesn't know she's dead.* "Who's the boss?"

Right on cue, she could hear a car coming up the road and stopping behind her. A car door opened and then slammed shut. Footsteps sounded in the crunchy gravel as Irelynn tried to look behind her. Hot breath blew on her neck as a man bent over and whispered.

"Hello, Irelynn. It's nice to see you again."

Irelynn sharply inhaled, and shards of fear crept down her spine. The man grabbed a fistful of her hair and yanked it back. Stunned, Irelynn looked up into the face of Mark Marchetti.

"What the actual fuck," Irelynn whispered.

"Surprised to see me?"

"Marchetti. You're their boss?"

"You've given us quite the runaround, Irelynn. I would have preferred to handle this in San Francisco. With that serial killer on the loose, your death would have been blamed on him. But seeing the great outdoors, it's much easier to dump your body here; you would never be found. The only problem is…you still have my property, and I want it back."

"Where's Rebecca?" Baltini asked. "She was with you."

Marchetti looked at Baltini with disgust. "Rebecca was a liability."

"Why don't you tell him?" Irelynn sneered.

Baltini pulled his gun and pointed it at Marchetti. "What did you do to my sister?"

Sister? "She's dead," Irelynn said.

Baltini turned his gun on Irelynn. Just as quickly, Marchetti pulled his and pointed it at Baltini.

"Don't be a fool, Baltini. Put your gun away."

"You took something from me; maybe I should take something from you."

Unable to breathe, her heart dropped into her stomach, and nausea rolled through her. Closing her eyes, she prayed.

Both men backed down and put their weapons away at the sound of another car coming up the gravel road. Car doors opened and slammed shut. Two voices she never thought to hear in this place chattered behind her. Irelynn closed her eyes and inwardly groaned at the danger they had placed themselves in.

"Far out. This place is the coolest," Elyse said.

Anablue held her arms out and spun in a slow circle. "We finally made it."

Turning to one of the men who ran up to them. "You have no idea what it took for us to get here," Elyse said.

"Who the fuck are you?" Baltini said.

"I'm Bambi, and this is Blossom," Elyse said.

Baltini scrutinized Elyse. "You look familiar," he said.

"Where's River? He's going to be so excited to see us," Anablue said.

"Oh, look. There are the girls," Elyse said.

Anablue stepped in front of Irelynn. Irelynn looked her up and down. Opening her mouth, she snapped it shut. She recognized the long black wig as Gramie's; her clothes and jewelry were a mix of Gramie's and hers from the back of the closet. Elyse was dressed in much the same way.

Elyse clapped her hands. "Oh, a game of tie me up, I want to play."

Irelynn blinked. Tie me up?

A long, drawn-out shriek sounded behind them, and everyone turned to look.

"Get them off of me," Sergio cried. He stood in the center of the yard, swiping at some unseen force.

Baltini looked at him in disbelief. "What are you talking about?"

Pulling a knife, Sergio twisted and turned, contouring his body to slash at the air. "Can't you see them?"

"See what?"

"Pinecone fairies. They're everywhere."

Baltini yanked Elyse and Anablue by the arms; hauling them across the yard, he shoved them into the women sitting on the ground by the picnic table. Elyse's wig came loose in Baltini's hands, and he staggered backward. He was looking at Elyse. "You?" he whimpered. Terrified at the wig he held in his hands, he tried to shake it off as he ran toward Marchetti. "Booker…," he sniveled.

Another guard started stripping off his clothes, pretending he was an airplane; he flew around the compound naked before climbing to the greenhouse's roof.

"It's a plane. It's a plane" Looking skyward, he stopped. "No," he screamed, "Run. It's a Pterodactyl." Screaming, he jumped and ran into the forest. His screams carried through the trees like a dying banshee.

From across the yard, Irelynn exchanged shocked glances with the other women. They all watched as a low flying crop duster plane buzzed the area. A third guard pulled his gun to shoot at the plane. Elyse picked up the eggs on the table and started lobbing them at the guard like hand grenades. Confused, the man dropped the gun, fascinated with the egg goo of each splat as it stretched and slimed across his face and body.

Marchetti whipped around, screaming at Baltini, "What the fuck is going on?"

Stopping short, looking behind Irelynn, his eyes filled with terror.

Baltini screamed like a little girl, "Big Foot."

Marchetti pushed Baltini to the ground and sprinted across the compound; the women screamed and rushed to a shed dragging Elyse and Anablue with them.

"No. We can't leave Irelynn," Elyse cried, pushing the hippy women inside the shed; she picked up the bag of flour.

Swinging, she hit Marchetti in the head. A cloud of white filled the air, coating Marchetti and Baltini in flour as Elyse and Anablue disappeared into the forest.

Irelynn heard him before she saw him. Looking out of the corner of her eye, he was massive. His hot breath on her neck, he sniffed her sending chills down her spine.

Fifteen hundred pounds of Grizzly Bear stood next to her, rocking back and forth on all fours. Irelynn didn't breathe or move. The full-grown Grizzly was a far cry from the cub she had rescued after his mother died. The last of his kind in these parts, he was wild, dangerous, and could snap her neck instantly.

"Big Ben," Irelynn whispered.

CHAPTER 39

Three pick-up trucks pulled off to the side of the main road. Brendan jumped out of the back of the truck to check the gravel road they were parked in front of. Their only lead was to check the gravel roads leading off the main paved road for tire tracks. Brendan kicked at the gravel in frustration.

"Nothing. How many more fucking gravel roads lead off this main road?" Brendan growled.

Ryan pulled his map out and spread it out on the hood of his truck. "We've got a few that aren't even on the map. This will teach me to keep my maps updated."

RJ pointed at the map. "The next road leads to the hippy commune to the east. West leads to Shadow Springs."

"That's what Irelynn said this morning," Brendan said.

"This commune. Tell us about it," Mac said.

"It's just a bunch of kids. Last I heard about seven of them, but they come and go," Ryan said.

"Are they on your property?" Mac asked.

"No. Their property butts right up to ours on the eastern edge of Sugar Mountain," RJ replied.

"Let's get Max to do a fly over of the commune," Brendan said. "Where's Donall?"

Mac lifted his walkie talkie. "Max, where's Donall?"

"On the other wing," Max replied.

Mac's eyebrows lifted. "Say again."

There was static on the line before Max replied. "Donall and I are strapped to the fucking wings."

"Roger that," Mac replied as his eyes met Brendan's, and he grinned. "That would be why Donall said you owe him."

"Coming up on your position," Max's voice came over the radio.

Looking skyward, Brendan lifted his binoculars hanging from his neck. "Fuck me. They're on the wings."

"Roger that."

Ryan lifted his walkie talkie, "Max. Who's flying that plane?"

"Agnes," Max replied.

"Jesus, Mary, and Joseph. It's supposed to be her grandson flying today with his two-seater. Agnes is too old to be flying, let alone giving rides," Ryan growled.

"Roger that," Max replied. "Actually, she's quite good."

"There's a logging truck coming up the road," Aiden said.

"What the hell? I thought Barney closed the road?" Ryan said.

The truck screamed by them, horn blowing, with Gramie hanging out the passenger window waving and yelling something about the commune. Right behind was Elijah's red Camaro; passing the truck, it raced past them. Barney's police car, red lights flashing, the siren wailing, came up behind the logging truck.

"Elijah. Wasn't that your car, dude?" Sean said.

Elijah's eyes followed his car up the road. "Are you fucking kidding me? I'm going to kill them both."

"Was that Gramie in the logging truck, screaming about the commune?" RJ asked.

"Yeah. And your mother was driving." Ryan replied.

"And we wonder where Irelynn gets it from," Jamie growled.

"Obviously, the women know something we don't," Mac said.

Brendan sucked in his breath. "Irelynn is at that commune." Twelve men looked at each in shock before scrambling for their trucks. Racing up the road behind Barney's police car, Ryan pulled up next to it. Brendan rolled down the passenger window. Lifting his walkie-talkie, "Barney, Irelynn is at the hippy commune."

"Ten Four," Barney replied.

Up ahead, the logging truck veered right, its load of logs shifting as it headed down the gravel road to the commune at a breakneck speed.

"Kill the lights and sirens. We're going to try and get ahead of that truck."

"Ten Four," Barney replied.

Ryan sped up, chasing down the logging truck; he veered off the road to pass the large truck. Brush and branches slapped at the truck as Ryan went back and forth from the road to the woods, avoiding rocks and trees in its path before it finally got ahead and slowed the truck down. Once it came to a complete stop, Ryan pulled off to the side of the road. Jumping from his truck, he stormed back to the driver's side and opened the door.

"Woman. What the hell do you think you're doing?"

Rachel flung herself into Ryan's arms. "Ryan. Thank God. Our baby is with the hippies."

"Why didn't you call me on the walkie-talkie?" Ryan said as Sean helped Gramie from the truck.

"I accidentally knocked it into the sink," Gramie said.

"Where did you get the logging truck?"

"I stole it. Gramie and I decided to sneak away to save Irelynn. Elyse and Anablue figured out our plan, and now they've put themselves in danger."

"We'll handle it from here. You two get in my truck and stay there. Keep Ralph and Soup with you," he said.

"But…" Rachel cried.

"No but's. Get in the truck and lock the doors," Ryan said. Brendan watched their interaction with a smile on his face. "Now you see what you're up against with Irelynn."

"Gladly," Brendan replied." Where are we?"

"We're uphill from the road into the commune," Ryan said.

Spreading out, they moved through the forest when a naked man came screaming through the brush.

"Pterodactyls. They're after me," he screamed. Running, he disappeared into the woods on the other side of the road.

Mac looked at Brendan. "Little old ladies stealing trucks. Naked dudes and flying dinosaurs. Do you get the feeling there's more going on here than we realize?"

"This whole thing is fucking insane," Brendan snarled.

"Michael, Matthew. Go catch that fruitcake and put him in he back of Barney's squad car," Mac said into his walkie-talkie.

With hand signals to the group, the men crept silently down the hill toward the commune.

"I see her," Mac said over the walkie-talkie. "She's tied to a chair."

Brendan inhaled sharply as he moved forward. Spotting Irelynn, his heart dropped into his stomach. "Roger that. What the fuck is standing next to her?"

"It's a Grizzly bear. A big one," Mac replied.

Ryan's frantic voice came over the walkie-talkie. "It's Big Ben. Whatever you do, do not shoot that bear. You'll only piss him off."

"Fuck," Michael's voice came over the radio. "That fruitcake doubled back on us. He's in the logging truck heading down to the commune driveway," Michael cried.

"Dad. He hit your truck with Mom and Gramie inside. Knocked it into the ditch," Matthew said.

"Oh shit. He rolled the logging truck and dumped the load. "Shit. It's rolling your way," Michael cried.

Brendan turned in horror at the sound of a logging truck sliding on its side down the hill with grinding metal on metal of twisted carnage, its load of logs bumping and rolling down the hill toward him. Whipping around, his eyes on Irelynn, the bear had charged, attacking someone out of view. Feeding off pure adrenaline, he raced down the hill toward Irelynn.

Big Ben pounded his paws on the ground. His teeth clacked, and he huffed. Lowering his head, he charged toward Baltini. Wild eyed and screaming about Bigfoot, Baltini danced around, unaware that the bear charged toward him like a runaway locomotive. Irelynn closed her eyes at the sickening crunch of his neck being snapped. Covered in flour, Marchetti took off into the forest with Big Ben giving chase. Of the other two men, one leaned against the women's greenhouse in a stupor, his silly gaze locked on the ground. The other man still swatted at imaginary pinecone fairies.

The sound of a crop duster plane overhead, and Irelynn looked up to see the plane with two men strapped to the wings. *Agnes is still giving joy rides.*

On the hill above her, a deep rumble echoed through the trees. Irelynn's eyes were drawn to the logs rolling down the hill toward her. Absolute terror gripped her as she tried to stand; lifting the chair again and again, she hopped backward toward an outcropping of rocks.

The first log bounced and rumbled, taking down trees and brush in its path before rolling past her to slam into the women's greenhouse. Back she scooted, her breath harsh and gasping as another log rolled past, missing her by inches. She looked up the hill; another log was shooting straight toward her. Brendan rode the log like a surfer riding the waves.

Oh my God... "Brendan," she screamed.

Catching himself on a tree branch, he swung wide, landing on his feet, he pounded through the camp, picking her up, chair and all, he pushed the two of them under the rock outcropping.

A dozen logs and unearthed rocks rolled past, slamming into the house and greenhouse, missing the other greenhouse and the shed. The tiny house groaned under the weight of the logs before collapsing with a scream of shattering glass and splintering wood.

Silence surrounded her. Eyes wide and filled with fear, Irelynn waited with bated breath.

Marchetti's far-off high-pitched screams filtered through the forest ending as suddenly as they began.

"Justice served," Irelynn whispered.

Her body shook, and her vision narrowed to the face looking down at her. "Brendan. Are you really here?"

"I'm here, Sparky. I'm here." Brendan whispered.

Irelynn closed her eyes; relief surged through her body.

The tears rolled down her cheeks as he freed her hands and feet, the broken chair tossed aside. Enveloped in Brendan's strong arms, the sounds of the forest returned as he covered her face with kisses. Running his hands over her, he checked for injuries.

"God. George," holding her to his chest, he sobbed. "I thought I lost you."

She ran her hands over his face. "I'm okay. I'm okay."

Brendan rose to his knees, pulling her up with him at the frantic calls from the men, and running feet filled the camp. Irelynn, on her knees, looked around at the devastation.

Elijah jumped from log to log, his panic, and desperation showing in every leap he took. "Elyse? Anablue?" he bellowed.

"We're here," Elyse called out as they climbed out from under another rock outcropping.

Ryan ran to Irelynn and pulled her into a crushing embrace, followed by her brothers. Gramie and Rachel, and the dogs, were guided down the hill by Matthew and Michael as Irelynn was passed from one person to the next.

The hippy women came out from hiding in the shed, directing Aiden and Collin to open the remaining greenhouse door releasing the four hippy men. Joined by their women, they wandered the commune in shock at the destruction. One long haired man picked up an empty cooking pot; disappointment flickered across his face as he dropped it and picked through more rubble.

"Oh my God. Look at this place," Irelynn said.

Logs were strewn about like Tinker toys. One log had impaled the greenhouse. Supple young saplings swung back and forth while the brute force of the logs flattened larger trees and brush on the hillside.

Elijah still had his arms wrapped around Elyse and Anablue while Aiden and Collin searched for Baltini's guards and found what remained of them crushed beneath logs.

Max's voice came over the walkie talkie as the plane circled above. "Everyone okay down there? It looks like a tornado flattened the forest and the commune."

Mac took a quick head count. "Roger that. We're good," he replied.

CHAPTER 40

Stepping from the shower, Irelynn dried off and quickly dressed. Gramie's house was full of family. Outside, the children played a game of kickball. Irelynn's sisters in law, Amy, Sherry, and Susie, were in the kitchen, prep- ping a meal to feed the hungry families. Busy with their children, they had kept the home fires burning during the search for Irelynn. After hugs and kisses, they denied her offer of help, pushing her outside with a tray of condiments.

Two large picnic tables were pulled together, the benches filled with family. Crossing the large deck, Irelynn carried the tray and set it on the table. Brendan's arm snaked out and pulled her onto his lap. Wrapping her arms around his neck, she looked into his crystal blue eyes.

"How do you feel?" Brendan asked.

"Other than a few bumps and bruises, I'm fine," Irelynn replied.

Mac picked up the bottle of ketchup. "Clever girl. Picking something so simple to use as a message."

"I had to think of something my mom would know related to me," Irelynn replied. "And, of course, we had plan B."

"Plan B?" Ryan asked.

Irelynn smiled. "The chicken stew was laced with psychedelic drugs, guaranteed to provide a wild trip. Truthfully, it was like a three-ring circus. I didn't know who to watch more. It was fascinating and… scary."

"No judgment here, but it's dangerous to dabble with drugs. We'll take care of them. Help them to rebuild the commune," Ryan said.

"It's the least we can do after all they did to help Irelynn," Rachel said.

"What about Big Ben?" Irelynn asked.

"Why didn't the bear attack Irelynn?" Mac asked.

"Hmm. Big Ben. She found him as a cub and hid him in her closet for two weeks. It's possible he recognized her scent, but it's most likely because she didn't move. He didn't consider her a threat," Ryan said.

Irelynn tensed up. "I don't want him destroyed." She relaxed as Brendan lightly squeezed her waist in support.

"You know I have no control over that, especially after he killed two men. If the game warden finds him first, there's nothing we can do. We've already put live traps out. If we can catch him, we'll move him further out into the Sierra's this time," Ryan said.

"Two? Did you find Marchetti?"

Ryan sighed. "Aiden, Collin, and RJ just returned from tracking Marchetti. They found his partially buried body. We'll set a trap there since we know Big Ben will be back to finish his snack."

"I still don't know what Marchetti or Baltini wanted," Irelynn said.

"Rebecca gave you a can of Mace. Inside that can was a list of double agents. Marchetti's name was on that list," Brendan said.

"So, he was playing both sides. Why would Rebecca give it to me?"

"We don't know why. She was probably holding out for money; maybe Rebecca thought hiding it with you would be safe," Mac replied.

"Baltini didn't kill Rebecca, she was his sister. Marchetti did it," Irelynn said.

"I'm not surprised, though I should be. I should have known when Marchetti showed up in Vietnam that something was off," Mac said.

"Where is that list?" Donall asked.

Mac grinned, "It was hand delivered to a trusted source in D.C."

"Who delivered it?" Collin asked.

"Just a couple of retired guys on vacation," Mac replied.

Lifting his cup in a toast, he smiled at Gramps and Pops.

"I intend to put it all behind me and look to the future," Irelynn said.

Hearing giggles from behind her, Irelynn excused herself and went to sit with Gramie, Elyse, Anablue, and Jane.

"Seriously, Irelynn. You hid a grizzly bear cub in your closet?" Elyse said.

"Oh, that's nothing. She had a family of orphaned baby skunks in there once, which was fine until they started spraying. It took months to fumigate her bedroom," Gramie said.

"After that, my mom started doing daily checks to see what was living in my closet," Irelynn said.

"I'll tell you another little secret. She used to call skunks fart squirrels."

"I still do," Irelynn replied, "Which reminds me, I haven't seen Penelope around."

"She was begging at your mother's back door last week," Gramie replied.

"Who's Penelope?" Anablue said.

"My pet skunk," Irelynn replied. "I've always had a soft spot for animals."

"So, that snake I killed really was a pet?" Brendan said, coming up behind her and kissing her neck.

Irelynn giggled. "No. The day we met; Brendan killed a snake that threatened me."

Rolling her eyes, "Vietnam is full of creepy crawlies. I had a shit list of bats, rats, spiders, leeches, snakes, and mosquitoes this big," Elyse said, spreading her arms wide.

"It seems to me the Marine Corps was on that shit list," Elijah said, handing a plate to Elyse.

"Your name was at the top," Elyse replied, looking at the plate. "What is this?"

Irelynn gave her a strange look. "It's a hot dog."

"Oh. I've heard of hot dogs, but, I mean, it looks different than what I expected."

Grinning, Irelynn handed her the bottle of ketchup. "You're going to love it."

"Hot dogs are as American as apple pie," Anablue chimed in.

"I've never tasted apple pie," Elyse said.

"I can see I sorely neglected your upbringing," Pop's said, shifting Bunker to his other arm.

"Oh, daddy. How could you have known? You ate dinner very late, and I had mine earlier. Except when there were parties at the embassy, and when you made pancakes for breakfast, I ate mostly Vietnamese food," Elyse said.

"Still better than eating a snake," Irelynn said, popping a grape from a fruit bowl into her mouth.

"I guess I'm going to have to bake some apple pies," Rachel said. "I'll have to buy more flour first."

Anablue giggled. "Especially since Elyse hit Marchetti with your ten-pound bag. You should have seen him covered in flour. He looked like a ghost."

"Lucky for us, it provided the cover we needed to escape into the forest. Then we circled to untie Irelynn, but Brendan beat us to her," Elyse said.

Donall set a tray of hotdogs and hamburgers hot off the grill on the table. "If the two of you would learn to stay put, you wouldn't need to escape anything."

"We still need to discuss taking my car for a joy ride," Elijah growled.

Anablue gave him a mischievous wink. "I did enjoy driving your car. She purrs like a kitten on the straight away."

"You're lucky there's not a scratch on it," Elijah said.

"Don't we know it," Elyse breathed a sigh of relief.

Donall shook his head. "I almost had a heart attack watching the logging truck sliding sideways down the driveway from up above."

"Stopping mere inches from my Camaro," Elijah said, "By the way, why were you radio silent during the whole rescue?"

"Dropped my walkie-talkie," Donall replied.

"Don't let him fool you. He was too busy screaming like a little girl," Max called out from the other side of the deck.

"That's a little like the pot calling the kettle black," Donall said, "Agnes is a great pilot, but that's one experience I don't want to re-live."

Irelynn leaned over, nodding toward the twins. She whispered, "How do you tell them apart?"

"I wanted to paint numbers on their foreheads, but they objected," Anablue whispered back.

"Elijah has a dagger tattoo on his forearm." Elyse grinned.

"Hmm. That helps," Irelynn replied.

Irelynn admired Brendan, his brothers, and Mac as they leaned against the deck rail. The brothers with their wavy black curls and Mac with his shock of red hair. All tall and broad shouldered, there was an easy camaraderie in their brotherhood. From there, her gaze touched on her brothers, two of whom wrangled their children to sit at the kid's table for the meal. Sean and Jamie were at the grill while Matthew held his tiny son. The older men chatted about football. Blinking back the tears in her eyes. Irelynn was grateful to everyone who had come to her rescue.

The doorbell sounded from the front of the house. A few minutes later, Susie led Father Andrews to the back deck. The priest paused when he spotted the six Corrington boys. His eyes fell on Elyse and Anablue, then to Gramps and Pops.

"I'll be... So much for peace and tranquility. It seems you boys are going to follow me to the ends of the earth," Father Andrews said.

Brendan grinned, "Father Andrews, I didn't realize that when you said you were retiring from the Corps, you were coming to Irelynn's parish."

"Trust me. If I had known, I would have run in the opposite direction. Of course, I'm kidding, but you boys seem to be my cross to bear."

Donall stepped up to greet the priest. "Nice to see you again," he said.

"Donall. I haven't forgotten your last trick. There's a

special place in hell for those who let sea lions knock priests into the bay."

"Sorry about that, Sir," Donall replied.

"I suppose I should forgive you, but I find myself looking over my shoulder whenever you boys are around," Father Andrews said, spotting Irelynn as he made his way toward her.

Reaching out, he patted her hand, "Ah, Irelynn. I came as soon as I heard what had happened. I thank the lord that you are safe."

"Thank you. I'm happy to be back, but we have a group of people in desperate need. The hippies at the commune, they lost everything."

"We'll do a fundraiser for them. I'm sure you and your family will help. Where are they now?" Father Andrews asked.

"My dad put them into two bunkhouses at the logging camp," Irelynn replied.

"Good. Now, I'd like to have a private word with you and Brendan."

Brendan stepped off the deck and held Irelynn's hand.

Brendan led the way out to the meadow.

"I know the circumstances of your marriage are a bit odd. I suggest a do over. You need the proper marriage license, so there is no question you're legally married. You can have a ceremony, big or small, whatever your heart desires. I'm sure both of you and your families would be relieved. Think about it and let me know," Father Andrews said as he headed back to the deck.

Looking down into Irelynn's upswept face, her eyes sparkled, shining with love. Caressing her, Brendan pulled her into his arms. She closed her eyes and leaned into his embrace.

"I know we got off to a rocky start. I know I've said it before. I intended to start slow. Take you on dates and spend more time getting to know each other. But I find myself just wanting you. Now and forever. I don't want to wait a moment longer."

Brendan pulled a small box from his pocket and dropped to one knee.

"What say you, George Irelynn? Will you marry me…again?"

"Another Montagnard wedding?"

"Only if that's what you want."

Irelynn snorted. "Oh my God, Brendan. Yes. I'll marry you again, but this time. Let's make it traditional."

Brendan swept Irelynn into his arms as loud cheering rose from the deck. Placing the ring on her finger, he smiled. An oval Amber stone offset by two twinkling diamonds in a gold setting sparkled from her finger.

"My father bought this ring for my mother when I was born. I know she would be happy to see it on your hand."

"It's beautiful," Irelynn cried.

"It reminds me of your eyes," Brendan replied.

"I want us to keep wearing our Montagnard wedding bracelets."

"Of course. And we'll still go out on dates and such."

"You'll buy me a real spaghetti dinner?"

"Minus the sedatives," Brendan replied, grinning.

"Will you travel the world with me, if need be?"

"I'd follow you to the ends of the earth."

"It's okay with you to wait for babies?"

"Someday, when we're ready, we'll settle down and raise a family," Brendan replied.

"What about you? What do you want out of life?"

"Other than you, I don't know yet. I need time to process Vietnam and the things I've seen."

"You seem to like being a deputy sheriff."

"I do. Come on. I'm starving. Those burgers and hotdogs smell amazing."

"I have one question for you. You looked like a surfer riding the waves when you rode down the hill on that log. Have you ever surfed?"

Brendan smiled from ear to ear. "In my younger days, I lived to surf."

"You were one of those groovy surfer dudes?"

Wiggling his eyebrows, Brendan laughed. "Oh yeah. I thought I was all that."

"This I've got to see. Now we need to go to the beach."

"We can honeymoon there if you'd like."

"Don't we need to plan a wedding first?"

"We do seem to do things out of order, don't we?" Brendan replied.

CHAPTER 41

"Irelynn. Are you listening to me?" Elyse said. Irelynn looked up from her morning coffee and gave Elyse a scathing glare. "I'm not awake yet," she muttered. "Ooooh, someone is Miss Crabby pants this morning," Elyse said.

"I'm sorry, we can't all be Mrs. Mary Sunshine in the morning," Irelynn grumbled.

Elyse grinned. "Well, I'll repeat it again. Good morning."

"If it were a good morning, I'd still be asleep in bed," Irelynn replied.

Elyse giggled, "Brendan was a little annoyed last night when he found out he had to wait to sleep with you."

Irelynn snorted into her coffee. "You could say that again."

"You know, that's exactly what you need."

"What?"

Elyse snickered. "An early morning roll in the hay to put a smile on your face."

Irelynn growled.

"As I was saying. You, your mom, and Gramie should come to San Francisco to shop for your wedding gown."

Irelynn rolled her eyes and glanced over at her mother at the sink. "Shhh. Mom's got full blown wedding fever," she whispered.

"Be grateful you have your mother to help you," Anablue said, dunking chunks of cheddar cheese into a bowl of peanut butter.

"I know. I'm sorry. I don't want this to be three hundred guests, with a six-foot wedding cake to accompany the full orchestra type of affair."

"You need to make your wishes known," Gramie said. "What are you eating, my dear?"

"Cheese and peanut butter. It's good like this, but better as grilled cheese and peanut butter sandwich," Anablue replied.

"Oh, let me try it," Elyse said, taking a bite. "Yum. This is good. I've been partial to burnt toast and Liverwurst this time around. Here Irelynn, try it."

Irelynn shuddered, "No thanks. I'll pass on the weird pregnant food. For the wedding, something simple. And the sooner, the better."

Elyse waved her hand in front of Anablue's face. "Are you daydreaming?"

"Yes. I'm dreaming how much of a six-foot wedding cake I can eat."

Elyse dropped some cooled scrambled eggs onto Bunker's highchair tray. "Here you go, sweetie, eat up. I swear he's a bottomless pit just like his Auntie Anablue."

Jane, fresh from her shower, pulled up a chair. "Ha. You've only filled up his chunky little thighs."

"I know. Bunker eats more than I do," Elyse said.

"Nothing wrong with a good eater. My Ryan was like that, couldn't fill him up," Gramie said.

"I hope the men are comfortable staying at the logging camp. We offered your fathers to stay at our house, but they chose to stay at the logging camp with your men," Rachel said.

"Each bunkhouse sleeps twelve. I imagine it's a bit like being in basic training again," Irelynn said.

"Elijah said they've almost got the commune cleaned up and ready to start building the new house," Elyse said.

"That's good. We've imposed enough on your family," Anablue replied.

"Nonsense. We've enjoyed your company," Rachel replied. "Mac, Brendan, and the sheriff are wrapping up their investigation. Elijah and Donall are interested in learning how to build a log cabin," Irelynn said.

"Donall is debating building one on our beach property," Anablue said.

"Aiden and Collin are heading back to San Francisco tomorrow, but I heard they may stay on for a while. They're talking about creating a rescue service to help people lost in the mountains," Elyse said.

"Gramps, Pops, Capt. Jack, Max, and I are leaving today. They need to get back to work, and I feel much better now. John should have the door to Elyse's house repaired by now," Jane said.

"Who's John?" Irelynn asked.

"Elijah has a crew building our new house and John is the foreman," Elyse replied. "Elijah hires mostly Vietnam vets."

"That's wonderful. So many of these men have no idea what they are going to do for a living once their home from serving," Gramie replied. "Much as in any war, I imagine they have to learn to pick up the pieces and rebuild their lives."

Irelynn drummed her fingers on the table. "Along with Elyse's story, which would make an interesting article. I need to get back to work myself," she mused.

"Now, Irelynn, before you run off, let's talk about your wedding," Rachel said.

"Think small. Brendan said we could do whatever I wanted.

We just need to tell him when to show up."

"Typical. How did you girls plan your weddings?" Gramie asked.

"Um. Well. Mine was a bit off the rails. It was at Vung Tao on base," Elyse replied.

"Who were your bridesmaids?"

"Six of the biggest badass Marines you could ever meet," Elyse replied.

"Damn," Gramie said.

Irelynn rolled her eyes, "Gramie, you're drooling." Gramie grinned and winked.

"Mine was elegant but simple. Between Mrs. Wang, Jane, and Elyse, we pulled it off fairly quick," Anablue said.

"It was lovely," Jane breathed.

"See. That's what I'm talking about. Something simple. With nature and the mountains as our backdrop, we could have the ceremony and party right in our backyard," Irelynn said.

"It's doable. Maybe by month's end," Rachel replied.

"Before Halloween," Irelynn said.

"I could have your father build an arch."

"No. Let's assign that task to Brendan. It will give him something to do," Irelynn replied.

"I have one question," Anablue said. "Whose paying who with the goats and chickens?"

The women in the kitchen erupted into bright laughter.

Irelynn's head was spinning with the whirlwind activities of the past two weeks, between the shopping, dress fittings, choosing the menu for the wedding dinner. Not to mention working. She sighed deeply; the only time she had been alone with Brendan was during the few trips to and from San Francisco either on his motorcycle or in her truck. Except for their first date, Irelynn's mind wandered to the night before.

Brendan's eyes lit up and caressed every curve and valley as she made her way down the stairs at Mrs. Wangs. Her midnight blue minidress sparkled with the light of a thousand suns.

"You're stunning," he whispered into her ear, his breath warm and caressing, sending whispers of thrills down her spine as he helped her with her coat. Irelynn's clip on earring popped off, and Brendan caught it mid air. Clipping it back on her ear, "You are forever losing your earrings Sparky."

"Rose and Carol were supposed to pierce my ears, but we never got around to it."

"We'll have to remedy that for you," Brendan said.

Dinner was at a restaurant on Fisherman's Wharf. Well known for its Italian seafood, its Crab Cioppino, and seafood sausage was to die for. Fresh warm bread and a full bodied white wine complimented the meal. After dinner, they had strolled the wharf hand in hand until he returned her to Mrs. Wangs. They had lingered on the front steps kissing and hugging until Mrs. Wang flipped on the front porch light.

"Donall did warn me about Mrs. Wang and her porch light," Brendan murmured in her ear.

Irelynn giggled. "Such is life at Mrs. Wang's home for wayward women,"

Brendan chuckled. I'm sure Anablue and Donall would agree with that comment.

A final kiss and Irelynn slipped inside. Sighing dreamily, she leaned against the door. The night was perfect. She eyed the stairs, just a little tipsy from wine and Brendan's heady kisses. "Four flights. I can make it."

Elyse snapped her fingers in front of Irelynn's face. "You're daydreaming again."

"Hmmm. Yes. I was just thinking about our first date."

"It was that good?"

"It was candlelight, with desert and two spoons good," Irelynn replied. "Did you know Brendan plays the violin?"

"I'm not surprised. Elijah plays the piano, and Donall plays the flute. I know they all play an instrument."

"Elyse also plays the piano and the guitar. You've married into a creative family," Anablue said as she sat at the table.

"Well, you paint. How about you, Irelynn? Can you sing or play an instrument?" Elyse asked.

"God, no. I'm tone deaf and squawk when I sing."

Anablue daintily unfolded her napkin, placing it in her lap. "Can you draw or paint?"

"I can draw stick figures and a cool horse lady," Irelynn replied.

"But you're an amazing photographer and writer," Anablue said.

"Speaking of art. Gramie invited us to her art class tomorrow," Elyse said.

"Oh boy," Irelynn breathed.

"We figured once we finish getting everything ready for the bridal shower on Sunday, it might be fun to check out her class," Anablue said.

Irelynn rolled her eyes. "You do know she uses live models, right?"

"It should be fun," Elyse said.

Irelynn's eyebrows raised into her forehead. Tempted to explain, the little devil inside her decided it would be more fun to see their expressions when the male model dropped his sheet. Grinning mischievously, "Of course," she replied.

"This is a lovely restaurant," Anablue said.

Irelynn looked around the magnificent restaurant. Columns of marble graced the perimeter, adding to the old-world elegance of the venue. Golden chandeliers of Austrian crystal hung from a stained-glass ceiling. She spotted Gramie and her mom making their way through the tables with crisp white tablecloths and sparkling crystal glassware.

"Gramie's Gramie used to bring her here for special occasions," she said.

"My twenty sixth birthday was my first visit," Gramie said as she settled into her chair. "It was quite the grand affair. I've many happy memories here with my mother and grandmother. And now, my daughter-in-law, granddaughter, and you two lovely ladies. It's too bad Amy, Susie, and Sherry are missing lunch."

"They had to work. We'll meet them at the dress shop later," Rachel replied.

Gramie sighed. "Where is the waiter? I know what I want."

Irelynn picked up her menu. "What's good here?"

"I insist that you all try the Candle salad. It's quite refreshing. That, and the finger sandwiches are delicious," Gramie said." And a Mimosa to wash it down nicely." She pointed at

Elyse and Anablue, "Except for you two. It's orange juice and champagne."

"I guess I will have the same," Rachel said. "Me too," Irelynn, Elyse, and Anablue replied. "Minus the champagne," Elyse pouted.

The ladies chatted about the dress fittings scheduled for later in the day as they waited for their food. When the waiter appeared with a smirk and a wink, he started placing the Candle salads in front of them. Irelynn, Elyse, and Anablue looked at each other, trying to compose themselves.

There on a crystal plate sat pineapple rings with a banana standing straight up. Placed on a decorative bed of crisp lettuce and a layer of cottage cheese. All topped with a maraschino cherry, creamy mayonnaise dripped down the side of the famous fruit salad.

Irelynn blinked before whispering. "What is this?"

Gramie's eyes twinkled in amusement. "Candle salad. See, the banana is the candle; the mayonnaise is the dripping wax."

Elyse leaned forward and whispered. "I must have a dirty mind. This looks like a penis to me."

Rachel snickered, Anablue covered her mouth to stifle her giggles, and Irelynn shook with laughter as her hands fluttered to cover her eyes and red face.

"This is right up there with Gramie offering to teach

Brendan the finer points of lovemaking," Irelynn said as she wiped the tears of laughter from her eyes.

"Say what?" Elyse said.

"The ladies and I offered to instruct Brendan since Irelynn fell asleep in his arms," Gramie replied.

"You don't say," Elyse replied with a gleam of mischief in her eyes.

Irelynn knocked her banana over to lay on its side. "Open mouth. Insert foot."

CHAPTER 42

*B*rendan growled as he threw a chunk of wood to the ground. "Measure twice, cut once," he grumbled. "I measured ten times, and I still fucked up." Behind him, watching his every move from his in-law's deck, his brothers and Mac howled with laughter.

"Hey Picasso, how's that arch coming along?" Mac called out.

Brendan's brow fell in a thunderous frown; turning to look at his work, he sighed deeply. "Why is it not straight? Three times, I've started over three times." *I am not a carpenter.* Brendan looked up as Elijah placed his arm around his shoulder.

"Brendan," Elijah chuckled. "Let's scrap this um…work of art and start over."

"Gladly," Brendan replied.

From inside the house, Irelynn pulled the kitchen curtains back and peered out the window. Grimacing as she caught sight of the arch. "I guess I assumed he was a carpenter like his brothers."

"Everyone has different talents," Rachel said.

"I feel bad. Brendan's trying so hard."

"He stepped up to the plate, didn't he? Well, Elijah's out there now. I'm sure they'll figure it out."

"Okay. I'm heading up to Gramie's. Elyse and Anablue should be settled in by now. Max and Jane will be arriving anytime."

"Would you mind taking this lemonade out to the men first?"

Slipping her camera over her shoulder, Irelynn picked up the tray. "Anything to help."

Tray in hand, Irelynn stepped out on the deck. Setting the tray on the table, she lifted her camera, intent on capturing the men on film. Snapping photos of the brothers as they posed and preened for the camera, leaving Irelynn laughing out loud at their antics. Once she had them lined up and leaning against the rail, she admired Brendan, his brothers, and Mac. Gorgeous. Sexy. Every single one of them.

"Okay, boys. Let's play twenty questions while I snap some

pictures. Aiden, tell me about yourself."

Aiden grinned. "What's to tell?"

"Name, former rank, the instrument you play, and let's go with favorite sport."

"Aiden Yarusso. Major, US Army. Cello, and wrestling in high school and college."

"Yarusso is that your real last name?"

"Mom was married before. My dad passed in a training accident when I was an infant. I was adopted by father right before Brendan was born."

"And here I thought you used a fake ID that night. I'm sorry for your loss," Irelynn said.

"If it wouldn't have happened, I wouldn't have this motley crew watching my six."

"Brendan, my love?"

"Brendan Corrington, US Army, Special Forces, Green Beret. Violin. Surfing."

Irelynn grinned. "A surfer dude. Remember, you promised to teach me to surf."

Brendan winked. "I'll be teaching you many things."

Irelynn felt the slow burn of embarrassment creep from her chest to her cheeks.

Flustered, she aimed her camera at Collin. "Aaaand…next."

"Collin Corrington, Major, United States Marine Corps. I play the viola, and football was my game of choice."

"Football? I'm surprised. I take you for the calmest of this bunch."

"Everyone needs to let their beast out once in a while." Irelynn moved her camera to Donall.

"Donall Corrington, Captain. Naval Aviator. I play the flute, and baseball was my game."

"A naval aviator. Very cool."

"Next."

"Elijah Corrington. Major, Marine Corps. I play the piano and the guitar. Basketball."

"And you wrangle Elyse," Irelynn smirked.

"A sport unto itself," Elijah replied.

"Last but not least. Mac."

"Seamus McLoughlin, Major, Special Forces. My voice is my instrument, and I played basketball with Elijah."

"You didn't mention the CIA."

"I can neither confirm nor deny," Mac replied to the amusement of the others.

"Whatever. And how did you end up with this crew?"

"I grew up next door to the Corrington's. After my mom ran off with a Jody and my dad died, I was raised by Aunt Meg and father. I may have different parents, but these assholes are my family."

"What's a Jody?"

"Another man."

"You know, I think I have heard that term before. I'm sorry."

"Don't be."

"Why do you guys call your dad father? It sounds so formal."

"Aiden started it. Fodder became father," Gramps said.

Irelynn turned as Gramps, Pop's, and Capt. Jack stepped out on the deck.

"That's really cute," Irelynn replied. "So, the bachelor party is tonight. Any girls popping out of a cake?"

"God, I hope so," Mac said.

Irelynn narrowed her eyes and glared at Mac.

"Don't give me the evil eye. Your brothers planned the party," Mac said.

Irelynn held up one fist. "This is six months in the hospital." She held up her other fist. "This one is sudden death. You guys decide which one you want if any girl pops out of a cake."

Brendan chuckled behind her as his hands gripped her waist, pulling her close. "Easy, Sparky. I think I can handle myself," he said.

Irelynn turned in his arms, plucking at the collar of his shirt; she sheepishly grinned. "I'm sorry. I know you can. I've got a bit of the green-eyed monster in me."

Brendan stroked her smooth cheek. "When it comes to you, I'm the same."

"I'm late for Gramie's class."

Jane and Max stepped out into the deck. Max grinned as he set a cooler of beer down. "Get your ice-cold beer here."

"You guys are starting early. Jane. I'm heading up to Gramie's now. Come on. I'll take you up there. Trust me; you don't want to miss this."

"I'm game. Let's go," Jane replied.

Irelynn slid into her seat in front of an easel. Up on a platform, a chaise lounge sat in the middle of the room. Spread out in front of the lounger, the women sat in a half circle in front of their easels as Gramie handed out sheets of crisp white drawing paper.

"I've got chalk, watercolors, charcoal, and pencils to choose from. Help yourself, ladies," Gramie said.

Sipping on a small glass of moonshine, Irelynn sat next to Jane directly across from Elyse and Anablue. The elder ladies: Agnes, Alice, Margaret, and Gracie, filled the chairs in between. Sipping their moonshine, they giggled in nervous twitters.

A young man entered the room. Shirtless, a sheet wrapped around his trim waist. He flirted outrageously with the elder ladies as he climbed the podium to stand in front of them before dropping the sheet to the floor. Irelynn snorted and choked on her drink at the looks on Elyse and Anablue's faces. Eyes wide, their jaws dropped. Jane's face turned red, and she fumbled with her pencil, looking everywhere but at the man who now lounged on the chaise.

"Well, this…is…um…unexpected," Elyse said. "It's art, my dear," Agnes said.

Next to her, Anablue, flabbergasted, barked out a laugh and covered her eyes.

"Come now, girls. You've all seen a naked man before," Gramie said.

"Just a peek," Irelynn mumbled into her glass before draining it.

"Only Donall," Anablue replied.

"You're forgetting Woodstock," Jane said.

"They did seem to enjoy running naked through the festival," Elyse said.

"If you've seen one, you've seen them all," Gramie said. "Of course, size does matter," Agnes twittered.

"Can you at least give him a pillow to hide his linke pinke and tickles?" Anablue said.

Elyse took a sip of her orange juice. "You mean his cock and balls?"

Irelynn giggled. "Tickles. That's a good one."

The old ladies chortled; picking up their pencils, they started to draw.

Irelynn reached down next to her chair and picked up a jar of moonshine. Filling her glass and Jane's, she looked at Jane's paper. "Can you draw?"

"Nope. I'm just here for the show," Jane replied.

"Here. Here," Irelynn replied as they clinked their glasses.

Rachel pulled open the door to the deck. "Is Irelynn still here?"

"She's gone to Gramie's," Brendan replied.

"Shoot. I forgot to give her the goodie basket and this box of jars," Rachel said.

"I can take them up there," Brendan replied.

"Are you sure you want to venture into Gramie's lair during art class?"

Brendan pulled a jar from the box. "Sure. Why not. What're the jars for?"

"Moonshine. Her customers drop the empties off here."

"Is that even legal?" Mac said, taking the jar from Brendan.

"She has a permit for the still," Rachel replied.

"And here I had visions of Deputy Corrington here taking an axe to the old lady's still," Mac said.

Brendan chuckled. "I have no wish to end up on the wrong end of Gramie's shotgun."

"You'd be picking buckshot out of your ass for decades," Mac said.

"Let's drop this stuff off and check out this art class," Brendan said, hefting the box to his shoulder. Mac, think you can handle the basket? Wouldn't want you to strain something."

"Remember that the models are nude," Rachel called after them.

Brendan's eyebrows lifted into his forehead. "Are you kidding me?"

"Watch yourselves. Those little old ladies can't keep their hands to themselves," Aiden called out.

"How do you know?" Brendan asked.

"Irelynn's brothers sent us up there our first week," Collin said.

"Barely got out of there with my pants on," Aiden said.
"Nude models? Anablue is up there," Donall said.
"Elyse, too," Elijah said.
"Let's go check it out," Brendan said.
Mac smiled. "This whole thing is right up your alley."
Brendan grunted. "It's been a while."

Jumping out of the back of the truck, Brendan signaled his brothers, Mac, and Max, for silence. Leaving the box of jars and basket on the front porch, intent on mischief, they snuck around the house, peering in windows until they found the women in the back of the house in the sunroom. Kneeling against the side of the house, they grinned at each other before slinking around the back to crouch below the house.

"The guy in there is definitely naked," Brendan whispered.

A big grin split Donall's face. "This isn't exactly painting flowers."

"It doesn't piss you off?"

"Hell no, but that doesn't mean I'm not going to give her shit."

Mac lifted his head to peer in the window. "Now that we're here, what the hell are we doing?"

Aiden bringing up the rear, sided up to Mac." There's a beautiful woman here that I don't recognize."

"Really? What does she look like?" Mac asked.

"Stunning.... absolutely stunning," Aiden replied before pausing, "Shh. Someone is following us." He looked up just as a broom came crashing down on his head.

Lilly Beauchamp adjusted her silk bathrobe around her body. How she let her cousin Brian talk her into this was beyond her, but desperate times called for desperate measures. They had driven the few hours north from San Francisco to pose for a bunch of old ladies. The client had requested both male and female models for her art class today. The old ladies tended to get a bit bawdy with Brian, though the few times she had posed for them, they had been respectful and sweet to her.

Running a brush through her long dark brown hair, she checked her make-up in the mirror. Her heart sunk into her stomach when she spotted the reflection of a man peeking through the window.

Thinking of Gramie and the other vulnerable older ladies, she growled. Quietly moving from the room, she slipped out the front door. Spotting a broom on the porch, she grabbed the broom as a weapon and snuck around the house. Peeking around the corner, she spotted seven men crouched down below the windows.

Lifting the broom, she brought it down on the closest man, the one who had peeked in her window. "Peeping Tom pervert," she snarled.

CHAPTER 43

*A*iden felt the first whap of the broom bristles across his brow. "Ow," he sputtered as he reached out to grab and missed the swiftly moving broom. Time, and time again, the woman pummeled him with the broom before he pulled it from her hands and tossed it away.

"Dirty pervert. I'll teach you to peep through windows," she cried as she swung a fist at his head. Ducking, he easily caught her flying fists and pulled to her his chest. She twisted in his arms, and her knee came perilously close to unmanning him. The two tripped, losing their balance; they rolled to the ground.

"Ow. You bit me," Aiden said.

"Serves you right, you snake."

Aiden rolled, straddling her at the waist; he held her

hands above her head. She bucked her hips, trying to throw him off.

"Alright. I'm sorry. Stand down," he said.

Her breath came in short gasps. Outrage flashed from her chocolate brown eyes. Creamy skin, red from exertion, she gritted her teeth as she continued to struggle beneath him.

"Need some help there, old man?" Brendan said.

Aiden looked over to see his brothers watching him with amusement.

"You sure you can handle the wee piece of fluff?" Mac asked.

"I am not a piece of fluff," she snarled.

Aiden rolled his eyes. "Not helpful, Mac."

"Aiden. What are you doing? Get off Lilly," Gramie said from the deck above.

Aiden looked down into the beautiful eyes of the woman beneath him. "Lilly. How perfect," he murmured. "I'm sorry. I didn't mean to spy on you." Holding his hands up in surrender, he moved off her and rolled to his knees between her thighs.

Lilly sat up, clutching her robe closer; she glared at Aiden. Jumping to her feet, she picked up the broom, running past the men and up the stairs to the deck where Gramie and all the women stood looking down at the men.

Handing Gramie the broom. "I'm sorry. I can't do this today," Lilly said as she escaped into the house with Brian, wrapped in his sheet, on her heels.

"It alright, dear. We'll see you two next time," Gramie

called after her. Frowning, she swung her broom in a threatening manner toward the men. "The seven of you better pray she comes back."

Eyeing the broom in her hands, the men held their hands up in surrender.

"Easy, Gramie," Aiden said. "We'll fix this."

"What the hell are you boys up to anyway?"

"Obviously, no good," Brendan replied, following the entire group inside.

"Now what? We've lost our models," Alice said.

Brendan smiled. "No, you didn't."

Taking Irelynn by the hand, he led her over to the chaise. "Sit, my love," Brendan said.

"Brendan, if you think I'm getting naked here. You're wrong," Irelynn replied.

"I'll get you naked one of these days, but not today."

With a gentle hand, he pushed her down on the chaise. Kneeling in front of her, he removed her boots and socks. Arranging her artfully, so she was stretched out on the chaise; he pulled her dress and bra straps off her shoulder so just a peek of her round breast was exposed. Pulling the binder from her hair, trailing a finger down her neck, he caressed her shoulder and smiled when she shivered.

"Don't move," he whispered.

Picking up a piece of black charcoal and paper from a tray, he sat in Irelynn's seat.

"I see the unspoken questions in your eyes, my love. There was a time in my life when I was torn between what I loved. Surfing and art. And my duty to my country and family. I wanted to go to art school, and in the end, I chose West Point and was accepted. I did eventually take night art classes. Yes, I've sketched many a nude model. I've always loved the female form, but I prefer them partially clothed when I draw. It adds more mystique and excites the imagination at what lies beneath."

He glanced up at Elyse and Anablue standing next to him, watching him draw.

"I remember my first nude model. Once you get past your initial embarrassment, the artist kicks in, and you forget the person is nude. All you see are the sensual lines of her hair, the angle of her chin, and the curve of her breasts and hips. The inner beauty shines through, and the artist finds themselves desperate to capture the model's essence. For me, it's like making love with each stroke of the charcoal."

"My God, Brendan. I had no idea you could draw like this," Elyse breathed.

"It's been a while. Go on and sit down, ladies. George Irelynn is a breathtakingly lovely model," Brendan said.

"It was your sketchbook in the drawer at the hotel in Da Nang," Irelynn said after a while.

"Yup. Never did ask you why you took my Captain bars and shirt?"

"Oh. Umm. Other men are less likely to bother you if you're wearing an officer's shirt. An officer's implied lover is off limits."

Brendan grinned. "You made that up."

Irelynn smiled back, "Maybe. It's possible I just wanted your shirt."

"I look forward to seeing you wearing nothing but my shirt," Brendan said. Looking up from his sketch, he caught the blush play across Irelynn's cheeks.

"Well, that just made my lady parts all tingly," Alice said.

"I must agree. My glasses are a bit steamed up," Agnes replied.

Raising an elegant eyebrow, Brendan looked around the room at the nodding old ladies. "Sorry, ladies. I got carried away." Spotting what he thought was a glass of water, he drained the glass before realizing it was pure moonshine. Trying to draw a breath, he coughed and grimaced as Jane pounded him on the back. "Where are my brothers?" he croaked.

"You kind of got caught up in your drawing; they left an hour ago," Jane replied.

"The ladies are getting heated up. This is the part where you should probably run," Irelynn said.

CHAPTER 44

Smoothing down the silk of her wedding gown, Irelynn's thoughts returned to the day of her first wedding. The red dress and shoes specifically. Smiling, it was funny that she hadn't known it was her wedding day until weeks after. Looking down, the tips of her red shoes peeked out from beneath her gown as she walked down the aisle. Recalling the wild race through the village with the bull chasing her. *These shoes are not very good for running, but I have nothing to run from today.*

Brendan stood at the end of the aisle with his brothers and Mac at his side. Elyse, Anablue, and her sisters in law stood on the other side of Father Andrews. If there was one person missing today, it was Sierra. She would have loved to have her standing alongside the women. Looking lovely in their matching red dresses, they smiled tearfully as she made her way down the aisle. One hand gripped the bouquet of red roses while the other rested lightly on her father's arm. Tunnel vision took over, and all she could see was Brendan at the end of the aisle. His eyes held her, dipping momentarily to her red shoes; he grinned before his gaze rose to hold her in a captive embrace. Soon, she was at the end of the aisle; her father kissed her cheek before placing her hand in Brendan's.

"Nice shoes," Brendan whispered.

"I thought you might remember them," Irelynn replied.

"Any bulls around here?"

"Nope."

"Then we should be good."

Brendan lifted her veil over her head. When her grandmother's clip on pearl earring shot off her ear, he deftly caught it mid-air and clipped it back on her ear with a grin.

Taking her hand in his, they stepped up to stand in front of Father Andrews and the arch lovingly decorated with red roses and baby's breath. They exchanged vows and placed rings on each other's fingers.

Irelynn felt a soft rubbing against her ankles. Looking down, she gasped as Penelope, the skunk, peeked out from under her dress and darted to the priest. Eyes wide, she caught the stunned expression on Elyse's face just as the priest pronounced them man and wife.

"Shoo. Shoo. Penelope," Irelynn whispered.

Catching Brendan's eye, they looked down and froze as the skunk weaved in and out of Father Andrew's legs.

"Penelope. Go home," Irelynn hissed.

Brendan slowly pulled Irelynn back. Father Andrews gave them a confused look before looking down in horror.

Mac and the brothers shuffled nervously and backed away. The skunk lifted its tail, and Elyse, Anablue, and the other women squealed and darted away from the arch. The groomsmen pulled further back as chaos broke out when the skunk shook its tail, spraying Father Andrews. Brendan scooped Irelynn up, throwing her over his shoulder; he ran down the aisle. The guests scrambled, and every able-bodied man scooped up little old ladies and children. Running up the aisle, they left Father Andrews standing alone beneath the arch. Father Andrews scowled at the crowd gathered at the far end of the aisle and snapped his bible shut.

Wrapped around Brendan's shoulders like a faux fur stole, Irelynn breathed. "Oops."

"Ryan. Get the tomato juice," Gramie bellowed.

Gramie lifted a glass of moonshine over the makeshift outdoor curtain. "Here, Father Andrews, drink this. It will make you feel better. Then hang your clothes on the end of this pole." She nodded and smiled at the coughing and choking coming from the other side of the curtain.

Rachel handed Ryan standing on a ladder, another can of tomato juice. "Douse him good. Make sure he scrubs good, then hose him off."

Taking the clothes dangling from the pole, Gramie

dropped them into a large steaming pot hanging over the bonfire. "We'll be lucky if he doesn't ex-communicate the whole lot of us," Gramie grumbled.

"Nah, he's pretty understanding," Gramps said. Taking the stick from her, he stirred the pot. "I've known Father Andrews since I was a recruit, and he was fresh out of the seminary. He's a fantastic priest. He'll get over it. He always does."

"He's sure got some colorful language."

Gramps chuckled. "He's still a Marine."

"I'm praying we can get the skunk stench from his vestments."

"I'm right there with you. Though, it's not the first time I've paid for replacements," Gramps said.

"Your boys?"

"I've always said, when it came to trouble, what one didn't think of, the others did."

Another string of colorful language came from behind the curtain as Ryan aimed the hose.

"We're all going to hell," Gramie said.

Sipping champagne, Brendan looked down into the shining eyes of his bride. "You look beautiful."

"Thank you. You're pretty handsome yourself," Irelynn replied.

"I want you to wait until after dinner, then go put your combat boots on," Brendan said.

"Why? I didn't think I would be running from you today."

"You'll be running with me, not from me."

"Who are we running from?"

"My brothers. I'm sure they have something up their sleeve."

"Elyse and Anablue told me what happened on their wedding nights and to Collin's wife."

Brendan grinned from ear to ear. "Epic. Though we didn't plan on Anablue getting in the wrong limo."

"So, you're saying that your brothers will be out for revenge?"

"I need you to know that whatever happens, I will find you."

"I know you will."

"Promise me you won't worry about it," Brendan said.

"I promise. A toast, my love. What shall we toast too?" Irelynn said.

Brendan grinned. "Spaghetti."

"Spaghetti," Irelynn breathed.

Sipping his champagne, he placed a seductive kiss on her shoulder. "Speaking of food. What the hell happened to the cake?"

"The baker almost hit a deer. The cake damn near ended up in the ditch feeding all my little forest friends."

"It looks like the Leaning tower of Pisa."

"Mom's frantic, but it will taste the same."

"Let's go eat. What are we having?"

"Spaghetti," Irelynn replied.

"No drugs?

"No drugs. Are you going to keep me awake this time?" she teased.

Brendan growled deep in his chest. "All night long."

Boots on and ready to go at Brendan's word, Irelynn smiled. Moving through the remaining guests, accepting kisses and hugs, she laughed and smiled while scanning the crowd for a glimpse of Brendan. He had gone inside a while ago and hadn't returned. Elyse and Anablue stood conversing with her parents beneath the bright white Christmas lights twinkling around the yard. A small band set up near the temporary dance floor still had a few people locked arm in arm, swaying gently to the sensual beat of the music. The children had all been shuffled inside, nestled snuggly into spare beds so their parents could enjoy the evening.

Irelynn looked around for Gramie, normally the life of the party; she couldn't imagine that she would have gone home already. Jane sat deep in conversation with Gramps, Pops, Father Andrews, and Capt. Jack. Brendan and his brothers, Mac, and Max were all missing.

The hackles on her spine raised as she realized something was up. Moving swiftly across the yard toward Elyse and Anablue, she paused in front of them.

"I'm sorry to interrupt, but have you seen Brendan or his brothers? They seem to be missing. Gramie's gone too," Irelynn said.

Looking around, Elyse frowned. "No. I haven't seen Elijah since we danced."

"The same with Donall. That was half an hour ago," Anablue said.

"I'm going to check the house," Irelynn said.

Elyse nervously chewed her lip. "We'll help you look."

Crossing the lawn, they made their way through the crowd of guests, their voluminous skirts swishing as they moved between the numerous tables set up for the party.

Making her way through the kitchen and down the hallway, Irelynn stepped over Ralph and Soup, guarding the bedrooms where the children slept. The women quietly peeked in each door.

Rachel followed nervously behind them. "Irelynn. I'd like to have a word with you."

Turning to look at her mother, noting the worried expression on her mother's face, Irelynn paused. Oh boy.

"Can you give us a few minutes?" Irelynn said.

"We'll check out the front and the garage. I know there were men out there smoking earlier," Elyse said.

Irelynn slipped her hand into Rachel's, allowing herself to be pulled down the hallway into her parent's bedroom.

Rachel nervously plucked at her hands. "George Irelynn. I wanted... well...I... it's your wedding night."

"Yes, mom."

"Brendan's a man, and you're a woman. Er.. I wanted to see if you had any questions. Um, questions about…tonight and…sex," she whispered. Irelynn picked up her mother's hand and patted it. "I'll be fine, mom."

"Of course, you'll be fine. I wanted to make sure you understood."

"Yes. Thank you for talking to me. It will be okay. You can relax now."

"I'm so relieved," Rachel replied.

"I love you, mom."

"I love you too."

"I could use a drink," Rachel said.

Grinning, Irelynn wrapped her arms around Rachel. "Me too."

Stepping out on the front porch, Irelynn gently shut the screen door.

"Everything okay?" Anablue asked.

"Yes, she wanted to have 'The talk.'"

"The talk? Oh…that talk," Elyse said.

"I kind of feel bad. She was probably worried about it all day," Irelynn said.

"No one's out here," Anablue said.

"My brothers were out back dancing. Where are the rest of the men and Brendan?" Irelynn asked.

"I get that the men would be gone. But… You're still

here," Anablue said.

"What does that mean?" Irelynn said.

"It means in a new twist on their games, they've kidnapped Brendan," Elyse said.

Brendan blinked at the bright lights as the hood was removed from his head. His mouth was covered with duct tape, his eyes frantically moved around the theatre. Duct taped to the middle seat in the front row; he struggled in the seat.

Three folding chairs were placed in a half circle in front of him as he became aware of people sitting behind him in the otherwise empty theatre. The scent of popcorn and fresh butter teased his senses as someone slurped their drink through a straw.

What the actual fuck.

Someone placed their hand on his shoulder, and Aiden whispered in his ear. "A little birdie told us that you desperately needed some education."

Next, Collin chuckled in his ear. "Revenge is a dish best served cold. Enjoy the movie, bro."

"Remember my wedding night when you put that duct tape across my stomach? I still have bald spots." Donald said, patting him on the shoulder.

"Lucky for us, Elyse talks in her sleep. There will be a question-and-answer session after the movie," Elijah said.

"We'll check with Irelynn tomorrow to see if you passed the test."

Question and answer? Test?

"Brendan, my friend. You should have come to me. If I had only known you needed help. Ah, well, this should clear things up," Mac said.

Max snickered behind him. "Sorry, dude, but I wouldn't have missed this for the world."

Their footsteps echoed up the ramp; laughing uproariously, they left the theatre.

The lights dimmed, and the movie started. 'Understanding Reproduction' glared on the screen.

Brendan closed his eyes, and he inwardly groaned. *Sex Education? Are you fucking kidding me? I saw this when I was, like, twelve.*

Fifteen minutes later, the movie was over, the lights came on, and Brendan blinked. Gramie and the ladies sat on the chairs in front of him.

"We were told not to remove the duct tape over your mouth. We understand you can't reply. You can nod your head yes or no," Agnes said.

"Brendan, your brothers, told us you have yet to learn how to please a woman," Gramie said. "Out of concern, they asked us to help."

No. Just no. I'm going to kill them.

"Yes. We heard Irelynn fell asleep in your arms," Agnes said.

What! No. We were drugged.

"We're aware the film only addressed human reproductive organs and their purpose, but we thought it was a good starting point," Alice said. "We believe in being open and honest about a woman's needs. We're not prudes."

"Do you know what a clitoris is?" Gramie asked.

Brendan leaned his head back and closed his eyes. *Oh, God. I'm done. Just kill me now.*

Agnes rapped his knuckles with a ruler, and his head snapped back up. "Pay attention. This is important."

"Back to the question. Do you know what a clitoris is?" Gramie asked.

Noting the sparkle of amusement in her eyes. Brendan narrowed his eyes at Gramie.

She's having fun with this. I'm going to play along to get through this; he nodded his head.

Oh, but you and my brothers are going to pay.

Gramie nodded in satisfaction. "Wonderful. There are a few sensitive places on a woman's body. Direct stimulation with your hands or tongue work best."

"Oh yes," breathed Alice. "You're going to want her wet."

Brendan closed his eyes and groaned. Wapp, the ruler slammed down on his knuckles again.

Owwww…

"Nipples. Don't forget about the nipples," Alice said.

"It should be pleasurable for both of you. We did show Irelynn how to practice on a banana," Agnes said.

Brendan's eyebrows reached for the sky.

"What is it they call it nowadays?" Gramie said.

"A blowjob. We called it dicky licking in my day," Alice said.

"Say's the queen of dicky licking," Gramie said.

I don't think I need to know this.

"I'm sure I've heard it called head," Agnes said.

"Now, don't forget. If you're not ready for babies yet, use a condom," Gramie said.

Alice sighed. "Or pull out."

"That's not very effective. I got pregnant with my Charles Jr. relying on that method," Agnes replied.

"They help prevent venereal disease, too," Alice whispered. "Bad stuff."

"He's a virgin. How would he know about that?" Agnes asked.

I am not a virgin. *And don't they have the pill now?*

"We drew pictures to show you where everything is located," Gramie said, holding up pictures.

You have got to be kidding me.

Alice leaned in and whispered. "Between you and me. You should tie her up and spank her once in a while. It's quite exciting."

Brendan rolled his eyes. *This… is going to haunt me for the rest of my life.*

"Oh, look at the time. I need to go home and take my pills," Agnes said.

"You're going to have to drive my car and take us home. None of us can see at night to drive," Gramie said, pulling the duct tape from his mouth.

"Thank you, ladies. That was very…educational," Brendan said.

"You're welcome, dear," Agnes replied.

The ladies had been delivered home safe and sound. He had walked each lady inside, checked in closets and under beds at their request to make sure they were safe. Now, he sat in Gramie's car right outside her house.

"You know that was all bullshit, right?" Brendan asked.

Gramie grinned and winked before getting out of the car. Leaning into the car, "What is it they say? The devil made me do it."

Brendan snickered. "Do you want me to walk you in?"

"Hell no. I'm more than capable."

"I know you are," Brendan replied.

"You take good care of my little George Irelynn."

"Until my dying breath."

"I do have to agree with your brothers. It was epic," Gramie winked again and shut the car door.

A car pulled into the driveway, and Brendan watched in amazement as the old doctor made his way up the walkway. The front door opened, and Gramie kissed the man before yanking him inside.

Sex into your eighties. I'll be damned.

Picking up the hand drawn pictures, he laughed till he cried. He had to hand it to his brothers and Mac; it was an epic prank. Not that he'd ever admit it. Tomorrow, he'd think about getting even. But tonight…He still had to find his bride and practice what he had *learned*.

"Assholes," he snarled. Wiping the tears of laughter from his eyes, he put the car in reverse and backed out of the driveway.

CHAPTER 45

Pacing back and forth on the front porch, Irelynn turned to Elyse and Anablue. "What do you know about this?"

"We don't. The guys are secretive about their pranks," Elyse replied.

"He'll be back. Meanwhile, we have a surprise for you," Anablue said.

"A surprise. What about Brendan?"

"He will find you. I promise," Elyse said.

"I know. I promised him I wouldn't worry about it, but now I have visions of them duct taping Brendan to the top of a giant redwood."

"They do love their duct tape," Anablue replied.

"That's not very comforting," Irelynn replied.

Peering out over the driveway, Irelynn spotted headlights coming up the road. "Is that them?"

"Yes." Hands on her hips, Irelynn watched as the car pulled up in front of them, and the men climbed out. Laughing at some joke, they quieted upon spotting her standing on the porch.

"Where's Brendan?" Irelynn asked.

"He'll be along shortly," Aiden replied.

Narrowing her eyes at the men. "What did you do to him?"

They all looked up to her with shit eating grins.

"Nothing much. We left Brendan enjoying a movie," Mac replied.

"A movie? The town theatre closed hours ago," Irelynn said.

"Special screening," Collin replied with a deep chuckle.

Elijah snorted and looked up at Elyse. "Is everything ready, brat?"

"Ready and waiting," Elyse replied.

The men whooped, and Irelynn squealed as she found herself blindfolded and flung over Mac's shoulder. RJ and Jane came from around the side of the house, carrying a few flashlights. The group cheered and moved to the back of the house and down the path through the woods.

The lively group crossed to the middle of the meadow, directly in front of Irelynn's giant redwood tree house; Mac set her on her feet. Smoothing out her gown and pushing everything back in place. "Seriously, Mac. Was it necessary to manhandle me like that?" Irelynn said.

"Can't have little people walking through the dark, scary woods on their own."

Irelynn rolled her eyes. "It's not scary. Besides, Elyse, Jane, and Anablue got to walk."

"Since I'm never getting married, I thought it would be a good experience to have a bride flung over my shoulder."

"Famous last words," Irelynn replied.

"Don't you go jinxing me too," Mac growled.

Irelynn giggled. "Wouldn't dream of it. Can you take the blindfold off now?"

"In a minute. We have to wait for Elijah and Collin to light the way."

A gasp escaped from Elyse, and Anablue standing next to her. "Oh, look. It's beautiful."

"Okay, turn around, and I'll remove the blindfold," Mac said.

Tingling in anticipation, Irelynn turned around. Mac's fingers fumbled in the dark as he untied the blindfold.

Even in the dark, Irelynn knew the meadow she stood in; her childhood hide out and old swing were behind her. Slowly she turned back around, and a soft gasp escaped her as she looked across the meadow. Instead of the old platform built into the side of the giant redwood, she saw a large tree house. Steps with a built-in railing for safety wound up around the old tree to a porch surrounding a screened in room. Coleman lanterns softly lit the room, the glow spreading across the meadow.

"Oh my god. It's a Tarzan in the jungle tree house. Brendan should be here to see this."

Irelynn looked around to see the rest of her family had joined the group.

"He will; we'll leave a breadcrumb trail so he can find you," Ryan said.

Rachel wrapped her arms around her. "I'll say goodnight now. Elyse and Anablue will help you prepare yourself. I'm not climbing those steps. I might not get back down."

Giggling, Irelynn kissed her parents and family goodnight.

Hiking up her skirt, Irelynn whooped. Racing across the meadow to the tree, giddy with laughter, she stopped at the steps waiting for the group to catch up.

"Holy shit. No wonder Brendan had a hard time catching you," Elijah said.

"Three-time track and field champion," Irelynn replied.

"It's how she outran the bull on her first wedding day," Mac said.

Irelynn smiled as she fingered her wedding bracelet. Holding Irelynn's hand, Aiden led the way up the winding stairs to the porch.

Irelynn walked around the porch admiring the limited view in the dark. She could see the occasional flashlight beam as her family returned to her parent's house. Collin held the screen door open as she made her way inside. She paused to admire the room, her eyes falling on the platform bed against one wall. Sleeping bags and soft down pillows filled the space with rustic, roughhewn nightstands on either side of the bed. Mosquito netting draped from the ceiling to cover the rose petal covered bed. A plate of strawberries and a bottle of champagne chilled in a bucket on a small wooden table and chairs.

"This is stunning. You guys built this for us?" Irelynn said.

"We figured since you're not going to a hotel for the night, you needed somewhere special to hide out instead of your cabin," Donall said.

"This is perfect."

"We got the inspiration from Gramie's old lumberjack pictures showing buildings built into the sides of giant redwoods," Collin said.

"Dad provided the plans and his expertise. Your new family here supplied the labor," RJ said.

"It's beautiful. You guys made the furniture too?"

"Aiden and Collin did," Elijah replied.

Elyse pointed toward the bed.

"We were going to haul a mattress up here, but we worried your forest friends might make it their new home."

"It might get chilly this time of year, so we brought lots of blankets and sleeping bags," Anablue said.

Mac snorted. "Brendan will keep her warm."

"Speaking of, where is Tarzan?" Irelynn asked.

Max looked at his watch. "We've got to go."

"Thank you, guys, for everything. I'm sure Brendan will feel the same."

The men laughed. "We'll see how Tarzan feels after Gramie and the ladies finish with his class," Aiden said.

"Oh my god. What did you guys do?" Irelynn said.

"Just a little harmless fun. Soon to be followed by some OJT." Mac replied.

After kisses and hugs, Elyse shooed the men out. "We need to hurry. Out you go."

"We'll…um…wait below for you," Elijah said, following the men out the door.

Pulling into his in-law's driveway, Brendan killed the engine. Racing up the front steps and through the front door, he impatiently paused to hold the door for the crew hired to serve the meal and clean up. Making his way through the house to the back deck, he found Rachel and Ryan enjoying a glass of wine. Rachel's legs were on Ryan's lap as he massaged her feet.

"There you are, Brendan. Don't mind us if we don't get up. My feet are killing me, and I'm enjoying my massage," Rachel said as she took a sip of her wine.

A grin split Brendan's face as he chuckled. "Not a problem. You both deserve to rest."

"Before I forget," Ryan said, handing Brendan an envelope. "Open it tomorrow."

"From the bottom of my heart, thank you for everything," Brendan said, sliding the envelope inside his jacket pocket.

"Any idea on where they hid my bride?"

Ryan and Rachal grinned.

Brendan gazed over the empty yard as Ryan handed him a flashlight.

"Follow the roses," Rachal replied.

Stepping off the steps and into the yard, Brendan aimed the flashlight toward the yard. There, he spotted a rose petal in the grass. Picking up the petal, he inhaled the sweet floral scent. Aiming the flashlight, he spotted another, then more scattered across the lawn.

A rose petal trail?

Following the trail onto a path, he made his way through the woods. The petals on the ground thickened as the trail wound playfully around trees and bushes before continuing back on the path. An owl hooted above, and the forest was alive with night creatures called as if taunting him to find his missing bride. Excitement built when he found himself on the edge of a familiar meadow. Soft light spilled out above the tree line; his eyes rose in amazement to the new tree house built into the giant redwood. There, leaning against the railing, was the curvy outline of a woman.

His breath caught in his throat. *Irelynn.*

CHAPTER 46

Illuminated by the light of the tree house, a mama deer and her twin fawns grazed in the meadow. Irelynn could not tell from the distance if it was Bambi, one of the fawns she had rescued and eventually released by the game refuge back into the wild. A bit cold, Irelynn rubbed her arms as she watched for Brendan from her bird's eye view. Her mind returned to the day's events, from Penelope spraying the priest to the leaning cake. The speeches after dinner had left her in stitches. Father Andrews's stories about Brendan, his brothers and Mac had her wondering how her father-in-law had survived the six boys.

Her perfect day had a few mishaps, but she had married the man of her dreams twice, and her happiness knew no bounds.

Her eyes caught the movement of a man jogging through the meadow.

"There he is," she breathed.

He stood beneath the tree a moment later, looking up at her. "Evening, Mrs. Corrington."

"Major Corrington."

"Are you going to stand down there all night? Or would you rather come up here and kiss me?"

"Oh, I'm coming up there," he said. Pulling off his tie, he slowly made his way up the steps toward her. "And I'm going to do more than just kiss you."

Irelynn nervously chewed her lip, running a hand down her curves, "Like what?"

"Like what? Hmm. First, I will kiss every inch of your luscious body."

"And then?" she seductively called to him, watching as he made his methodical way up to her.

"How about I show you?" Brendan said as he made it to the top of the stairs.

Slowly backing up, a smile lit her face. "It's about time you got here, Tarzan."

Closing the distance between them, "If I'm Tarzan, what does that make you?"

"Jane?"

"Nah. George of the jungle," Brendan said. Running a finger along her shoulder to the edge of her nightie. "Leopard print. It goes nicely with the tree house." "I think they had a theme going here."

"As long as it doesn't involve me in a loincloth," Brendan chuckled, glancing around. "This tree house is pretty cool."

"Come on. I'll show you." Taking him by the hand, Irelynn led the way inside.

Shrugging out of his jacket, he flung it on a chair. "I don't want to see that stuff now,' Brendan said.

"No? What do you want to see?"

"As lovely as you look, I want to see you shimmy out of that nightie."

"What about the cool pulley system to haul supplies up here?"

"Nope."

"Or the furniture your brothers made?"

"Tomorrow."

Irelynn giggled as she backed away from him. "Would you like some champagne and strawberries?"

"Later."

Brendan kicked off his shoes and unbuttoned his shirt while advancing, his smile a mile wide. Irelynn's eyes widened at the bare expanse of his chest as he flung his shirt away. He dropped his pants, kicked them away, and peeled off his socks. Irelynn's eyes dropped to his visible bulge, which seemed to grow by the minute. Inhaling sharply, her heart pounded in her chest, and her body quivered with nervous energy as her eyes rose to his.

Pulling the nightie off her shoulder, she hesitated a moment before letting it drop to catch on the curve of her breasts. Brendan reached out, tugging at it. It fell to pool in a silken swirl at her feet.

"You are stunning," Brendan said.

"You think so?"

Brendan lifted a lock of her chestnut curls before running his hand along the curve of her breast. "Spectacular," Brendan replied, pulling her into his arms.

Wrapping her arms around his neck, Irelynn grinned mischievously, memories of their first wedding filling her thoughts. "My ta-ta's did look spectacular in that red dress."

"Even better now." his mouth found hers sending shivers up her spine.

Goosebumps dotted her arms as he plundered her mouth, his deep kisses probing. Her nipples pebbled hard against his chest. She wasn't sure if it was from the cold or the burning ache deep inside her core. His hands slid down her waist to squeeze her bum; lifting her, she settled around his waist, wrap- ping her legs around him as he carried her to their makeshift bed. He laid her on the bed; Irelynn giggled when a little poof of rose petals rose to land gently on her face. Irelynn's eyes crossed as she tried to blow a rose petal from her forehead. Brendan grinned as he brushed the petals from her face and hair.

"How did you find me?"

"They left a trail of rose petals through the forest," Brendan said.

Irelynn bit her lip. "That's sweet."

"Not as sweet as that lip you're chewing on," Brendan said as he trailed a finger across her plump, quivering lips before lowering his mouth to hers.

"Or this shoulder," he murmured, placing a light kiss on her shoulder. "And these curvy mounds with their pink tips."

Irelynn moaned as she arched into him, gripping his shoulders with her hands; his mouth worked its magic as his tongue moved back and forth between each rosy crest.

Her hands trailed down his arms as she explored his body, and the soft black curls on his chest contrasted with the power radiated through him. Her toes curled, and she softly moaned at every sensation. Brendan whispered sweet words as his mouth and hands slipped lower to her smooth belly, then lower as he pulled her silk leopard panties down her quivering thighs. His mouth found hers as he teased and plundered her body, leaving her with driving anticipation and a sense of urgency.

Long into the night, Brendan loved her until, exhausted, she'd fallen asleep in his arms. Pulling her close, he tucked the blankets around her before brushing the rose petals from their pillows. A rose petal stuck to his fingers; shaking his hand to remove the stubborn petal, he brushed his hand against the side of the bed before reaching over and diming the lantern. He lay in the darkness listening to the sound of the forest and

Irelynn's steady breathing. He grinned at the occasional light snoring that escaped her lips.

He chuckled lightly. "I think I passed the test."

At some point, his breathing steadied, and he drifted off to sleep.

CHAPTER 47

Wrinkling her nose at the tickling sensation, Irelynn opened her eyes to see Brendan resting on his elbow. Rose petal in hand, he trailed it across her lips and down to circle her taut nipple.

"Morning, beautiful," Brendan said.

"Morning," Irelynn grumbled as she tried and failed to burrow back under the warmth of the blankets.

"A little birdie told me you're grumpy in the morning."

"I'm pretty sure I told you that back in July."

"I have the perfect thing to cheer you up?"

"Does it begin with a C?"

Brendan threw back his head and roared with laughter. "Actually. It does."

"Oh my God. I meant coffee."

"And I meant this…"

Rolling her beneath him, nuzzling her neck. He paused; a look of consternation crossed his face.

"Have you grown fur on your legs overnight?"

"What?"

"Don't move. There's something in our sleeping bag."

Brendan leaned over, lifting the sleeping bag; they looked down between their feet.

"Penelope. How did you get in here?" Irelynn said. "I'm sorry. She thinks she's a dog."

"Can we get her out of there before she sprays the family jewels?"

Giggling, Irelynn lifted the skunk from her warm snuggly spot. "Naughty girl. Outside with you," she whispered. Pulling a blanket from the bed, she covered herself before padding to the screen door to set Penelope outside.

"We didn't lock the screen door last night. We're lucky it wasn't Big Ben."

"I'm sure I would know if there was a grizzly parked at my feet."

Irelynn rolled her eyes.

Brendan crooked his finger and patted the bed. "Come here so we can greet the morning properly."

Clutching the blanket around her chest, Irelynn tossed him a playful look as she backed away. She squealed when he jumped from the bed and stalked her with the skills of a predator.

"Coffee," Irelynn said.

"Later," Brendan replied, catching the edge of her blanket, he gave a tug. Leaving him holding an empty blanket amidst a stream of laughter, Irelynn raced to the bed; diving across the bed to the other side, she rolled to stand up. She wrapped another blanket around herself as Brendan snatched her by the waist, and they tumbled back onto the bed.

Brendan's deep voice chuckled as he snuggled her neck. "New rule. No blankets allowed in the bedroom."

Irelynn snorted as she wrapped her arms around his neck. "I'll freeze."

"No, you won't," Brendan said as he nudged her knees apart.

"I'm going to keep you so hot those beautiful eyes of yours are going to shoot sparks of amber."

"Like fireworks? Or a powder keg?"

"More like an ammo dump going up in flames." Irelynn chewed her lower lip.

"Like last night?"

"Last night was just the beginning," Brendan said as he lowered his lips to hers.

EPILOGUE

Irelynn lifted her camera to snap a shot of Brendan. They sat in Istanbul drinking Turkish coffee in an outdoor café on the Sea of Marmara. Brendan reached out and stroked her hair, pushing a strand behind her ear. "The hoop earrings look perfect."

Irelynn gave him a dazzling smile. "You did a wonderful job of piercing my ears. All with a needle, a potato, and some ice."

"I'm kind of missing those days of catching flying earrings."

Irelynn raised her camera again. "You got pretty good at it."

"Put the camera down, Sparky, and drink your coffee before it gets cold."

Irelynn grinned. "I can't help it. You're just so handsome with your hair growing out."

Brendan brushed his black wavy curls back. "I look like a long-haired hippy freak."

"It's perfect for the hippy trail."

Spreading a map across the table, Brendan grinned. "Thanks to the honeymoon trip from your parents."

"That envelope the day after the wedding was quite the surprise. I can't believe we've been gone five weeks."

"Istanbul to Beirut, then on to Tehran and Kandahar. Kahir, Delhi. Kathmandu, my favorite. Bangkok and Goa. Now back in Istanbul before heading to London. It's been an adven- ture with trains, planes, and a broken-down double decker bus teetering on the side of a mountain, but I'm ready to go home."

"Speaking of, let's see the letters we picked up at the Poste Restante," Irelynn said.

Brendan handed her a letter. "Letters from your parents, father, and Mac."

Irelynn scanned the letter from her parents. "They caught Big Ben. Before he left, Mac set up a military chopper to trans- port him to Yellowstone for release. My dad said he'll find many pretty girl Grizzly's there."

"Even giant Grizzly's need loving. He'll be happy there."

Father says he thinks Aiden is searching for Lily."

"Lilly? After Gramie's art class, I'm not so sure she wants him to find her."

"She does swing a wicked broom. All is well, except Collin went back to Nam with Mac."

"Did he re up?"

"No. He went as a civilian. I'm assuming to patch things up with Belinda."

"I thought she was in Taiwan. Do you think he's working with Mac now? I wish we knew more about that."

Brendan shrugged his shoulders. "It's Collin's story to tell."

"And Mac went back for Molly?"

"And Sierra."

"Sierra. Is he serious about her? I know Mac kissed her, but she's not his type."

"Sometimes you don't know your type until cupid hits you with a two-by-four."

Irelynn grinned. "She's a little spitfire. I'm not so sure he can handle her. Read his letter."

Brendan ripped open and scanned Mac's letter. He looked up at Irelynn. "Sierra is missing. Wait. Mac wrote the first half of this letter. Sierra wrote the second half. She says Mac is miss- ing. What the hell is going on? And where is Collin?"

"What do we do?"

"This letter was dated almost three weeks ago. Let's get to the airport. We're due to catch our flight soon, and I need to make some calls."

"Vietnam. Here we come. Again," Irelynn breathed.

Brendan raised an eyebrow before lowering it in a thunderous frown. "George," he growled.

"Don't think for a minute that you're going without me," Irelynn growled back.

Brendan pulled her in for a kiss. "God Sparky, you drive me crazy."

MIDNIGHT MIST IS COMING SOON

DA NANG AFB, SOUTH VIETNAM OCTOBER 1969

Opening the door to peer out into the deserted hallway, disappointment filled Sierra Byrne as she closed it and crept through the anteroom outside of Colonel Bragg's office. Her hand tightly gripping her shoe, her eyes followed the silver-dollar sized spider as it climbed the wall.

"*Incy wincy spider climbed…up the water…*" she softly sang, kicking off her other shoe; hiking her skirt up mid-thigh, she climbed on the chair.

Aiming the shoe, she squealed as the spider scurried up the wall.

Shaking off the heebie jeebies shivering down her spine, she climbed over the arms and onto the next chair. "*Spout…*

down came the rain... Fifteen thousand men on base, and ye think I could find one ta kill this spider?"

She climbed up on the chair's armrests; balancing, she swung at the creepy crawly.

"Gotcha, ye wee bastard."

She screeched as the spider sprang at her, and she toppled backward, landing squarely in the arms of a man, knocking them both to the floor. She rolled over to look at her rescuer and found herself lost in green eyes sparkling with amusement.

"You've got it all wrong, love. It's; 'Itsy Bitsy Spider,'" Mac chuckled as he tightened his hands around her waist.

"Ye sing it yer way, and I'll sing it mine," Sierra replied. Shaking her head, her black curls bounced as she pushed off his chest. Kneeling between his muscular thighs, her skirt hiked up to show creamy thighs and a white garter belt visible above her silk stockings. Her eyes roamed his handsome face and the shock of red hair trimmed high and tight to his head before she realized where his hot gaze touched her exposed thighs. Scrambling to her feet, her cheeks pink with embarrassment, she cleared her throat and pushed her skirt down to cover her legs.

"Mac. Yer back and still sneaking up on me," she stammered.

"Miss me, love?" Mac asked.

Her face flushed with pleasure, and the shoe still in hand, she swung around, looking for the spider.

"Damn it. I'm not going ta be able ta work in here until that sspider is dead."

Seamus McLoughlin, known as Mac to his family and friends, rose to his feet. He smiled, taking her shoe from her hand as her gaze drifted up his muscular six-foot-four frame.

Jesus, Mary, and Joseph. He's a handsome one in his fatigues.

"You're afraid of a wee spider?"

"Wee sspider? The beastie was so big I almost had ta wrestle it ta the ground," Sierra retorted.

"I'd pay to watch that match," Mac said.

Sierra snorted. "Ye would." Picking her other shoe up off the floor, she stalked the office searching for the offending pest.

"Come out... Come out... Wherever you are..." she softly sang as she peered behind a chair. She peeked out of the corner of her eye at Mac while he prowled around a filing cabinet and roguishly ran her eyes down his broad shoulders and back.

"Sso, how's Irelynn and Brendan?"

Mac turned to her, "They're good. Happily married, legally. They went on their honeymoon right before I left the states."

"I'm happy for them," Sierra said.

"We missed you at the wedding."

Sierra blushed and turned toward her desk on the far wall.

Mac grinned as his gaze caressed her backside. She was small, maybe five foot two, with curves galore.

He ached to reach out and run his hands along her tiny waist and the curve of her hips. Her breasts, more than a handful, drew his eyes, and he abruptly turned his back on her. Drawing from his willpower to curb his lustful thoughts. Mac loved women, but seducing virgins crossed the line. His mind traveled back to the day he had left Vietnam with Brendan when he had kissed her, a mistake on his part. With nothing to offer her, not marriage, a home, or love. He didn't have it in him. Oh, but that kiss, a taste of honey. Now, he couldn't get Sierra off his mind. It irritated him, yet he couldn't help himself from wanting more.

"What are ye looking at me like that for?" Sierra said.

"Sorry, love. Daydreaming."

"Well, daydream with yer eyes off my chest," she retorted.

Mac grinned, *God. I love her spunk.*

The door swung open, and Colonel Michael Bragg stormed into the anteroom.

Mac and Sierra snapped to stand at attention.

"Mac. It's about time you got your sorry ass back here. Kitten, go get us some coffee," Colonel Bragg ordered as he went into his office.

Sierra narrowed her eyes, "Yes, sir. Your most exalted lordship," she mumbled under her breath.

Mac grinned, reached above her head, and smashed the spider on the wall. He handed the shoe back to her, complete with spider goo. Sierra grimaced as her eyes were drawn to the remaining goo on the wall.

"Dolt. Now I have ta clean the wall," Sierra hissed as Mac went into Bragg's office and shut the door.

ABOUT THE AUTHOR

Leesa makes her home in Minnesota with her husband and their two dogs Rosie and Jax. When she isn't writing, she enjoys gardening, painting, and reading romance novels. She and her husband also enjoy music, movies, traveling, and entertaining.

Leesa's favorite romance authors are Kathleen Woodwiss, Christine Feehan, Johanna Lindsey and Dianne Duvall.

Printed in Great Britain
by Amazon